H/

By

Peter S. Barnes

This book is a work of fiction. All names, places and events are fictional and are products of the author's imagination. No portion of this book may be reproduced without permission from the publisher except by a reviewer who may quote brief passages in a review.

Published in the United States by
PB and J Publishing CA 2018
PB and J Document Services

Hard Rock
ISBN: 978-1-7326822-0-7
Library of Congress
TXu-1-628-814

www.hardrockthebook.com

For Mom and Dad

PROLOGUE

HE LAY BACK in the chair with his eyes closed - though he couldn't feel the chair anymore - it was more like some kind of floating sensation. Total euphoria. Suspended animation. At times like this, he would pinch himself to see if it was real. He forced the nail on his right forefinger into the fleshy part of his thumb and opened his eyes.

It wasn't a dream. They were still there.

These were two of the finest specimens he'd ever seen, and he'd seen a few. The brunette was now down to a g-string and the blond completely naked. A thousand guys would probably give their life to be the brass pole that was separating the two - separating not being the correct word. They gently kissed each other, playfully giggling and stealing glances at him.

He didn't know their names nor did it matter. The brunette pushed off the pole and crawled toward him with that stripper crawl. Like a lioness hunting prey. Her lips lightly brushed against his.

She was perfect. They were both perfect. The drugs made everything perfect.

Never breaking his trance, he found his pipe, ran a flame under the glass bulb and breathed in as deeply as he could. The rush came over him like waves of warm water crashing over his body. The brunette knelt down in front of him, unbuttoned his jeans and took him in her hand. As he let his head fall back, he pinched himself again to see if it was still real.

The rock star life, baby…

ONE

THAT PATRICK PEARSON was born with a God-given gift was not something that the people in his young life would try to debate. The boy had been humming and tapping out complex rhythms in the back seat of the family station wagon as long as anyone could remember.

He was good too – a 'natural talent' according to his trumpet teacher Mr. Left, who also ran the music program for the local school district.

Pat's mother and father provided for him well. His home couldn't have possibly been any more middle class than it was - a typical San Fernando Valley ranch style with large picture windows and a double front door. The neatly manicured yard boasted two beautiful weeping willows that provided a sleepy lakeshore feel that offset the fact that the neighborhood was surrounded by the sprawling city of Los Angeles. All the other houses in the development looked like his; as if someone had taken a giant cookie cutter and created a baked neighborhood that allowed each homeowner to add his own frosting. It was a nice place to grow up.

Maintaining the scenery that gave the family home its character was a joint effort by Pat and his father. They spent what time they could together mowing and trimming on warm summer weekends.

They would make small talk; his dad would question about school, music and the possibility of sports in his future as any dad would. Pat's mind however, drifted far away from those subjects – it was fairly consumed with girls.

He probably thought about girls more than even Freud would expect from a pre-adolescent boy and definitely more than his father would which was not at all, and since Pat was in no way prepared to share his fascination with the fairer sex with anyone, small talk was all Dad was ever going to get out of him. The subject of girls had never been breached in the Pearson household, and well-behaved Pat surely wouldn't be the one to stir up the picture-perfect family.

On one of those warm summer days, Dad reached down and mussed Pat's bushy blond hair. He loved Pat more than anything in this world.

"Your mom and I are really proud of you, bud. Mr. Left told us that he believes you to be a natural talent. He says he can tell that you've been doing a lot of practicing."

Pat just smiled and nodded in agreement, looking up with his pale blue eyes and thinking to himself how easy it was to please this man.

At just twelve years old Patrick had already figured out how to exploit his gift and had been relying on it for some time. Instead of affecting the required two-hour practice sessions each night mandated by his father, he had recorded himself playing scales on his new stereo and played back the tape over the speakers with the door to his room closed. His mother was none the wiser and left Pat to his hard work, which had turned from rehearsal exercises to the admiring of the naked bodies of beautiful women on the pages of his father's pilfered Playboy magazines. Fortunately, when it came to testing at school, and even to individual recital of said scales and exercises, Pat never missed a beat in spite of his lack of practice.

Pat knew his theory. He knew how to solo and how to improvise well. He had good discipline, good lips, and good chops. It wasn't long before Mr. Left advanced him to the high school marching band even though he was not yet in high school.

"Playing in the marching band with the high school kids is a privilege and must be taken seriously Mister Pearson," said the bushy-bearded and bow-tied Mr. Left in the same stern tone that he used whenever he discussed music. "You have earned this opportunity through your hard work. You have the potential to be anything you want to be if you don't let things distract you from your goals."

"Thank you for the opportunity Mr. Left. I won't let you down."

Whether it was knowing the appropriate words to say or knowing the appropriate notes to play, young Pat was charmed indeed, especially when it came to performing music. He appeared cool and focused and played smoothly and deliberately. That is, until the marching band. Practicing on the football field after school he first noticed them practicing too.

Holy shit…

They sure didn't look like that in middle school. Their bodies had curves; like that of a Corvette or maybe a Porsche. And those outfits - those tiny miniskirts and tank tops! It was the most incredible thing he'd ever seen.

*Look at their legs and boobs…*he thought to himself. *And their eyes…they're wearing makeup… It makes their eyes look… sexy? Is that the right word? Oh man, you can see their underwear when they do their routines. The way they move, the way they dance…*

It was a good thing Pat was naturally talented because while marching in step, maintaining formation, and playing simultaneously might be a real challenge for most mortals, Pat seemed to be able to handle it all while still watching his favorite girl's ass moving around the field, save for an occasional missed note here or there.

Her name was Darcy - one of his bandmates had provided him with the info - also adding of course that his chances of ever talking to her were about as good as his chances of jumping the Grand Canyon on his Huffy bicycle. But anything was possible in a charmed life, and Pat wasn't deterred from studying her so intensely that he probably knew her cheerleading routine better than she did.

Someday I'll talk to her...Someday soon...

"Mister Pearson!" snapped Mr. Left as he interrupted Pat's daydream with the wave of a finger, "If you think I don't hear you missing notes out there, you are sorely mistaken. There is no room for distraction in this program, my friend. You need to get focused on your own or tell me why it is that you can't."

Pat gave a stunned look. Mr. Left put a kind hand on his shoulder and squeezed for effect.

"Whatever it is that is causing you distraction needs to be dealt with, Mister Pearson. It's time to grow up, son. Now pack up and go meet your mom."

"Yes sir, Mr. Left."

"Good night, Patrick."

As Pat waited for his mom to pick him up from school, he fell into one of his familiar dreamy states, fantasizing about what it might be like to talk to Darcy. To touch her. To kiss her. He lay across a bus bench and closed his eyes. He pictured her hair, her smile, her eyes gazing into his. What a feeling it must be to have sex with a girl like that! He'd seen magazines; he figured he'd know what to do.

I'll kiss her and hold her and feel between her legs... I'll reach down and...

Startled by the sound of voices, Pat sat up suddenly.

"Bye, Tiffany, I'll see you tomorrow."

"Bye, Darcy."

There she was - right there, not twenty feet away! She turned straight for him and looked in his direction. He couldn't help but stare - she was so beautiful. She began to speak...

"What the fuck are you looking at, you little faggot?"

He almost choked.

"I…I …think you are pretty…" It just came out. He couldn't believe it.

Oh God…

"You think I'm what, loser? You wouldn't know what to do with a girl if you got one! Keep your eyes to yourself, you little queer!"

♪♪♪

"Please just tell me what's wrong, honey," his mother pleaded in a concerned tone.

"Nothing's wrong, Mom! Just leave me alone!"

The ride home from school had been almost entirely in silence. Pat went straight to his room, buried his head in his pillow and cried himself to sleep.

His mother later cracked open the door to his room.

"Patrick, it's time for dinner."

"I'm not hungry, Mom."

She let herself in and sat down next to him on the bed, checking the temperature on his forehead as mothers do.

"Honey, whatever it is that's bothering you, you can always talk to me about it. Anything, Patrick."

"I'm fine, Mom…I just wanna crash."

"I'll leave something out for you on the kitchen counter. Patrick, I don't know what's bothering you, but I want you to remember that you are a very special and talented kid. You can have anything you want in life, and your father and I love you very much."

"I love you too, Mom. Goodnight."

He lay awake in the dark, the disastrous scene playing relentlessly over and over in his head.

"What the fuck are you looking at…you little faggot…you little queer…"

How could she treat me like that?

He was more than heartbroken; it had been love. And it wasn't the first time he'd fallen in love - there were the girls in the magazines too. He wished he could see them now, his girlfriends, but Mom and Dad were home.

He'd been in love many times but never felt it returned. What might it be like to have girls love him; to be popular and have lots of friends? He was special - his mother told him that a lot and he wanted to believe it more than anything. She said he could have anything in life. If that were true, then why couldn't he have the one girl he wanted? Didn't any of the girls out there realize how special he was? Why not?

Rolling over on his bed, he tried to make out the glowing numbers on his digital alarm clock through his watery eyes. 11:41. Johnny Carson had just started. Wiping his nose, he got up and turned on his little black and white TV. After a brief warming up process and a couple of commercials, the familiar set of the Tonight Show filled the small screen. He'd already missed the monologue, his favorite part.

Hope he's got some decent guests on…

"Ladies and gentlemen," Johnny announced, "please welcome, from the rock band Van Halen, David Lee Roth, and Eddie Van Halen!"

Eddie Van Halen strutted onto the stage dressed in ripped up jeans and a sparkly shirt. His long brown hair flowed over his shoulders, and he had a lit cigarette hanging from his lips.

That is so cool…

Then David Lee Roth walked on set. Leather pants, sunglasses, long blond hair and a beautiful girl on each arm. These girls looked even better than the high school ones - tight short shorts, long tanned legs and huge breasts - just like the ones in the magazines. Pat was entranced.

"So Dave, what's with the ladies here?" asked Johnny.

"I always hang out with two of them 'cause it's better for conversation," said Dave with a grin, "You see if there winds up being any, I don't have to be involved!"

The roar of the crowd coupled with Ed McMahon's hearty laugh distorted the tiny speaker on Pat's little TV. Both girls kissed Dave on the cheeks and began to dance around as the studio erupted with laughter. Eddie puffed on his smoke. It was the coolest thing Pat had ever seen.

"It's the rock star life, baby!" Dave said.

It was right then that Pat knew.

The next day he and his mom picked out an electric guitar.

♪♪♪

The dark-haired girl stood over him, champagne dripping off her sparse pubic hair; her perfectly tanned skin glistening in the soft light. She kissed his neck, slowly working her way to his mouth. He could taste the champagne on her lips. The blond was now between his spread legs sucking him and stroking him with her hand, her long hair falling across his thighs, sending shivers through his body. The brunette pushed her aside, straddled him and slid him inside her.

"Fuck me, Patrick Pearson."

He felt in awe of his own virtuosity. He went over the events from the last few nights in his mind as she rode him: Denver, Vegas, San Francisco and finally Reno, the last stop. The last show is always best. Reno was crazy; the crowd had gone totally insane. The Crystal Meth in Reno was the best in the country. And these girls - these girls were incredible.

The album had gone platinum and the tour had been flawless. The perfect tour, the perfect show, the perfect night.

The band, and he were becoming colossal.

He pinched himself again.

♪♪♪

"It's too hard!" Pat exclaimed. "It doesn't make any sense, and I can't do it."

Eric smiled as he looked Pat and his guitar over. He was a soft-spoken and patient man - a fantastic guitar teacher who truly cared about kids and loved rock & roll.

"Look buddy, it's only as hard as you make it. You're a talented kid Patrick - you've proven that with the trumpet. This is simply an instrument that reads in a different key signature. And, yes, you have chords too, but it's not any different from classical music. It's all universal, amigo! You just need to transpose what you already know and develop some muscle and dexterity."

"But even when I do read the notes right, my fingers just don't do it. I can't push down on all the strings! It's too hard!"

Eric took a moment to consider his student and then spoke softly. "Patrick, what do you want out of your music? Not your parents or instructors, but you?"

Pat answered without hesitation. "I want to be a rock star."

"Do you know what it takes to be a rock star?"

Pat wiped his eyes. "I don't know," he whined.

"A lot of musicians have an undeniable natural talent. Others, Patrick, don't have the natural talent, but they work their butts off. They practice like there is no tomorrow. A real star has both, work ethic and talent. A guy like that will eventually find the zone. And once he does, anything is possible."

"What's the zone?"

"The zone is that place where your mind goes when everything clicks effortlessly. When something else takes over. I like to believe it's God. Musicians, athletes and artists can sometimes feel it. However, some do and some don't. If you can, and I believe you probably already have with the trumpet, then you can be anything you want."

Pat looked confused. Eric tried to find the best words to make the young boy understand.

"Patrick, when you improvised with the jazz band, was there ever a time that you did it without thinking about it? You know, like during a solo? Think about it and tell me how it felt."

Pat stared at the floor trying to understand. He shifted a guitar pick back and forth between his fingers. "I don't know…sometimes I can play while I think about something else."

"That's kind of it, only you get so far into concentration that you feel nothing around you. It's just you and your instrument, and something takes over and directs your hands to do things even before you think of them. At that moment, you are truly blessed, and at that moment, you are in the zone."

Pat thought he understood. At least he felt from what Eric had said that there must be some kind of different world he could tap into. And he wanted it. He stared at the pick rolling in and out of his fingers lost in thought. Eric broke the silence.

"Okay amigo, lesson's over for this week. Take those scales and arpeggios home and practice. Practice like your life depends on it. And do not look at the fretboard while you do it - look into a mirror. Watch yourself as if you are watching your hero. Look into that mirror and see who you want to be. See it. And let God do the rest."

♪♪♪

Pat closed his eyes and visualized the part in his head. He thought back to what Eric had said about God and the zone, just as he did every time before he played. He put his fingers to work. The notes flowed. He was feeling something. Tonight was the night.

He slid open the door to his old Chevy van and walked across the parking lot to the bar's back door. Holding his breath for a moment, he pushed it open and shuffled inside. The music was booming and causing everything around him to vibrate tediously. He sat down on a wooden bench in a hallway, leaned his guitar against the wall and listened.

Pat wasn't allowed in front of the backstage area because he was too young to drink. He stared at the cracked yellow-brown walls in the hall and inhaled the typical bar scents of old stale alcohol mixed with cigarette smoke. The queasiness began. He waited for his turn.

The guy that was on stage was doing Van Halen's 'Eruption' - pretty much a staple for all guitarists, but Pat always figured if you don't have a band backing you so you can segue into 'You Really Got Me', it kind of sucks. Plus it never really sounded like Eddie Van Halen anyway - because nobody has Eddie's gear but Eddie - although Pat's friends had told him that if Eddie ever died, he should be the one to step in. But that was in Pat's bedroom. Pat had never played in a band. Or in front of a crowd for that matter.

He peeked around the stage entrance into the main room. It was packed. People were standing around tables covered in glasses and beer bottles. It was dark except for the glow on the crowd from the stage lighting. Weird colors and shadows flashed across peoples' faces making them look like monsters. They were rowdy; some cheering with hands in the air, some booing and waving body parts in more threatening motions. His heart and mind raced. The nausea. He knew he shouldn't have looked in there.

Shit, I can't do this...

He fell back onto the bench and stared up at the stained popcorn ceiling.

All these people... oh man...I shouldn't have written my own thing...it sucks...this sucks...

The guy that was on stage raised his fist to the crowd. Another triumphant end to 'Eruption'. He strutted offstage, and the M.C. took over the microphone.

“Thanks again for coming out and supporting local SoCal’s local music scene! Next up in Pirate Radio’s guitar wars, Mister Patrick Pearson…Give it up!”

Pat climbed the stairs to the stage and froze, feeling his dinner coming up. He swallowed and wished he had never signed up for this stupid contest. He was shaking like a leaf.

“Go on bro, you’re up!” someone said giving him a shove.

Oh God...

He walked onto the stage. The lights were blinding; he couldn’t see for a second or two. It was hot as hell. A Marshall Stack guitar amplifier sat on the stage - it was taller than he was and he feared it might fall over and crush him at any moment. He sheepishly shuffled over to it and plugged in his guitar. A loud crack followed by a screech of feedback resonated through the building making the crowd cringe. He turned the volume knob on his guitar clockwise, and his throat went dry.

Okay, here we go...

At some point - he didn’t know exactly where - he had stopped thinking. A strange feeling of calm swept through his body. He heard nothing nor saw anything in front of him. Gazing directly into the spotlight, a smile slowly began to form on his lips. His fingers kept moving. And moving. Control was relinquished somewhere along the way, and it felt euphoric. The notes flowed like water down a river. The crowd was enchanted and screaming with enthusiasm, but he was unaware of it. God had become his copilot. He was in the zone.

TWO

PAT WAS A cute kid. He had a great physique and bushy blond hair, a soft face, and high cheekbones. As he got older, a strong jawline filled in and his hair turned long, curly and slightly darker with blond highlights. He had the body of a surfer, toned but not too cut, and his bronze skin completed the package.

Today he looked nothing like that. Today he was a wreck. His face was pale white with dark bags under his eyes, and his hair looked frizzed and almost gray. What a difference a day makes.

"Dude, are you okay? C'mon man, wake up!"

Pat stirred a little. At least Chris knew he was alive.

"Dude, get up! It's two in the afternoon!"

Pat rolled over.

"Get out of here, Chris…"

How Pat got from the bus to the hotel room, Chris had no idea. Why he'd want to leave the only tour bus with a built-in stripper pole, Chris didn't know either. How he was going to get Pat out of this hotel room and back on the bus without any Crystal Meth, Chris did not even want to think about.

"Pat, we were supposed to be on the road by ten! Everyone wants to get home. And your wife keeps calling."

"She's not my wife, asshole…"

Pat pushed one of the two ladies from the previous night aside and was now sitting up. "Where's my shit?"

"I don't know man, but I can tell you that if you and these broads smoked everything that you had, then we're out."

Pat pushed the other girl out of the way, climbed out of bed and immediately fell to the floor. The bed sheets were knotted around his legs, and the rest of the room didn't look much better. Fortunately, the lack of light afforded by the opaque hotel room curtains hid some of the disaster. He staggered back to his feet.

"We gotta have some dope – where's it at?"

"I'm telling you," Chris said, "if you don't have anything then we're out."

Pat's face instantly turned angry. "There better be some fuckin' dope around here!"

He looked down at the two naked girls on the bed like he was looking at a couple of thieves. He jabbed at the sleeping blond. "Hey, do you have my shit?"

The girl was interrupted before she could even comprehend what was being said.

"Forget it. You two gotta go. Get the fuck up."

Pat began tearing apart the room. He wasn't frantic yet, but it wasn't far off. His head pounded; he was so hung over that his hair hurt.

"Dude, there's got to be some dope around here!"

Chris picked up an article of clothing off a table and held up a Ziploc bag containing some Crystal Meth residue. "Here's a scraper," he said proudly.

"Sweet," said Pat, "You get to scraping that baggie. I'm going to go throw up. And get these freeloading sluts out of here."

He went to slam the bathroom door but it simply hissed closed, further irritating him.

Chris pulled open the drapes and the brutal sunlight poured in making everyone's eyes sting. He casually put on his shades.

"You heard him, ladies. Grab yer shit and split!"

Chris sat down at a small table, ran his hand through his spiky black hair, adjusted his lip ring and commenced to scraping any possible Meth residue out of the Ziploc. The girls slowly gathered their things and began to get dressed.

♪♪♪

"Are you Christopher Martinez?"

"Who wants to know?"

"I'm Officer Sanchez and this is Officer Davis. We're with the CHP."

"That explains the uniforms. What do you want?"

"Christopher, may we come in?"

"Do I have a choice?" Chris sneered as he reluctantly opened the heavy crystal-inlaid door to his home.

The two officers looked around and back at him, no doubt puzzled at what a chubby, tattooed Latino kid in a Metallica T-shirt was doing in a house like this.

The home was beautiful, large even for the suburban San Diego neighborhood of Mount Helix. The huge marble entryway was lined with exquisite hardwood molding. A spectacular staircase wound its way toward the second floor. Chris stood under a chandelier in the middle of a large oriental rug nervously playing with his lip ring and staring at the two cops.

"May we sit down?" asked one of the officers.

"I don't think so." Chris nervously answered. "What's this about? I haven't done anything wrong."

"Chris, if I may call you Chris, are any other family members home?"

"Yes, you can call me Chris, and no, nobody is home. What's going on?"

"Chris, we want you to understand that this is the hardest part of our job."

Chris's stomach dropped. For once the visit wasn't about him.

"Chris, your parents have been in an automobile accident. We're terribly sorry and we'd like to sit down and explain the circumstances."

Chris stood in silence, staring down at the crimson patterns in the plush rug.

"Chris? There's a police car in the driveway!" his sister Maggie exclaimed as she walked through the open front door. "What have you done now?" She turned to the two officers. "You aren't taking him to jail are you? He's been going to his classes."

"No Ma'am, we were speaking with Chris about something else. Ma'am, if we could just all sit down for a minute."

"Why?" Maggie said in a shaken voice, "What's going on here? Has something happened?"

"Ma'am, can we please sit down…"

"No! What is going on?"

"Ma'am, we were just explaining to your brother that your parents…"

"No! No, goddammit!"

"Ma'am, there's no easy way to say this. There's been an accident and your parents were involved. Please understand how sorry we are…"

Maggie looked at Chris in disbelief. "This is your fault, you fucking asshole!"

Chris just stared at the floor.

"Ma'am please, it's not his fault. It was a traffic accident on highway sixty-seven. We need to sit down so we can explain the circumstances."

Maggie slapped Chris hard on the side of the head. One of the officers grabbed her from behind and pulled her away.

"You fucking asshole! You did this! You told them you wished they were dead! You fucking drug addict! I hate you!" Maggie fell to the floor sobbing. "You did this…"

"Please, both of you, we need to sit down and discuss…"

"Get out," Chris said.

"Sir, we…"

"Get the fuck out!"

♪♪♪

"Where are you?"

"I'm at Grandma's."

"Don't forget to pick up the rest of your stuff from the house. The new people take possession this weekend."

"Thanks a lot."

"Chris, you did all of this to yourself. If you weren't such a loser you'd be reaping the benefits of Mom and Dad's estate, but you chose instead to be a drug addict. Dad said if you didn't change you were to get nothing. It's your own fault, so don't act like a victim."

"Don't be such a cunt."

"Goodbye, Chris. Say hi to Grandma."

"Bye, Maggie."

Chris's older sister Margarita was named the executor of the estate and had elected to sell the family home and move to Arizona. She had actually given Chris a fair chance to 'clean up his act' in accordance with her father's wishes, but Chris was unable to make the commitment and was therefore excluded from any inheritance.

Having no place to go, Chris found his way to his grandmother's mobile home on the Pala Indian Reservation, about thirty miles north of San Diego tucked back in the hills along a river. The mobile home would have had a beautiful view if not for all the broken down cars and garbage strewn across the property.

Chris's grandmother was from his immigrant father's side of the family and did not speak any English. To make matters even more difficult for Chris, she also had the preliminary symptoms of Alzheimer's creeping on. Some days were better than others, but the disease was progressing rapidly and she would occasionally wake up screaming at night or wander off into the woods, giving Chris, a nineteen-year-old drug-dependent high school dropout, quite a bit more to deal with than he ever bargained for at this stage of his young life. Chris was unwittingly positioned into the role of keeping Grandma from 'going off the reservation' so to speak.

In the early nineties, San Diego County became a hotspot for Indian casino activity. Downtrodden, low-income reservation properties like Grandma's were prime for Vegas-style casinos, providing the locals with fresh opportunities.

Chris was way too irresponsible and chemical dependent to become a card dealer or work in a casino in any capacity that would require him to come to work on a regular basis. However, Chris was not without his niche. Part-time work as a bouncer at a casino bar fit well with his nocturnal schedule, and more importantly, provided him with exposure to a culture that was often in need of some kind of pick-me-up during a night of drinking and dancing and whatever else. Chris was able to capitalize on this need well and soon was able to keep both he and his grandmother medicated on a regular basis.

As progress would have it, the Indian casinos soon gave forth to gigantic resort hotels complete with outlet stores, PGA golf courses and huge show venues that began booking local and national music and comedy acts to rival Las Vegas, and a whole new world opened up for the area's musicians. Local bands were offered the possibility of national exposure by being paired up with an established touring act.

One of the first bands to take advantage of this opportunity was called Blacklist and featured a lead singer/guitarist by the name of Patrick Pearson.

On one particular night when it came time to find that extra boost needed to get through the afterparty, Chris was introduced to Pat as a reliable source for the much-needed goods.

The two hit it off immediately. An outsider would have never known that Pat and Chris had grown up a hundred miles apart - they appeared to have known each other their entire lives. They had listened to the same music, watched the same movies and TV shows and done the same drugs. When they were together, nobody could utter a word without the two of them ganging up - quoting lines from Caddyshack or Ghostbusters and clearly poking fun at the expense of anyone who was not hip to Conan O'Brien or Howard Stern.

The two of them continued to party together non-stop until it seemed like the logical choice for Chris to accompany Pat on the road with the band. Of course there wasn't much to do back then; unload trucks and connect some gear occasionally, and there wasn't much money either, but Chris was loyal nonetheless. So when the time came, Pat snuck Chris into his contract as his 'personal assistant' and as long as there were drugs around, Chris would be very happy to be Pat's road dog. And Pat could do no wrong. Every aspiring rock star needs his own 'yes man'. Especially a 'yes man' who can score dope.

♪♪♪

Chris sometimes missed taking care of his grandma. She was usually easier to deal with than Pat.

Exiting the bathroom with a treacherous scowl on his face, Pat flopped down in a chair across the table from Chris and drew a huge hit off the dirty glass pipe, holding his breath for a few seconds and releasing a cloud of smoke thick enough to blot out the light streaming in behind him from the window. You could see the color returning to his face, and he almost smiled.

"Man, what a night. Thank God for scrapers. I think I can feel my headache dissipating as we speak."

"Amen, bro..." Chris lowered his sunglasses. "Look, we gotta get moving. Everyone is ready to go except you."

"Okay… do we have enough shit for the trip, or what?"

"I doubt it."

"What do you mean you doubt it? We had plenty last night and now we don't have any? You had some to hold for me! Where the hell is it?"

"Pat, you took it all before you locked me out of the bus last night. I know you don't remember but..."

"But nothing! Come on, man!"

"Pat, I don't have any."

"You're a fuckhead, Chris! You better get on the phone and find me some! We got like five hundred miles to drive and I am not gonna make it! We must know somebody in Reno… Don't we?"

"Pat, listen, by the time we found anything here it would be way too late a start to get everyone home tonight. We've got a little bit in the pipe and you can nap on the bus. I'll make some calls and it'll be waiting for us when we get back. It'll be an easy trip, okay man? Are we cool?"

Pat unenthusiastically agreed to the terms. "Yeah, we're fuckin' cool," he grumbled. "Let's just fuckin' go."

♪♪♪

Once back on the bus, Pat went straight to the back and passed out on the bed. Chris took a seat in a captain's chair behind the driver. The band's manager, Steve Stanford, poked his head through the open bus door.

"So dipshit's on the bus? Can we finally leave, or do I have to catch a fuckin' plane?"

"Yes, Steve, he's here," Chris said sarcastically.

Steve was one of the most well-known entertainment business managers in California, and truth be told, the guys were very lucky that he saw anything in them at all. His client list was mostly pop acts, but he'd been working with Blacklist for a while now. And he was not pleased with the direction things were going.

"Don't give me attitude you little fuck! Do you guys give two shits about what happens to this band at all anymore or is it just about your crack pipe? That fuckin' idiot is going down and taking everyone else with him and you enable him every step of the way. I'd beat your drug-addict ass if you weren't part of his contract!"

"Well, as you know, I am. So blow me. And find your own ride."

Chris reached over the driver's shoulder and pulled the door lever, causing it to close on Steve's arm.

"You fucking cocksucker!" Steve screeched as he pulled his arm free of the door.

"Let's go..." Chris told the driver, who put the bus in gear.

Chris spun around in his chair and looked into the back of the bus. The A/C felt good, and only the perimeter 'mood' lighting was on. The bus looked very peaceful and comfortable. He was glad they were leaving for home.

Finally...I can relax...

Sometimes Chris wondered why he even bothered. Being the liaison between Pat and everyone else was starting to take a toll. Things had really changed. It was now the new millennium, and Blacklist was huge. And as Pat grew more famous, they grew further apart. What Steve had said wasn't too far from the truth – it did seem that it was all about the drugs these days. He and Pat used to relate in so many different ways. Now the only time they seemed to have any contact at all was either when they were hardcore partying, or when he was trying to keep Pat from blowing a gasket.

The road was tough on everyone.

*We'll chill out on the dope and drinking...*Chris thought to himself as his eyes began to feel heavy. *We'll clean up a bit... get a place on the beach... like a vacation... It'll be relaxing... Yeah, life will be different at home...*

Chris fell asleep dreaming of that life.

THREE

"PUNCH IT BITCH!" Otterpop hollered with delight.

Garrett stomped on the gas and cranked the wheel of the Mitsubishi 3000GT hard right; the rear tires broke loose and the car drifted around a corner. He spun the wheel left and corrected, squashing the gas pedal.

"This car kicks ass!" Garrett exclaimed with a smile.

He got it up to about seventy miles per hour and pulled on the emergency brake, drifting another sharp turn. The car stuck to the asphalt like glue.

"I can't believe you got this thing for a half ounce of dope!" Otterpop laughed. "It's *my* dope, brother!" Garrett replied with a grin.

He stabilized the car and hit a freeway ramp, weaving past slower traffic thoroughly amused. His phone could be heard ringing from somewhere in the speeding automobile.

"Hey, get that phone will ya?" Garrett yelled over the cabin noise.

Otterpop reached down into the console and picked up the cell phone.

"What's up Chris?"

"Hey bro, is Garrett around?"

"Yeah, he's here, but he can't talk right now, he's got my dick in his mouth!"

"Give me that fuckin' phone," Garrett said, slapping Otterpop on the side of the head with one hand and trying to control the car with the other. Otterpop playfully smacked the back of Garrett's head as he tossed him the phone.

"Hey, man, it's me. What's up? You guys on your way back?"

"Yeah, and thank God you answered. We're totally out of shit and Pat's gonna start trippin' any time. He's crashed out in the back of the bus right now and when he wakes up I want to be able to say I already talked to you."

"Yeah, bro, it's all good," said Garrett as he nearly clipped the back of a Ford Explorer, "Come on over anytime tonight. I got bitches at the pad and freshy-fresh shizznit. How far out are you guys?"

"A few hours or so, but we gotta unload and return the tour bus and shit. Then we'll be over."

"Don't trip man; you guys always have a pass."

"Cool, see you tonight."

Garrett threw down the phone and punched the gas. They flew up Interstate five at a nice one hundred mile per hour clip, weaving in and out of traffic like the freeway was their own. Otterpop's buzz was suddenly shattered as he looked to an exit.

"Dude, slow down, there's a fuckin' cop over there!"

Garrett hit the brakes.

"Did he see us?"

"I don't think so. You know, this car is kind of a cop-magnet, being bright red and whatnot."

"I hate fuckin' cops," Garrett muttered.

"Have you ever considered that the only reason you hate cops is because whenever you come in contact with them, you're always doing something illegal?"

"Have you ever considered that you're a dick?"

♪♪♪

For most drug dealers, life was tough. Just as with any business, you had to make good decisions, watch your bottom line and surround yourself with trustworthy people if you intended to be successful. Unfortunately, when everyone – including you – are high all the time, decisions weren't that good and people weren't that trustworthy. And then there was the whole 'it's illegal' thing. However, every so often you'd find a guy who seemed to make it work, and Garrett Kinglsey was that guy. Garrett seemed to find a balance – he was a ruthless businessman when he needed to be and a likable guy when that was the ticket.

Garrett hailed from a long line of slick businessmen. His father, a diamond expert, had emigrated from England in the mid-1970's and built himself a fine jewelry business in Pacific Beach.

Young Garrett, a blond-haired, blue-eyed kid with a very fair English complexion, would hang around his father's jewelry shop after school on most days. The precious gem business attracted a diverse crowd, all of them being wheeler-dealers. He would sit behind the countertops admiring stones through a gem scope while his father haggled for hours with the Jews from the San Fernando Valley and the Italians from Downtown. His father would say to him in his thick English accent, "Garrett, don't go into a business where you can't trust people. Salespeople are not noble. Gems and metals are no good to anyone; they just perpetuate greed. Please, always stay away from selling goods."

Apparently, Garrett did not heed his father's words but listened instead to the banter that made him the businessman that he was. Only for Garrett, his business happened to be drugs, and Garrett proved to be quite good at his chosen profession. He had cultivated the best source – pure shit straight from Mexico – better than even the local biker gangs could provide. He had a loyal client list that he'd built up over several years. He had a trustworthy inner circle. Business seemed to be booming; in fact, Garrett proved that if you are good enough at this particular profession, it is possible to live a life not far away from that of a rock star.

And live like a rock star he did. He had money. He had perks. He had rock star friends. He *always* had drugs. In fact, Garrett sometimes had more perks than his rock star friends.

FOUR

IT HAD BEEN a long trip, and Pat was miserable. Tweekers don't get dope sick like heroin addicts do, they just become absolutely unable to function. Pat heard his phone ringing but pretended to be sleeping. Chris snatched it up thinking it might be Garrett calling back for some reason. It wasn't.

"Chris, where's Pat?" said the voice at the other end.

"I think he's sleeping, Christine."

"Are you guys driving?"

"Yeah."

"Chris, please wake him up…"

She was crying again. Chris didn't know what to do – he liked Christine a lot and felt bad for her, but now was definitely not the time for those two to talk. Not with Pat coming down off dope.

"Please Chris, I need to talk to him…"

"Okay, hold on Christine..."

Against his better judgment, Chris jogged to the back of the bus and nudged Pat.

"Dude, your wife's on the phone."

"She's not my fuckin' wife, asshole, and I'm not here."

"C'mon, man, she knows you're here. We're on a bus."

Pat sat up. "Dude, why did you even pick up the phone? You are such a fuckin' idiot."

"Whatever, man." Chris tossed the phone into Pat's lap and walked away.

Pat put the phone to his ear with a pre-argument grimace on his face. "Hello?"

"Pat, we need to talk..."

Christine Johnston and Patrick Pearson had met back in the bar days before Pat was with Blacklist. Pat was young and on a roll, just learning to take advantage of all the benefits of being a musician until he met his match. Christine refused to play along. She wouldn't sleep with him, touting that she was not that kind of girl and she didn't date guys in bands, but Pat always took that as a challenge. He would tell her, "Just wait, I'm going to make you fall in love with me."

It took a little while, but that is exactly what he did. Playing the romantic, he would come to her window in the middle of the night after gigs and beg to come in until she finally agreed. He'd bring a rose or one of those stuffed animals that one can win in those machines they have in every bar, though usually the bar manager would open the machine and let him retrieve it himself. She'd let him stay the night much to the dismay of her roommate who was leery of musician types. They'd fall asleep on the couch in each other's arms.

Eventually, Pat proposed to her and suggested that they run off to Mexico and get married, which they did. They held hands on a beach in the moonlight as a Padre said something in Spanish that they did not need to understand. Christine was head-over-heels in love.

In fact, Christine was so in love that she refused to see the obvious, that Pat was becoming more and more self-centered and narcissistic, borderlining on sociopathic. When Pat enjoyed some element of success, he began to alienate anyone who cared for him. For a sociopath, success was in itself a drug. Add actual drugs, and you had a recipe for disaster.

He'd disappear for days and even weeks at a time, obviously sleeping with other women. She'd get upset with him, saying that he wasn't being the husband he promised her he'd be. He'd say the marriage wasn't legal because it was in Mexico.

When the heavy touring started, he spent more time away than at home. She cried herself to sleep on many nights, her heart shattered. She would have left him for good if not for the pregnancy. He said he'd be there for her no matter what she decided, so she decided that they'd be a family eventually. Only Pat never got the memo.

Pat slipped completely out of her life, completely out of his mind, and did not plan on coming back.

"Pat, when are you coming home? I can't do this all by myself. I need you here for Tommy even if you don't care about me anymore. It's not fair to him."

"I'm coming home tonight. Just be patient. I've got some important stuff I have to do when I get back, and then I'll call you."

"Call me? What do you have to do that's more important than seeing your son? Do you have to go score dope? I swear, Pat, your priorities are way out of whack."

"Christine, I'm not in the mood for it right now, okay?" Pat's head began to throb.

"You're never in the mood for anything, Pat. I have hardly any money and the insurance isn't covering Tommy's last trip to the doctor. I have to work, get groceries, deal with daycare…I have nobody to help me! And all you care about is your drugs and your stupid band." She was now sobbing.

"I'll write you a check as soon as I get back."

"It's not about the money, you selfish asshole, it's about your son! It's about making time for your own child!"

"What do you fuckin' want from me?" Pat hollered, his head pounding even harder.

"Pat, all I ever wanted was for you to be there for us."

Pat held his breath. His head was about to explode. He didn't know what to say. Yes, he loved her – at least sometimes he did. But not right now.

Why does all this shit seem so overwhelming right now? He couldn't think. The headache.

"Just leave me the fuck alone!" he screeched as he threw the phone to the floor.

God just get me home...

♪♪♪

Finally back in town, Pat and Chris rented a compact car and commenced the trip across town to Garrett's place. The only thing that kept Pat from jumping out of the car onto the freeway was the promise of drugs waiting for them.

They could hear music and voices coming from the back of the house as they got out of the car and dragged themselves up to Garrett's front door.

"Whazzup my homies?" Garrett exclaimed as he opened the door. "You guys look like shit. Come on in and partake in the partay!!"

Pat and Chris both gave quick hugs to Garrett and walked through his living room and into the backyard. Pat looked around and soaked up the scenery. He was always amazed at how well Garrett did for himself as a dope-slinger. His home was beautiful.

The backyard had a wet bar and a hot tub that was occupied by a couple of ladies, who of course were currently sans clothing and clearly willing to do whatever it took to get high and stay that way. A natural gas fire was burning in the center of the patio, around which were several comfortable chairs and a glass table.

On the table was a mountain of Crystal Meth in its purest form. It resembled what shattered glass looked like and was the most potent version available. The crystal shards glistened in the light of the fire. All the necessary utensils, from straws for sniffing to a water pipe for smoking, were placed in close proximity to the enormous pile of dope. Pat's mouth literally began to water. It was a beautiful scene.

"Go ahead guys, help yourselves," said Garrett as he prepared to hop back into the hot tub. "We'll talk business later. And tell Otterpop what you want from the bar."

Otterpop clapped his hands together; the blue tattooed flames on his arms that resembled the color blue of the frozen children's treat he was nicknamed after emphasized his presence.

"What can I get you fellers from the cellar?" he asked.

"Beer for me," said Chris, as he pulled the glass bowl out of the plug on top of the water pipe in preparation of loading.

"Same," said Pat.

Otterpop tossed the beers to Pat. Chris slid an open matchbook under the pile of Meth, picked up a good half gram and dumped it into the bowl of the water pipe.

"Time to live up to your rock star reputations, my brothers!" Garrett laughed from the hot tub.

Chris eased the bowl back onto the bong and prepared for the first hit. Pat took a seat next to Tina, a mutual friend of he and Garrett's.

"What's up, Tuna?" Pat asked.

"So the rock star returns." Tina laughed.

Tina was dressed impeccably as usual – a tan suede miniskirt and blazer, white blouse and matching pumps. She was an attractive girl with long jet-black hair, pouty lips, long legs and perky breasts. With the exception of the slight acne, a byproduct of Meth use, she had a classy East Coast look to her – a far cry from the typical tweeker chicks that frequented Garrett's house. But then Tina was not your typical tweeker chick. In spite of the fact that she was equally as dependent on the drugs as anyone in Garrett's little circle — and made most of her money selling them — Tina saw herself as a step above functional. She saw herself as successful, this because she worked part-time as a pseudo-paralegal for Ron Goldberg, a criminal attorney who was very well known in the dope circles as both a savior and a customer alike.

Some tweekers would take electronic things apart or obsess on fixing cars that weren't in need of repair. Legal research was Tina's thing. The Meth gave her delusions of grandeur, and she errantly believed she *was* an attorney, and tried desperately to live the part. With her wardrobe and her beloved Jaguar, most people bought into her charade almost immediately, but for those who knew her, there were a lot more sides to Tina.

"So how was the tour, Pat? Bring home anything that can't be cured with penicillin?"

"Nothing nearly as nice as what I could surely get from you, my love."

There would always be some sexual tension between her and Pat. They'd had their moment together, but Pat found Tina to be a bit much for his tastes. Behind closed doors, Tina was very dominating to the point of inflicting pain through various strange means. Unlike dominatrix types that do it for money because men are such easy marks for that sort of thing, Tina did it for her own pleasure. Pat could also never wrap his head around the idea that Tina preferred sex in the rear end instead of the traditional way.

Tina had also had short stints with Garrett and Otterpop alike but soon became more like just one of the guys due to her strong personality. She was not shy about cutting up with the boys or voicing her opinion, and she could take a joke with the best of them. Her sense of humor, thick skin and loyalty made Tina a great friend.

"Seriously dude, you look beat up from the street up." Tina's face expressed genuine concern. "Are you okay, Pat?"

"I'm good now," said Pat, blowing a huge hit out of his mouth and nostrils. "This is some bomb-ass shit."

"Yes it is. So tell me about the trip. You guys did like ten cities this time, didn't you? And how's the wife and kid?"

"Tina, can I be perfectly honest with you?"

"Of course."

"Tina, I literally don't remember anything from the trip except yesterday and today. I 'd never been so high in my whole life – it was insane. But this morning I'd never felt so miserable in my whole life. And then Christine calls and starts beating up on me. My son, you know? She's pissed because I'm never there. And she's right, but how can I possibly face her or even talk to her when I'm coming down? And I sure as hell can't face them when I'm high. I don't know what the fuck to do…" He stared into the fire. "I have to change something, but how can I be a father when I'm a dope fiend and I love it! I'm a fuckin' rock star! How can I possibly be a dad?"

"Is the pig developing scruples?"

"I'm serious, Tina."

"Pat, you are one of the most narcissistic people I've ever met. I'm just like you. I really wish I had some answers for you, but it's gonna take a miracle for me to quit doing this shit. I love my lifestyle, and I'm betting yours is a whole lot more fun than mine. Drugs and fucking and money, who wants to give that up?"

"You're some help."

"Hey, I'm just being real. There's no sense lying to yourself."

Pat felt a wet hand on his shoulder.

"I don't know what kinda downer shit you guys are talking about, but I'm thinking it's time for an attitude adjustment," a dripping wet Garrett laughed. Pat was relieved that his conversation with Tina was interrupted before it got too much deeper. "Everybody gather around!" Garrett exclaimed. "It's fogger time!"

The fogger Garrett was referring to was a giant glass hookah pipe, modified specifically for smoking Meth. It was the size of a small beach ball and had six hoses, making it look like a big glass octopus. Garrett poured a massive amount of Meth into the huge bowl. Pat, Chris, Tina, Garrett and the two completely naked ladies all grabbed a hose. Otterpop worked a torch.

"Ready everyone?" said Garrett. "This is going to make you sweat!"

They all breathed in deeply.

Wow, what a rush. Incredible...

They smoked until they couldn't smoke anymore.

♪♪♪

Pat opened his eyes. He was lying back in a lounge chair, watching Garrett being ridden by one of the naked girls. The other one was between Pat's legs, working his manhood like a porn star. Tina, Chris, and Otterpop were in the hot tub doing who-knows-what.

Garrett turned to Pat. "It's the rock star life baby!"

Déjà vu...

♪♪♪

Chris handed Garrett a wad of money. "Thanks for a sweet welcome home, my brother."

"Yeah, man," Pat added, "Thanks for the hospitality. You've got a great place here."

"No sweat. Call me anytime. I stuck a little bundle of coke in the bag too. Enjoy."

"You're the best, Garrett..."

Chris and Pat shuffled down the steps and got into the car.

"Hey Chris, I'm sorry for being such a dick to you on the bus, man," Pat said, feeling a lot of artificially induced love.

"It's cool bro, I totally know what you're going through and I understand."

"You understand me more than anybody – I know I can count on you for anything. I hope you know you can count on me too, bro. I love you man."

"I love you too, dude." Chris steered the little rental car onto the freeway. They were both just high enough to be happy. More importantly, they had enough drugs to last a few days.

"Bro, what are you going to do about Christine and your son?"

"I don't know, man. I really do love Christine, but she and Tommy don't deserve the life I'm leading. How can I possibly be a dad with all the shit going on in my life? I got recording sessions, rehearsals, tours…"

"Drugs, bitches, more drugs…"

"I know, man, I need to stop."

"You do need to stop."

"I will. *We* will, right? Check it out man, we got the show here in San Diego and then the schedule is clear for a while, right? We'll wean ourselves off the dope. We'll take a break."

"I was thinking we should get a beach house or something. Take a vacation."

"Dude, that's awesome. Maybe we'll get out of town. Hawaii or something."

"That would be awesome."

"We'll bring Christine and Tommy. No drugs. I'll go see them tonight and tell them. I'll be a dad!"

"Lots of rock stars are also dads too, bro."

"Right! I can do this. We can do this. We party our asses off till the Coors Amphitheater show, and then that's it. We go out with a bang. I'm all in. I feel real good about this. In fact, I'm calling Christine as soon as we get home."

"I'm feelin' good too, man. Now pass the pipe!"

They laughed — and partied — all the way home.

♪♪♪

Garrett stepped out of the shower feeling refreshed. He grabbed a towel and stopped to look in the mirror.

Man, I look good... he thought to himself. His arms and chest were nicely cut, and the moisture on his skin made his muscles glisten. He wrapped the towel around his waist and strutted into his bedroom. Peeking out the window onto the patio, he could see Otterpop collecting bottles, cans and empty drink glasses, and a girl vacuuming naked.

I've definitely got the life...

He opened a dresser drawer and grabbed a pair of shorts and a T-shirt, pulled them on and walked out into the living room, taking a minute to admire his huge entertainment center and the built-in glass shelves around it full of his knick-knacks.

Being from England, Garrett was very fond of soccer, and most of his trinkets reflected that. Like most transplanted Londoners, Manchester United was his club. He picked up his favorite item, a crystal soccer ball he had found on a trip to Scotland with his family. He thought about what Pat had said; how impressed he was with his setup. Garrett was proud of his success and loved to flaunt it, so to hear that from a bona fide rock star was pretty gratifying.

He sat down at the bar and the naked maid walked out and gave him a kiss.

"Is there anything else we can do for you?" she asked as the phone rang.

"Oh definitely… Just let me get this,"

He picked up the handset. Dead air. He paused for a second with the phone in his hand, feeling a little puzzled.

A deafening explosion shook the house. He whipped the girl behind him to shield her and turned his head from the flash of the blast. His ears were ringing. The girl that was inside the house ran out the door and fell to the ground holding her ears and screaming in terror. As Garrett looked inside, he could see smoke filling the room. His heart pounded. The sound of glass breaking echoed throughout the house. Another explosion. Footsteps running through the house. More screaming. Garrett stepped in front of the doorway, and there it was.

Through the billowing smoke, he could see the barrel of an assault rifle with a bright red laser shining directly into his eyes.

"On your knees! Hands on your head!"

Garrett dropped to his knees and slowly laced his fingers behind his head as a tear ran down his cheek. He watched as his beloved crystal soccer ball shattered on the ground.

FIVE

TINA GAZED INTO the rearview mirror in disbelief. One, two, three cars, maybe four – she couldn't keep count. Cops were running all over the place. They swarmed the house, smashing windows with the butts of rifles and tossing in concussion grenades. The force of the explosions could be felt inside her car as she drove away.

The first black and white to appear on the scene sped directly toward her, racing down the opposite side of the street nearly hitting her head-on. Two more marked cars could be seen approaching in the distance behind her. By the time she reached the end of Garrett's street, it was completely blocked and smoke was billowing out of his front door. Officers were out of their cars with the doors open and guns drawn as if they were in a movie standoff. The view in her mirror was surreal. She nearly sideswiped a parked car as she tried to steer and stare into the mayhem commencing in her mirror at the same time.

This cannot be happening...

She turned onto a main road leading into Pacific Beach, breathing rhythmically in an attempt to prevent herself from hyperventilating. Still in shock, she continued down Grand Avenue perplexed and fumbling for her cell phone.

What am I going to do?

She spilled the contents of her purse onto the passenger seat, driving with one hand and searching frantically for her phone with the other. Her tweeked out mind raced.

I've got to call Ron Goldberg, but first I have to find out what they've done with Garrett... I've got to find somewhere to chill... God, I've got no place to go... what am I going to do? And where's my phone?

The only reason she'd even left the house in the first place was to go pick up breakfast. She wasn't sure whether to be glad she'd gotten out of there just in the nick of time or be totally panicked about the fact that she now had no place to return to.

And what about Garrett and Otterpop? Oh, God...

She took a deep breath.

Think, Tina, think...

She continued to drive, though her destination was yet to be determined.

And where is my fucking phone?

Tina had moved out of her apartment two weeks prior and put everything into a storage unit. She'd more or less been loitering around Garrett's ever since, helping him with business and sleeping with him when it was convenient.

Tina had no girlfriends, as she had always felt that she was too good for the women she came in contact with — 'bag whores' she'd call them — she believed most other women were beneath her, as she was *going* to go to college and *going* to become a lawyer. Tina believed she had a future. What that future held now was anyone's guess.

Tina, you need to get a grip...

She pulled into a Chevron station, parked the Jaguar parallel to a cinder block wall away from the gas pumps and focused on the contents of her purse further. She took a quick inventory.

Okay...makeup, cigarettes, lighter... a bag of dope... Good, that's one less thing to worry about...Now where is my...

She bent over and tried to see under the passenger seat.

There you are, you little bastard...

She reached under the seat and worked the phone into her hand with her fingertips. Relieved, she sat up and flipped open the phone to look through her contact list. It was then that she looked up and noticed the red lights in her rearview mirror.

♪♪♪

Pat's home in North San Diego County was a very comfortable and relaxing place. His cul-de-sac he shared with three other houses was very quiet most of the time, that is, unless Pat was having one of his infamous afterparties.

The large Victorian style home on the corner to the left was owned by an older couple that had retired and spent ninety percent of the year traveling the country in their big diesel motorhome. The property to the right down a long dirt drive was owned by a world-renowned motocross rider. The people across the street only used their home during racing season at Del Mar, which was from roughly July to September.

Pat's house was a beautiful, modern two story of beige stucco and glass; a sweet floor plan that included four bedrooms, formal living areas and a lower level used for throwing parties. The pool and hot tub were accessible from nearly every room.

Pat's 'party room' had comfortable couches throughout, TV's everywhere and all the amenities like a foosball table, a pool table, and a completely stocked bar. A few steps up from the party room was another sliding glass door that led into Pat's pride and joy, the garage.

The ceiling was at least twenty feet high, and the floors were all checkered tile. The huge space was equipped with hydraulic lifts and every tool imaginable. The collection included an array of motorcycles, a '68 Chevelle SS hardtop coupe and a bright red Dodge Viper. But Pat's one and only true love sat in the third spot; a gold metal flake 1970 Oldsmobile Cutlass 442 convertible that was given to him by his grandfather. The four-barrel four hundred cubic inch engine was polished so clean that you could see your reflection in the high-rise intake manifold. Pat loved his toys.

Chris and Pat pulled up to the house, leaving the rental car parked on the street for easy pick up by Enterprise. It was midday and the spring sun was shining down on the long stone driveway. Pat walked casually over to the keypad mounted on the wall and punched in the alarm code. As they stood waiting for the garage door to finish rolling up, they both thought about how great it was to be home. Pat admired his prized machines as they walked through the sliding glass door into the party room and flopped down onto a leather couch. Chris picked up the remote control to fire up a TV.

"You know what is really strange," Pat observed as he sank into the cushions, "is how badly I've wanted to get home, but when we finally get here the first thing that pops into my head is, like, now what?"

"I'll tell you what's popped into my head, bro…poppin' some rock hits!"

"Handle it. I'm gonna grab a couple of hits, then it's time to make some calls and let everyone know we're back."

"You gonna call Christine?"

"I guess I gotta. But gimme that pipe first."

♪♪♪

"Driver of the Jaguar, turn off your ignition, throw the keys out the window, and place both hands out the window where I can see them!"

Tina was terrified. She looked back, trying to see what was going on behind her, but was quickly blinded by bright white and red lights. Her stomach was knotted, her throat dry, her body frozen. A bag of dope lay next to her on the passenger seat. She was screwed. There were two clear choices — submit or run. She looked through the windshield; all was clear in front. To her left, an SUV was gassing up at the pump; to her right, a wall. She squinted into the rearview mirror trying to make out how many lights there were. Her stomach had now moved up into her chest.

Let's see...one, two on top, and the red one in the middle...one set of high beams...

There was only one police car behind her. One of the lights suddenly lost its focus and moved its beam. The left side door was opening on the police car, and the officer was getting out. She slowly set down her phone, picked up her driver's license and stuck it in her bra.

"You, in the Jaguar," the officer yelled, "I'm going to ask you again, please turn off the engine and throw the keys..."

She slammed the car into gear and stomped on the gas pedal. Thc Jaguar jumped like a cat, squirting gravel from the rear tires as she flew out of the parking lot and into the street leaving a trail of sparks behind her. She could see the cop jumping back into his car as she picked up speed, recklessly weaving in and out of the slower moving cars in front of her. She shot through a stop sign sending cars skidding to a stop in both directions. Never letting up on the pedal, she spun the wheel to the right as the car loosely followed her command, sending her squealing around a corner. She counter-steered fast enough to avoid hitting a whole line of parked cars on the other side of the street just as a truck clipped her left rear fender.

Screaming out loud, she sailed down Pacific Beach Drive narrowly avoiding obstacles on both sides. She could just barely make out the flashing blue and red lights in her rearview coming around the corner in pursuit. She chose another left – this one being onto a main street into Mission Bay.

If she could cross the bridge ahead, maybe she could lose him in one of the resort hotels or at Sea World. They couldn't chase her into an amusement park – it would be too dangerous.

Jamming the pedal all the way to the floor, the V12 engine of the Jag responded just as the advertisers would have you believe it would. She pushed her way into the left lane passing cars like they were standing still. Glancing into her mirror she could see that the cop had just made the corner. The curvature of the bridge blotted his lights from the horizon; she figured she had about a quarter mile on him. She laughed to herself.

Tina, you might just pull this off yet...

The car began to shudder as it approached a hundred miles per hour and a traffic signal. The signal turned yellow, then red.

*Oh, God...*She closed her eyes tightly, held her breath, and waited for impact.

♪♪♪

The boy had his elbow locked, and all of his upper body weight was pressing down on her mouth. Screaming was futile, but she could and would fight.

She'd seen the boy around school before. He wasn't ugly or anything like that; in fact, she'd even smiled at him once or twice. But now his eyes displayed anger like she'd never seen in her life.

Tina clawed at his arm, drawing long red lines down the inside of it with her fingernails. He recoiled in pain, allowing her to turn her head and free her mouth from his smothering. She didn't scream; instead, she cursed him.

"God will make you pay for this, you bastard!"

He sneered and cupped his bloody hand around her throat, cutting off her ability to breathe. Her eyes widened with fear.

"Don't worry, you're going to like this, you little bitch."

The boy ripped her underwear from her body; there was no way for her to stop him as fighting for air was much more important at the moment. His hand worked its way between her legs as she kicked and fought for breath. She felt one of his fingers inside her.

God, please help me...

Tina reached above her head, grabbed the leg of the table that the boy had pushed her under, and pulled with everything she had.

The table slid forward and suddenly the boy's head fell forward with a thump. He jumped back, grabbing the back of his neck with both hands and wincing in pain. A heavy brass paperweight in the shape of an iron that her homeroom teacher used to press flowers inside the pages of books clunked to the floor. Tina and the boy stared at each other in amazement.

Winning the short battle of reflexes, Tina dashed for the classroom exit, threw open the door and bolted down the hallway. As the school's exterior doors grew nearer, she could hear the footsteps and heavy breathing of her pursuer gaining fast. She lowered her shoulder and threw her body into the heavy metal door. It impeded her progress just long enough for her to feel the clasp of the boy's hand on her shoulder.

"No, goddamn you!" she screamed as she squirmed herself loose of his grip and flew down the steps and into the street; a truck missing hitting her by inches.

Her would-be rapist was not so lucky. The huge grille of a Dodge pickup mowed him down with screeching brakes; the locked up left front tire ripping his grated torso all but in half.

Looking back in disbelief, Tina ran straight into the arms of a tall black woman and began to cry. The woman knelt down, shielding Tina's little head from the gruesome scene. She took Tina's head in her hands and looked into her face, as a crowd began to gather around the truck.

"Baby, are you okay?" the woman asked.

"That boy tried to rape me," Tina sobbed.

The woman looked over Tina's head at the boy's mangled body sticking out from under the truck, then back into her eyes. "Sweetie, the Lord works in mysterious ways."

♪♪♪

The car shook violently as it scraped the ground and bounced into the air, careened through the intersection and slammed down hard enough to jar her eyes open. Cars on both sides of the street screeched to a halt. Never letting off the gas, she looked back over her shoulder in disbelief; she had made it through the intersection.

Thank you, Lord...

As she turned her head around to face forward, she saw red and blue lights now approaching in front of her.

Son of a bitch...

She cranked the wheel right, turning onto a main road that led into the Pacific Princess Resort on Vacation Island. Moving way too fast, she plowed over the median taking out an entire row of palms and other foliage – her vision now completely impaired by the fronds all over the windshield.

Just as the windshield was freed of debris, a hotel maintenance golf cart pulled out directly into her path. She let out a wail, pulling on the wheel as hard as she could and simultaneously jamming on the brakes. It wasn't enough.

The Jag skidded sideways, the right rear door of the car squarely hitting the little cart. The impact forced the car over the golf cart and through the air, rolling over and over again in a blur of metal, plastic and shattered glass. Finally, the momentum tossed the car right side up again, slamming it down with a deafening crash on top of the hoods of two parked cars.

Tina opened her eyes and looked down into her lap. No blood. She felt no pain. She peeled her shaking hands off the steering wheel and slowly began to look around. Feeling like she was still floating through the air, she shook off the effects of the impact and realized that the car was about three or four feet off of the ground.

Damn, look at that...there's my phone!

Laughing to herself she picked up the phone and stuffed it in her bra, released her seatbelt and grabbed the door handle. She held her breath and pushed the door with her shoulder.

Holy shit, it opened...

She jumped down from the Jag and ran. Behind her she could hear people screaming, sirens wailing, cars skidding and a helicopter thumping in the distance. But it was all behind her, and she wasn't looking back.

Nope, you're not stopping till it's safe...

She ran until her lungs hurt, hurdling bushes and shrubs and darting between buildings until the beach blocked her from going any further. She then took off up the beach toward some little rental bungalows and ran up to the patio of one, checking the sliding door. Locked.

Shit...

She pushed her way through the shrubbery to another bungalow. Back door this time. She tried the lock. No dice.

Shit!

She grabbed the knob again, twisting as hard as she could, and slammed her left shoulder into the door. She flew through the doorway, falling hard onto the tile floor.

Astonished, she quickly got herself up and slammed the door behind her. Leaning with her back against the door she caught her breath and looked around as her eyes attempted to adjust to the light. She assessed her situation. A sofa bed, a nightstand, a TV and an armoire. All the curtains were closed. Nobody was here. Another door led into to the master suite. There was a suitcase open on the bed and the sheets and covers were a mess. Clothing was strewn around the room. Yet another door. The bathroom. She couldn't hold out any longer. She stood over the toilet and threw up.

♪♪♪

"Yes, I'll be there, I promise." Pat hung up the phone and tossed it on the couch. "So what's the deal man?" asked Chris, his eyes never leaving the TV.

"I told her I'd be there around one o'clock. I'm freaked out, bro. I can't face her and the boy high."

"What's your alternative…not high? I'm thinking that's pretty much out of the question." Chris laughed. "You need to man up, brother. Go see your son."

"You're going with me."

"No I'm not."

"Dude, I feed you, I clothe you, I buy your fuckin' drugs, and you can't do this?"

"Pat, be real. This is *your* family. You need to step up to the plate sometime. If you choose a life of sex, drugs and rock n' roll that's fine with me, but you still have an obligation to see your kid and deal with Christine. Nobody can do it for you dude, it's something you gotta do yourself. So just fuckin' do it."

"When did you become so righteous?"

"I'm just being real."

Pat got up slowly and meandered toward the garage. He stood there for a moment, lost in thought. His nerves were shot.

What if his son didn't like him? He'd never been there for either of them, and Christine wouldn't let him forget that for five minutes. He wanted to try to get to know Tommy, but he knew that she'd start into him almost immediately, he'd go on the defense and it would turn into an argument. He'd wind up writing a check and leaving. If she'd just cut him a little slack, let him settle in before complaining then maybe he'd get the chance to feel this 'bond' with his son that everyone speaks of. He didn't understand anything about kids; he'd never experienced them. All he knew how to do was play music and party. What did she want him to do anyway? Just sit around with him? He's only three…what the hell do you do with a three-year-old?

Man, I'm just not dad material. I'll just look foolish, and she'll hate me even more...

He considered walking back inside.

"Dude, get going!" Chris said, sneaking up behind him and jarring him out of his spell.

"Fuck, man, I'm going…"

He climbed into the Oldsmobile, tossed his cell phone onto the passenger seat and started the car. The engine responded with a happy roar. It really was a beautiful day. He put down the top and backed out of the garage. Chris was mockingly waving goodbye as he started up the driveway.

Asshole...

He left the cul-de-sac and turned onto a quiet street – he was actually feeling pretty good. He felt the sun on his face, the wind in his hair – maybe this wasn't going to be so bad after all. As he rolled through the neighborhood toward the freeway, his phone rang. He picked it up and looked. Tina.

Man, I can't even deal with her antics right now... I gotta stay focused on what I'm doing with my family. Family? Did I just say that?

He powered off the phone.

♪♪♪

Please...pick up the phone you asshole!

She slapped the phone shut and sat on the bathroom floor, her back against the door. She could hear sirens and a helicopter circling above. She was never going to get out of here – she was on an island for God's sake! One way on and one way off – pretty easy for the cops to contain. Nobody was answering her calls. There was nobody to help her – she was going to have to figure something out on her own.

She picked herself up off the bathroom floor. Her mouth tasted like vomit. She turned on the sink, ran some cool water into her hands and drank, then splashed some on her face. She looked at her reflection in the mirror. Her mascara had run and her hair was haggard – she made a feeble attempt at fixing herself up.

What have you gotten yourself into?

She opened the bathroom door and walked into the bedroom, taking inventory of the room. A suitcase, women and men's clothing around it on the bed. An empty beach bag, some towels strewn across the floor – probably a happy couple on vacation. There was a drawer ajar on the dresser. She slid it open. Socks, underwear, spare room key, a watch, loose change, shades, keys…

Keys?

She scooped them up and held them up in front of her face.

Nice...

There was a BMW key on the ring. She began to frantically go through the clothing in the drawer and found a floral sundress and a matching scarf.

Color coordinated... Must be quite the lady...

She quickly stripped out of her own clothes, rolled them up into a ball and stuffed them into the bottom drawer. She had to move fast if she was going to get out of there, not only before these people came back, but before the cops had blocked off every possible escape route from the island.

She put on the sundress, wrapped the scarf around her head, reached back into the drawer and pulled out the pair of oversized sunglasses. She put them on and checked the mirror.

Perfect...

She reached back into the drawer a third time, grabbed the spare room keycard and stuck it in her bra. Cupping the keys and her phone in her fist, she gingerly cracked open the door, peering outside and letting her eyes adjust. Nobody near. She slowly stepped out, leaving the door ajar in case she had to go back in. She noted the room number on the door and started toward the nearest parking area.

I don't look right without a purse...

There were several BMW's in the lot.

Crap…

Looking at the keys in her hand, she smiled at the sight of an alarm remote. As she pressed the button, the lights flashed and the horn chirped on a silver 540i.

Sweet, my kind of car…

She got into the driver's seat, inserted the key, and started the car, finally letting out the breath she'd been holding.

Thou art definitely with me...

She backed the Beemer out of its space and began to follow the signs to the exit. Her jaw dropped at what she saw next.

There were more police cars then she could count. There was a fire engine, ambulance, and two tow trucks. Like the wake of a tornado, she could see her own path of destruction. The golf cart – or what was left of it – was over on its side with the top missing. There were palm fronds, shrubs and dirt everywhere. Her once beautiful Jaguar was now perched precariously on the hoods of two parked cars.

It appeared that whoever was driving the golf cart must have gotten away unscathed as she didn't see paramedics tending to anyone on the ground – she truly hoped that was the case anyway. Up ahead of her a cop was unrolling yellow tape across the exit lanes. She sped up to get past him before he completely blocked both lanes. He raised a hand as she tried to pass, setting down the tape roll and walking around to the driver's side of the car.

"What happened, officer?" she asked in the best curious tourist voice she could muster.

"An accident Ma'am. Where are you headed if you don't mind me asking?"

"Just to the store to pick up a few things – my husband is getting our boat ready for a day trip." She wondered to herself if she'd just volunteered too much information.

"And where are you staying Ma'am?"

"Bungalow number 123. It's right on the beach. It's just beautiful."

"Do you have your room key?"

"Of course..."

She pulled down the front of her dress exposing way more cleavage than she needed to. She smiled as she retrieved the keycard from above her right breast.

The officer leaned in closer but looked past her breasts to the passenger seat. He noticed her dress was without any pockets, and the absence of a purse or wallet on the passenger seat concerned him.

"Don't you need your purse if you are going to the store?"

Tina gasped.

I knew it...

She looked over her shoulder into the back seat and there it was. A brown leather purse on the floor of the rear passenger side.

Holy shit... Thou art seriously with me...

"It's right back there on the floor, officer."

The cop paused for a moment, looked into the back seat, looked back at Tina, and spoke. "Okay ma'am, but I'd hurry back; we are most likely going to be closing the resort for an investigation. Nobody gets in and nobody gets out without ID, so be prepared to show your room key and driver's license when you get back."

"No problem, officer. I hope everyone is okay. Thanks."

Tina put the car in gear and drove out of the resort.

♪♪♪

Pat sat across the kitchen table from Christine. She looked as beautiful as the day they'd met, her thick auburn hair flowing over her exposed shoulders, her big blue eyes gazing at him. Tommy was crawling around on the floor playing with a Tonka truck.

"You know, everyone says he looks just like you."

"He does, the handsome devil. I hope you're keeping him clear of all the little girls, I don't want him out there breaking hearts."

"Like you did mine?"

"C'mon Christine, don't start with me. Let's just have a nice visit, okay?"

"I'm sorry. What do you want to do?"

"I dunno... should we get him some ice cream or something?"

Tommy's little ears perked up. "Ice cream, ice cream, c'mon Daddy!" he exclaimed.

Daddy? He'd never heard that before. It made his heart swell a bit.

Tommy came over and tugged on his pant leg. "Can we, Daddy? Pahleeze?"

He almost melted. Last time he saw Tommy, he didn't talk much.

"Of course we can. Let's go."

Christine grabbed her purse and the three of them left her condo. The beautiful Olds convertible glistened in the sunlight.

"Daddy, Daddy, is that your car?"

"It surc is."

"I wanna ride in it…please, please…"

"Okay," said Christine, "let me get your car seat!"

She reached into the back of her car, retrieved the child safety seat and strapped it into the back of the convertible.

"Daddy, pick me up."

Pat picked up his son, lifted him into the back seat and belted him in. He was giggling and cooing over the large shiny automobile, exclaiming 'Nice car!' over and over. Christine got in the passenger side.

"He's definitely yours, no doubt in my mind now!" she laughed.

"Why, was there any?"

"Come on, Pat…"

He really missed the way they were – when they were happy. When he was happy. He looked at Tommy in the rearview mirror, his happy little face soaking up the sunlight. Was this his so-called family? *Maybe I could do this after all…*

He backed out the car and they hit the road. Tommy was laughing out loud.

"Faster, faster!" he cried.

Pat stepped on the gas, and the car leapt forward. They all felt elated as the warm wind blew by. He had not felt this free in a long time. It really was great to be home.

They drove and drove through the San Diego foothills. They stopped for lunch and some window-shopping; Pat carrying Tommy on his shoulders almost the entire time. Tommy got his ice cream and they started home. The sun was low over the hills and the high clouds were turning a bright pink color. As they pulled up to her condo, Christine took Pat's hand. He smiled, leaned over and gave her a kiss.

"Eeeeww!!" Tommy exclaimed from the back seat. They all enjoyed a laugh.

"I have to get back, honey. Chris is waiting at the house and we've got things to do."

"Chris? What do you guys have to…"

He put his finger up to her lips.

"Come on…don't ruin this day. I'll be down again tomorrow. I love you."

She sighed. "Really, Pat? If you tell Tommy that, you can't let him down. You have to be honest with us — and yourself — about what you are really capable of right now. If you can't come back down tomorrow I'll understand, but he may not. I just want you to be there for him. Don't tell us you're going to be here if you're not."

She was right. He had just begun jonesing for dope, and he wasn't sure what he was capable of either.

"Look, I'll call you tonight after I assess my schedule."

She rolled her eyes. "Schedule…" she said sarcastically.

He put his hands on her shoulders and looked deep into her eyes.

"Listen, I want you to know that I want you and Tommy in my life. I'm going to try real hard. After this week, the schedule is open. I was thinking of taking us all on vacation. You guys can come stay with me. I'm thinking of taking a real hiatus."

"Not with Chris. You'll have to kick him out first."

Pat laughed. "We'll cross that bridge when we get to it."

He crouched down in front of Tommy. "Hey dude, I love you. I gotta go now but I'll see you soon."

"No, no, Daddy, no don't go…" Tommy started to cry. "Please don't go…"

Pat was floored. He didn't know how to react. "I'll see you soon, don't worry, I'll call your mom tonight."

"No…Daddy, don't go..."

Pat began to cry as well. He picked Tommy up and held him tight. Christine was crying too. "Don't worry you two, I love you both… I'll see you tomorrow, okay?"

♪♪♪

Pretty much passed out on the couch, Chris opened one eye just enough to see the TV. The early news was on. There was a helicopter circling Mission Bay and he, like everyone else, loved a good police chase. He sat up and turned up the volume.

"A high-speed police pursuit ended in a spectacular crash today as officers chased a car through the streets of Pacific Beach and into the Pacific Princess Resort on Vacation Island. The car's driver lost control sending it sailing into a group of parked cars where the driver then escaped into the resort. Officers are still searching for the suspect, who they believe to be a Hispanic female. Police have issued a statement confirming that the car chase was related to a number of drug raids that were conducted locally by the joint effort of the San Diego Police and Sheriff's departments, the Narcotics Task Force. Vacation Island will be closed pending a door-to-door search and investigation, and police say it is very fortunate that nobody was hurt. Join us for more tonight at five."

Chris rubbed his eyes in disbelief. *That sure looks like Tina's car... Drug raids? Oh crap...* He laughed to himself uncomfortably. *What the hell happened?*

He searched around for his phone and found it buried between the cushions on the couch. He flipped it open and dialed Pat's phone. Directly to voice mail.

Shit...

He dialed Garrett's number. Busy.

Where is everybody?

He sat back down and began channel surfing for more info on the news story he'd just seen.

♪♪♪

It was getting to be a long ride home. Pat stared at the back of the car in front of him, once again consumed by his thoughts. How could he make everything work? He knew there was no way he could stop using dope. He was hurting for it right now, and it had only been about four hours or so since his last hit. He could not even comprehend the idea of living the life he lived without it. The road and everything – there was no way he could continue to burn the double-ended candle of rock stardom without using.

But it wasn't always like this. He was in love with her at one time. None of the other women even came close. She was perfect; beautiful, responsible, easy to get along with. They flowed naturally. She was the perfect mom. She deserved a perfect life in a perfect home. How could he provide that in his condition? And Tommy...

Tommy...

The connection was undeniable. Just leaving him was the most difficult thing he'd ever done.

I need that kid in my life...

As he pictured Tommy's face, he began to cry again. They were meant to be a family. The thought of any other man replacing him in that boy's life made his blood boil.

He took off his sunglasses and set them on the passenger seat, realizing just then that he had turned his phone off, and that it had been off all day. He pressed the power button and waited for it to boot up.

Man, I need to get high...

♪♪♪

Tina sat on a cliff staring out at the ocean. She'd driven the now stolen BMW to Sunset Cliffs and parked in a lot at one of the vista points, watching the sun set over the Pacific. She doubted they'd look for her at the beach. She'd been sitting on the hood of the car trying to contemplate her next move for the last two hours. She lay back on the hood of the car and closed her eyes.

God, I really need to get high...

♪♪♪

The phone rang. Chris snatched it up on the first ring.

"Yellow?"

"Hey, it's me. I'm on my way home."

"Dude, where are you right now? Are you near a TV?"

"I'm in traffic. Why, what's up?"

"Something's gone down, man, something crazy. It's on the news. There was a car chase in P.B. and the car involved was Tina's!"

"Shut up."

"Dude, I shit you not, it was definitely her car. And there were a bunch of drug raids..."

"Have you talked to her?"

"I don't have her number in my phone, remember? I just got a new one."

"Dude, you're not yanking my chain are you?"

"Bro, would I make this up?"

"I'll call you back."

♪♪♪

Tina flipped open her phone.

"Hello?"

"Tina, it's Pat. What the fuck is going on?"

"Pat…oh my God… Garrett got raided…he's gotta be in jail… I ran from the cops and smashed up my car… I stole a BMW…they're looking for me I'm sure… Fuck, Pat, I don't know what to do!" She started sobbing.

"Tina, listen to me. Where are you?"

"The beach."

"Can you drive right now?"

"Yes."

"Look, just get to my house. We'll talk about everything when you get there. It may not be such a good idea to use the phone. It'll be okay. I'll see you there."

SIX

A COUPLE OF hits of Crystal Methamphetamine, and it didn't matter whether you were a dope addict trying to cope with the idea of fatherhood, or you just outran and were hiding from the police – big problems became small problems once you got high.

Pat, Chris, and Tina had been sitting in front of the TV getting high and flipping back and forth between local networks watching coverage of the chase that had occurred in San Diego earlier that day. Pat and Chris particularly enjoyed Tina, who was very Caucasian, being referred to by the newscasters as 'Hispanic female'.

"Hey, holmes," Chris began, tapping Pat on the shoulder, "Remember Single White Female? The movie?"

"I got you…SHF…single Hispanic female!"

"Yeah… single Hispanic female seeks new Jaguar!"

"Single Hispanic female seeks defensive driving classes!"

"Single Hispanic female seeks sugar daddy for casual relationship, and to help support dope habit! Enjoys hiding at the beach and wearing other people's clothes!"

They all laughed.

"Tina, you have got to be the luckiest girl on the planet!" observed Pat.

And she was too.

She'd arrived around five-thirty, beating Pat to the house by ten minutes or so, just as it was getting dark. They quickly jockeyed cars around, put the stolen BMW up on a lift in Pat's garage with a cover over it and closed the garage doors. They were a bit paranoid at first; shutting off all the lights and peering through the blinds, but the paranoia soon wore off as more dope was smoked, lines were snorted and drinks were drunk. Before long, they'd settled into the big cushions of the couches in the party room relaxing in front of the TV.

As they surfed for news, Tina recounted the day vividly. Pat and Chris were dumbfounded at how the series of events had enabled her to escape the island and the clutches of the SDPD.

"Yeah, you've definitely got someone or something looking over you," Chris noted.

"It's God," Tina said, "She's always watched over me since I was a little girl."

"She?" laughed Pat, "Oh, here we go…"

"I think the only one really watching over you is your ex-husband," Chris added, "The rest is pure luck."

Chris was right on the money with his observation. After seeing the news, Tina had called Craig her ex-husband and he agreed to go with a cooked up stolen car story. Hell, in his eyes the damn thing had pretty much been stolen since she moved out anyway; all he ever got out of it was an occasional parking ticket. At least this way he wouldn't have to talk to her as much and he'd most likely get an insurance settlement. Win/win for him, he figured.

And with the police knowing her only as 'Hispanic female suspect' she appeared to have made a clean getaway.

"Yeah, Craig's a good guy," Tina agreed.

"Well, my favorite Hispanic female," Pat said, "it's been all sorts of fun and games, but we've got to get rid of that car you brought here, and we need to do it ASAP. I want it out of here tonight."

"I know, Pat. And we also need to find out what they've done with Garrett and Otterpop and call an attorney."

"What are we going to do with the car?" asked Chris.

"I don't know… We just leave it somewhere tonight," said Pat.

"But it's got my fingerprints and hair and stuff in it. We have to clean it, right?"

"Oh, I forgot, you're a lawyer and a CSI."

"Seriously, Pat, I don't want to take any chances of this thing coming back on me."

She looked worried and began to cry.

"Hey, I'm sorry."

She sobbed. "I'm the one that's sorry... It's just... I have nothing. My car is wrecked; I have no place to go...I don't even have the things that were in my purse."

"Listen, everything's going to be fine...I've got some chick clothes here; you can pick out whatever you want to wear. And we'll go shopping tomorrow." Pat turned to Chris. "C'mon bro, let's go find some shit to clean that car with. I want it outta here tonight for sure." He turned back to Tina. "Did you try to call Ron Goldberg again?"

"Yeah, but he's not answering. I left a voice mail."

"What about the Sheriff's website? Garrett's got to be logged in there."

"Good idea..."

"Okay, you do that, Chris and I are going out to the garage to clean up your mess."

"Pat," she said, "Thank you."

"No sweat."

♪♪♪

Oh my God...

Tina yelled down the stairs to the garage, where Pat and Chris were diligently wiping and vacuuming every surface of the stolen 540i.

"Pat, come up here, you have to see this!"

"What's up?"

"Look, I found him."

They both stared at the computer monitor.

"Are those the charges?" Pat asked in disbelief. "He's screwed!"

"They always stack up charges like that initially in anticipation of his attorney cutting a deal. The more charges, the better the chance of making something stick. Ron will get it knocked down to one or two items. If he didn't have a lawyer he'd be fucked, that's for sure."

The list of charges looked pretty impressive on the computer screen. Possession of a controlled substance with intent to sell, sales of a controlled substance, trafficking of a controlled substance, conspiracy to traffic a controlled substance, maintaining a fortified residence to aid in committing a crime, four counts of possession of a firearm with a controlled substance, and manufacturing.

Tina, speaking to nobody in particular, began to run it all down.

"The conspiracy, trafficking and manufacturing charges will be dropped. The possession with sales will stick, and the actual sales will stick if he sold to a cop. I'm not sure what a fortified residence is, but I'd imagine it has to do with weapons in a house. The real issue here is the firearms and drugs charges. Anytime you have guns and drugs together, they'll nail you to the wall for it. Judges hate drugs, hate guns, and hate both together even more. They do however, love convicting people of those charges. Those gun charges add up to a three-year enhancement per firearm. That's twelve years on top of the three to four years for selling the dope. You guys and your fucking guns."

Damn… Pat thought. He and Garrett loved their guns.

Pat had purchased his first firearm a good ten years ago and had been hooked on them ever since. Not for hunting – he couldn't bear to kill anything; just target shooting and the feeling you get when you held one. It was pure power.

Back when Pat did bar gigs and they got paid in cash, he met a sheriff's deputy who helped him get a concealed carry permit for protection when he left the bars late at night with expensive gear and money. He'd been carrying ever since. Whenever he was home in San Diego, he'd keep a piece under the seat of his car.

Garrett caught him carrying one night, and it was discovered that they both shared the love of guns. They'd go shooting at the local indoor range regularly, and up in the mountains on more than a few occasions. They were always trading and trying out each other's weapons.

Pat began to wonder if he'd left any of his guns at Garrett's house. That would really suck.

Damn...

Chris came in from the garage.

"That car's as clean as it's going to get. What's up in here?"

"We're looking at how fucked Garrett is," said Tina.

Chris leaned over, squinting his eyes as he looked at the monitor.

"Damn. He's proper fucked," Chris said in a cockney accent.

"Yeah, it's going to be a challenge, but I bet Ron can get him like eighteen months in the pen if he doesn't have priors. Ron is awesome. It won't be as bad as it seems right now."

Pat nervously ran his hand through his hair. "Hey guys…where are we going to get our shit from?"

There was a long silence. Nobody had thought about it yet.

"Why, how much do we have?" asked Chris.

"It doesn't really matter how much we have, it will run out eventually."

"Everyone I know pretty much hooks up through Garrett. He's the connect."

Tina looked deep in thought. "I don't know…let me think about it..."

She got up from the computer, walked downstairs and out into the driveway for a little fresh air. Thoughts were racing through her head. Without Garrett on the streets, she not only had no place to go, she also had no way to earn quick cash. She was worried that the police may have identified her from Garrett's house and was concerned they might pick up her scent from the stolen car. And she couldn't expect Pat to take care of her; he already had Chris as a dependent. Yes, at the moment, Tina was almost as screwed as Garrett.

The makeshift job as Garrett's assistant had allowed her to network with some of Garrett's clientele, who would surely soon be hurting for Meth just as bad as she and the guys. Additionally, at one point she had met Garrett's connection. It was a quick meeting but she remembered him nonetheless. She knew what he looked like and she knew his name was Carlos. She also knew that he was well connected with the Mexican drug cartels and was not to be messed with.

She had listened to Garrett complain about Carlos on many occasions. Business was done very differently in Mexico than in the United States. Garrett described in detail a ruthless, perpetually angry person who did not care about humankind at all. As long as things always went in Carlos's favor, he was a reliable connection with the absolute best drugs money could buy. But if things did not go Carlos's way...

He'd described stories Carlos had told him about putting guns to people's heads that owed him money and torturing them. Those who knew of Carlos said he had no problem killing anyone who crossed him.

Tina took her cell phone out of her purse and stared at it. A few days ago she and Garrett had been riding in her car and Garrett used her phone to call Carlos. That meant that Carlos's phone number was probably logged into her call history. It would be easy to find too, as that particular call was an international call to Mexico.

Could she call Carlos and score directly from him?

Hell, no, he'd never talk to me... Not a woman...

Tina knew better than to expect him to remember her and to trust her anyway. And if she did mess with him, she'd be in too deep.

You can't screw with him ... Not to worry, Pat's got plenty of dope anyway...at least for now...

♪♪♪

"Well, we have to come up with something." Pat was getting irritated. "We don't need to dump it in a lake or anything. We just need to park it somewhere. Like we're returning it."

It was about one AM, and they'd been discussing what to do with the stolen car for six hours now. And getting high. And shooting pool.

"Okay, we'll just leave it in the Vons parking lot," Chris suggested for what seemed like the tenth time. "Tina, you drive it, Pat and I will follow you in the truck."

"Why me? They might still be looking for me."

"Well, I'm not driving it. You're the one who took it!"

"Fuck, I'll do it," Pat said. "You guys can follow me in my truck."

"No argument here," said Chris.

"Pat, I'll ride with you," Tina said, "We'll go together and Chris can pick us up."

"Awesome. It's settled then. We're all going to Vons in a stolen car at one in the morning," Chris said sarcastically.

"You make that sound like a bad thing," cracked Pat.

Chris was right. It was stupid.

"Okay, tomorrow. First thing. That's it."

They all agreed to the plan.

♪♪♪

Pat pulled his hair into a ponytail, backed the stolen car out of the garage and pulled into the street. Tina had her feet up on the dash and was twirling her hair nervously. The mid-morning sun was bright and they both had shades on.

"Tina, it's gonna to be fine. After all you've pulled already, this should be easy breezy."

"I'm cool, Pat. Just drive."

They pulled out onto a busy street and turned north toward the grocery store.

"Pat…"

Tina grabbed his hand. There was a Sheriff's car pulling out of a driveway right across from the Vons.

"Just act like it's our car. It's all good."

They pulled into the parking lot and found a space right in front. They apprehensively looked toward the street out the corners of their eyes. The cruiser had turned and driven away. They looked at each other and smiled. Pat took out a blue bandana and wiped off the steering wheel, then casually worked his way around the door handles. They strolled into the grocery store, grabbed a twelve pack of Corona and headed back out the door. Chris was waiting in Pat's truck, and they climbed in.

"See, that wasn't so bad, was it?"

"Shut up, Chris," Tina said.

"Home, James!" said Pat from the back seat.

And home they went.

♪♪♪

The day proved to be gorgeous; the sunlight shimmered off the pool and reflected on the big glass windows of the house. A cooler of cold beer sat between Chris and Tina as they lounged in the hot sun. The rock star life, baby.

"Man, I'm bakin'," Tina said, shielding her eyes from the water's reflection.

"I'm eggs," joked Chris.

Pat walked out of the house, oblivious to the sun and obviously aggravated.

"You guys, this dope isn't going to last. I cannot run out. We need to take some action now or it's going to get ugly, 'cause before I run out, you two get cut off. So let's consider our options."

Chris sat up in his lounge chair.

"Everybody we know is in the same predicament. With Garrett gone, we're screwed."

"Bro, we got high before we knew Garrett. We know tons of people. There's got to be someone else."

"Yeah, if you want bunk waste-of-money shit. I could maybe get some more coke…"

"No, I don't want bunk shit and I don't want coke!" Pat was getting angry. "We have to find some good Meth."

Tina rolled over, sat up and slid her sunglasses up onto her forehead.

"I might have an idea."

"I'm listening…" Pat said in an annoyed tone.

"Well…I've actually met Garrett's connect before."

"There we go! Call him!"

"Pat, it's not that easy. He's connected to the Mexican Mafia. This guy's like a Tony Montana type. I only saw him one time. He probably won't even remember me."

"Do you have his number?"

"I don't know…"

"*Do you*? You do!"

"Well… I could probably find it… Garrett called him from my phone last week… I just don't know if I should…I mean, he's Garrett's guy…"

"Hey, you brought it up. Besides, what else are we going to do? You know Garrett would be cool with this under the circumstances – hey, you could probably even get the shit cheap and turn it over to some of the people you know from him… make some money, right? I'll even finance it for you!"

"I don't know, Pat…the guy is scary. Rumor has it he's killed and raped. Do you want me to get raped?"

"You can't rape the willing…"

"Fuck you, Pat."

"Tina, c'mon, I'm just kidding. Gimme your phone. I'll dial."

"He's right, T," Chris agreed, "we gotta do something. This could be a good opportunity for you and me. Maybe we could pull our own weight around here."

"That'd be nice for a change," Pat said as he playfully grabbed Tina's phone and started punching buttons.

"Pat, give it to me…" She jumped onto his back, grabbed his arm and snatched the phone before pushing him off the lounge chair and onto the ground. He laughed.

"I'll find the number. You assholes back off."

Chris and Pat watched attentively as she punched buttons on the phone. She navigated through the menus to her call history and began to scroll down.

There it was: 011-525-5399-6070

She looked at the phone, contemplating. Her hand began to quiver.

"Boo!" Pat made her jump.

"Pat, knock it off. This is serious shit. If I do this, you guys need to shut up. And you need to support me no matter what happens."

"You have my word."

"Mine too."

"Okay. Be quiet."

Her thumb hovered over the send button. No turning back. She pushed it.

The phone rang. Once…twice…three…

A voice answered.

"Bueno?"

SEVEN

HE WAVED HIS pistol recklessly around the room. The workers were on the dirty cement floor crouched under folding tables and trying to hide in corners. They were in a state of absolute terror. There was no escape. Men were trembling and women were crying. The dusty adobe building had only one door and no windows. A fan was running but it was disgustingly hot and everybody was dripping in sweat.

"I take care of you fuckers! All of you pinche perros! You'd be living in slums if it were not for me! And this is the thanks I get?"

Carlos Castillion looked down and pointed his pistol directly at the cowering man at his feet with his fingers laced behind his head. Another man in a dirty black suit had one hand on his shoulder preventing him from moving.

"How can you fucking steal from me?"

"Carlos, I swear, it wasn't stealing. I was going to pay it back. There just wasn't enough time."

"Pablo, how long have we known each other?"

"Since we were children."

"And I give you all of this. A shop to run. People to work for you. I compensate you well, no?"

Pablo nodded his head, "Yes, Carlos."

"And did you not think you could ask me for the money? If you needed money, all you had to do is ask. Why wouldn't you ask me?"

"Carlos, I..."

Carlos swung the pistol and hit Pablo square across the jaw. His head snapped violently to the side, and the bone-crunching sound of teeth being dislodged echoed around the room. Blood began to pour out of a deep cut below his lip left by the barrel. He began to weep.

"Because you chose to become a greedy fucking thief! That is why! How can I let this go? In front of all these people that work for you? They will think I'm weak and stupid. They will think it is okay for them to steal from me too, no?"

"No, Carlos, these are good people, they work hard for you."

"Cállate, puto! Why should I believe that? You are their boss and you steal."

"Carlos, I was not stealing…I was going to pay it back…It was a small fraction of what we produce for you daily…"

Carlos pointed the pistol down and fired, hitting Pablo just above the knee. Blood splattered across the floor, and onto the leg of Carlos's suit. Pablo bent over and grabbed his leg screaming in pain. Everybody in the room fell to the floor and started to wail.

"Tell me you were not stealing from me again!" Go ahead; tell me again you fucking dog!" He waved the pistol around the room again. "Listen to me all of you! You people do not produce shit! I have four factories out here, and this one makes me the least money. If you want to continue being paid, you people must work harder. This is not some fucking joke. Do not make a fool out of me. And let this be a lesson about stealing."

Pablo was in the fetal position holding his thigh and sobbing. Carlos looked down at him, reached into his pocket and pulled out a roll of hundred dollar bills. He tossed them at Pablo, hitting him in the face.

"Go to the doctor. I need you at work tomorrow."

"Thank you, Carlos, thank you…"

Carlos turned and walked out of the room followed closely by his henchman. They weaved through drums of chemicals, piles of steel pans, propane tanks, and other assorted waste products associated with Crystal Methamphetamine manufacturing. He turned to his henchman as they approached a dirty black Mercedes.

"That's the last time anyone in this factory shall steal from me, these fucking worthless pigs. I wish somebody would make an obvious mistake at one of the other factories so I can put the fear of God into them too."

He wiped the sweat off his forehead with a handkerchief and ran his hand through his greasy black hair. He was not a large man, in fact, he looked somewhat diminutive; but his dark, pockmarked complexion and low brow line made him appear perpetually angry and ominous. He looked at the blood on his pant leg.

"Pinche puercos. My suit is ruined. I should have just killed him."

His driver put the Mercedes into gear and they drove off down a bumpy dirt road toward the highway.

"Why don't they fix this fucking road?" Carlos complained as the Mercedes was tossed.

"You hear about the latest raids in San Diego, Mr. Castillion?" asked the henchman.

"Yes, Jose, I have. And I'm very troubled. It is this fucking Narcotics Task Force! They are slowly cutting off all of my good contacts in San Diego. Señor Arellano-Felix is very unhappy. The war against these fucking Tijuana pigs is one thing, but on the American side, there is only so much we can do. They have the San Diego Police and the Sheriff involved in this shit. As if the DEA was not bad enough."

"I know sir. And the border patrol…"

"Don't talk to me about the fucking Border Patrol," interrupted Carlos, "these dogs have taken three of my burros in the last month. Now I again have to worry about who is smuggling for me. Smugglers are fucking thieves. The Border Patrol are fucking thieves. All Americans are fucking thieves!"

He pounded his hand against the dashboard. He was seriously upset and with good reason. In addition to running his four meth factories and managing connections in San Diego, he was also the one responsible for the Cocaine, Marijuana and Methamphetamine trafficking operations through the Otay Mesa border crossing. The agents that Carlos had in Customs and Border Protection had been compromised, part of a cooperative operation between the DEA and the San Diego Police and Sheriff's Departments' joint venture, the Narcotics Task Force. As a result of the NTF's operation, agents were snitched out, smugglers were given up, and raids were conducted.

All that Carlos had been in charge of had remained unaffected during this ongoing drug war until now. But with the raids and the problems with Customs and Border Protection, Carlos had to work fast to find new contacts. He had to also find some new smugglers, or burros as he liked to call them. Product needed to be moved in a timely fashion without loss, or Carlos would once again be answering to the Arellano-Felix brothers, who had much more important things to worry about. Carlos did not want to lose his job, or worse.

"Jose, we need to find out who is still uncompromised in the Customs office. Find out who's left and how much it is going to cost me to get more contacts."

"Yes sir, Mr. Castillion. What are we going to do about burros?"

"Don't worry about that Jose, burros are a dime a dozen. Everybody wants to make a peso if it is a sure thing. Just relax and let the burros come to us."

Carlos's phone rang. It was from the United States. He picked it up.

"Bueno?"

♪♪♪

"Hello? Is this Carlos?"

"Who is this?" said the voice at the other end.

"This is Tina; I'm a friend of Garrett."

"Garrett? Who the fuck is Garrett, and why do you call this phone?"

"I'm a…business partner …of Garrett's. I met you a couple of weeks ago. Long black hair, light skin, gold Jaguar?"

Pat looked at Chris and whispered, "Business partner?" and they both laughed. Tina shushed them angrily.

"What do you want, Miss *Tina*?"

"I just thought you should know that Garrett was compromised. And I would like to continue his business with you…"

"You call my phone to tell me that our associate was raided, like I wouldn't already know that and already know who was responsible as well? And then you tell me you want me to do business with you? How do I know you aren't the police? Listen you little panocha, I don't know who you are, and I don't know any Garrett. I have no use for you. Do not call this phone again."

"Wait, please, I need your help."

"Why should I help you? Do you meddle in business? Does Garrett even know you are calling me?"

"Not yet, but my attorney, Ron Goldberg, is defending him. I work directly for Ron. I have no connection to the cops. I'm totally cool... I swear, Garrett's going to be protected, and you will be protected."

"You think you actually know something about business, eh hermana? You are a joke. I could find you and crush you right now just for calling me! The only reason I don't is the fact that I do remember you from Garrett, and I trust Garrett."

"Thank you, Carlos."

That was the right thing to say. Carlos was always pleased when somebody thanked him after he threatened them.

"Do you have something to write with?"

"Yes."

"You go buy a new phone. You call this number: 619-255-4464."

Tina scribbled the number into the palm of her hand.

"Let it ring twice. Somebody will call you back. Do not ever call this phone again. Do you understand?"

"Yes, I…"

Carlos hung up the phone.

"So what did he say?" Pat asked, eagerly awaiting her response.

"Pat, this is not a good idea."

"C'mon, Tina, what's up with that number you wrote down?"

"He didn't want to talk to me. He told me to go buy a new phone and call this number, let it ring twice and I'd get a callback. This number has a local area code. It doesn't make sense. This whole thing is weirding me out."

"He's probably paranoid. He might think your phone isn't safe because of the raid on Garrett."

"I guess so."

"Well let's go get you a phone!" said Pat, already tossing his car keys to Chris.

They drove to 7-Eleven and bought a pre-paid cell phone, inserted the sim card and went through the activation process. Tina typed the number Carlos had given her into the new phone. She pressed send. As instructed, she let it ring twice and then hung up. They sat in the truck waiting. Nobody could think of anything to say. It was a brutally long ten minutes. The phone finally rang. A raspy voice with a heavy Spanish accent spoke:

"This is Tina?"

"Yes."

"What you want?"

"I want to do business with Carlos,"

"No Carlos here. How much do you want?"

"A…a…quarter?"

"You know where the last U-turn to the USA is on the five freeway?"

She looked at Pat with a confused expression and repeated the question. "The last U-turn to the USA on the five freeway?" Pat looked at her and nodded that he knew where it was.

"Yes, I know where it is,"

"Bueno. Go there. Drive straight through the intersection and into the border parking lot. Park your car and wait by the parking money deposit stand." He sounded as if he was reading a script. "Be there tonight at six. Alone. Bring money."

"How much…"

He hung up before she could finish.

Tina looked at Pat and Chris and snapped the phone shut.

"Well, I guess I'm doing something… I'm not sure what…"

"What do you mean?" asked Pat.

"Whoever it was on the phone — and it wasn't Carlos — wants me to meet them at the border at six. And he said to bring money."

"Sweet! So we're hooked up then!"

"I guess."

"How much are we getting?"

"That's the thing Pat, he wouldn't specify any amount of money. He hung up on me before I could say anything. I don't know how much to bring or anything. I'm telling you, I don't feel good about this."

"Well, you'll feel a whole lot worse if we run out of shit."

"I know Pat, and I'm willing to do this. I'm just not very happy about it."

"Hey, I'm paying, so I'm the one taking the real risk."

"Whatever, Pat. I don't want to talk about it anymore. Let's just get the cash."

"Okay, you said a quarter, how much is a quarter ounce?"

"I don't know Pat, these guys dealt with Garrett. It was usually in pounds. Maybe he thought I meant a quarter pound."

"A quarter pound? How much does that cost?"

"From them? I don't know, fifteen hundred, maybe two thousand."

"Are you kidding me? Fuck that!"

"What do you mean fuck that? I called this dude, he said to bring money, and now we don't have it? Don't fuck with me on this Pat!"

"I thought a quarter ounce…like two-fifty or something."

"We don't know for sure, but we gotta be ready for whatever he brings us. I don't want to piss this guy off. He hurts people, Pat!"

"Well I'm not giving you two thousand dollars. You're insane."

"What do you want to do then?"

Pat thought for a moment. "I'm starting to agree with you. This whole thing is too shady."

"Well it's too late to back out now. So tell me what to do."

"I'll give you a grand."

"Fine. Whatever. I have to be at the border at six."

"Okay, we'll leave at four-thirty."

"We? No, he said alone."

"Alone? And just what do you plan on driving, Miss Daisy?"

"I need one of your cars."

"So you just want me to send you off in one of my cars, after you smashed yours, with a thousand bucks, to Mexico."

"Just to the border."

"The border."

"That's the gist of it."

"I must be the biggest idiot on the planet."

"I have a bad feeling you might be the second biggest."

♪♪♪

Tina backed out of the drive in Pat's big Ford F250 with a thousand dollars cash in the pocket of her jeans. She headed to Interstate 5 and went south. There wasn't much traffic; rush hour was over and the afternoon sun was sinking fast. Her heart was thumping as she kept going over and over in her mind the possible consequences to this excursion. Would she be robbed? Busted? Raped? Killed? She felt more and more uneasy as she got closer to her destination.

International Border 5 miles

The signs marked her progress, and with each one her blood pressure increased tenfold.

International Border 2 ½ miles

Then there it was…

Last U-Turn to USA
1 mile

She exited the freeway, drove straight through the first intersection and into the first parking lot. The parking lot deposit stand was right where the voice had described and she parked next to it. She slipped six dollars into the slot, leaned back against the truck's tailgate and looked at her watch. Five fifty-six.

Exactly three minutes later, a beat-up white van stopped abruptly in front of her. The side door slid open. The man in the passenger seat rolled his window down and yelled to her.

"Get in."

She hesitated, trying to decide if she should just run. It wasn't too late to back out; she could still get away if she wanted to. She was terrified.

This can't be happening... I can't be this stupid...

"Get in the van, Tina."

As she climbed into the van, the man in the passenger seat pulled on a rope that was hanging behind his right shoulder and the van door slammed shut. It made her jump. She looked around the van. There was dirty brown carpet beneath her with greasy stains of many different colors and shades all over it. She wondered what the color of blood might look like when it dried. There were miscellaneous car parts on the floor and a rusty toolbox chained to the left panel. The van stunk; of what she wasn't sure. She turned toward a brown vinyl bench seat stretched across the width of the van in the far back when the passenger spoke.

"Give me the phone you called me on," he said.

She fished into the pocket of her skin-tight jeans and handed him the pre-paid cell phone.

"Give me your wallet."

"Why do you need…"

"Just fucking give it to me," the man interrupted.

"I don't have one…I lost it."

"You better not be lying. Where is your driver's license?"

"Here…" She slipped her license out of her bra and handed it to the man.

"Now go sit in the back."

As she climbed toward the back of the van, the driver stepped on the gas, making her fall on all fours. She grabbed the edge of the seat and pulled herself up. Her stomach knotted up as she hung on for dear life. The driver was getting onto the freeway, heading straight for the border crossing. The passenger appeared to be closely scrutinizing her driver's license.

"Where are we going?" she asked, her voice trembling.

"Mexico," the passenger said, and then began to laugh. It was a raspy fiendish laugh, the kind you hear in horror movies right before somebody gets an ax in the forehead.

The van pulled into one of the inspection lanes leading into Mexico. The driver nodded his head, and the soldier at the crossing nodded back. They drove through and into Mexico.

Seeming utterly oblivious to her presence, the driver stomped on the gas and dove confidently into the Tijuana traffic. They went round and round on freeway overpasses and underpasses for what seemed like an hour. Tina was thrown back and forth across the bench seat and began to feel sick. The van slowed down at a traffic light, just enough for her to look around. She recognized the road; they were headed toward the coast.

"We're almost there," the hoarse voice from the passenger seat said.

Tina could see the lit up border fence on her right and slums and cottages on her left. The driver made an abrupt left turn into a dusty alley. The bumps in the dilapidated road were greatly amplified in the back of the van, nearly tossing her into the roof. She was sure she was going to throw up when suddenly the van stopped. The man in the passenger seat turned, got out of his seat and crouched in front of her on the van's floor, looking straight into her eyes.

"Take off your clothes," he said.

♪♪♪

Dude, relax, it hasn't even been two hours yet," said Chris.

Pat was pacing back and forth. He'd sit down at the bar, sip his drink, take an occasional hit off the pipe and begin to pace again.

"If it was your forty-thousand dollar truck and thousand in cash headed to Mexico, you'd be pacing too, man!"

"She's not going all the way into Mexico, just to the border."

"Yeah, and how long does that take?"

"Bro, it's an hour just to get there. Relax, everything will be fine."

"A fuckin' courtesy call would be nice."

"Dude, just let her do her thing. She's cool. She'll call as soon as she knows something. Think about the big fat shiny shards she'll be bringing back! Straight from the source bro, the best of the best!"

"Yeah, that'll be awesome."

The phone rang and Pat swept it up without hesitation and without looking to see who it was.

"Tina?"

"No, who's Tina?"

"Oh, Christine. Hey…"

"So who's this Tina you are so anxious to talk to? One of your groupies?"

"No, Christine, she's not one of my groupies."

"Whatever, Pat. You said you were going to call us today. Once again…"

"Honey, I'm sorry… I just got tied up with business. I was going to call tonight."

"Pat, as I was going to say before you interrupted, once again you made a promise to our son and you broke it. What would you like me to tell him?"

"Honey please, I've been stressed about other things. We got the record coming out this summer and Steve's been bugging me about re-recording and stuff. I'm sorry – it just slipped my mind."

"I know, Pat. Out of sight, out of mind."

"Honey, it's not like that. I'll make it up to you. I'll come down tomorrow."

"Don't tell me, tell him…"

Pat could hear her in the background yelling for Tommy to come to the phone. *Man, that's dirty…*

"Daddy? Daddy is that you?"

"Yeah, Tommy, I'm here."

"Daddy, where are you? Are you coming over?"

"Not tonight buddy, I'll see you tomorrow, though…"

"Daddy, you said tonight."

"I know son, but I have things going on right now."

"Like what, Daddy?"

Oh, if they only knew…if they only knew what a piece of shit you are… Staying home waiting for dope is more important than seeing your family…

But it was a fact and it was what it was.

"I've got music stuff going on bud, I have to work. But I'll see you tomorrow, I swear." *Nice… Lying to a three-year-old… You're quite a guy, Pat…*

"How long is that, Daddy?"

"What, you mean…in like… hours?"

"Yes, in hours."

"I don't know. I guess it would be like twenty-four hours. That's how many are in a day."

"That's too long, Daddy. Come tonight."

His heartstrings were being stretched, but not enough to pull him away from his current predicament.

"I'm sorry son, I'll see you tomorrow. Let me talk to your mom."

"I love you, Daddy!"

"I love you too, son."

Tommy yelled for his mother.

"Nice kid huh?" said Christine.

"Yeah, nice work, Mommy."

"I do what I can. What did you promise him?"

"Tomorrow night."

"Don't break his heart, Pat."

"I won't."

♪♪♪

"Take off your fucking clothes," repeated the man.

He was disgusting. He wore a stained wife beater and sunglasses although it was dark outside. She now knew what the smell in the van was.

"Please don't hurt me… I have money; you can take it…just leave me alone."

She had started to cry.

"I don't want your fucking money."

He ripped open her blouse. She started screaming and tried to hit him, but he grabbed both her arms in mid-flight.

Oh God... I don't want to die...

"Stop! Leave me alone!" she cried.

The driver of the van had climbed into the back and was now pointing a pistol directly into her face. She looked down the barrel and felt numb – she thought she was going to pee herself. She screamed louder.

"Cállate! Shut up, bitch!" snarled the driver, as he pressed the gun's barrel into her cheek.

She stopped fighting. "Why are you doing this?" she sobbed.

"Mira, we need to check you. Take off your fucking clothes."

She reluctantly took her blouse off, kicked her shoes off and stripped out of her jeans. She was crying uncontrollably.

"The bra and chonies too."

Tina slowly undid her bra and slid down her panties. She was entirely disgusted to be naked in this dirty van, in the presence of these dirty men. She wished she were dead.

The driver put the gun in the waist of his pants and reached toward her. She flinched.

"Relax, guera."

He lifted her long brown hair up, looked at her necklace and neck, and laid her hair back down.

The other man had gone thoroughly through her pockets and tossed everything she had into a pile onto the van's floor. Keys, driver's license, phone and a thousand dollars in hundred dollar bills, which oddly enough he seemed to ignore completely. He was now focused on her shoes. He shook her blouse out and felt her bra like he was kneading dough, then picked up her panties and held them up in front of his face. He smiled, and then tossed them to her.

"Get dressed," he said.

♪♪♪

"Yeah, she seems okay," the man said to the person on the other end of his phone.

"Si, muy bonita," he laughed, looking back at her as she got dressed.

The man said some more in Spanish into the phone, and then turned to the driver.

"Go ahead, drive."

The van pulled out of the alley, made a U-turn in the street and got back on the highway headed toward downtown Tijuana and the border.

"Bueno," the man said and hung up the phone. The van continued to bounce uncomfortably down the road. Tina was now dressed in the back seat, wiping her eyes. Her mascara had run all over her face. She was still too scared and confused to speak. The passenger turned toward her, tossed her a box of Kleenex and spoke.

"I hope you understand that this was all just business. We had to bring you down here because you could not be followed, and even if you were, nobody can help you here. We had to search you to make sure you weren't a cop."

She sniffled.

"Carlos did not get where he is by being stupid, guera. He asked me to check your ID and telephone to see if you were for real. And we had to scare you to see if you reacted like a cop would. Just by the fact you are alive right now, you know you passed our tests."

“Thank God,” she said under her breath, her voice still a bit shaky.

They drove past Tijuana, and around the highway interchange to a taxi drop off point just before the border.

“You can go now. The border is over there. Just follow the crowds.”

“But…did you guys bring the drugs? I brought the money,”

“No, we had to check you out first. Carlos will be calling you. Keep that phone close by.”

The passenger reached back, grabbed the van door handle and slid the door open.

“Nice to meet you, Tina.”

The driver and passenger both laughed. The van door slammed shut behind her, and they drove away.

♪♪♪

She opened the door to Pat’s truck and got inside. She was still shaking. Did all that really just happen? She took a deep breath, put the keys into the ignition and started the truck. It was nice to be back in the United States, even if she was only gone for…how long was she gone? She looked at the clock on the dash. Ten o’clock?

Holy shit…

It all seemed like an hour. She was still in shock. She pulled the truck out, found the freeway entrance and headed for home, dialing the phone with her free hand.

“Fuck, Tina…where are you?” yelled Pat.

“I’m on my way back.”

“Yeah, five hours later! What the hell, you couldn’t even call?”

She calmly closed the phone, turned it off and set it down. She’d deal with him when she got there.

♪♪♪

Pat wasn't sure whether to be pissed off or relieved. On the one hand, his money and truck had returned from Mexico without a problem, and more importantly, Tina was okay. But she had no dope. *No dope.* And she was noticeably shaken up. Even more than when she'd ditched the cops in her Jag.

Man, what happened down there?

"I'm glad you are okay T, I just have a hard time understanding why everyone went to so much trouble, and there was no dope at all. Seems like a big waste of time."

"I know Pat, I'm as confused as you. If you think I had any idea what was going to happen..."

"Man, the shit you seem to get into!" laughed Chris. "You are trouble walking!"

"I don't ask for any of this shit. Gimme a break, will you?"

"Sorry, T. You know I love you." Chris gave her a bear hug. "You'll always be my one and only Hispanic female. Hey, you should blend right in down there, come to think of it!"

Tina punched Chris in the shoulder.

"So when's he going to call?" Pat asked.

"Pat, I told you guys everything just as it happened. You know as much as I do."

Pat flopped back onto the couch, letting out a big sigh.

"Don't be so dramatic, Pat, he'll call."

The prepaid phone rang and they all looked at each other. Pat and Chris smiled. Tina didn't. She picked it up and answered.

"Hello?"

"I guess you met my friends, eh?" said Carlos.

"Yes."

"They liked you, my friends, they'd like to see you again," he laughed.

She didn't know what to say.

"I'm sorry, I'm kidding you. I'm also sorry if they scared you, but I have to be careful, no?"

"Yes, Carlos, I understand."

"You forgive me, then!"

"Yes."

"Mui bueno, mi amor. I would like to meet you, guera."

Tina's eyes lit up – Pat and Chris could see it.

"And I would like to meet you," she said.

"Fine, it's settled then. We will meet. I need you to drive south on the toll road from Tijuana to Primo Tapia. You know the toll road, yes? Highway One?"

"You mean in Mexico?"

"Yes, mi amor, you are coming to me. Is that a problem?"

"I guess not..."

"Good! Mira, it's about twenty-five kilometers south of Rosarito. There you will exit the toll road to the right onto Camino Benito Juarez. Park at the Pemex petrol station and wait for my associates. Be there at 10:00 AM tomorrow. Alone. Don't worry about the border, everything will be taken care of. Bring money for whatever you want. Do you understand?"

She repeated the instructions back to Carlos.

"Good. What will you be driving?"

"A blue Ford truck," she said.

"Bueno. I will see you tomorrow, mi amor."

"Thank you, Carlos."

He hung up.

"Holy shit, that's it?" Pat exclaimed.

"I guess so. We're meeting tomorrow," said Tina.

"Sweet! That means we'll have plenty of dope for the gig on Friday, so tonight we party out on the town! It's all on me. Ruth's Chris Steakhouse baby!"

"Really?" asked Chris.

"Yup. And we're breaking out the hookah. Call up some bitches, too."

"Done," Chris said.

"Sorry, Tina, no more swingin' dicks allowed. Ladies night. Too bad you aren't into chicks. But how 'bout I make it up to you with some new clothes tomorrow? I promised you we'd go shopping. I'm gonna hook you up, my love."

"Thanks Pat," Tina said, her voice a bit solemn.

"Come on cheer up. Life is a party, babe!"

♪♪♪

Tina knocked on Pat's bedroom door. No response. She knocked louder. Still no response. She cracked the door open. The room was dark and messy; there were sheets on the floor and clothes tossed everywhere.

"Pat!" she called out.

"In here…" Pat answered.

She walked into the master bathroom. The master bath had a huge Jacuzzi tub, which was currently overflowing with bubbles. There was a TV above it playing a cheap porno movie. Pat was lying with his back against the rear of the tub, with a girl lying back against his chest. Her huge boobs bobbed in the sudsy water.

"Hi, I'm Raquel…"

Man, if I was into chicks… thought Tina.

"I'm Tina. Pat, it's almost eight. I'm getting ready to go."

"Okay, hold on."

He jumped up out of the tub and walked into the bedroom, grabbing a towel on the way.

"What do you need from me, sweetie?"

"Nothing I guess, I'm gonna take the truck. I've still got the thousand bucks from yesterday, you just want me to take that?"

"Yeah, that's cool. Hey, there's a gun under the seat of that truck. You can't have it in Mexico. Take it out and put it under the seat of the Chevelle, okay?

"Sure, Pat."

"Hey, good luck. I love ya."

"Thanks, Pat. Ditto. See you in a few hours. I'm thinking two hours or so down, and the same back, I should be back by two or three, right?"

"Yup…and then the party really begins, babe! We're going non-stop till the gig. It's gonna be an awesome couple of days. Just get back here safe, my dear."

"I will."

EIGHT

IT ALWAYS MADE Americans feel uneasy - the sight of soldiers holding machine guns. In the United States, there was no need for military policing mainly because the local and state police forces tended to work well. The same was not the case for third world countries and despite what the Mexican Tourism Board would have tourists believe, Mexico is a third world country. The reputation of the Mexican Federales was legendary in Southern California. Tourists came back from vacations in Mexico spinning yarn of run-ins with the Federales or the Tijuana Police and the stories rarely were happy ones; tales of extortion, bribery, jail conditions and beatings, most of which unfortunately were true. Sometimes people went to Mexico and simply never returned at all.

Tina passed by a uniformed border guard holding an M-16, and though she wasn't doing anything wrong, she felt as if he was eyeing her.

I guess they're probably supposed to look that way...

She continued into Mexico through the busy Curcuito Bursatil interchange and down Calle 2da. Taxicabs and beat up cars and trucks surrounded her and were cutting her off at any opportunity. It was like they were alive and their mission was to run her off the road. She was hot and tense; driving in Tijuana was a battle. Finally, she got a little relief as she made it out of the heavy Tijuana traffic to the Careterra Tijuana-Ensenada, or the Tijuana-to-Ensenada toll highway. She sat back, cranked the A/C, hit the cruise control and let the truck do the driving while taking in the odd Mexican scenery.

The beach side of the highway looked no different from Malibu in some places. There were well-constructed homes and condos with huge satellite dishes on the roofs. In contrast, on the inland side, cardboard and wood shacks with corrugated aluminum roofs dotted the landscape, which wasn't much but dry brush. She thought about how strange it was that this was not a hugely developed area. It seemed sad that they did not allow American companies to own property here. They could build beachfront resorts where these people could work.

She pictured in her mind what it might look like with huge hotels and casinos placed majestically on the cliffs, with green parks, golf courses, and well-groomed white sandy beaches. For a moment, she almost forgot why she was there.

The truck's tires made crackling noises on the gravel as she pulled into the Pemex service station in the grimy little town of Primo Tapia and parked next to a phone booth. She turned off the ignition and stepped out into the hot, muggy air. She wiped the sweat off her brow with the back of her forearm and started toward the store for a drink. Two men in an old yellow Chevy pickup appeared out of a dust cloud.

"Que paso, guera. You Tina?"

"Yes."

"Mira, you follow us, por favor."

"Okay..."

The old Chevy belched a huge cloud of black smoke as she followed it out of the gas station and onto a dirt road.

Tina was glad she had Pat's truck – the road was so long and pothole-riddled that she didn't think anything but a truck could make the trip. She followed the men down dirt roads for what seemed like an eternity, passing burned-out buildings, piles of garbage, and the carcasses of vehicles and animals alike. They wound through mountains and rolling dry fields, finally arriving at a high wooden fence. The passenger in the old yellow truck jumped out and pushed the gate open, motioned Tina to pull in and then locked the gate behind them. She was then instructed to park the truck next to a barn.

She stepped out of the truck and took in her surroundings. The barn next to her looked rustic and burnt, like something out of a ghost town, and the several small outbuildings around it were similar in condition. The fence that surrounded them looked equally as rickety save for the shiny razor wire atop it. Between the barn and the outbuildings, she could see a white stone structure and a brown adobe situated near what she would consider the rear of the property. There were three cars parked next to the white building; an older Japanese compact, a black Mercedes-Benz, and a police car. Her first impression of the situation was not promising.

Police car? God... now what am I into?

The men from the Chevy pointed to the white stone building.

"Aqui, over there. Go."

The now familiar sick feeling was once again working its way out of her stomach and into her throat. The men escorted her past the cars and opened a large wooden door, motioning for her to step into a dark room.

As her eyes adjusted, she found herself in a room with two windows, both covered in foil, one of which had a small air conditioning unit in it that was struggling in vain to make a difference. The bare concrete floor was covered with stains and what appeared to be several dead cockroaches – at least she hoped they were dead. There were cabinets and a sink on one wall and some rusty metal file cabinets on another. A hanging bulb above the table provided the only light. She felt hot and uncomfortable.

"Bienvenidos, guera, we've been waiting for you! Please, come in and sit down!"

This was definitely the man with whom she had spoken on the phone. Carlos.

He sat at a wooden table with two other men. One of them was a giant of a man in a dirty black suit. The other was wearing a military uniform and had on mirrored aviator sunglasses that were nearly swallowed by his huge bushy eyebrows and matching mustache. He reminded her of Saddam Hussein. He removed his hat and stood up as she approached the empty chair.

"Where are my manners? Jose, please get her chair. Would you like a drink, Miss Tina? We have Coca-Cola, and whiskey and Coca-Cola!"

The other men chortled.

"Just a Coke is fine."

Jose walked slowly to a small refrigerator, extracted a small bottle of Coke and set it down in front of her. He pulled out a knife and popped the top off with the blade.

"So how was your journey Miss Tina? I hope it wasn't too long? I know it is quite a distance but I must stay out of the spotlight, you know? This place is very difficult to find, no? In fact, I'll bet you could not find your way out, nor could anybody find *you*, eh?"

She was taken aback by the very true statement Carlos had just made. She was also troubled by the fact that every statement Carlos made was in the form of a question.

What is this? Mexican Jeopardy?

She tried to think of a response. "I suppose it is off the beaten path a little," she said as she wiped a bead of sweat off her temple.

"Miss Tina, you are very pretty…mui bonita, yes? Do I make you feel uneasy?"

"I'm just a little nervous about being in Mexico, with all the stories I hear…"

"Nonsense! Mexico is the safest country in the world, right commander Gonzales?"

The man in the military uniform laughed heartily.

"Oh yes, perfectly safe. Nobody can hurt you here! Nobody gets hurt here!"

They all began laughing. She laughed uncomfortably along with them. Carlos leaned over the table and withdrew a large serrated knife from inside his suit jacket, pressing the tip of the blade up to Tina's throat.

"Nobody gets hurt if they do what I say."

♪♪♪

"Give me the keys to your truck," snarled Carlos.

He had the tip of the knife digging into her skin. Not hard enough to break it, but hard enough that it hurt. He looked directly into her eyes. She was too petrified to move or look away.

"Please, Carlos…I…"

"Just give me the keys."

She reached into her pocket, found the keys and handed them to Carlos.

He took the keys with one hand, and slowly lowered the knife with the other, never breaking eye contact.

"I have a proposition for you, guera."

She was now sobbing. She'd been sobbing a lot lately.

"I'm not going to hurt you. I need your help. You need my help. Maybe we can work out a deal so that we both benefit."

"I have…money…I just…"

"I don't need your money. I need you to do something for me. I need you to bring some items across the border."

"What items?" She wasn't sure why she asked – she knew exactly what he was talking about.

"I could make you a lot of money, guera. You and I can do business like you asked… Like your friend Garrett. You have nothing to worry about."

"I can't – I'm not a smuggler…I wouldn't know what to do…"

"I'll offer you five thousand cash and all the drugs you want. You just drive across. That's it."

"Drive across in what?"

"In the truck you drove down here."

"I can't Carlos, it's not my truck."

"Even better, guera. Whose truck is it?"

"It belongs to a friend."

"Does your friend have a fucking name?" said Carlos, raising the knife to her again.

"Pat...his name is Pat Pearson," she sobbed in a panic. "It's his truck, not mine..."

"Where have I heard that name before? Who is this Pat Pearson?"

"He's a celebrity...plays in a band...He's a rock star..."

Carlos began to laugh, "A fucking rock star? This truck belongs to a fucking rock star? Is this who you were buying drugs for? This is unbelievable! A pinche American rock star!" He was now laughing uncontrollably, and all the other men were following suit. Tina was crying.

"Don't worry Miss Tina, you still have a choice," Carlos said as he positioned the knife in front of her face so that the light reflected off the blade and into her eyes. "You can do this thing for me and make five thousand dollars – or I can slit your throat, take the truck and do it myself. You want some time to think about it, guera?"

♪♪♪

Pat, Chris, Raquel and one of her friends sat around the hookah. The third girl sat on the bar and watched – she'd never smoked meth before. Pat lit up the bowl, and everyone inhaled. They all let out huge clouds of smoke and lay back watching as the smoke settled like a fog around the room. Only meth smoke does that. They'd been up partying all night – and all day.

"So Pat, are we all going backstage to the show tomorrow night? Can the girls come with us?" Raquel asked.

"Of course baby, anything you want," said Pat.

"Raquel, I have to go home, it's almost four," said the girl on the bar.

Pat sat up suddenly.

Four o'clock...holy shit, is it four o'clock? Where the hell is Tina?

"You guys take my car. I'm staying here with Patsie," Raquel said as she cuddled up to Pat. "Can I ride to the concert with you in your limo, Patsie?"

"I don't know if I'm getting a car, sweetie, I like to drive myself to local shows."

"Can I ride with you?"

"I don't know baby, we'll see – but for now you stay here. I'll get you home in the morning somehow."

"Okay, sweetie." Raquel gave Pat a kiss and tossed her keys to the girl still sitting on the bar.

The girls gathered their things and Chris showed them out, thanking them for a great night and then some.

"Chris, it's after four. She's been gone for like eight hours."

"I know, I was thinking about that."

"Call her phone, see if she's on her way."

Chris dialed the phone.

"Who are you guys trying to call?" asked Raquel.

"Nobody, sweetie."

Chris was listening to the phone.

"Nope, no answer."

"Fuck!" said Pat, trying to stay composed. "Okay, I'm not gonna trip… Everything's going to be fine, right?"

"Yeah dude, you know how long the lines to get back across the border can be. She's probably in traffic."

"You, my friend, are absolutely right. And you, my darling," Pat said turning to Raquel, "I'm not done with you yet!"

Raquel giggled and grabbed Pat's hand, leading him off the couch and toward the stairs.

"Okay bro... I'll probably just hang down here 'till she gets here. Maybe grab a shower and watch some tube."

"Whatever, man!" Pat said, smacking Raquel's ass as they ran up the stairs to the bedroom.

♪♪♪

Carlos watched as his crew worked. They were truly amazing, he thought to himself. This particular crew had become a well-oiled machine. They could completely dismantle a car and put it back together in about four hours.

It was a sight to behold. The truck was almost completely disassembled – all the panels were off, tircs, bcdliner, seats and tailgate removed; everything laid out in a very organized fashion. The dope was on a folding table, all fit into custom shaped packages designed specifically to be hidden in this type of vehicle. Each package was marked with the location that it was to be hidden in. No panel, nook or cranny was left unused. Every installed package of drugs was sprayed with a cocktail of filtered coffee and a type of dog repellent. They even installed 12-volt transmitters into the truck's wiring harness that emitted a high-frequency sound to further confuse the drug-sniffing dogs.

Pleased at what he saw, Carlos strolled from the barn back over to the stone structure, walked in and took a seat next to Tina at the table. She was clearly irritated and terrified at the same time, two emotions that Carlos enjoyed evoking in anyone. She had her Coke bottle positioned right under her chin – a subconscious attempt to block Carlos's blade from coming near her neck.

"Almost done guera. Not much longer now."

She couldn't help herself.

"Why do you keep calling me *wetta*?"

"Guera is a term of endearment mi amor. You are my girl…" he laughed. "You *are* my girl, aren't you?"

"Carlos, please don't make me do this. I'm not the right person for this job."

"Guera, by the fact that you are alive right now, your choice has already been made. It's easy money, as you Americans love to say. You do nothing and get paid for it. It's the American dream! Why would you deny yourself the American dream?"

"Carlos..."

"Shut up!" Carlos said angrily. "There will be no more discussion. This is what you are to do. Pay close attention, guera, I do not want to repeat myself."

Tina reluctantly listened.

"My men will lead you back to the highway. From there you will drive back through Tijuana to the Otay Mesa border crossing. You don't want to get pulled over, eh guera? You better drive carefully. When you get to the Otay crossing, you must cross in the fourth lane from the right between eight and nine o'clock. The Customs agent in that lane will wave you through. Do not be earlier than eight and do not be later than nine. If you are early or late, you risk being pulled into secondary inspection. As long as you are on time, my people will be there. Do you understand the importance of this, guera?"

"Yes."

He reached over and grabbed her by her hair and pulled her face up close to his. She could smell his breath.

"You'd better fucking understand! You have thirty kilos of pure glass in that truck! You go to secondary and you'll either die in prison or die by my hand! You fucking understand now? Comprende?"

"Yes, Carlos, I understand."

He let go of her abruptly.

"Good guera. Now after you pass through into America, you drive to your rock star boyfriend's house, take him his little bag of mierda and have a good time, puta! Act like nothing's happened. Tomorrow night my associates will come and take his truck and leave your five thousand dollars. Will your boyfriend be home tomorrow night guera?"

"No, he's playing a concert."

"The rock star is playing a concert! I wonder if he'll make enough money to buy a new truck?"

Carlos and his cronies began laughing again. It made Tina want to strangle him.

"You'd better stay home from the concert, eh guera? Now you write down your rock star boyfriend's address for me. My men will come when you call them and tell them it is safe. You better call them, puta – and you better not tell the rock star anything. If anybody finds out what you are doing for me, I will kill you *and* your rock star boyfriend. Comprende?"

"Yes, Carlos."

Tina looked at her watch. Nine PM. She'd been gone for over twelve hours. The guys must be freaking out. A tear rolled down her cheek. She was immersed in fear, this time not only for herself, but also for Pat and Chris.

♪♪♪

"Dude, wake up!"

"Damn, did I fall asleep?"

"Yes, you fell asleep," Pat whispered. "And where's Tina? Have you heard from her?"

"No, I fell asleep," Chris said sarcastically. "Why are you whispering?"

"Have you tried to call her?"

"Bro, I said I've been asleep! What's wrong with you? Where's Raquel?"

"Dude, I just passed out on top of her! I need some more shit, fast! She said I was out for like five minutes!"

"Are you serious?"

"Shhhh! She might be able to hear us…Yeah, is that classic or what?"

They both made a valiant attempt to control the volume of the giggling.

"Chris, call Tina again."

He dialed the number and got no response.

"No answer, dude."

"Are you sure she didn't try to call while you were asleep?"

"I don't think so." Chris checked his call history. "No, she hasn't called on my phone. What about yours?"

"I checked it. Not my cell. You were responsible for the house phone, sleeping beauty."

"Hey, a brother's gotta sleep sometime..."

"Dude, are you aware that we've been up for like three days?"

"Yup. And I'm also aware that if Tina doesn't surface soon, we, my friend, will be in a world of hurt, because, there ain't going to be enough drugs to get us through all the way till tomorrow night. Face it, we sleep now, you ain't getting up.

"I know, bro, I don't really know what our next move is. I really hope nothing has happened to her. I'm in no condition right now to face anything stressful, that's for sure."

The house phone rang and Pat leapt for it, fighting Chris off in the process. Chris fell off of the couch and landed on the floor with an amusing thud.

"Sheeellow?"

"This is the last time I'm going to call you, Pat."

"Christine! Hey, what's up?"

"You know damn well what's up. Or do you? Do you even know what day it is?"

"Christine, I…"

"It's Thursday night, Pat! You were supposed to be here, remember? You *promised* your son you'd be here, and once again you've let us down. That's it. I'm done."

"Christine, listen…"

"No Patrick, you listen. You are a fucking wreck. I can hear it in your voice. You've probably been up for a week – you can't even put two words together. There is no way, even if you wanted to, that I'd let you see Tommy right now. You've hurt us too many times."

"But, wait…"

Pat, just get it together. Don't bother calling until you do."

"Christine, please…"

She hung up.

♪♪♪

"Havc a nicc trip, gucra," said Carlos, tapping his knife on the truck's windowsill. "Don't forget to call my associates. If they don't hear from you tonight, I will find you myself… Oh, and this is for your rock star boyfriend." He tossed a big bag of Meth into her lap and laughed.

She shot him a final look of disgust and drove away, following the old yellow Chevy back down the dirt road. She rolled the windows up to keep the dust out. It was shaping up to be a very nice day — weather wise anyway — the early morning sun shone brightly in the clear blue sky.

Unfortunately the weather was the last thing on her mind – she was now driving a truck stuffed to the gills with illegal controlled substances. She was drained. She knew that she had to psyche up for the mission – to get out of the mindset of fear and into the mindset of determination. Tina was a headstrong woman, and she believed she could do anything if she put her mind to it. Even this.

You are a smuggler... the best smuggler the Cartel has ever seen... You will not get caught... You will do this and do it right... You're the best... Calm, cool, collected... God is watching out for you...

She followed the other truck back to the toll highway then continued north on her own.

It's all you, now... Just be cool...

The ride up the toll road was uneventful, but as she made her way into Tijuana, the traffic began to get heavier. She hated traffic in the United States and the traffic in Tijuana was unbearable. Cars darted about without rhyme or reason, with complete disregard for lanes, lights or any traffic laws. But the other cars had immunity. It was she who could not get pulled over.

She fought her way onto Circuito Bursatil, through downtown Tijuana and into the business district. The whole city was disgusting. She got on Avenida Internacional which would take her to the Otay border crossing.

Working her way down the avenue, she was once again fascinated by the Mexican scenery. To her right was the Tijuana International Airport, teeming with Mexican and American commuters and to her left was the border fence. In between was exactly what you might expect – a dirty road lined with homeless people huddled under blankets and eyeing the fence; determined to wait for that one opportunity when some kind of diversion might cause the Border Patrol to turn their heads for a precious moment.

Nestled between the airport entrance and the parking garage were two Tijuana Police cars. The officers leaned on the hoods of their respective cruisers — old dirty Ford LTDs from a decade ago — discussing something that Tina assumed was probably not about proper law enforcement.

All these Latino cops look the same... the mirrored shades, military-style uniforms, thick mustaches and eyebrows; just like the cop with Carlos... A bunch of Saddam Husseins... All crooked sons-of-bitches, too...

Their mirrored shades followed Tina as she passed by. She thought she saw one of them stand and reach for something on his belt.

Don't start trippin' out on everything, Tina... Just drive...only about a mile and a half to go...

She checked her mirrors as she rounded the east side of the airport.

Shit...Is that a cop?

Sure enough, a dirty white police cruiser was rapidly approaching from behind. Her heart began the familiar race that she'd become so accustomed to.

He's coming up awfully fast...

Preoccupied with the police car in her rearview, she failed to notice that traffic had come to a dead stop. She slammed on the brakes; the tires letting out a screech so loud that it could be heard over the airport noise. The truck stopped inches from the rear bumper of a Tijuana Taxi. The obnoxious screeching noise came with an equally obnoxious cloud of smoke, leaving no doubt in anyone's mind that she was responsible for the shriek. The police cruiser approached from behind, overhead lights now ablaze. Her body went rigid; she was afraid to look.

Oh god, what am I going to do?

The car chirped its siren and pulled up right beside her. The cop looked up at the truck and waved for her to pull over, yelling something in Spanish. She obliged and began to move the truck toward the right curb. He chirped the siren some more and yelled in Spanish at the car ahead of her; continuing the procedure until he had pushed his way through the traffic, the intersection, and had sped off in pursuit of something other than her.

Stunned, it took the horn of the car behind her to shake her back to reality and get her to move back into traffic. She breathed in and out in an attempt to slow her heart as she merged back into the left lane and made the last tricky turn onto Garita de Otay.

What she saw next made her want to cry. Trucks. Huge oversized monsters with cars, pickups, and RVs nestled in between, lined up as far as the eye could see. And this traffic did not move. In fact she was still unable to see the border crossing from where she was.

God, how long is this going to take? She looked at her watch. 7:58. One hour.

♪♪♪

"This is way fucked up, man, way fucked up!"

"I don't know what you want me to do."

"I'm not asking you to do anything, asshole!"

Tina still hadn't been heard from and it was nearing a full day that she'd been gone. Tensions were running high. Pat was on a rampage and Chris was getting the brunt of it.

"Dude, I seriously think something might have happened. My truck is missing, my thousand bucks – and Tina! What are we going to do?"

"Dude, you're asking the wrong guy…I know as much as you do. Now quit yelling at me!"

Chris's tone caught Pat off-guard. "Don't tell me what I can and can't do, you dick! I support your freeloading ass!"

"Fuck you, Pat." As Chris got up to leave the room, Raquel came down the stairs.

"What's going on down here? Is everything all right?"

"Get out of here, you fucking cunt!" Pat couldn't believe what he'd just said. It just slipped out.

"Fuck you, Pat!" said Raquel, turning to go back upstairs.

"Wait, Raquel, I'm sorry, I didn't mean that… I'm just a bit on edge...please…"

"Pat, you've got a serious drug problem. You really need to get it together."

"Now you sound like my fucking wife!"

Shit, now what the hell did I say?

"Your wife?"

"I mean my kid's mom. We're not really together..."

"You have a kid?"

"Well…um…yeah..."

"Pat, you're a fucking mess. If you're a father, you *really* need to get it together! And you know what else? Nobody calls me a cunt, you bastard. I'm outta here – I'll get myself a ride."

She stormed back up the stairs.

"Go then, you fucking bitch! I don't need your bullshit either. I got plenty of problems besides dealing with *your* ass!"

Chris was standing by the bar staring at him, astounded by what Pat had become.

"What the fuck are you looking at?"

He just shook his head and walked out the sliding door into the yard.

Just then the phone rang, causing Pat to cringe. *Christ... now what?*

"Hello?"

"Pat, it's Steve."

Oh, fucking great... "Steve, this is not a good time, man."

"Never is," Steve replied. "Look, I'll make it quick. I need you at a meeting tonight before the show to discuss the record release and some other stuff. You guys don't have to soundcheck so we'll have the meeting at seven thirty. You with me so far?"

"Yes, Steve, I'm not stupid."

"That's debatable. Anyway, be at Coors by seven fifteen and security will let you know which meeting room we'll be using. Pat, please be on time. This is important."

"I will, I will."

"Okay, see you there."

"Later."

Pat lay back on the couch and nervously looked around – it was a rare occasion that he was all alone. He picked up the pipe and took a big hit. Everything was fast becoming a daze.

♪♪♪

Tina inched her way from the ramp onto the street. She stuck her head out the window and squinted, trying to see the border crossing. She could barely make out the overhead pedestrian bridge. She looked at her watch again. 8:08.

Ten minutes to go fifty feet? I'm never going to make it...

The two left hand lanes were moving at a slightly faster crawl than hers prompting an attempt to move over. The car in the next lane completely ignored her as she attempted to auger the big Ford in, causing her to impulsively lay on the horn. A vendor carrying a bucket of wilted roses ran up to her window and began tapping on it.

Oh come on...

"You want buy? Three dollars! You want buy?"

"No, no, nada!" Tina yelled through the truck's window, furiously waving her away with her hand as the lane next to her opened up. "No, get out of the way!"

"You buy...two dollars!"

I'm gonna run this bitch over...

She cracked the window and screamed over the glass.

"Get the fuck out of my way!"

The lady finally backed off and moved on to another car and Tina made her lane change.

I can't take this shit...

This lane was moving along a little better. She looked at her watch again. 8:15.

Forty-five minutes left. She sat in the crawling traffic, her heart beating out of her chest.

God, get me out of this circus...

Lanes were ending on one side and opening up on the other; cars and trucks were merging randomly. She had no idea in which lane she was going to wind up.

Vendors were running around everywhere selling pottery, stuffed animals, flowers, and churros. The thought of food in the midst of all the chaos made her feel sick, not to mention the smell of unregulated Mexican exhaust that penetrated the truck even with the windows rolled up and the A/C on. She subconsciously drummed on the steering wheel with her fingers, trying not to look at her watch. 8:27.

More lanes opened up and traffic began to move a little faster. She could now clearly see the bridge, and through the windows in the bridge the crowds of people moving across, no doubt happy to be home in the United States. She could see the red and green lights blinking over the lanes in the distance. Stop, go, stop, go. She began to count the lanes, ensuring that she was in the right one. Number four.

One, two, three, four... Wait a minute...

There was no traffic signal above lane number one.

Shit...lane 1 is closed... Does that mean I go to lane five? I mean, they aren't numbered or anything... crap... Lane four or five? Lane one still counts, right? We'll go to lane four... Or three...God, this is bullshit!

She pushed her way into what appeared to be the fourth lane. As all the tractor-trailers and RVs started to separate from the rest of the vehicles her view got clearer and up ahead she could now see all sorts of activity. Homeless people were going from car to car knocking on windows and there were ladies dressed up in nurses' uniforms collecting donations in plastic buckets. Beyond that, men in uniforms were walking dogs around the cars and trucks.

Dogs? God, this can't be happening!

She kept inching forward toward the bridge. 8:40. Twenty minutes left to go about five hundred feet - she should be okay if her head didn't explode. The uniformed men were weaving through the cars. The dogs would sniff around for a minute and move on.

They're searching for their toys, the poor animals... They have no idea what they're actually here for...

She inched forward a little more. 8:48. She stretched out her neck and lifted her head to see over the truck in front of her and tried to count the cars in her lane.

One, two, three... The cars in the lane she was in were veering off to the left.

I'm in the wrong lane!

There was nowhere to go. Cars surrounded her on all sides and nobody was moving. They were getting too close to the cement medians at the inspection kiosks for people to merge. Those in their respective lanes were pretty much committed at this point.

Should I try to push into the next lane? I have to...but I can't make a scene...the guys with the dogs...I have to stay blended in... God help me...

Delineation was only about six car lengths away. She rolled down the rear window of the truck and waved at the driver behind her and to the right. He ignored her. The car in front of her moved up. She had to pull forward. The car to her right began moving forward as she tried to push over and cut her off. Five car lengths. 8:52.

Dammit! Fuck this!

She slammed the transmission into park, jumped out of the truck and walked purposefully over to the car behind on her right. She knocked on his window. Startled, he only rolled it down a crack.

"Please sir, I need to move into this lane...I can't explain why, just please let me over!"

"No ingles, Señora... no speak..."

This is unbelievable... Doesn't anybody speak English anymore? Oh, I'm in Mexico... She almost laughed out loud. "Please let me move over...let me in...move over! Aqui!" She waved her hands like a madwoman, pointing over and over at his lane.

"Aqui?" he said, pointing over his dashboard.

"Por favor, aqui, please… please sir…" She put her hands in a praying position as if to plead with him.

"Si, aqui…" He nodded his head in understanding. At least she hoped he understood.

"Thank you! Gracias! Thank you!"

She ran around the back of the truck to the driver's side and jumped in. The car in front of her had moved, and the truck behind her was now honking his horn.

Fuck you, you son-of-a-bitch… Please don't let this guy make a fucking scene…

She stuck her hand out the window and flipped him the bird while steering the truck into the next lane. She finally made her merge. The driver behind waited patiently; smiling and giving her the universal OK sign.

*Gee, thanks, asshole…*she smiled.

Three car lengths. 8:55.

As she continued forward she was surrounded by big metal boxes and cameras mounted on poles. She tried to look into the boxes but they had dark tinted Plexiglas covers. She couldn't see what they were. They made her feel like a target.

Just remain cool Tina, they look for nervousness…

She tried not to move her head when she looked around. She attempted looking nonchalant — even bored — like she was a commuter who'd had it with the traffic. She wiped her palms on her jeans and glanced around at the cameras, the big creepy machines and her rearview mirror.

The dogs…

They were right behind her. Two car lengths. 8:59. The dogs were right at the truck's tailgate sniffing around. One of the dogs started to whimper.

You've got to be kidding me …

The dog let out a yelp and pulled its owner toward a car in the next lane, as if it feared Tina's truck.

One more car. 9:00.

The light turned green and the agent in the booth waved the car in front of her through. As she moved up the light turned red. She stopped at the yellow line just before the booth. The agent in the booth waved her forward, lowering his sunglasses a little, and almost appeared to smile at her.

This is it...

She rolled forward, but as she moved up another agent came from the right and held his hand up in front of her. She hit the brakes. The agent crossed in front of Tina and walked to the booth, still holding his hand up and saying something to the first agent. The agent in the booth responded by removing his fluorescent safety vest and handing it to the other agent.

Oh god, I'm too late... They're changing shifts...

♪♪♪

Pat used to believe that when a person drank — or used — alone, that it was proof of that person's life completely unraveling. A point he'd never reach because he was smart enough and strong enough to quit way before things ever got that bad. Drugs were meant for partying and having fun with other people, not for hiding from life's problems.

Yet Raquel had gotten a taxi home and Chris had gone somewhere — Pat wasn't sure where — and alone he sat, just he and his drugs. The reality was that he was never really alone. It was scary.

He wiped his wet eyes and decided to call Christine.

I'll just call and apologize...set something up with them for Sunday...

He picked up the phone and dialed.

"Hello, Pat..."

"Hey, honey, I just wanted to call and say sorry, and see if maybe we could get together on..."

“Pat, save it. I don’t want to hear from you until you do something about your problems.”

“Babe, I’m totally going to mellow out… Right after the gig…Hey, where’s Tommy?”

“He’s at my mom’s. And I wouldn’t let you talk to him right now anyway.”

“Why not? I just wanna…”

“Pat, stop right there. I do not trust you, nor do I believe anything you say. You’re just lonely right now for some reason, so you’re calling me. You do this all the time.”

“It’s ‘cause I love you, honey…”

“Pat, get some help. I’m going out.”

♪♪♪

Tina stared at the two agents through the windshield. Nobody had looked at her yet. They were discussing something.

They all wear the same fucking sunglasses…

She pulled her hands off the steering wheel and looked at her palms. There were indentations in them from her nails. She almost wished they’d just take her to jail so this whole ordeal would just end.

What is going on?

The second agent lowered his hand and started to laugh. He then turned and ran back over to the main building on the right. The first agent waved her forward.

Here we go…

He leaned over to her window as if to look into the passenger seat.

“Country of citizenship, Ma’am,”

“Uh, United States?”

“Is that a question or a statement?”

“I’m sorry, United States, sir.”

“ID, please.”

She reached into her bra, slid out her driver's license and handed it to him. He looked it over and handed it back. He leaned closer.

"Do you have any idea what fucking time it is, you stupid bitch?"

"Uh…I…"

"Get the fuck out of here."

The light turned green and he stepped back and angrily waved her through. Tina drove through a maze of cement barricades and onto Interstate 5. As soon as she felt that she was out of view of the border she pulled over to the side, opened the truck's door, leaned out and vomited.

NINE

PAT LAY ON the couch attempting to distract himself from the boatload of problems he faced by watching 'Clear and Present Danger' on Cinemax. He liked action movies. It was at the part where Harrison Ford's character Jack Ryan had just ratted out the intelligence officer of a Mexican drug cartel to the cartel's leader. Gunfire had ensued, and the cartel leader was killed.

His sleep-deprived delirium had turned his anger into distress. He began to think the worst that — like she had said there was the possibility of — that Tina been raped or killed. Should he call the cops and report her missing? Maybe report the truck stolen? What if she was just fine and they found her and pulled her over with his drugs on her? Then she'd be arrested. He definitely couldn't chance involving the cops, but what was the alternative? Go look for her? How? And where?

I've got to play this gig tonight... How am I supposed to focus on playing after all this? And how the hell am I even going to make it to the gig without any shit? Why do I do this to myself? Is dope that important?

It was.

The phone rang.

Dammit! What now?

"Hello?" he answered.

"Pat, it's me."

"Tina! Oh my God! Are you okay?"

"Yeah, I'm fine...I'm back in the USA..."

"What the hell happened? Where have you been? Why couldn't you call? Fuck, Tina, I didn't know what to do!"

"Don't worry, I'm fine. I just had some problems finding my way around and stuff. There's no cell service down there. But I'm on my way back."

"Do you have it?"

"Yeah, I have it."

At that very moment, Pat's world turned from purgatory to paradise.

"Awesome! Tina, just be careful and get back here safe, okay?"

"I will. I'll see you in an hour or so."

"Cool. Love ya, babe…"

"Love you too, Pat."

♪♪♪

Tina drove up the freeway at sixty-five miles per hour; no less, no more. Both hands were on the wheel. She was exhausted – she couldn't even remember the last time she'd slept or done any dope for that matter. What she did know was she'd had enough stress in the last three days to last her a lifetime, and that things couldn't possibly get any worse. She just wanted to get to where she was going and relax. God knew she deserved it.

She thought about what to tell Pat about the trip – she didn't want to lie to him, but she certainly couldn't tell him the truth. If that ever got out, they'd both be dead.

Everything will be fine… They'll take the truck, Pat will call his insurance company and get a new one… All of this will be over… No harm done, right?

Then why did she feel so horrible?

She thought about her story. She was lost in Tijuana and couldn't get hold of Carlos because her cell didn't work down there. She had had to find a payphone to call Carlos. Once she had, his people came up and led her back to Ensenada where she had to wait for a long time because he was out shit (everyone knows how drug deals go) but finally she got the dope and got lost again coming back. She was tired and scared, but she finally found her way back to the border. What a horrible experience.

No shit... if they only knew...

The story would work; it didn't really have to be elaborate – Pat and Chris would just be happy to see the dope.

The dope...Shit, the bag was free...what do I do with the money? How would I explain the dope if I give his money back? I can't just steal his money...

She decided to keep five hundred, give five hundred back and say they gave her a really great deal on the dope because of her inconvenience.

Shit, that's a laugh... my inconvenience...

Feeling a little bit loopy she giggled to herself. She was almost home free.

♪♪♪

"Hey man, it's Pat."

"What's up, Pat?"

"Where you at, bro?"

"Does it matter where I'm at, Pat? I'm just a freeloader, right?"

"Come on, dude, I was upset. Tina was gone, my truck, my money, Christine, Raquel…I was just stressing out. We've been through worse than this, bro…"

"Whatever, Pat. I'm just getting sick of it. You're getting worse and worse. You treat people like they're beneath you and your mood swings are insane. You gotta chill out on the shit, man."

"Hey, Tina's coming back, I just talked to her."

"Well, why didn't you say so…I'm on my way!"

They both laughed.

"Dude, I'm sorry," said Pat. "I'm done after the gig. I'm quitting. I can't live like this anymore. And if I can't do it myself, I'm gonna get help."

"I'll do it with you."

"Okay, it's a deal. But tonight..."

"Tonight it's on like Donkey-Kong!"

"Exactly. Now get your ass back here."

♪♪♪

Tina pulled into the driveway just as the morning sun peaked in the sky. Like a dog that hears its owner's car drive up, Pat and Chris heard the sound of the truck's big diesel engine and ran out into the driveway as excited as kids at Christmas.

Tina climbed slowly out of the truck, her cramped legs slowly adjusting to the outside world. She hadn't looked in a mirror since yesterday morning, and mascara was still smeared all over her face from crying.

"Man, Tina, you look shot out!" Pat said.

"Yeah, from the rot out...!" Chris added

"Beat up, from the feet up!"

"No...beat up from the *street* up!"

"Reelin' from the feelin'!"

"Would you two idiots shut up?" Tina finally said. "I've been through way too much to be dealing with the likes of you right now."

"Are you okay?" asked Pat. "Let me look you over." He spun her around, pulled her to him, and gave her a big hug and kiss. "Seriously, Tina, I was freakin' out. I'm glad you are okay."

"Thanks, Pat."

"How's my truck?" Pat climbed into the front seat and looked around.

"It's fine, Pat, just a little dirty..."

"Why does it smell like coffee?"

"I…I spilled a cup of coffee in it."

"In my new truck? Where?" He started looking around.

"I mean…I had a cup sitting in there for a while. I threw it out."

Pat looked at her, one eyebrow askew. "You're delirious, sweetie...let's go inside and see what you brought home for daddy!"

They walked back into the house and sat down, all letting out exaggerated sighs of relief. Tina stood up and began to unbutton her jeans.

"Sweet! Table dance!" Pat said.

"Haven't I already asked you to shut up?"

She reached down into her crotch.

"You're not going to pull out a dick are you? Oh my God, you got a sex change while you were down there! No wonder you were gone so long!"

Chris and Pat high-fived and started cracking up.

"I'm glad you guys amuse yourselves because you don't amuse anyone else," she said, trying not to smile as she pulled out a Ziploc bag almost completely full of shiny amber colored shards of pure Crystal Methamphetamine. She tossed the bag onto the coffee table.

"Holy crap!" Pat exclaimed. "How much is here?"

"I don't know," she said as she fished half of Pat's money out of her pocket and tossed the cash on the table next to the bag. "But it only cost five hundred."

Pat jumped on Tina, kissing her profusely. "I looove you! Please, my darling let me show you how much!"

"Show me with the hookah, you freak!" said Tina, pushing him away.

"And I love you too…" said Chris, leaping on her as well.

"You guys are retards!"

"Yeah, but in a good way!"

Pat opened the bag and spilled out the contents. He lovingly rolled one of the huge amber chunks around between his fingers, admiring the quality.

"This is the real deal, bro. Hard rock."

They got out the hookah and smoked until they couldn't smoke any more.

♪♪♪

"Come on, we gotta go! I go on at nine. You guys are riding with me, right?"

"I'm not going, Pat," said Tina.

"Why not? It's gonna be the party of the year – hometown gig, baby! Everyone will be there!"

"I can't, Pat…I just don't feel good. There's no way I could handle the whole party thing tonight. The Mexico trip killed me Pat, I'm too beat."

"Okay, suit yourself. If you decide you want to go later, call a cab and I'll pay for it. Get hold of Chris and we'll arrange for you to get backstage, okay?"

"Thanks, Pat, but I'll just see you guys tomorrow."

"All right, come on bro, let's go."

Pat and Chris headed out into the garage to select the appropriate vehicle for the night's festivities.

"What're we driving' bra?" Chris asked.

"The mighty Chevelle. We haven't even tried out the new engine. We're gonna rock that 560 horsepower bitch to the show tonight, my friend."

"Are you sure you're cool to drive? I'm high as fuck right now. Maybe we should get a limo."

"Oh, I'm good bro. Never been better!"

They got into the Chevelle, and Pat cranked her over. She came to life with a roar; a symphony of power. The car's exhaust gurgled beneath them, shaking the seats.

"God, this car is sick!"

"No shit…Just take it easy on the way down…we don't need to get pulled over."

"They gotta catch us first!"

As they got on the freeway, Pat stomped the gas and the car screeched and leapt forward in a huge cloud of smoke. By the time they were at the end of the ramp, they were already going one hundred miles per hour.

"I think my dick is getting hard," Pat yelled over the roar of the engine. "This is going to be a night to remember my friend!"

With a blatant disregard for public safety, they made it to the Coors Amphitheatre in record time.

Pat maneuvered around the traffic and entered through the VIP gate where he was waved through by security. They parked the car near the backstage entrance. The opening act was pounding out one of their big radio singles. The crowd sounded primed. Pat was stoked. There was no sound in the world like a raging crowd. He and Chris jumped out of the car and trotted toward the artists' backstage door. They were cheerfully greeted by security.

"Hey Pat, what's up man?"

"Livin' large and lovin' life my friend. How's the crowd?"

"Shit man; just listen to 'em..."

The band had just finished a song, and the applause was thunderous.

"Damn!" Pat exclaimed with a grin.

"Yeah, just imagine how they're going to be for you guys!"

The guy handed Chris and Pat their passes and lanyards.

"Have fun tonight, man!"

"Oh, we will, my friend!"

They walked down the hallway past empty Anvil hard cases and other gear bags toward the dressing room area. The doors to the green room were propped open by a couple of freestanding cement ashtrays. Inside, there must have been sixty or seventy people.

There were catering trays with cold cuts, sandwiches and all sorts of other goodies. A bartender was working a full-service bar near the back of the room, and trashcans full of bottled beer sat in either corner. Comfortable couches were placed in the center of the room, with all sorts of folding chairs and tables around the perimeter. Video monitors on each side of the bar displayed the activity on the stage.

There were friends of the band, friends of friends, and friends of friends of friends. It was awesome. Everyone in the room was smoking and drinking; it was quite a scene. Pat and Chris sauntered in, dressed to the nines and fashionably late.

"Hey, Pat," said a lovely young lady in a black dress and stiletto heels.

"Hey, Karen, what's up?"

The room suddenly erupted. A crowd instantly formed around Pat and he ate it up as usual, shaking hands, giving out hugs and kisses and even signing a few autographs. You couldn't pry the smile off his face with a crowbar. The other band members were sitting on the couches, slightly less enthusiastic about his entrance. Pat walked over and flopped down on a couch, his arms around two giggling ladies.

"Grab us some drinks, my brother," he said to Chris.

"You got it, bra!"

He looked at his bandmates and gave a mock salute. "What's up fellas? You guys ready for the best gig in a long, long time?"

"You missed the meeting tonight, Pat," said Mike, the band's rhythm guitarist.

"Oh, shit… I guess I did! Fuck, sorry dudes. Did I miss anything important?"

"Pat, we need to talk. Before the show."

Jay, the bass player, stepped into a corner and whispered into his cell phone. "Hey guys," Jay said, waving them over, "let's go into the dressing rooms where we can all talk in private."

They all exited the green room for the dressing room lobby. Everybody found seats on couches or pulled up chairs.

The lighted mirrors and vanities in the adjacent dressing rooms could be seen through the doors that lined the far wall, and the other walls were decorated with pictures of Marilyn Monroe, James Dean, and other classic stars. A couple of acoustic guitars sat on stands in one corner of the room, a fake palm sat in another. Steve walked into the room, pulling the doors closed behind him. He looked at Chris like he was the antichrist.

"Chris, get the fuck out of here. This is band business."

"Whatever," Chris said, heading for the door. He could feel several sets of angry eyes burning holes in his back as he exited.

Steve found a folding chair in one of the dressing rooms, brought it out into the lobby and sat down directly in front of Pat. He put his elbows on his knees and his head in his hands. He looked up and let out a deep breath.

"Okay, here we go…First of all, you're late again."

"I'm supposed to be late, bro, I'm a rock star," Pat said, looking at a picture of James Dean instead of at Steve.

Several disgusted sighs echoed around the room.

"You're not serious, right?"

"I'm an entertainer, Steve, an artist. People admire that part of me because they can't do that in their own lives. It's important for my image."

Steve was aghast at the words coming out of Pat's mouth. "What it is, is inconsiderate and irresponsible, you misguided little fuck!" He stood up. "So what you are telling me Pat, is that you knowingly blew off the meeting tonight because you feel that it is important to your rock star image to be late?"

"Whoa, listen Steve, I'm sorry, man, I didn't just blow it off," Pat said half-smiling as if he were joking about the whole thing. "I just forgot – I had other stuff going on. Can you fill me in?"

"No, I can't fill you in. I can't fill you in because we had people from the label here to meet you. The European distribution deal, you idiot! People who now think you are as much of a flake as your reputation says."

"Dude, I'm not..."

"Shut up!" Steve screamed, standing up and stepping threateningly into Pat's personal space. "Shut the fuck up! Leo was here waiting for you too. He had the photographer for the album art here with him for a backstage shoot but you weren't here for that either, Pat! And he left! They all left! Because you wasted their fucking time, Pat! Do you have any idea how much money you may have cost us tonight?"

"We can find another photographer. Shit, I can find a new agent..."

"A new agent? Are you high right now?"

"So what if I was?"

"You are one defiant little prick."

"Look, I'm kidding, man, I'm sorry..."

"Save it, asshole. You can't do this anymore. Your excuses aren't going to cut it this time. We took the meeting time we had without you and had our own discussion. So here it is...Clean up or get out!"

Pat looked around the room and laughed.

"What is this, an intervention?"

"Call it what you want," Steve said.

He laughed again, although this laugh came out differently; maybe a bit less confident.

"Pat you're a mess," Mike interjected. "We used to be best friends. We don't even talk anymore. We don't write songs anymore. We don't even communicate."

"Are you guys giving me an ultimatum? You can't give me an ultimatum – it's my band!"

Jay jumped up out of his chair and got into Pat's face.

"No Pat! It's not your band! We hired you!"

"I have a contract," Pat snapped back. "You can't fire me. I can do whatever the fuck I want!"

"That's where you're wrong, asshole!" screamed Jay. "You never show up to rehearsals, you never show up to meetings, and you're always having to be dragged off the buses by your little bitch Chris just to get to the shows! You're a worthless fucking tweeker!"

"I'm not a tweeker, asshole."

"Are you kidding me? Look at you! You've probably been up for a week! You look like a battered housewife! You're a fucking tweeker!"

"Don't call me that, Jay..."

"I call it like I see it. Everybody knows it Pat. Even your wife says you've become a piece of shit!"

Pat jumped up and shoved Jay across the room.

"You're just pissed because I fucked yours!"

Jay lunged for Pat, and Mike and Billy the drummer jumped in to hold him back.

"Come on, Pat, you fucking pussy! Bring it on!"

"Goddammit, everybody sit down and shut up!" screamed Steve. "You guys are acting like children! Now shut up and let me talk."

Jay angrily pulled loose of his handlers and stormed out of the room.

"Look, guys, everything has changed and not for the better. And Pat, no matter what you say right now, you know damn well it's because of the drugs. You've alienated your friends, your family, your business associates, even your kid. This band is on the verge of superstardom and we cannot let it slip away because of your drug habit. The line is drawn. It stops now."

"I know...I know..." Pat said reluctantly with his arms crossed like a child who had just been scolded.

"Look Pat, we're not trying to put you on the defense, we're trying to save the band. Save the business. We're just getting strong. We can't let this happen."

"Pat, we miss having you around, dude," said Billy.

Mike put a hand on Pat's shoulder.

"Billy's right, Pat, we do miss you. You can call this an intervention or an ultimatum. The bottom line is that we're afraid that you won't show up to the next gig because you'll be in jail…or worse. We're afraid of what you're into, Pat."

Oh, if they only knew…

They were all absolutely right, just as were Christine, Raquel, his parents, and even Chris.

Shit…everyone…

There was no sense in lying to himself anymore.

"Okay, guys. Monday, I go get help."

"Tomorrow, Pat," said Steve.

"Fine, tomorrow. But tonight I'm going out with a bang."

♪♪♪

Tina stood at the window in the guest bedroom over the garage and stared out at the truck parked in the driveway. She wanted to cry. Pat loved his truck, and what Carlos was forcing her to do was not fair to her or to Pat. But she also knew that there was no way around it. She had to do as she was told if only to protect Pat, Chris and herself. She couldn't wait until it was all over. With tears in her eyes, she picked up the phone and dialed the number Carlos had given her.

"Bueno?"

She recognized the voice at the other end – it was one of the guys that had her trapped in the van in Tijuana the other day.

"It's Tina."

"Hola, Tina. It looks like you made it home!"

"Yes, and the truck is here."

"Good, guera. I will call Carlos and call you back."

She closed her phone and sat back, still staring out the window.

It will all be over soon…

The phone rang back almost immediately.

"Que onda, guera…"

"Hello, Carlos."

"I take it you made home, guera."

"Yes, Carlos, I made it here and the truck is here."

"Very good guera, I'm impressed. Your boyfriend is gone, yes?"

"Yes, I'm alone."

"Bueno. My men will be there around midnight. Is there anything they should know? Any pesky neighbors to look out for? Will there be anybody home, guera?"

"Just me, Carlos. Pat's gone for the rest of the night. It's a very quiet street. Nobody is around."

"The rock star stays out all night, eh guera? My men will come and take the truck and leave you your money. Where is the truck, and where do you want your money left?"

"The truck is parked in the driveway and the keys are in it. I don't want the money. I just want this to be over with."

"Don't be foolish, guera. You did a good job for me…take your money and maybe we can do this again, eh?"

"I don't think so, Carlos."

"Never say never, mi amor… I can always find you… Buenos noches, my love."

"Goodbye, Carlos."

She took a last look outside at the truck and went downstairs. She checked her watch. 8:59. Pat should be going on stage any time now. She wished she were there instead of here.

♪♪♪

"It's dipped, bro!"

"What?" Pat was having a hard time hearing Chris over the roar of the crowd.

"I said it's dipped! You know, laced!"

"Laced with what?"

"Heroin!"

Chris was referring to the joint he had lit and ready to go.

"Puff, puff, pass! I've still got the encore to do!"

"We said we were going out with a bang, right?"

"Oh, definitely, my friend…"

Pat was just offstage behind the right speaker tower toweling off and getting ready for the last encore. Pat's guitar tech was checking the tuning on his main guitar, a beautiful vintage sunburst Les Paul. The crowd was going wild. Pat took a big hit off the joint, a gulp of his drink and strapped on the guitar. He looked over at the stage manager and waited for his cue. The crowd began chanting and clapping in unison. The sound echoed through his head – he couldn't remember the crowd ever being so raucous. Numbness began to creep over his body.

He was so amazed at what this had all become – there were people as far as he could see and they were all his. They'd do whatever he asked. They'd tear the place down in a riot if he wanted them to. It was an exceptional feeling to have that much power over that many people. The sound of the clapping seemed to be music in itself — much like when one listens so intensely to the sound of an engine that music can be heard in the din — it was resonant music created by the energy of the crowd noise.

Resonant crowd energy... Psychoacoustic response is the people responding to the sounds I create...where are these words coming from? Why am I talking to myself? Man, am I fuckin' high...

The lights came up and the stage manager waved them on. The stage shook from the explosion of the crowd as they jogged back out. Security was trying to fight off the front rows from completely engulfing the buffer space in the front of the stage and they finally lost the battle. The crowd rushed the stage.

"I love each and every one of you motherfuckers!" Pat screamed to the crowd. "Thank you so much for being here San Diego, my homefucking town!"

The crowd responded with a tumult like he'd never heard before. He reached down into the crowd and pulled a beautiful blond girl up onstage, who quickly gave Pat a kiss, then turned and pulled up her shirt. The place erupted. The band members laughed as security chased her around the stage.

"Thank you folks for making this the best show ever..." Pat hollered into the microphone, as he simultaneously cranked his volume knob clockwise and let his guitar scream, the feedback echoing throughout the venue. He began to play – the notes flying through his fingertips at a superhuman rate. Mike stood watching with his mouth hanging open. This was not part of the show.

Pat stared straight into the spotlight, blinded and losing touch with all that was around him. He felt as if he were on fire. As he closed his eyes, he saw the colors left by the remnants of the spotlight dancing in his head. The music flowed through him. The zone.

He opened his eyes, ran over to Mike, looked him in the face and began to riff out the guitar solo to Led Zeppelin's 'Whole Lotta Love'. Mike read him perfectly as if the whole thing was planned out and waved in the rhythm section flawlessly. Jay was hammering out the bass part with intense accuracy, and Billy rolled through the John Bonham drum fills as if they'd rehearsed it all that very same night. Pat belted out vocals that would have made Robert Plant himself stop to listen. The entire band was in the zone as they'd never been before.

As they segued from the Zeppelin into Lightning Strikes, their biggest single, the crowd lost all control. The strobe lights emulating lightning from the stage made the crowd appear as one gigantic entity, moving in waves like an ocean that had come to life. Guys were climbing up on the stage and diving off, and security had given up trying to stop it. Pat danced around, laughing and high-fiving them. The energy was electrifying, and the heat was intense. Then, in an instant, it was over.

Pat threw his guitar up in the air, letting it crash onto the stage. He ran over and hugged Jay, shouting 'I'm sorry' into his ear over the crowd noise. Jay reciprocated in mime, and the two joined Mike and Billy at the front of the stage for a bow. The smoke settled and the night reached its culmination with a resounding thunder of applause. They all smiled, waved, and walked off the stage.

The band was welcomed back into the green room with more applause.

"Best fuckin' show ever, guys! Did you feel that shit?" Pat exclaimed.

"I sure did," said Mike, "It was truly awesome. It'll be nice to have you back, Pat…"

"Hey, not so fast! I still have one more night! And I'm going out with a bang!"

Mike chose to ignore that comment.

"Where's the afterparty going to be?" Chris inquired. "They'll kick us out of here by midnight! We should get a hotel or something."

"Fuck, that! My house, baby! Afterparty at my house!" Pat yelled across the room. "If you know where I live, then you're invited! If you don't, then you're not!"

Everybody in the room cheered. The words 'party at Pat's house' seemed to be getting passed on and on. Chris whispered an observation in Pat's ear.

"Hey bro, if the party's going to be at your house, we better get there before everyone else so we can get high."

"Dude, worry not…did you forget what we drove here? Now where's that special joint?"

♪♪♪

Tina shuffled out to the driveway for some air. She looked at her watch. It was 11:35. She figured she knew Carlos well enough to know that his men would not be late. She walked over to the truck and pulled on the handle. It was locked.

Oh shit, Tina...

She put her face up to the window with her hands around it to quell the reflection of the light behind her, trying to see where she had left the keys. She saw a glint of something shiny. They were still there.

How the fuck did this truck get locked? She walked around the truck, trying all the doors. *Pat must've locked it...I know I didn't...did I? Shit, I better call these guys...* She opened her cell phone and dialed the number to Carlos's henchmen.

"Bueno?"

"Hey, it's Tina."

"Is there a problem, guera? We're already on our way."

"The truck is locked"

"Carlos told you to leave us the keys, you stupid puta!"

"Listen, the keys are in it. But it's locked. You'll have to get it open,"

"Oh we'll get it open … any other problems?"

"No, just that."

"Okay, we'll see you soon."

"No, you won't."

She hung up.

As she stepped back to admire the truck for the last time, the motion-sensing light above the garage suddenly went out and startled her. Without that light — which wasn't much — the driveway was almost pitch black with the except for the shadows formed by the moonlight through the trees. A light wind caused the shadows to move eerily, and she suddenly felt frightened. She waved her hands around, trying to get the motion sensor to activate. It finally did after some coaxing, and she utilized the light to find her way back into the garage and close the door. She walked upstairs to Pat's study where she had a clear view of the driveway, dimmed the lights, turned on a small desk lamp and waited.

♪♪♪

The lines on the freeway went solid. Everything flew by in a blur, including other cars that were probably already going sixty or seventy.

"How fast now?" Chris screamed over the engine's howl.

"I don't know – it's pinned! Maybe a hundred thirty? This is fuckin' intense! I don't think I've ever gone this fast before!"

"This is so sick!" agreed Chris, "I think I'm gonna shit myself!"

The car sailed down the freeway at such a rate of speed that the bumps on the road could no longer be felt. It was like floating, especially to Pat and Chris who had just finished smoking a heroin-dipped joint and a bowl of meth.

"What's the time?" asked Pat

"Eleven forty-nine."

"Where are we?"

"Passing Del Mar."

"I told you, man! Chula to Encinitas in twenty minutes!"

"Not yet! You only got three minutes left!"

"Well, why didn't you say so?"

He pushed the pedal down further.

"Dude, don't miss the exit!"

"What's the time?"

"Eleven fifty-one."

Pat screamed. "Yeeeeeaaaahhh!"

"Okay! Time! Time! Slow down! It's our exit!"

Pat hit the brakes, slowly at first and then with a good jab. The car tracked beautifully. He jammed the tranny down into second and brought her down to a suitable speed for the ramp.

"Whoo! You see that shit? I am amped!"
"Me too, brother!"

♪♪♪

Tina saw something out of the corner of her eye and looked up from the magazine she was reading. A pair of headlights were slowly creeping around the corner – she couldn't quite make out what kind of car it was. As it got closer its lights dimmed and she could see it in the moonlight.

The white van. How could I forget that piece of shit?

A bright flashlight beam lit up the side of the house for a moment and almost immediately was extinguished. The van continued around the cul-de-sac and parked parallel to the driveway facing the direction from which it came – its only escape route. It sat dark and still for a moment, then under the van's interior light a figure exited the passenger side and scurried down the driveway.

He was wearing a black hoodie and black pants making him barely visible in the shadows. Staying hunched over, he made his way toward Pat's truck. He paused behind the right side of the truck for a moment, then worked his way around the front to the driver's side. The van remained idling on the street at the end of the driveway about forty feet up, just out of the thief's line of sight. Tina could see a small flashlight beam and something shiny come out of his pocket. He forced what looked like a slim piece of metal down through the gap between the window and the door and began to work it back and forth in an effort to pop the lock. He paused for a moment to look down the street. There was a car coming.

♪♪♪

The Chevelle drifted sideways around the corner, the rear tires slipping free as Pat steered straight for his driveway, laughing so hard his eyes were watering. Chris was still holding on for dear life. The car bounced up the curb, passing an old white van that was parked on the street. Pat slammed on the brakes, and the Chevelle came to a well-deserved rest about twenty feet or so behind and slightly to the left of his truck.

"That's the shit I'm talkin' about!" Pat exclaimed as something caught his eye on the left side of his truck as he killed the engine and headlights. He turned to Chris.

"Hey, did you see something over there by my truck or am I just seeing shadow ghosts from being so high?"

"No bro," Chris whispered, "I saw it too."

"Dude, what's the deal with that van back there? Is someone trying to break into my house or something?"

"If they are, they picked the wrong night!" Chris said as he reached down and pulled Pat's .45 caliber nickel plated Springfield 1911 pistol from under the Chevelle's seat. It was a beautiful and powerful weapon.

"Dude, what are you doing?" whispered Pat.

"Don't trip! I'm just gonna to scare 'em."

Chris slowly lifted the handle on the passenger side door. It unlatched with a loud click, making him wince. He stuck his head out of the passenger side holding the pistol in front of him, and Pat slid over and was now in the passenger seat peeking over the dash. Chris knelt down with the gun in his hands pointed at the sky with his arms resting on the hinges between the car's windshield and door like a standoff cop. It was absolutely silent except for the idling motor of the van behind them at the top of the driveway. They could see through the Ford's back window and the windshield to the front of the truck. Something in front of the truck moved.

♪♪♪

Oh my God, Oh my God... Tina was kneeling down at the window, mouth agape.

What the fuck are they doing here? They were supposed to be gone all night...

She could just make out the two dark figures moving around in Pat's car. She could also see the man hunched down in front of the truck. He was trying to see around the driver's side. She looked back to Pat's car. The interior light in the Chevelle had just gone on. Somebody was getting out.

Tina was about to jump out of her skin. She felt her heart skip; not believing what was unfolding in front of her.

Chris... What is he holding... is that a gun?

♪♪♪

Armando crouched in front of the truck's grille. The car that had driven up was blocking him in – there was no way to back the truck out even if he did get inside it. The Slim Jim was still sticking out of the driver's door. He had one hand on the truck's bumper, the other hand on his Berretta 9mm semi-automatic pistol that was in the pocket of his black hooded sweatshirt.

What the fuck am I to do? These pinche putos... I'm taking this fucking truck for Carlos...nobody can stop me... I'm going to have to deal with these fucking gringos...

He slowly moved to the driver's side of the truck, the hand in his pocket gripping his weapon as he cautiously peered around the truck's left fender at the car parked behind. The interior light in the car had come on, and he could clearly see a person inside the car shuffling over to the passenger seat. As he leaned out a little further exposing his face, he saw another person, and the shiny barrel of a gun pointed at him. A bright light suddenly illuminated the whole area. He pulled out his Berretta and jumped out from behind the truck.

♪♪♪

The motion sensing light on the garage went on.

"Fuck, he's got a gun!"

Chris had the gun aimed at the sky with his finger on the trigger. Pat grabbed Chris's arm in a narcotic-evoked panic.

"Dude…No!"

The muzzle flash lit up the driveway, the house and the entire cul-de-sac like a thousand camera flashes and the crack of the .45 echoed through the trees. Tina stood up and put her hands on the window in awe. The dark silhouette in front of the Ford stepped forward, shuddered and fell to the ground. She screamed in terror. The van at the top of the driveway screeched away. The last thing Armando saw was the bright flash.

The bullet hit him in the neck, snapping his head back. It didn't really hurt, but he grabbed at it anyway. His hands felt wet. He tried to run, but he couldn't; his legs were numb. Becoming instantly dizzy he began to lose sight. He fell forward onto the driveway.

Pinche gringos…

TEN

CHRIS SLOWLY SET the smoking gun down on the floorboard of the car. He was stunned by the discharge of the weapon and rattled by the screaming he heard coming from inside the house. As his eyes tried to re-adjust to the darkness after the gun's muzzle flash, he was able to make out the lump on the ground beside the truck. The cul-de-sac had gone deathly quiet except for the pounding inside the house of Tina running down the stairs, which he could barely make out over the ringing in his ears and the thumping of his heart.

Equally stunned, Pat slowly climbed over the gun and stumbled out the passenger side of the car.

"Dude, what just happened here?" he said, his ears also ringing from the crack of the pistol.

"I...I...don't know..."

They both began inching their way around the front of the car and toward the left side of the truck. They cautiously approached the dark lump on the ground just as the motion-sensing light turned off. They both jumped.

"Fuck! Stupid fucking light!" Pat yelled, stomping in its direction and waving his hands wildly in an effort to activate it. The garage door suddenly began to rise and Tina came running out, banging her head on it in the process and sobbing uncontrollably. The light went back on.

"Oh, God..." Pat turned away, gagged and threw up.

Tina put her hands up to her face and began screaming. Chris just stood there, unable to move at all.

“Oh my God, what have you guys done? Oh my God!” Tina screamed.

Pat turned toward Tina still half hunched over from puking.

“Hey, stop screaming! What is wrong with you? He’s a fuckin’ burglar! Oh, man… we gotta call the cops.”

Wiping vomit from his mouth he turned back to look at the mess on the ground. The body was lying face down. The hoodie had ripped clear of his head and about half of his neck was missing; a chunk of mutilated flesh was hanging in its place. The puddle of blood continued to expand and there was spatter all over the place.

“Oh, fuck…I…this…We…We have to call the cops. Shit, we’ve got dope in the house. Chris, go get the shit and flush it.” Pat got out his phone and began to dial 911.

Chris just stared at the body, still frozen.

Tina snatched the phone out of Pat’s hand and closed it.

“Tina, what the fuck are you doing? Gimme that phone!”

“No, Pat, you can’t…”

“Tina, you need to mellow out! He’s a burglar! He was on my property and there’s a Slim Jim sticking out of my truck! It’ll be okay…we have to call the cops!” He turned away again. “God, I can’t look at this shit.” He grabbed for the phone and Tina dodged out of the way, holding the phone at arm’s length.

“Pat…listen,” she said in between sobs, “you can’t call the cops!”

“Tina, stop acting crazy! We have to! A guy’s been shot, Tina! What are you worried about – the dope? We’ll just get rid of it.” He turned to Chris who was still in shock. “Dude, wake up! Listen to me! Go grab the sack and flush it. Take the pipes and shit and smash ‘em.”

Chris nodded.

“Pat, you don’t understand…you can’t…” Tina begged.

“Fuck, Tina! What is there to understand? I’ve got a dead guy in my driveway! We’re calling the fuckin’ cops! Okay?”

"Pat, your truck is full of dope!"

Tina was shaking and crying her eyes out.

Not quite sure of what he had just heard, Pat's voice suddenly dropped an octave.

"Tina, what are you talking about?"

"I'm sorry, Pat... I'm so sorry! They forced me...they said they'd kill you!"

"Tina, you're hysterical," Pat grabbed her by the shoulders. "Look at me... What the fuck is going on?"

She pointed at the body on the ground.

"Pat...that guy is a member of the Mexican Mafia...He was stealing your truck because it's packed with dope!"

Chris let out an uncomfortable laugh. "Holy shit!"

Pat was still trying to process the new information. "I...What...Tina, say that again..."

"Pat," she continued sobbing, "I'm so sorry...they made me do it."

"So my truck was used to smuggle dope? Is that what you're saying? And this guy is a Mexican mob guy?"

"Yes... Pat... I'm so sorry...nobody was supposed to get hurt...Carlos said he'd kill all of us if I didn't do it."

"Wow...this is pretty bad," Pat said to nobody in particular.

They all looked down at the bloody lump in the driveway.

"What do we do?"

"I don't know," Chris said, "but whatever it is that we're going to do, we'd better do it fast because we're hosting an afterparty."

Pat tried to swallow but couldn't. "Shit, he's right! Anybody that is anybody is on their way here right now!"

Tina started up again. "Oh, my God, Oh, my God...We're so fucked...what are we gonna do?"

Tina's crying was ringing through Pat's head.

"Tina, stop! We have to do our best to think semi-rationally!"

"Even though we haven't slept for about four days?" Chris added, "Rational..."

"Let's get this body out of here," Pat said.

"To like, where, dude?" asked Chris.

"We'll put it in the garage for now."

"The garage…Okay…"

"Chris, don't argue. We don't have time. Go get that piece of carpet that I lay down when I work on the cars and bring it here."

Chris ran into the garage and retrieved the carpet while Pat and Tina stared at the body in disbelief. He brought it out and laid it down next to the corpse.

"Okay, we have to roll him onto it, and then we can drag him into the garage and lock the doors."

"Are you serious? I'm not touching that dude."

"You shot him."

"I didn't mean to."

"What the fuck does that have to do with anything?"

"I don't know…"

"Quit being a fucking idiot! Come on, let's just roll him over."

They both got between the body and the truck. Pat was at the shoulders and Chris at the hips.

"Okay, one, two, three."

They pushed him over. Blood squirted out of his neck. His eyes were still open and blood was running out of his nose and mouth. Tina screamed again and Pat began to dry heave. Chris simply jumped away. The lifeless body lay on the carpet in a position that was not natural. At least not natural for a living person. Pat turned back around, grabbed the carpet and flipped the loose side over the body so they didn't have to look at it.

"Come on, grab a corner."

Chris and Pat dragged the body across the driveway and into the garage, dropping it in the spot normally allocated for the Chevelle. They looked out into the driveway.

Tina was staring at the blood puddles and vomit all over the ground.

She sobbed softly. "What are you going to do about all that?"

Pat looked around.

"We'll park the Chevelle over it."

Pat got into the car and parked it next to the truck, strategically placing it directly on top of the mess. He slowly climbed out of the car, put his arm around Tina and the three of them walked into the garage and watched the roll-up door go down.

"Do you think anyone heard the gunshot?" Chris asked.

"No, all my neighbors are out of town and I don't think anyone any further away than that would be all that alarmed. This area's so exclusive, nothing ever happens around here."

"Okay then, what next?" asked Chris.

"You pull the blinds at the garage sliding glass door closed and I'll lock it from this side and leave through the roll-up door. I know it isn't necessary to say this, but I'll say it anyway…we can't let anybody go into the garage."

Chris gave a slight grin in acknowledgment.

"Listen," Pat continued, "we're going to be cool until we can get everyone the fuck out of here. Right Tina?"

She looked up at him with a sad mascara-covered raccoon face. "Yeah."

"Okay then. You guys get in the house, clean up and get ready."

"Hey, Pat…" Chris said

"Yeah?"

"You might want to wash your hands and change that shirt."

Pat looked down at his shirt and hands and gagged. He ran over to a washbasin in the garage and ripped off his shirt, furiously scrubbing his hands under scolding hot water. Tina and Chris went inside. Satisfied with his hands, Pat walked over toward the sliding glass door that led into the party room to lock it. He looked down. Bloody footprints.

Fuck! Please be me and not them! Not in the house…

He looked at his shoes. It was him. Taking off his shoes while attempting to stay in stride, he tossed them into the washbasin with his shirt, ran over to the sliding glass door, locked it from the garage side and opened the roll-up garage door. He walked out into the driveway searching in the dim light for remnants on the ground. Fortunately, they were mostly covered by the Chevelle.

A car came barreling down the driveway and parked right behind Pat's cars. Pat hit the outside garage button. The door slowly began to roll down as the door of the first partygoer's car swung open.

"Hey…Pat! What's up?" a cheerful voice yelled.

Pat didn't recognize it. He looked back at the body wrapped in the carpet, and at the garage door closing agonizingly slow.

Fuck…Hurry up dammit…

The person was walking in Pat's direction.

Oh, fucking great…

"Wow, am I the first one here, man?"

The garage door putted along. *Come on…This fucking door…*Pat moved in front of it. "H… Hey, man, how are ya? Welcome - mi casa es su casa!" Pat said as the door finally closed behind him.

"Thanks man, I'm Dave, remember? I met you backstage with Karen? She's meeting me here…"

He looked Pat up and down, probably wondering why he had no shoes and no shirt on. Pat had no clue who he was, but it didn't matter – Pat gave him his warmest handshake. "Oh yeah, Karen – of course. Nice to see you again, Dave…" He put a friendly hand on Dave's shoulder. "Hey, why don't we head up to the front door? I'll show you around. We'll grab a beer."

"Wow! Thanks, man!"

Pat led the guy into the house. "Hey, bro, head down those stairs over there and you'll see my buddy Chris. He'll get you a beer. I'll be with ya in a few. Cool?"

"Okay. Thanks, Pat!"

"No sweat, brother."

Pat walked into his bedroom and shut the door behind him.

Holy shit... How the hell did all this happen?

He could hear cars pulling up outside.

How am I gonna get these people out of here?

Doors were opening and closing, and more and more voices could be heard in the house.

Time to go down and be the life of the party... Good luck with that...

He splashed some cold water on his face, put on a clean shirt and some shoes and checked himself in the mirror.

Okay, here we go...

He took a deep breath and opened the door.

♪♪♪

Tina sat on the bed in the guest room with her head in her hands. She was all cried out. She sat up and stared at the wall, reflecting on the events of the past week or so.

So far this week she'd outrun the police, totaled her car, smuggled dope across the international border and gotten somebody killed – who it just so happened, was connected with the Mexican mob. And yes, it probably would get worse.

And don't forget Tina, you've also pretty much signed the death warrant on yourself, Pat and probably Chris too... Oh, and totally betrayed your best friend's trust... Nice work, Tina...

She tried to cry some more but the tears wouldn't come – just the headache that went along with being unable to cry anymore. She stood up, went to the bathroom and looked in the mirror. *Whoa, somebody needs some sleep...*

She got her makeup bag and tried to clean herself up but was not satisfied with the results. She lay back down on the bed. She could hear the music pounding downstairs.

I am not going down there... No way... I can't take any more of this shit...

There was a knock at the door.

"Go away!"

"Tina, it's Pat…"

She opened the bedroom door and was suddenly able to work up some tears.

"Hey, calm down, girlie. Sit down. It's cool."

"Pat…I'm so sorry…"

"Hey, I know you are. Just tell me everything that happened from beginning to end."

She did. She told him about the two guys in the van and the trip in the back of it through Tijuana. She told him about her meeting with Carlos, the knife to her throat and everything he had said with it there. She told him about the stuffing of his truck with the dope, the smuggling of it over the border, the five thousand dollars and the threats to kill them both if she didn't oblige. She told him of the plan to steal his truck and the hopes that it would finally end this nightmare for her.

Pat just sat there listening, completely blown away by the incredibly hopeless situation they'd gotten themselves into.

"Wow, I guess you were right, maybe we shouldn't have called him, huh?"

She socked him in the arm and they laughed. He pulled out a loaded pipe.

"Grab a hit."

She took a big hit off of the pipe and let out a deep breath. She felt better. Pat looked into her eyes. "Listen to me. We are going to get through this shit. We're going downstairs, and we're going to act completely natural and have a good time. We're going to party, get everyone the fuck out of here, take a nap and deal with all this shit in the morning. Are we cool?"

"Like the Fonz…"

Pat took her hand and opened the bedroom door. They walked arm-in-arm down the stairs.

♪♪♪

"Patrick, you rock!"

"Great show tonight!"

"You guys are fuckin' awesome!"

"You shred, Patrick!"

The compliments came over and over and over. Pat didn't eat it up like usual though – tonight was different. His smile felt very fake to him; however, it did seem that it fooled everyone except Chris and Tina, who seemed to be wearing the exact same fake smile.

"Hey Patrick, wanna smoke some chronic?"

"Hey Patrick, how about another shot?"

He must have smoked twenty joints and had twenty drinks. He could not seem to get high.

"Patrick, when are you guys playing again?"

"When is the new album coming out?"

"How was the tour?"

Why can't everyone just shut the hell up? What time is it anyway – don't these people have homes?

The party was in full swing. A few of the other band members were there along with some local celebrities; ladies were topless in the pool and hot tub. People were lounging around the bar and the TV, shooting pool and playing foosball; all in all, it was quite the shindig.

Pat walked upstairs to catch his breath. Two people were making out on the living room sofa.

"Hey, douchebags, downstairs!"

Pat followed them downstairs to make sure they got there. Chris ran up to him out of breath.

"Hey bro, Travis is here." Chris was talking about Travis Barker of Blink 182 who lived nearby in neighboring Rancho Santa Fe. Travis and his girlfriend strolled over to say hello.

"Hey, Travis, what's up, man?" said Pat.

"Not much, bro…Saw your show tonight. Fucking incredible, man, you guys are super tight."

"Thanks Trav. How are the guys?"

"We're on hiatus right now – working on the next album."

"Us too – I can't wait. Maybe we could do some shows together – you know our manager Steve Stanford, right? Have your peeps give him a call."

"I will. Hey, I heard you have a ZX6 that Jamie Hacking built. Is that true?"

"Yeah, I love that bike! It's out in the garage."

Oh my God, what did I just say? The garage? You fucking idiot!

"Can I check it out?" Travis said enthusiastically, "I love crotch rockets!"

Pat looked at Chris, and Chris looked back at him like the idiot he was.

"Uh…um…" he gazed at Chris with big 'help me' eyeballs.

"It's… in the shop…new tires," Chris interrupted.

"Oh yeah, I forgot," Pat said, "the tires…the tires were kinda worn... I'm getting them replaced. And a performance tune-up. Can't be too careful, right Trav?"

"Oh yeah, of course, man. Well what else you got in there? I love toys; let's see what else you've got."

"Um, I can't…uh…"

Think of something you idiot!

"…the garage is being fumigated."

"What?"

"I mean the garage is being re…done. The tiles…the tiles were coming up off the floor, so I'm having it resurfaced. All the bikes and cars are in storage. We can't go in there. It's like a construction zone."

Travis gave Pat a look as if to say he understood that Pat was just living up to his druggie reputation. "Okay man, maybe next time."

"Yeah, for sure, we'll go ride the canyons sometime."

"Sure, Pat. Hey, great party. I'm gonna go get a drink."

"Make yourself at home, my friend…"

Travis walked over to the bar and joined the rest of the party.

Pat grabbed Chris's arm and pulled him close. "Dude, I can't take this shit," he whispered, "we gotta get these people out of here or I'm gonna fuckin' lose it."

"I feel your pain, bro…" Chris agreed.

"Patsie!" a deliriously happy voice squealed from behind him. He turned around. It was Raquel, obviously drunk. Pat looked at Chris, who shrugged his shoulders with a smirk.

Raquel looked incredible. She had a tiny little dress on with six-inch heels. Her huge boobs were pouring out of what little clothes she had on.

"Hey, I'm so sorry about the little tiff we had this morning sweetie. Will you forgive me?"

She leaned up against him, rubbing her boobs on him and playing with his hair.

"Uh, yeah, of course I forgive you."

"I love you, Patsie; you looked so sexy on stage tonight."

"Uh…thanks." Pat gave Chris another 'help me' look. This time Chris just smiled.

Raquel put her arms on Pat's shoulders and gave him a big wet kiss. "Hey, would it be okay if I stayed with you tonight, sweetie?"

"I…uhm…"

She interrupted him before he could muster up an answer. "Patsie, I want you to meet my friend Jackie."

Jackie was a tall, thin girl with long black hair and a beautiful face. She was dressed as if she'd just gotten off work at the Spearmint Rhino.

"Hi Pat, nice to finally meet you," she said, twirling her hair around her finger nervously. "Raquel's told me all about you."

"Uh…nice to meet you too."

Raquel leaned in close to Pat and whispered in his ear as he eyed Jackie's long curvy legs.

"She's never been with a celebrity before, Patsie. *And* she's never had a threesome before!"

You've got to fucking kidding me! Tonight? Come on!

"That is, before tonight, baby…"

God, you are a cruel one…

"Uhm…I …I'm really tired tonight, Raquel…"

"Oh come on baby…look at her…" She pulled Jackie close to her. "How can you resist this beautiful girl?" She gave Jackie a long passionate tongue kiss.

Okay, God, this is no longer funny. You can quit anytime…

Chris just stared, not believing his eyes. Pat wanted to go find the gun and shoot himself.

"Sweetie, I'd really love to…In fact, you have *no idea* how much I'd love to, but I've been up for days and I'm crashing soon. In fact, this party is going to be winding down any time now."

"That's fine… We'll just wait for you upstairs."

"Really, I'd love to, but I just can't. Not tonight."

"You can't be serious."

"I'm sorry. Maybe another night?"

"Whatever, Pat…I guess we'll just have to find some other lucky guy…"

She grabbed Jackie by the arm and walked away.

Pat turned to Chris.

"Just kill me now. Please."

"Yeah, that's all I need. A second body to dispose of."

They looked at each other and started laughing hysterically.

"My brother, we got to get these people out of here."

"You really want them out of here?" Chris asked.

"Dude, do what you have to do."

Chris walked over to the bar, grabbed the remote control and killed the TV and stereo. He then made the announcement.

"Ladies and gentlemen, we thank you for coming over tonight but it's time to start heading for the door. We've got a few people who are feeling a little under the weather, so we're shutting down. It's been great having you, but get the fuck out!"

The crowd let out a collective sigh with a couple of chuckles and slowly began to filter toward the door. Chris went out to repeat his announcement to the pool area. The collective sigh was heard again.

"Hey, thanks for coming," Pat repeated for what must have been the hundredth time.

"Great to see you."

"See you soon, thanks for being here."

Partygoers never leave quickly. Pat repeated his goodbyes over and over during the next hour or so. He and Chris had to physically push some people to the door and call cabs for others. It was agonizing.

Finally, it was just the three of them again. The unwelcome glow of daylight was rearing its ugly head outside. They lay on the couch in the party room, completely exhausted. Pat spoke first.

"I know what we have to deal with guys, but I just can't do it right now. None of us have slept for I don't know how long. I don't know about you, but I have to crash. I just have to."

He looked over at Tina and Chris for a response, but Chris was already snoring, and Tina was passed out on his shoulder. Pat didn't make it to his bed either.

ELEVEN

PAT SAT UP and looked around. Sunlight shone straight into his eyes, making him put his hand up in front of his face to block it. He looked to his right. There they were, still sound asleep. It wasn't a bad dream. It was real. He knew he didn't have to pinch himself.

He stood up slowly, dug into his pockets for his cell phone and looked at the time. 3:02.

Oh, shit...Three o' clock?

He thought about the gruesome scene inside his garage. What the hell were they going to do? He nudged Chris.

"Hey! Hey man, wake up."

Chris stirred and then slowly opened his eyes. The afternoon sun had the same effect on him that it had on Pat. He shielded his eyes from the light like a chubby Latino vampire.

"What time is it?" Chris groggily asked.

"Three. Dude, what are we going to do?"

"So it wasn't a dream?"

Tina stirred. "That's what I was hoping too."

"No, it wasn't a dream," Pat said. "I'm gonna grab us a bowl to smoke, and then we have to figure out what we're gonna do about this shit."

"Hey, you wanna know something ironic?" Chris said.

"What?"

"You were supposed to go to rehab today!"

"Shut up, asshole."

"I'm just sayin'..."

They got high until they were once again able to function and then decided to go get something to eat, further avoiding the garage. They walked outside to the Chevelle. They all paused, each waiting for the other to look underneath the car. Pat decided to take the problem head-on.

"All right, we all know what's under there." He tossed Chris the keys. "Dude, back up the car. I'll get the hose."

Chris backed the car up, exposing the mess beneath. They all had to turn away. Pat mustered up all the bravado he could and began hosing the blood and vomit down the driveway drain. The stone came clean but the grout was stained. It looked a little like oil. Pat wasn't too worried about it; presently there were much larger problems at hand. He inspected his work, and satisfied, he rolled up the hose. They all got into the car and drove to Denny's.

♪♪♪

"I'll have the ham and cheese omelet, white toast, hash browns and coffee," said Pat.

"Okay, I'll be right back with your drinks," the waitress said, with a huge smile on her face, letting them all know she recognized him.

"Knock, Knock," said Chris.

"Who's there?" replied Pat with a smile.

"Omelet."

"Omelet who?"

"I'm o' let Tina suck my dick tonight!"

Pat and Chris laughed hysterically. Tina just gave Pat a look of desperation.

"Okay. We have to get serious," Pat said. "Has anybody thought of anything?"

"Yeah, we're fucked," Tina said, beginning to panic. "There's blood spatter everywhere and probably hair and carpet fibers on the driveway and on us and our DNA is on the carpet and him, and…"

"Hold on there, Detective, we need to think a little more positively. How do you get rid of a body anyway?"

"Aren't you supposed to submerge it in lye?" asked Chris. He and Pat began to banter back and forth.

"Lye? What's lye?" asked Pat.

"You know, in movies they put the body in a 55-gallon drum and fill it with lye and the body just disintegrates, right?

"I thought it was lime."

"Is it? It might be. Or hydrochloric acid, right?"

"Where would we get a 55-gallon drum and hydrochloric acid?"

"Home Depot probably has all that shit."

"And wouldn't we have to cut the body up to fit it in the drum?"

"I guess so…"

"I wonder what kind of saw you'd use. We'd probably need a tarp."

"Visqueen."

"What?"

"Visqueen. That's what they call that plastic sheeting."

"Maybe we should Google it… How to get rid of a body."

"Don't they trace that kind of stuff on the internet? They'd find your computer if you typed that in."

"Who's they?"

"I heard somewhere that pigs will devour an entire body in fifteen minutes."

"Seriously?"

Tina could take no more. "Are you guys for real? What are you talking about? Cutting up a body and putting it in a drum? Feeding people to pigs? Googling it?"

"Shhhh, Tina, we're just kidding! Keep it down, people are looking."

Pat and Chris were giggling. The waitress came back, and Pat read her nametag: Mandy.

"Here's your drinks, and your coffee, sweetie…"

"Thank you so much, Mandy."

She blushed. "My pleasure, Patrick…"

"My pleasure, *Patrick…*" Tina mocked sarcastically with a goofy grin on her face. "God, these groupie whores make me sick."

"You once loved me too, in fact, I know you still do…don't try to deny it! Besides, Mandy may be a very nice girl."

"Pat, I just felt so sorry for you that I let you have me once," said Tina, laughing with them now.

"Don't do me any favors, single Hispanic female!"

"Shut up, tweeker."

"Don't get me started!"

Tina's cell phone rang.

"Hello?"

"Que paso, guera, you remember me?"

Tina's blood drained right out of her face. She felt dizzy. "Carlos…I…"

"Shut up, you fucking cunt. Your rock star boyfriend killed my man, guera. You and the rock star are dead."

"Carlos, it was an accident…"

"I will find you. I can find you anywhere. Maybe we'll get on the news, eh guera?"

"Please…"

"I'm going to watch you suck my dick before I kill you. And I'm going to cut off your boyfriend's huevos. Don't bother hiding, I will find you no matter where you go. Goodbye guera."

Tina began to cry.

"Tina, what did he say? Are you okay?" asked Pat.

She just shook her head unable to speak. Holding her hand to her mouth, she jumped up and ran to the restroom.

Pat turned to Chris. "Dude, we gotta stop joking around. This shit is way too fucking serious. We have to figure out what to do with that body and my truck, and we have to figure it out now."

"Hey, I have an idea. Give me your phone – I left mine at the house."

Pat handed Chris the phone.

"You'll have to power it up…I've had it off 'cause I really don't feel like dealing with all those people I told I'd be going to rehab today."

"Yup, looks like today ain't the day," Chris said, turning on the phone and dialing.

"Hey, Cheeto, what's up, it's Chris… Chris Martinez, remember? Yeah… Hey, I have a problem I need your help with… No it's a bigger problem than that… No, I'm on my friend's cell phone…yeah, okay, I'll do that…thanks man, I'll make it worth your while…okay, later." Chris slapped Pat's phone back down on the table.

"Who's Cheeto?" Pat asked.

"He's a guy I used to roll with back in the day. He's into everything, drugs, guns, stolen property, everything. He'll know what to do."

"Well, what did he say?"

"He won't talk on your phone. He said to go buy a new prepaid and call him back."

"I seem to be acquiring a lot of new phones this week."

Tina came back to the table, ghostly pale.

"T, what happened?"

"It was Carlos, Pat. He said he is going to kill both of us…" She started weeping quietly, trying not to make a scene in the restaurant.

Pat just sat there. He didn't have a reply for that.

"Pat, he's seriously connected. We have to get out of town or something."

Again, he couldn't reply.

"Pat, do you understand the magnitude of this? He will find us."

"I'll hire a bodyguard. Protection. He won't get us, he'll get his. But first, we have to deal with the problems at the house."

Mandy returned with their food and a big smile. Pat suddenly didn't really feel like flirting with her. He seemed to have lost his appetite too.

♪♪♪

They pulled up to the house as the evening sun was creating long shadows across the driveway, making every crevasse in the tile grout look dark and stained. Chris was in the back seat attempting to open the hermetically sealed package containing the new pre-paid cell phone.

"Fuck, why do they have to seal these things like this?"

Tina didn't hear him at all. Her eyes were fixed on the garage door. They stepped out of the car but instead of taking the normal path through the garage to the party room, they turned up the driveway and entered the house through the front door. Tina followed Pat into the kitchen and Chris sat down on the living room sofa to finish his battle with the phone's packaging.

Pat grabbed a couple of beers out of the fridge, and he and Tina sat down on the stools at the kitchen counter.

"So, Pat, what was with that comment Chris made about you going to rehab?"

"Last night at the gig the band pretty much gave me an ultimatum. Or an intervention – I don't know what to call it. Anyway, we all agreed I'd be going to rehab today."

"No shit."

"Yeah. And the day before, I pretty much promised Christine and Tommy that I'd do it too."

"Were you serious or just blowing smoke? No pun intended."

"I guess I was serious… I mean, shit Tina, I've got so much; a great career, great people in my band, a great girl, my son, my family… I've got everything in the world going for me, but it's inevitable that I'll become just another statistic if I don't slow it all down."

"Ya think?"

"That's what I mean. Because of drugs, I have a fuckin' dead body in my garage. I can't do this anymore. We have to get through this shit and it's all got to stop."

"Were you going to tell me about rehab?"

"I hadn't even thought about it. All this shit happened so fast – I haven't been thinking at all. Everything is upside down. Had things not transpired the way they did in the last day, of course I would have told you. My hope is that you and Chris would clean up with me. You guys are literally my best friends."

"Pat, I had dreams of becoming an attorney. I even had some connections. I probably could have done it too, but the dope… I have to stop too. This life has gone from heaven to hell. I can't handle it any more either. I'll stop with you."

"So, we'll all stop this shit as soon as we get through this."

"Are we going to get through this? Pat, I'm really scared."

"I am too, T."

Chris came running into the room.

"Guys, I talked to Cheeto. He said we need to bring the body and the truck to his warehouse. He said we can work all this out."

"Who's Cheeto?" Tina asked.

"Some guy Chris knows from way back. Dude, how well do you know this guy?"

"I used to know him pretty good – I bought shit from him before I met Garrett."

"But how well do you *know* him? I mean, look what you're trusting him with. We have some serious shit going on here. He's not going to get mixed up in this for his health. Why is he helping us? What's in it for him?"

"I kinda promised him the dope."

"The dope in the truck?"

"Yeah."

"Chris, that dope belongs to the Mexican mob," Tina said. "Did you tell him that?"

"I might have left that part out."

"How much did you tell him there was?"

"Thirty keys."

"How could you say that? We don't know how much there is, do we?"

Tina nodded yes. "I told him, Pat. I don't know where you were at the time, but yeah, there's about thirty kilos according to what Carlos said."

"How much is that worth?"

"My math isn't very good, but I'd bet it's a few million bucks."

"And you think Carlos will just let that go? You think he doesn't already have people coming to get it?" Pat blanched, completely aware of the very uncomfortable silence initiated by his last statement. "Look, we have to get the fuck out of here, and we have to do it now. Chris, go to my safe. The combo is 06-21-38. Get all the cash, documents and guns and bring it all to the kitchen. Then grab my guns from in my cars and bring them in too. Tina, go into the hallway closet and grab the empty suitcase and duffel bags and bring them here. Then both of you grab enough clothes and shit to last a day or two and pack. I have to make a phone call."

Pat ran upstairs to his office and dialed the phone.

"Hello?"

"Hey, it's me."

"What do you want, Pat?"

"I need to come over."

"No, not tonight. Tommy's just getting ready to lie down. I don't want him getting all riled up before bedtime. If you come over, he'll never go to sleep. And I don't want to see you anyway."

"Christine, you don't understand – something really bad has happened, and I just need to stop by for a few minutes. I'm not asking you, I'm telling you."

"What happened Pat? What have you done?"

"I can't talk about it on the phone, Christine. I'll be seeing you in an hour or so. You have plenty of time to put Tommy down if you need to."

"Pat, this is…"

"Christine, please don't ask questions and don't argue. I'll see you in a bit."

He hung up the phone and started collecting anything related to personal finances from his study. He jogged them back down into the kitchen meeting Tina and Chris there. Chris had the contents of Pat's safe spread out on the kitchen counter.

"Dude, how much is here?" asked Chris.

"A hundred fifty grand."

"How many guns do you have?"

"Eight or nine."

"Damn bro, I never figured you for the Armageddon type."

"You never know, my friend. Here, put all this shit into the suitcase except for the two .45's and the Glock. We'll keep 'em out and load 'em. The ammo is in a plastic storage bin under my bed. Oh, and there's a shotgun in a guitar case under there – grab that too." He then turned to Tina. "Tina do you know how to use one?"

"A gun? Not really, Pat, and I don't really want to."

"Babe, at this point you don't have much of a choice. We don't know what the future holds for us and I don't want any of us to wind up dead."

The Glock was already loaded. He picked it up and dropped the clip, racked it back and popped a round out of the chamber, catching it in mid-air.

"This is a Glock 17L nine millimeter. It's super light and easy to use. Most cops carry ones like this. It weighs just over two pounds and it won't kick that hard. You push the clip in like this, pull the slide back until it clicks, and let it go. This gun is now ready to fire. It's semi-automatic, so the slide comes back every time it's fired. The safety is right here – always leave it on unless you intend to use it. It's tucked under here so it can't be accidentally turned off. You hold it like this…" He showed her. "Here, take it."

Tina reluctantly took the weapon and held it like Pat showed her.

"I'm not going to go into a bunch of target shooting tips with you – just point it, push down the safety and pull the trigger. It'll flash, it'll kick, it'll be loud, and it'll be scary. But it might save your life."

He took the gun back, demonstrated how to unload it, and had her do it a couple of times.

"This one's yours. Stuff it in your jeans or whatever feels comfortable."

Chris came back with the ammunition and the shotgun in the guitar case. They each loaded a .45 and put them behind their backs in their waistbands. Everything else went into the suitcase.

"I'm going to grab some clothes and stuff. You guys grab everything else and I'll meet you guys at the garage."

Chris and Tina looked at each other, and then back to Pat.

"Yes, this is it," Pat said. "We have to do this. I'll see you at the garage."

Tina and Chris shuffled slowly outside and down the driveway to the garage door, carrying the suitcase and duffel bags. It was now almost dark outside, and it made them feel even more ill at ease than when it was still daylight. They were suspicious of every shadow and any movement. They stood by the garage door waiting for Pat.

"Do you think it smells yet?" Chris asked Tina.

"Why do you feel it necessary to ask me that?"

"You're the only one here. Who else would I ask?"

The front door slammed and Pat came down the driveway with a duffel bag of his own.

"Where is Cheeto's warehouse anyway?" Pat asked.

"Near the 54 and Highland Avenue in Chula Vista."

"We're making a stop at Christine's on the way down."

"It's gonna be a long night."

"We're used to it."

He dropped the bag and punched the code into the keypad thus opening the garage door. They collectively held their breath as the door slowly rolled up.

The garage was just as they left it – two feet hanging out of a folded piece of carpet and bloody smudges and footprints all around on the checkered tile floor. They all breathed in, subconsciously checking for the smell. Although it wasn't rotting, they thought they could smell death as they stood staring.

"We've got to get it into the back of the truck."

"How?"

"I don't know. I guess we'll have to wrap it in something and lift it."

"We could just leave it in the carpet."

"It's not wide enough to roll up enough to be secure. We have to be able to lift it in without him slipping out."

"What else you got?"

"There should be a big ass tarp in that cabinet over there." Pat pointed to a cabinet inside the garage. "Third shelf."

Chris went over and retrieved the tarp, laying it out on the tile floor next to the body in the carpet.

"Okay, we have to roll him onto the tarp and wrap him up."

"Okay…"

They attempted to psyche up for the task. Finally, Pat pulled back the carpet. The fluorescent lighting in the garage made the body's face look milky white with almost a purple tint in certain spots. There was dried blood on his goatee and chin. His eyes were still open about halfway, making him look as if he were a stoned dead body. They tried not to look at his mutilated neck. Blood was dried all over the carpet, making it stick to the wound and his clothes. The sight was unreal.

"Should we close his eyes or something?" asked Chris. "You know, like they do in the movies?"

"Go ahead if you want to – I'm sure as fuck not doing it," answered Pat.

"I guess not."

They knelt down next to the body, and trying not to get too close, Pat and Chris tucked the tarp under the part of the carpet that he was laying on.

"Okay, let's grab the carpet and roll him off of it and onto the tarp," Pat said.

"Will do."

Tina just stood by staring with her arms crossed, unable to say or do anything.

They pulled the carpet up, and the body rolled right onto the tarp, and onto its side.

"Sweet. That worked well. Okay, let's wrap him up."

They pulled the tarp tight, folded the ends up over his head and feet first, tossed a loose side over the body, and rolled him up like a big blue burrito. They used bungee cords to secure the tarp around him tightly. They stood back and admired their work, dusting off their hands like they'd just completed a home improvement project.

"Good. Now we have to get him into the truck. I'll back it up."

Pat backed the pickup into the garage. They looked at the back of the pickup. With the truck's custom suspension lift, the tailgate was almost up to Tina's breasts.

"Tina, you're gonna have to help here."

She reluctantly agreed.

Pat grabbed the shoulders, Chris the torso and Tina the legs. They lifted.

"Fuck, how much does this guy weigh?" Pat exclaimed.

Pat's section was on the tailgate and Chris almost had his up when Tina lost her grip, and the body was sent falling to the ground with a clunk.

"Hey, remember Weekend at Bernie's?" Chris said, almost chuckling.

"Yeah," Pat said, chuckling a little himself.

Tina wasn't laughing. "Come on, let's try again, we've got to get out of here." Her voice was quaking.

"Okay, this time get up under him. One, two, three..."

The body rolled onto the tailgate. They pushed it back into the truck's bed. Pat jumped up into the truck bed and rolled it up against the cab.

"We've still got to cover the back of the truck," Chris noted. "You have any more tarps?"

"There's one over the WaveRunners on the side of the house. We'll use it."

As they walked out of the garage into the driveway the motion-sensing light came on, making then all nearly jump out of their skin.

"Fuck!" squealed Chris.

"I'm gonna shoot that fucking thing," Pat said.

They continued to the side of the garage, pulled the tarp and bungee cords off the watercraft and brought them into the garage.

"Let's put the suitcase and duffel bags up there too."

They tossed all the luggage and the guitar case into the back of the truck and closed the tailgate. They then stretched the tarp across the truck's bed and secured it tightly with the remaining bungees.

"Chris, take that bloody carpet, fold it up, and stuff it in one of the trash cans. I'm going to hose down the garage. T, would you be so kind as to grab the floor scrubber over there?"

"Sure Pat..."

They cleaned the garage floor until it looked shiny new. At least the white checkers did.

"Good enough…" said Pat. "Let's get the hell out of here."

Pat closed the garage, locked the front door and set the alarm. They climbed into the truck; Chris in the driver's seat, Pat shotgun and Tina in back. They finally drove out of the cul-de-sac.

As they turned left onto the main road out, two black Ford vans passed them going the opposite way at a rate of speed that was excessive for the neighborhood. The vans turned into Pat's cul-de-sac.

"Did you see that?" Chris said, "Where the hell do you think they're going?"

"The Mexican mob?" Pat asked.

"Dude, where else would two black vans be heading on your street, where everyone is out of town except you?"

"Oh, man…we got out of there in the nick of time. But, my house! Maybe I should call the cops."

"I'm not so sure that wasn't the cops, Pat," said Tina. "That's the same kind of vans they had when they raided Garrett."

"Cops? Oh great! I don't know what's worse."

"What do you want to do?" asked Chris.

"Nothing. Cops or mob, we got to go …just keep driving. And speed up; they might have recognized the truck."

Chris continued driving toward the freeway, eyes glued to the rearview mirror. Tina and Pat could not stop looking back through the truck's rear window. Every pair of headlights they saw creeped them out more.

"Fuck man, are they following us?"

Chris took a left onto the freeway. A pair of headlights followed. They appeared to be from a truck or van. Chris instinctively sped up.

"Wait, dude, don't go over sixty-five!" yelled Pat, "There's a dead body back there!"

"And thirty kilos of dope," Tina added.

Chris slowed to the speed limit and chose the second lane. The headlights were right behind them. It was definitely a van. It got closer. It was now right on their rear bumper. Chris could not and would not speed up.

"Fuck, why doesn't this prick just pass us?"

"Cause it's them, man, it's them!" said Pat, starting to lose it. "We're so fucked! They're going to kill us."

"Should I try to lose them?" Chris suggested. "Should I drive to a police station or something?"

"Come on, man! You know we can't involve the cops! Hell, they might *be* the cops!"

"Well, we've got guns…let's get off the freeway and drive somewhere isolated and take them by surprise!"

"Are you fucking kidding? We're not getting into a gunfight with anyone! And they might be cops! Come on, Chris!"

"Well, I don't know what to do!"

"I don't know either!"

Tina began crying and talking to herself. Praying.

"Maybe drive to someplace public," Pat yelled in a panic. "They can't just shoot us in front of people! Can they?"

"How the hell should I know? Where do you want me to drive to?"

"I said, someplace public!"

"Well, where the fuck is that?"

"I don't know, Chris! Think!"

"I can't think! This fucker is all over my ass! You think!"

"Fuck, a grocery store or something! Someplace busy!"

"Where? You want me to exit now?"

"I don't know!" Pat screamed, now almost crying himself. "I don't know!"

Suddenly a barrage of red lights came on in their mirrors. The entire truck lit up. A siren went on.

"Oh, my God!" Tina screamed.

"Fuck man, they've got us. I don't know how, but they've got us," Pat sobbed, "Just pull over, man. There's no escaping them now. We're totally fucked. Just pull over, Chris. We have to give up."

Chris pulled to the right, and the ambulance that was behind them sped on by.

"Holy fuck, holy fuck, holy fuck!" Pat screamed.

God, thou art with me... Tina thought to herself.

"That's right! That's right!" Chris laughed. "Whoa, man! I think I just pissed myself. We gotta pull over. Pat, you gotta drive. Fuck this."

♪♪♪

"Hi."

"Hi, Pat."

"Where is he?"

"In his room sleeping."

"Can we come in for a second?"

"Do I have a choice?"

They all walked into Christine's condo. It was a nicely decorated place, very clean and very homey.

"Hey, Christine," said Chris uncomfortably, knowing how she felt about him.

"Hi, Chris."

"Christine, this is our good friend Tina."

"Nice to meet you, Christine," offered Tina, "I've heard nothing but good things about you."

"Likewise, I'm sure," said Christine with a skeptical look. "Look Pat, I'm sorry to be a bitch but Tommy's asleep and I wasn't expecting company tonight. Can we get right to the point?"

"Can we talk in your room?"

"Okay, Pat."

Pat picked up the suitcase he walked in with and followed Christine upstairs. Chris sat down on the sofa. Tina picked up a picture of Christine, Pat and Tommy.

"She's pretty."

"She's a good girl."

Pat and Christine went into her room, and Pat closed the door behind them. He looked troubled.

"Okay, Pat, tell me what is going on."

"I don't even know where to start, Christine, I'm in so far over my head." He looked like he was about to cry. "I'm so sorry…I should have listened to you… I should have stopped the drugs…I'm so sorry…"

"What happened Pat? Are you in trouble?"

"I'm in so much trouble, Christine. I'm not sure if I'll get out. That's why I needed to come over."

He opened the suitcase.

"Pat, what is all this?"

He began taking items out.

"This is all my financial stuff. Everything I own. Titles to the cars and the house, bank stuff and will and trust. Please keep them safe."

"Pat, what is going on?" She began crying.

"Babe, I can't involve you. It's best that you know nothing, that way you'll be safe."

"But, Pat…"

"Christine, just take my stuff and take care of it. There's some cash here for you and Tommy. It's a hundred grand. Stash it away in your bank account."

"Pat, you're scaring me."

"Lastly, I need you to take this gun. You may need to protect yourself or Tommy sometime." He went to hand her a 9mm.

"Pat, I'm not taking any gun! What is happening? What have you done?"

He grabbed her and held her close. They both hugged hard, crying together, not saying anything for a few minutes.

"I'll be okay, babe. This is all just precautionary."

"Would you please tell me…?"

"No, honey. I have to go. I'm planning on going to rehab as soon as I sort some things out. Maybe sometime this week. I already promised the guys I would too. That's good news, right?"

"I suppose, Pat. Whatever you're doing, just be careful. Please. Tommy needs you and so do I."

"Thanks honey, I will. I love you."

"I love you too, Pat."

"I need to see him."

"Okay."

They walked across the hall to Tommy's room and slowly opened the door. He was sleeping soundly under a Lightning McQueen blanket, curled up to a stuffed dog. Pat sat down on the bed next to him. He reached over and cupped Tommy's head in his hand and brought him up to his chest, hugging him tight. Tommy woke up.

"Daddy?"

"Hey, buddy!"

"Daddy, what are you doing here?"

"I just came by to tell you I love you."

"I love you too, daddy. Can I get up? Is it morning?"

"No son, it's late and I have to go to work. I just wanted to see you."

"Daddy, can you come over tomorrow? We can play cars!"

Pat started to cry again. "We'll see buddy, we'll see."

"Be careful at work daddy. Sometimes people get hurt at work. Like construction workers."

"I will, buddy. Now go back to sleep."

"I love you, daddy."

"I love you too, son."

Pat slowly closed the door to Tommy's room and walked back down the stairs.

"I'll call you tomorrow, okay?"

"Don't just say it, do it," Christine replied.

He took a long look at her, held her auburn hair in his hands and gave her a soft kiss on the lips.

"Fine. I'll talk to you then."

Pat, Tina and Chris walked back out to the truck and got in.

"Wow, Pat, I've never seen you so sappy!" said Tina.

"Shut up, Tina…"

They resumed their journey.

♪♪♪

"Hey, man, the tarp is flapping around back there."

Man… what now?

"How bad is it?"

"I don't know bro… It's getting worse… it might blow off if we don't fix it."

"All right, I'll pull over."

Pat pulled the truck onto the shoulder and turned on the flashers. He and Chris got out of the truck to check out the problem.

"Where's the bungee that was back here?"

"Musta blown off."

Upon further inspection Pat and Chris found that the tarp had torn, causing the slack and allowing one bungee to pull too tight and the other to blow away. The grommet holes were still there – they just needed another bungee and to cross them over so it wouldn't flap around anymore.

"Can we take one from another spot on that side?" Pat yelled across the bed of the truck over the traffic noise.

"I don't know where, dude, they're all holding the tarp down. If we take one from here, the tarp will flap on this side."

"I guess we'll have to take one from the you-know-what."

"Hey, at least we have 'em," offered Chris, "We don't really need 'em on Bernie with the tarp over the back."

"You're calling him Bernie now?"

"Why not?"

Pat shook his head. "Whatever…Let's pull the tarp back."

They pulled the tarp back about halfway. Pat lowered the tailgate, climbed over the duffel bags and into the back of the truck. He undid a bungee cord from the body and climbed back out. He and Chris each grabbed a side and pulled the tarp back over the length of the truck bed, strapping it down tight as they went.

Fuck, what else could possibly happen tonight?

No sooner had that thought passed through Pat's mind that a pair of headlights lit up the back of his truck. As Pat turned to look, a set of spotlights came on.

Are you kidding me?

The car slowed to a stop about twenty feet behind Pat's truck. Pat dropped what he was doing and stood up straight, trying to make out the vehicle. It was definitely a police car.

The car's door opened and the officer stepped out and walked toward them.

"Everything all right, guys?"

"Yes, sir…" Pat answered in his best ass-kissing voice. "Tarp just came loose. We didn't want it to fly off on the road."

"That would definitely be bad," said the officer. "You guys have any ID?"

"Sure," Pat said, taking out his wallet and trying to control his shaking hands in the process. Chris followed suit, fishing his license out for the officer.

"Anyone in the truck, guys?"

"Yes, my girlfriend," Pat replied, hoping he said it loud enough that Tina could hear him.

"Mind if I go and say hello?"

"Sure, she's in the back seat…"

"You guys stay here. Just lean up against the truck, okay?"

"No problem, sir…"

Chris and Pat looked at each other. They both wished they were dead.

The cop pulled out his flashlight and shined it into the truck hitting Tina right in the face. She smiled. He opened the back door.

"Hello, Miss. Everything okay tonight?"

"Yes, sir," Tina replied, her stomach up in her throat again.

God, please help me...just once more...please God...

The officer shined the flashlight through the front seat and back to the rear seat.

"May I ask your name, Miss?"

"Sure, It's Tina Stickney."

He took out a little notepad from his shirt pocket and scribbled down her name.

"Thank you, Miss Stickney – just sit tight, okay?"

"Yes sir."

The officer holstered his flashlight and walked back over to Pat and Chris, who were trying their best to look nonchalant even though they both wanted to puke. The cop looked over their shoulders at the tarp on the back of the truck. He then walked around to the open tailgate of the truck and eyeballed the luggage.

"What's with the luggage, guys? Where you headed?"

"Vegas, sir," Pat said as if it were true. "We're picking up Chris's girlfriend and then heading to Vegas!"

"Is that right?" He glanced in Chris's direction.

"Oh yeah. And this time we're gonna win big!"

The cop chuckled. "Well, I hope so, boys. Have a seat on the tailgate. I'll be right back."

The officer began walking back to his car but something made him stop. All the lights on the police car were blazing into their eyes – all they could see was his silhouette. He put his hand on his holster, turned and stared at them for a moment then walked back over and looked Pat right in the face.

"You're Patrick Pearson, aren't you?"

"Yes, sir..."

"Hey, I saw you guys play at Coors Amphitheater last night. You were awesome! Best concert I've been to in ages."

"Thanks, man, we definitely appreciate the support of America's Finest."

"Oh yeah, helluva show. Just let me run your IDs and you'll be on your way, okay? It's just standard procedure. I'll be right back."

"No problem, officer..."

"Jackman, Mike Jackman. Nice to meet you, Patrick."

They shook hands.

"You too, my friend."

The cop walked back to the car, disappearing into the bright lights, which hc dimmcd aftcr hc got in.

"This is un-fucking-believable, bro," Chris said to Pat sideways out of his mouth, "Un-fucking-believable."

"Dude, if we get out of this one, I'm never doing dope again. I swear to God."

"Me either."

The cop got out of his car and walked back to the truck.

"Here's your IDs. Everything checks out. Here, let me help you guys with this."

The cop pushed up the tailgate and helped them pull the tarp tight.

"See, the problem is your tarp is torn right here. Cross these bungees over and connect them on the bumper like this. There, that ought to work."

"Officer Jackman, I don't know how we can thank you."

"Hey, call me Mike. Have fun in Vegas, guys."

"Thanks, Mike. You have a safe evening."

Officer Mike blocked for them as they pulled off the shoulder and back into traffic, continuing their agonizing trip to see Cheeto.

TWELVE

SPECIAL AGENT KIBBLEMAN stared at the monitor. Nobody spoke a word or made a sound. It was too risky. They only used hand signals.

They'd been inside a twenty-foot box truck parked across from the warehouse for four hours now. No food, no drinks except for water and no bathroom breaks. Just sitting in complete silence, watching the monitors.

The guys were restless and uncomfortable in their gear. They wanted to get this raid over with. There was another van just down the street with six more agents also waiting for Kibbleman's go ahead, but nobody was moving until the shipment got there.

Agent Kibbleman had been with the ATF for seventeen years and he'd worked hard. It took a long time to come up through the ranks, but this year he finally made Commander. It was a job that he felt he earned and he took it very seriously, demanding respect from anyone under his command. And he got it. His men felt he was probably the most talented and hardworking ATF investigator that the Southern California region had ever seen.

He'd been watching these gunrunners for months now. He knew where the guns came from, where they were going, and who the players were. They'd already had an undercover man in place for almost a year when this case was dropped in his lap. He had lists of names, evidence, sources and buyers. His man was set up to do one more buy, and the mastermind of the whole weapons ring was handling it himself this time. Time to drop the hammer.

The man was Alex Kaskariyan, an Armenian gunrunner from Los Angeles. Alex had ties to the Russian mob, and if he talked, he could possibly bring indictments on many of their leaders, including Arbi Barayev, a known Russian mafia boss and his clan of arms dealers on the west coast. At the very least, this operation would stop the flow of Russian assault weapons through San Diego and into Mexico. It may even create more information on the buyers, who were primarily the Arellano-Felix Cartel.

Kaskariyan was scheduled to meet Kibbleman's undercover man at a small time middleman's warehouse that night. The place was tucked away in a business district and was easy to surveil. The undercover agent and a small time crook named Eugene Carver, but who went by the street name of 'Cheeto,' had been there for several hours now smoking weed and waiting for Kaskariyan to show up with the load of weapons from Los Angeles.

"Any word yet chief?" said the voice at the other end of the two-way radio headset that Kibbleman was wearing.

"Just sit tight guys, it won't be long now."

Where are these fucks?

A pair of headlights appeared and turned onto their street.

"You see that, Chief?"

"Yeah, everybody stand ready. This has got to be them."

A brown panel van not unlike a UPS truck rolled up to the doors of the warehouse. They could see on the monitors that it was Kaskariyan in the passenger seat. They waited for the doors to the warehouse to open. Kibbleman felt a drop of sweat run down his nose. He watched it drip onto the monitor.

This is it... I've finally got you, you motherfucker...

The doors to the warehouse opened, and the sellers and buyers greeted each other with hearty handshakes. Cheeto motioned for the driver to pull the van into the warehouse.

"Now Chief? Are we go?"

"Wait for the van to pull in. I'll give you the go..."

The van pulled toward the doors.

"Chief, are you seeing this?"

"Yeah, who are these motherfuckers?"

A lifted Ford pickup pulled up beside the panel van blocking Kibbleman's view of Kaskariyan. Cheeto trotted over to the passenger side of the Ford.

♪♪♪

"Hey, Chris, long time no see!"

"What's up Cheeto…how's life been treating you?"

"Like I slept with its wife!" Cheeto laughed "Hey, pull your truck in first in front of this van. They'll probably leave before you do. Where's the stiff?"

"She's in the back seat."

Cheeto poked his head in the window and saw Tina.

"Very funny, asshole," Tina grumbled. Chris and Cheeto laughed.

"I guess you haven't lost your sense of humor…"

"Nope… Bernie's in the back of the truck. Along with all sorts of other problems."

"So I understand." Cheeto turned and looked at Pat. "You Patrick Pearson?"

"Yeah."

"I've got your first CD – I like it better than the newer stuff, but you guys still rock."

"Thanks, man."

"Just pull the truck in. We'll have to deal with the problems a bit later. I got some other business going on."

"Okay, cool."

Pat pulled the truck into the warehouse.

♪♪♪

“I don’t recognize any of them Chief, maybe they’re here by chance. They might just be civilians.”

“Well I don’t give a rat’s ass. I’m not letting a year of police work go down the drain because of some stupid fucks that showed up in the wrong place at the wrong time. If they’re here, they’re guilty of something as far as I’m concerned.”

“Then we’re go?”

“We’re go!”

♪♪♪

Pat hopped out of the driver’s seat and looked toward the door. He was looking straight at the explosions. The sound rattled his brain and he became dizzy. He couldn’t see at all – he was completely blind and his ears were ringing. He grabbed his ears in a panic when something hit him from behind, knocking him to his knees. He felt pain in the back of his head. Disoriented, he fell to the ground and rolled over onto his back as he began to recover his eyesight. He could barely make out a tinted black helmet. A rifle was pointed at his face. A voice screamed at him from behind the mask.

“You move, you die!”

THIRTEEN

KERRY PARKER SAT in the back of the van looking carefully over the items in his tool bag and listening to a walkie-talkie. He had his Pacific Bell shirt on over a long sleeved t-shirt that covered his tattoos. His ID badge looked authentic and his white hard hat completed the ensemble.

The white van had ladders and magnetic signs on the doors. His flashers were on and safety cones out; to any passerby he was just a phone technician doing routine maintenance. His walkie-talkie chirped.

"There's a fiber line," said a voice at the other end of the walkie, "and there's six phone lines, from what I can tell...Stand by for a second, I'm gonna pop open the network interface boxes."

"Roger.... Take your time, brother, there's still people in the store. I can see the doors from here."

The grocery store closed at midnight, but there were always stragglers until at least twelve-thirty. This wasn't the first time Kerry and his crew had hit a Vons – he knew what to expect.

As the last customer left, the night manager would lock the night crew inside the store. The night crew at this particular store consisted of a lead and three stock guys. The night manager would empty the drawers, make the drop into the safe, pull all the receipts, checks, and credit card transaction printouts, audit each open register and punch out with the last cashier at around one-fifteen. That would give Kerry and his crew ample time to take care of the technical aspects of the job, and be ready to go in.

The walkie chirped.

"Hey, it looks like the alarm is on line six, and the pair they're using is purple – copy?"

"Roger that. I'm gonna re-route line one, cut lines two thru five, and line six is the alarm, right?"

"Ten-four."

"Okay, I'm going up the pole."

Kerry strapped on his climbing gear and tool bag and climbed the telephone pole across the parking lot from the store. He noticed an employee; a young girl had come out for a cigarette and was watching him. That was sort of unusual for this time of night in San Clemente.

Fuck it...

He belted in and went to work. He popped open the splice block enclosure on the pole and located the correct wires. He then slung a pack of equipment over the strand that supported the feeder lines between the poles. The pack contained a modem, a wireless transmitter, and a battery; the modem with leads that were connected to their respective voice input ports. He attached the leads to line one and cut the phone lines. The modem lit up indicating that the proper connection had been made. Now, any calls made from the store's phones would be routed wirelessly into the van to a voicemail system that would give an 'all circuits are busy – please try again later' message. Any employee making a call from the store would believe the phone company was having line trouble.

He then routed the alarm line to a dial tone emulator. The alarm system was tricked into believing it was still connected to a phone line, so cutting the line did not activate it. In addition, if the panic button that normally sent a silent alarm to the police was pressed, the system would be fooled into believing it had reached the monitoring center when in reality no such alarm had gone out at all.

I'm a fuckin' genius...

Kerry smiled, descended the pole and got back into the van. He pulled a mirror out from under the seat next to a rack of equipment and snorted up a huge line of coke. Wiping his nose, he double checked the blinking lights on the gear and picked up the radio.

"All good over here. Come on back."

"Ten-four."

A big black dually pickup with a covered load in the bed rolled up quietly behind the Pacific Bell van. Kerry welcomed the two guys who hopped out. "Everything's on point, my brothers!" Kerry said. "Everything ready to go?"

"Yeah, man..." said Johnny, a 'business partner' of Kerry's. "We're ready to rock."

"Okay, then. Now we wait."

They all climbed into the big truck; Johnny in the driver's seat, Kerry shotgun and Wheels in the back.

"Hey, you want to move the seat back, dog?" said Wheels. "I got plenty o' room back here..."

"Yeah, thanks, brother."

Though he and his crew ran most of their hustles in south Orange County, Kerry was still tied to San Diego through his ongoing affiliation with the local motorcycle gang, though he wasn't what you'd call a charter member. Kerry had voiced his discontent with the club over what he called the "un-evolving racketeering groupthink," and it was mutually decided that the nomad version of the patch would suit him better than a full-fledged San Diego Mob membership. Kerry was headstrong, intelligent and liked to be his own boss.

Kerry was also a big guy, not out of shape, just big. He had a huge belly and bulging biceps to match. Almost every inch of his body was tattooed. Both arms were sleeved, and he boasted a giant "1904" in old English lettering across his vast midsection. The number represented San Diego County in prison – the letter S being the nineteenth letter of the alphabet and the letter D being the fourth. His complexion was almost always bright red, reminiscent of an alcoholic, though the thought of alcohol made him sick. His head was completely shaven, emphasizing his perpetually angry eyebrows and giving him a menacing look. All in all, he would make an intimidating nemesis for anybody shy of Hulk Hogan.

In contrast, Johnny was tweeker skinny and Wheels was crackhead skinny, although it wasn't the drugs that made them do jobs like this, it was the high. Kerry preferred their kind; the guys that did crime to do crime were usually better at it than the ones who did it for drug money. And they were also a more honest criminal, if there was such a thing.

"Hey, look," Johnny said, "there go the last of the customers."

Kerry sipped his coffee.

"Patience, brother. It'll be time soon."

The front of the Vons store had two entrances. Both entrances were sliding double doors placed to the left and right with a series of windows between them. The windows were all covered with advertised specials and the like. There were four pillars in front of the store, one on either side of both sets of double doors. The pillars were about four feet wide and nicely obstructed the view of the street. The doors on the left had already been chained shut for the night, leaving the doors on the right as the only way in and out from the front.

The girl had come outside again. She leaned against one of the pillars, smoking her cigarette and looking around. It almost seemed to Kerry as if she was purposely avoiding looking in their direction.

Fuck it…

"Wheels, let's get this truck around back."

Kerry and Johnny exited the truck and climbed into the van, and Wheels drove the pickup around back into the alley and parked right outside the back door next to the loading dock, shielded from direct light by a large industrial trash compactor.

As the girl walked back into the store, the manager met her and locked the doors behind her. The store was secured for the night.

Kerry checked his watch. 12:45.

I'll give these guys about twenty minutes to do their jobs, and they'll be punching out and leaving...

Kerry and Johnny sat in the van waiting. Kerry never took his eyes off the front door. He had a sixth sense for this kind of job, and when he worked, he was in the zone. Johnny knew better than to even try to talk to him at this point. 1:01.

"Let's get ready," Kerry said right before the lights in the store dimmed.

"Man, you are good," said Johnny.

They climbed out of their seats and into the back of the van where they put on black jackets and ski masks and picked up two sawed-off Mossberg 12 gauge shotguns. They opened the back door to the van and looked out. Everything was quiet.

"Let's go," Kerry whispered.

They closed the van's rear doors and ran as fast as they could to the front of the store, each taking up a position behind the pillars. Kerry looked inside. Clear. He signaled Johnny, and they moved to the sides of the double doors, still being blocked by the pillars from the street's view. They waited.

♪♪♪

"There you go brother. All set."

"Thanks, Kerry," said the huge biker as he handed him two hundred bucks.

"All you do if it gets shut off is call me, and I'll get you a new card. You just slide it back into the slot and the receiver will pop right back on. Every channel, every time."

"Awesome, brother. Where did you learn all this anyway?"

"I don't know...Just seems to come naturally to me."

"Well, you're a genius. You say you'll have some CD players tomorrow?"

"Most definitely. They're Akais – pretty hard to get."

"I want 'em for sure."

"They're yours. I'll see you tomorrow."

Kerry shut the garage and walked back into the house, locking the door behind him. He knocked on the bedroom door.

"Hey, Pops…It's me."

The door abruptly swung open. Pops grabbed Kerry by the hand and yanked him inside, locking the deadbolts behind him.

"Kerry, I have a signal! This could be it!"

Kerry smiled.

"Gee, that's great Pops. What frequency?"

"295 Gigahertz! That's not of this world!"

"Are you sure it's not from a satellite?"

"No way! It's them! I know it!"

Kerry looked around the room. Every inch of it was covered with electronic devices, some he understood, and some he didn't. Hundreds of miles of wire crisscrossed any available space. Fans hummed everywhere, giving the feeling of being inside of a giant beehive. Aluminum foil covered every inch of wall space. Pops stared at a monitor through his huge coke-bottle thick glasses.

"That's great Pops. You want a sandwich or something?"

"Shhhh!"

"Okay, Pops, I'm going back out."

Pops hurried Kerry out of the room and quickly locked the door behind him.

Kerry began coming over to Pops's home as a little boy. Pops always had some fascinating new video game on his computer that nobody else had ever seen. In fact, a lot of people in that neighborhood had never even seen a computer at all in those days. Kerry firmly believed that pops somehow built them himself even before the days of the Commodore 64, but Pops never confirmed nor denied. Kerry was never allowed in 'the room' where all the answers were.

Pops pretty much adopted Kerry after his father went to prison. Kerry was a teenager and was in desperate need of some kind of guidance as school had become boring and tiresome; the result being that he didn't bother going anymore. It was then that Kerry began to assist Pops in his lifelong quest to contact the extra-terrestrials.

Hunting extra-terrestrials did not come without a price however, as of course the government would surely lock up anyone with the knowledge that Pops was privy to. And since Pops could not expose himself to all the government agencies that were of course watching his every move, Kerry moved into the role of chief breadwinner.

With no formal education or work experience, Kerry parlayed what he learned from being around Pops into a lucrative business of dealings with illegal electronics. And business was good.

Kerry giggled to himself as he made a sandwich. Pops contacted the aliens at least once or twice a week. Though the "signal" usually turned out to be from a satellite or a solar flare, Pops always got just as excited when he found one, and Kerry enjoyed seeing him happy. He heard a knock on the back gate.

"Hey, man, I'm outside," said a voice from the other side of the gate.

"I'll be right out."

Kerry grabbed his sandwich and a Coke, and strolled out to the garage.

"What's up Jeff?" Kerry said to another large biker. "What are you looking for?"

"Black boxes for Dimension Cable. Got 'em?"

"Does a squirrel have nuts?"

Kerry pulled up the garage door and the two quickly slid inside. They sat down at Kerry's desk, surrounded by all sorts of electronic components, tools, and stacks and stacks of books and manuals.

"You actually read all that shit?" the biker asked.

"Every one."

"You're crazy, man."

"Probably, brother, probably."

Kerry went into a stack of equipment and extracted several Zenith cable boxes.

"They've all been chipped. Should work great. Six hundred."

"Kerry, I have a proposition for you."

"What is it?"

Jeff slapped down a huge bag of cocaine.

"The Prez wants me to give you this. It's pure Peruvian flake. He is suggesting we start taking things to the next level. You are in line to be patched in. What do you think?"

Kerry stared at the bag. He'd never tried anything but weed before, but of course felt the same curiosity that any high school age kid did.

"I don't know, man…I don't really do drugs."

"Have you ever done this shit?"

"No, actually…"

"I'll tell you what… I'll give you the cash and we'll party a little and I'll let you decide. You got a lot of talent and a lot of connections. You can be an asset to the club."

Kerry was like any other kid. Afraid, but more intrigued. He had been riding his dad's '46 Knucklehead Bobber since he went to prison. He always wanted to be a biker. This was his chance.

"Yeah, okay…let's party."

Kerry watched intensely as Jeff poured out the substance, chopped it into a fine powder and lined it up. *Just like in the movies,* he thought.

"Okay man, sayonara!" exclaimed Jeff.

Here we go…

Kerry put the straw to his nose, bent over the mirror, and inhaled.

♪♪♪

The double doors suddenly slid open.

"Goodnight, see you guys tomorrow!" said a voice coming through the doors.

Kerry and Johnny jumped in front of the doors and pushed the man back into the store.

"Get the fuck inside! Get back inside now!"

Kerry shoved the man to the floor. He was by himself.

"Please, please don't hurt me!"

"Shut the fuck up! Where are the keys?"

"Right here, right here…"

The manager had the keys around his neck on a lanyard. Kerry ripped the keys loose, snapping it. He turned around and locked the double doors.

"Get the fuck in the back!" He yelled, pushing the guy with the barrel of the shotgun. "Go!"

Johnny had already run into the back of the store and burst into the stockroom screaming commands at the workers.

"Get on the fucking floor! Don't move! On your faces! One move, you fuckin' die…"

All of the workers lay face down on the floor. Kerry came into the stockroom kicking the manager, who was whimpering. He took quick inventory of the scene.

"There's only four of you here! Where the fuck is your lead?" He leveled the shotgun at the stock boys and manager. "Tell me or I'll kill you!"

"Please sir," stuttered the manager, "she went out front…she's pulling out pallets…she's somewhere in the store."

Kerry turned to John. "Find the bitch."

Johnny bolted out of the room.

Kerry turned to the people on the floor.

"Look, we're not here to hurt you, but we will if we have to. So don't fuck us around. Understand?" He waited for a response, but all he heard was sobbing. "I said, *understand*?" He let a shotgun blast fly at the ceiling.

"Yes…yes…yes." They all sobbed in unison.

"Now all of you sit up and turn toward me…"

They did.

"Everybody empty your pockets. Money, phones, wallets, keys, everything. Don't worry, you'll get it all back when we leave. But if I search you and find *anything* on you, I'll kill you. Do you understand?"

"Yes," they all said as they emptied their pockets.

♪♪♪

Kerry hit the guy with everything he had. Left, right, left. The guy fell to the floor and Kerry leapt on top of him. The guy was clawing at the ground, trying to get away. Kerry hit him in the groin, and he abruptly stopped moving.

"What did you call me? Say it again!"

"I'm sorry!"

"Say it, motherfucker!"

"I told you, I'm sorry!"

The guy was holding his testicles and bleeding out of his nose and mouth. Kerry climbed onto the guy's chest and punched him square in the nose. The crack of breaking bone was heard throughout the crowd. Everybody cringed.

"Cops!" somebody yelled.

Johnny jumped on Kerry's back, pulling him off of the guy.

"Dude, stop man, the cops are coming!"

The alarm went off, and the announcement came over the speakers:

"Lockdown, this is a lockdown…in your cells now!"

Everybody ran just as the Sheriff's deputies stormed the jail module in full riot gear. Inmates ran to their cells and pulled the doors closed behind them. Anybody who didn't make it suffered the consequences.

The guards fired rubber bullets, hitting the only two inmates that hadn't made it to safety. The inmates fell cowering in corners on the floor as the deputies maced them, beat them repeatedly with their rubber clubs, hogtied them with giant zip ties and dragged them off screaming to the hole.

Johnny turned from the tiny window in his cell door back to his cellmate and threw his hands in the air.

"Dammit Kerry, look what you've done! God knows how long this lockdown will last! The whole module will be out to kick your ass! And if that punk snitches on you…"

"I know, brother, I know…"

"Well, what's your problem, dude? You're getting out next week! Why would you risk catching another case in here? You can't just suddenly attack people! You're not thinking straight!"

"I know, bro…I don't know. I'm afraid."

"Afraid? Afraid of what?"

"Afraid of what I'm going to do when I get out."

"You of all people? Come on, man! You're like the smartest one in here! You'll have no problem coming up with a hustle. You're gonna be fine, bro. I can't wait to get out so we can hook up and run some scams!"

"That's not what I mean, brother."

"What're you talking about?"

"You know why I'm here, right? I told you the whole story didn't I?"

"Well, you don't talk about it much. I know it's a strike, and I know it was violent. I know you nearly killed the guy."

"That's what I'm worried about, brother."

"What, the person you assaulted? Is he dangerous or something?"

"You don't know, do you?"

"I guess I don't."

"It was my dad."

"Your dad?"

"Yeah, and I'm afraid I'll kill him next time I see him."

"Well, if you act like you did today with that punk, then you might. What did he do to piss you off, anyway?"

"He called me worthless. That's what my dad called me the day he killed my mom."

♪♪♪

Amanda knew it was coming. The phone company van, the black truck parked with it. She knew there would be a robbery and she knew there would be no escape. But she also knew that she should at least try to get a call out to the police. She'd tried the store phones just before the thieves had come in but the phone lines were down. She did however, have her cell phone in her pocket.

She hid behind the deli counter listening to one of the burglars running through the store checking the aisles. He was calling out to her in a sick tone.

"Come out, come out, wherever you are… Don't make me kill you sweetie!"

She was terrified. She knew there wouldn't be any time to make an actual call before he found her, so she decided to dial 911 and leave the phone open, hoping they could trace it and find her. Slim chance, but she'd take it anyway – she didn't have much of a choice as she could hear his footsteps approaching the other side of the counter. She quickly took out her cell phone, dialed 911, hit send and put it into a cabinet under the deli counter. The footsteps were now right on top of her. She scurried away on her hands and knees trying to get away from the counter. As she rounded the corner, she heard the robber's voice right behind her.

"Shit, you're kinda cute. It'd be a shame to blow your pretty little head off. Why don't you get up and come with me, huh?"

Johnny pulled Amanda up by her collar, walked her across the store and shoved her into the stockroom with the rest of the staff.

"Got her, boss."

"Good."

Kerry looked into her eyes. She looked back into his. There was something going on. He could feel it.

Fuck it...

"Did you search her?" Kerry said to Johnny.

"No, not yet..."

"Are you fuckin' retarded? Search her!"

"I'd love to." He turned to her. "Must be my lucky day! Empty your pockets, sweetheart, unless you want me to do it for you..."

She obliged. Johnny patted her down, paying close attention to her breasts and crotch. She stood perfectly still and squeezed her eyes shut tight.

"Okay, kids," said Johnny, "everybody kneel down, and put your hands behind your heads."

Johnny took off his backpack, reached in and pulled out a package of large zip-ties. He went one by one, methodically tying each employee's hands safely behind their back. When he was finished, he yelled to Kerry, who was out in the store.

"All done here, boss!"

"Good. Put 'em in the fridge."

"You heard him, kids!"

Johnny walked the staff in a single-file line into a walk-in cooler, closed the door and put a zip-tie through the hole where a padlock would go. He walked over to the customer service desk, where Kerry stood inspecting the store's safe.

"All secure, boss."

"I sure fuckin' hope so."

Kerry keyed up his radio.

"All clear."

"Ten-four, dog!" answered Wheels, "I'm backing up now."

Kerry used his shotgun to blast the padlock off the roll-up door at the loading dock. He hit the green button next to it, and the door slowly rattled its way up. They walked outside to where Wheels had just backed up the truck. The big Dodge was lifted to exactly match the height of the loading dock. They rolled the equipment out of the back of the pickup, onto the dock and into the store, and closed the door behind them.

"I got it, dog," said Wheels as he pushed a heavy device through the store and over to the location of the safe.

The device was originally an electric hydraulic compressor from a boom truck, later custom fitted with iron blades thin enough to fit under the type of safe that the Vons stores used. They rolled it over and pushed the blades under the safe. Kerry plugged it in and picked up the controller.

"Okay, here we go…"

The machine slowly lifted with a whirr, bogged down for a moment, and then with a whine and crack of breaking metal, the safe pulled right up off of the floor.

"Fuckin' awesome, dog!" Wheels exclaimed, just as he did every time they pulled this job. Kerry simply leaned on the counter and smiled.

Wheels and Johnny propped up the safe, slid a pallet jack under it, and the two of them pulled the safe out of its home between the wall and customer service counter. It was heavy, at least four feet tall and two feet wide, with an equal two feet of depth. It had an electronic lock on the front as well as a keyed lock and a wheel. The electronic portion had a digital display window and a standard twelve character keypad. There was also a phone line and power cord connected to the back of it, which Kerry promptly severed with a pair of bolt cutters. Kerry wasn't worried about the locks or connections; he'd have no problem opening the safe back at his garage.

Wheels pulled the pallet jack down the aisle toward the stockroom and the loading dock, Johnny following with the hydraulic machine. Kerry strutted confidently behind them, his bolt cutters resting on one shoulder, his shotgun on the other.

God, this is getting to be sooo easy...

Wheels pushed the safe into the back of the big Dodge, followed by Johnny with the machine. Kerry tossed the bolt cutters into the back of the truck, and they secured their haul and pulled a tarp over it. Kerry walked back into the store and pressed the red button to close the roll-up door and exited through the side door, casually locking it behind him with the manager's keys. He got into the truck, which Wheels already had running and in gear.

"Nothin' but gravy, baby," Kerry said, taking off his ski mask. "Let's go."

They drove around the side of the store to the van. Kerry climbed out of the truck and walked around to the driver's side, bootlegging his sawed-off against his leg like a quarterback.

"Nice work gentlemen, see you back at the..."

Suddenly a police car came screeching around the corner right in front of them, lights blazing and sirens screaming.

Oh, fuck...you gotta be...

Another came sailing across the parking lot to their left, and two more right up behind them. The place was suddenly lit up like a stadium.

"Just go...*go*!" Kerry hollered at Wheels, who put the truck into drive and punched the gas. He maneuvered the truck around the van, where he was cut off by another cruiser and plowed into it head-on. The huge truck's front end lifted up onto the hood of the car high-centering it.

Whoa... didn't see that coming...

Kerry turned toward the car coming across the parking lot and leveled the shotgun, squeezing off a round. The police car's right headlight exploded and the car skidded sideways to a stop. He ran and took cover behind the van, his back up against its side door.

There was about an alley's width between the van and a six-foot, wooden security fence.

Motherfuckers...I am not going back to jail...

The two other cars were approaching from behind the van fast. He could hear the cops whose car he shot at, shouting for him to come out and drop his weapon.

Yeah, right...

He looked around for any place to escape. Cops to the left in front of the van, cops to the right behind the van, cops on the other side of the van, and a six-foot fence in front of him.

Fuck it...

Still holding the shotgun, he pushed off from the side of the van gathering as much momentum as he could, and with a loud scream, lowered his huge right shoulder and threw all of his two hundred seventy pounds directly into the fence. It gave with a loud crash; its slats splintering all around him. He fell to the ground dazed for a moment but recovered quickly, rubbing his aching shoulder. He was in a small enclosed patio; the only exit from which he could see was a sliding glass door into a house.

Double fuck it!

Kerry lowered his head again and barreled straight through the sliding door in a thunderous explosion of shattering glass. He continued through what ended up being a bedroom, down a hallway and into a living room. The two people sitting watching TV screamed at the sight of him and ran into their kitchen, cowering in a corner next to a refrigerator that was covered with family memorabilia.

"Which way out?" Kerry screamed at them.

Too afraid to speak and never taking their eyes off of the shotgun that Kerry was holding, they pointed to the front door. Kerry swung the door open and flew through the threshold, down the walk and out to the street.

He paused at the curb listening. There were sirens coming from nearly every direction, and he could feel the low beat of a helicopter's blades in the distance. The street was dark save for a few lights on garages.

I go left, deeper into the neighborhood. Right, out to a main boulevard. Make a decision now, Kerry...

He chose the neighborhood. Running up the sidewalk in the shadows he could hear the ensuing chaos in the house he had just run through, as the police had simply followed his wreckage. He assessed his options as he darted through the darkness, looking carefully at the houses and the cars in the driveways.

He came to a house with immaculate landscaping with the lights still on inside showing through a flimsy screen door. There was an 80's Buick sedan parked in the driveway, and it looked very well maintained.

Definitely an elderly person...perfect...great car to blend in with, too...

He ran up the walkway, kicked the screen door open and leveled the shotgun, turning toward the TV that was on in the room.

"Don't fuckin' mo..."

A huge black man reached beneath the sofa he was relaxing on and pulled out a weapon of his own.

"Fuck you, motherfucker!"

He fired his pistol, missing Kerry's head by inches and shattering the window on the open front door.

Stunned, Kerry lost his balance, stumbled backward out the door and fell onto one knee on the walk.

Shit! What the fuck?

The man in the house was up on his feet and heading for the door, gun in hand.

Kerry regained his balance and staggered down the walkway back toward the street, his head ringing from the blast of the man's gun. He could just barely make out the figures of men running toward him up the street holding flashlights, and the helicopter was now almost on top of him.

"Over here, the motherfucker's over here!" The man in the house was yelling as he came flying out the door.

Kerry turned up the street just as the helicopter's spotlight hit him. A police car turned onto the street in front of him. He ran across the street, diving between two parked cars and still trying to shake off the effects of the shot taken at him.

Musta been a big fucking gun...

He jumped out from between the two cars and ran up a driveway to another house, taking refuge between a thick hedge and the house's wall. The helicopter was hovering directly above him. It looked like daylight. He tried to see through the leaves of the hedge. Over the noise of the helicopter, he heard a strange sound; like the jingling of keys. It got louder. Then the pain.

Oh fuck...

The dog pulled his leg out from under him, and he crashed up against the wall behind him and down onto his back. The dog was snarling and tearing at his right calf, trying to pull him out from under the bushes by his pant leg. He kicked at the dog, trying to free himself.

Fucking dog...

He lowered the shotgun and put the barrel directly up to the dog's head.

Fuck you...you motherfucker...Oh, goddammit, I can't...

He tossed the gun to the ground and attempted to shelter his body and face from the dog as officers swarmed him, grabbing him by every limb and pushing his face into the dirt.

FOURTEEN

PAT RUBBED THE back of his head with his left hand. His right was handcuffed to the wooden bench he was sitting on. The room was small – only about six by six feet square, and was made of thick glass on one side, making him feel as if he were staring through an aquarium. The door to the holding cell was also thick glass and was propped open enabling Pat to hear conversations outside and feel the bustle of activity, but due to the partition across from the door and the inability to move from the bench, he couldn't see anything. He could hear a three-person conversation happening, and from what he'd heard so far, he figured one of the voices to be the man who was in charge of the raid or whatever it was, and another voice to be a different police detective that they'd called in after he, Tina and Chris were arrested. The third voice seemed to be some kind of superior – he didn't really know what to make of him yet.

"Yeah man, who'd have thunk it, huh?"

"I know, right? These bozos drive right into a raid with a dead body and a truck full of Meth! Talk about your dumb luck!"

"You know, right before we went in, I even said to my guy, 'If they're here, they're guilty of something!' Boy was I right about that one."

They all laughed.

"Do we know how much dope yet?"

"No, they're still dismantling the truck. They're finding a new surprise behind every panel, though!"

"Hey, you know who the long-haired guy is?"

"Who?"

"Patrick Pearson. From a band called Blacklist. He's a rock star."

"Never heard of him."

"I hadn't either, but I know the band."

"Any good?"

"Yeah, I suppose."

"You talk to him yet?"

"No. Sheriff's deputies are still at his house in Encinitas trying to figure out what happened. They're pulling evidence from everywhere. We're waiting for the okay first."

"Is he clean?"

"Yeah, no record, but he does have a reputation in the media for being a druggie."

"What about the other two?"

"The Latino guy has a bunch of petty shit, traffic tickets and stuff. Had a DUI back in '94."

"And the girl?"

"The same. All misdemeanors. Once beat the crap out of her ex-husband from what I understand. She also has a druggie rep. The Narcotics Task Force is trying to connect her to a bust that was done a week ago. They say she might be a suspect in another crime, but they didn't elaborate."

"Well, we won't need any help with these idiots. They're buried."

"No doubt."

"They ID the body yet?"

"Still working on it."

"And the guns?"

"The guns we found in the truck are all registered to Mr. Pearson. We're still processing them, but it looks like we may have our murder weapon. Only the guns in the truck are connected to our case, the rest are part of the ATF sting."

"Good. Okay, you go ahead and start talking to the rock star. I'm gonna put Jackson on the Latino kid, and we'll get Ms. Hunter to talk to the girl. Let me know immediately what the Sheriff digs up. And the minute they ID that body, I want to know about it."

"No problem, boss."

"Nice work."

"Shit, what work? They drove themselves to us. Thank Mr. Kibbleman and his guys for being there!"

"Thanks, Commander. Good luck with your investigation."

"Likewise, Mike, it's been a pleasure."

Homicide Detective Luis Moreno walked over to the coffee station and grabbed himself a fresh cup. He'd been woken up out of bed around midnight to respond to an ATF operation in his district. Agents had come across a dead body during a gun smuggling bust. They called in the local cops, and upon his arrival, he'd found two men and a woman being held by San Diego uniforms. The body in question lay wrapped in a tarp in the back of a pickup owned by one of them. Dogs were brought in, and it was discovered that the vehicle they were driving was used to smuggle drugs. A lot of drugs. Enough drugs that somebody would be missing them. A bag full of guns was also found in the back of the pickup; one of which had been recently fired and appeared to be the weapon that killed the victim. Uniforms ran ID on them, made the arrests and brought them back here to Moreno's division. Now he'd have to work in tandem with the Narcotics Task Force and the Sheriff's department to get answers.

Detective Moreno scratched his head as he pondered all the nagging questions. Who was the dead guy, why was he killed and who pulled the trigger? Where did the drugs come from and who did they belong to, and what part did each of these seemingly small-time drug users play in this scenario?

His focus right now was going to be Patrick Pearson. It should be easy to get him to talk; he obviously wasn't much of a criminal. From the info Moreno had, and from his experience, he figured

Patrick was probably a spoiled rich kid who grew up to be a more spoiled rich kid. He probably felt due to his celebrity status that he could do whatever the hell he wanted. He was probably a dope addict and got in too deep somehow in his efforts to maintain his drug habit. The best angle was going to be to make Patrick feel like he was receiving special treatment. Get his trust.

He's been in the cell for four hours now; lots of time to stress over the situation... Moreno thought to himself. *He's also most likely coming down off of dope. He'll be tired, scared and confused, just the way he should be... Hopefully, he's naïve enough not to want an attorney and hasn't watched too much 'Law and Order'...*

Moreno sipped his coffee and slowly walked over to Patrick's cell. He tapped lightly on the glass wall next to the door.

"Hey, buddy, you okay?"

"Yeah, I guess so..."

Patrick looked Detective Moreno over. He was wearing faded blue jeans and a flannel button-down shirt, with a badge on a chain hanging around his neck. He had bushy salt and pepper hair and a goatee. He was quite a bit less intimidating than the uniformed officers.

"Can I get you anything, Patrick? Water, soda, coffee?"

"Some water I guess..."

"No problem...I'll be right back."

Detective Moreno walked over to the water cooler.

This is going to be a piece of cake...This guy is scared out of his mind...

He grabbed a cup and poured Patrick some water and walked it back over to the holding cell. He took a seat on the bench next to Pat.

"Here's your water, man. Hey, let me loosen you up there."

He reached over and uncuffed Pat's wrist from the bench.

"You're not going to run off on me, are you?" he said with a smile.

"No, I won't…" Pat rubbed his right wrist.

"I'm Detective Moreno." He shook Pat's hand. "Luis Moreno. You can call me Lou if you want…"

"Okay…"

"Hey man, I want to talk to you about what we found in your truck. You could be in a lot of trouble, and I want to help you. If you're honest with me, I probably can."

"Where are my friends?"

"They're in jail, Patrick. The only reason you aren't is because you have some celebrity status. I don't believe you had much to do with this mess, and I'm trying to keep you safe. Celebrities don't do well in county jail, Patrick, so if you just talk to me straight, I can help, but if you don't, I can't. You understand, buddy?"

"Yeah."

"So, do you want to tell me where all the drugs came from?"

"I don't know."

"Patrick, you have to help me help you. How about the guy in the back of the truck, Patrick. Who is he?"

"I don't know."

"I think you know a lot more than you are telling me, Patrick."

"I really don't. He was breaking into my truck."

"So you shot him?"

"I didn't shoot him."

"Somebody shot him Patrick. It was your gun. Your fingerprints are on it. It's your truck the drugs are in. Patrick, you could be in a lot of trouble. Who shot the guy?"

"I don't know…Look, don't I get a lawyer?"

Oh, here we go…

"Patrick, this isn't a movie, bud. You can't just ask for a lawyer. You still have to talk to us."

"Don't I get a phone call?"

"Okay, Patrick, let me see what I can do."

He reached over and cuffed Pat's wrist to the bench.

"Too tight?"

"No, it's okay…"

"Okay, I'll be right back."

Detective Moreno walked over to the coffee station and poured out his cup. He poured himself a fresh one, and slowly spiced it up to his liking with cream and sugar. He stirred it slowly, put a lid on it and meandered slowly through the office and back to Patrick's cell. He sat back down beside Pat.

"Hey man, I talked to my boss, and he said he can't let you make any calls. He said after you are booked into county, they have phones there, and you get a free phone call in holding. I tried to reason with him, but he's not bending."

"So I'm going to jail?"

"Well, like I told you, if you help me, I will help you."

Pat stared at the ground, tears welling up in his eyes. He was completely worn out. He wanted to collapse.

Should I be honest with this guy? Pat thought to himself. *He seems like he wants to help me…like he cares…He knows who I am…But I should know better…everybody knows you never talk…I need a lawyer…Any lawyer would be pissed if I talked…But jail…Oh God…*

"I can't go to jail…"

"Then talk to me, Patrick."

"You have to promise me I won't go to jail!"

"Patrick, it's not my call. But if you talk to me, I can make it much easier on you. Please Patrick, you gotta talk to me, bud…"

Pat was now crying.

"No…Promise me I won't go to jail…"

"Patrick, let me go talk to my boss again, see what he says about all this. I can tell you though, he's gonna want solid talk from you. Good information. Understand?"

"Yeah…"

"Okay, I'll be back."

Moreno walked out of the cell again, feeling a little like a car salesman. He walked around the corner into the office area and sat down on another detective's desk.

"Hey, Steve-o, what's happenin'?"

"Not much," the detective answered.

"I need you to do me a favor."

"Sure."

"Give me about a minute in the holding cell with this kid I've got, and then call my cell phone."

"Done."

"Thanks."

"No sweat, Lou."

Moreno walked back to the cell, where Patrick was eagerly awaiting his news.

"What did he say?" asked Pat, wiping tears away from his eyes.

"Patrick, the boss said he'll do his best to keep you out of jail if you cooperate, but only if you cooperate. He seems to like you a lot, Patrick, and so do I. Like I said before, help us help you."

Detective Moreno's phone rang.

"Hang on Patrick, I need to get this..."

He opened his phone. "Moreno here."

"Oh...oh really...at his home...fingerprints...okay...right... okay...thanks, I appreciate the call...okay, talk to you soon.

"Patrick, it seems that your fingerprints are on the gun that killed the victim and they found his blood all over your house. Your two friends are also saying you did it. Now you either talk to me now, or you're going up for murder. You won't be getting out."

Patrick knew instantly that Moreno was full of shit. Tina and Chris would have absolutely no reason to implicate Pat, especially since they all knew what the truth was, and there was really no reason to lie about it. And there was no blood inside the house either; the body never made it past the garage. He knew Moreno was just trying to get him to incriminate himself. Now he absolutely couldn't talk. He had to stick to his guns no matter what, and he had to accept the fact that he was probably going to jail.

"You're lying. I'm not talking to you anymore."

"Patrick, do you really think your friends give a rat's ass about you when it comes to looking at prison time? They gave you up, dude, and I'm giving you one chance to tell your side of the story. You need to tell me where the drugs came from and who shot that kid."

"I told you I don't know. I want to call a lawyer."

Moreno turned around and closed the glass door. He reached over, grabbed Pat by the shirt collar and pushed him up against the wall.

"Look you little shit, we've got a man with half his neck missing, and you fucking did it. You're going to prison for a long, long time, and if you think the fact that you are a celebrity will get you out of it, you're dreaming. I love putting little spoiled-ass fucks like you in prison. And you know what happens to cute guys like you in prison, don't you, Patrick?"

"I want a lawyer," Pat sobbed.

"I don't care what you want. This is your last chance to tell me what happened."

"I want a lawyer."

He went to backhand Pat across the face. *"Tell me now!"*

Pat flinched in fear.

"You're not worth it, you little fuck. Have fun in jail. Nice talking to you."

Moreno walked out the door and closed it behind him. Pat put his head in his hands and started to cry again. A few minutes later, a uniformed cop read him his Miranda Rights.

♪♪♪

"Okay gentlemen, and lady, what have we got so far?" asked Captain Mike Harrington, as he and Detectives Moreno, Jackson and Hunter pulled up chairs at the big oak conference table.

"Martinez is the shooter," said Detective Jackson. "He copped to the shooting without any coercing. He said it was an accident; that they caught the guy breaking into Pearson's truck."

Captain Harrington reclined back in his chair and laced his fingers behind his balding head.

"Any proof?"

"Yeah, both his and Pearson's fingerprints were on the gun, so we did a GSR on Martinez and he was a match. The Sheriff already found the casing, and the examiner is working on the match."

"Fast work. I like it. So we have a confession and most likely supporting evidence?"

"Yes sir…"

"Excellent. I'm not sure I buy the 'breaking into the truck' bit. Any possibility of a real motive? Does Martinez have any ties to the victim? They're both Hispanic; any gang ties or relatives? Drugs?"

"I don't think it's related boss. Martinez's history is pretty clean aside from a DUI and a possession of weed conviction. Petty shit. He grew up in East County and his home address for the last few years or so is on the Pala Indian Reservation. Pretty far away from our victim."

"And who is our victim?"

"Identified as Armando Romero of San Ysidro. Nice guy too, this Romero. Two striker; been to prison twice. Gang ties all the way to the Arellano-Felix Cartel, international watch list, and a laundry list of convictions. These folks probably saved the taxpayers a bunch of money by shooting him."

"So no chance of it being personal between him and Martinez?"

"I don't see it. Martinez doesn't run those circles. We had the Sheriff search his last known address, his grandmother's house, but they didn't come up with anything of interest. His grandmother said he hasn't been around much lately; that he pretty much lives with Pearson now. He hangs around with rock stars, not gang bangers."

Captain Harrington turned to Detective Moreno.

"And what is the story on our rock star?"

Detective Moreno shuffled through his notes.

"The Sheriff finished the search of Pearson's residence, and they found the victim's blood on the driveway, in the garage, and on a piece of carpet in the garbage, presumably used to move the victim. Got the shell casing like Jackson said. Looks like he was shot in the driveway, moved into the garage and then moved into the back of the truck. Three sets of footprints and three sets of fingerprints, all belonging to our new friends. If the shooting was an accident as Martinez would like us to believe, I'm not sure why they went to such great lengths to hide the body and went to no lengths to alert authorities. I'm still thinking it was a dispute over the drugs."

Harrington rubbed the bridge of his nose. Moreno continued.

"The search didn't turn up much more than that. The inside of the house was a mess like they'd just thrown a party, and the deputies did find miscellaneous drug paraphernalia in the home, but not much else."

"Is he talking to us at all?"

"No, he's crying about a lawyer already. Too much TV. Pearson is just your typical rich kid who acquired a nasty drug habit and thinks he's above the law."

"So why then have they gone to so much trouble to cover up a crime scene that appears to be an accident?"

"The drugs. A lot of them. The drugs were obviously smuggled by people who know what they're doing, probably the cartel that Romero has ties to. The Narcotics Task Force says there were over thirty kilos professionally packed into that truck. I just don't see this bunch as drug smugglers. Who knows? Maybe they got involved in this in an effort to make some cash to pay for their habit. Money talks."

"I'd be inclined to agree with that if we were dealing with street urchins, but Pearson is a celebrity, right? I'm assuming that means he has some money… can't he just buy drugs? Why would he get caught up in some harebrained scheme? Is he broke?"

"Drugs make people do stupid shit."

"Amen. Check his financials. And we need the source. Who is going to give up the source of the drugs?"

"Maybe Martinez will. Like I said, Pearson's crying for an attorney, but I'm sure I can get him to talk if I get rough with him."

"Don't bother." Harrington turned to Detective Hunter. "Let's hear about the girl."

"You're gonna love this, cap. Miss Stickney's fingerprints are a match with the prints found in that car that led SDPD all over Pacific Beach last weekend!"

"The chase that was on TV?" interrupted Jackson.

"You bet."

"You're shittin' me!" said Harrington.

"Nope. And she happens to be the ex-wife of the guy who owned the car she used in the chase. The one who reported it stolen."

"Who is he?"

"Craig Stickney of La Jolla. He's a restaurant owner. Squeaky clean. SDPD brought him in and it turns out that he has no contact with her anymore with the exception of alimony checks which he mails to a post office box and the use of the car. He claimed he reported it stolen and agreed not to say anything to authorities just to get her out of his life. He came clean. The interviewing officer believes him. They charged him with obstruction of justice and insurance fraud and let him go home."

"Wow, small world," laughed Harrington.

"That's not all, sir. The NTF has ID'd the car and Tina from a raid earlier that same day."

"So *she* might be our missing link?"

"Maybe."

"Okay guys, we have to get one of our new friends to tell us where the drugs came from. That's going to be the key. I want names. I want a trail to chase. Hunter, you're going to have to put the screws to Miss Stickney."

"Yes, sir."

Harrington turned back to Jackson.

"Jackson, what about Martinez? He'll be getting manslaughter at the minimum. Make him think you are going to cut him a deal. Give him the business. He'll say anything."

"You got it, cap."

"Okay, here's how it'll go. You guys let Mr. Pearson and Miss Stickney know that Mr. Martinez has already copped to the shooting, and see if you can get them to match his story. If the stories match, and it is an accidental shooting, Martinez gets manslaughter plus the drugs. If there is any question or discrepancy in the stories, he gets murder one, plus all the charges related to the drugs, and we dig deeper. So far Mr. Pearson gets accessory and criminal negligence, plus all the drug and gun charges. The guns were his, right?"

"Yes sir."

"Okay, Miss Stickney gets the same minus the guns, and we'll have to get with SDPD and the DA to see what charges need to be filed with respect to that car chase." Harrington took a breath and laughed. "Man, I still can't believe that shit! Moreno, you start the booking – I'll talk to the DA today about how they want to proceed. Jackson, you and Detective Hunter find out where the drugs came from. Do whatever it takes. Let's move this along as fast as we can. Is there a potential for media?"

"Not sure, sir."

"No talking to the media until the booking is done and we talk to the DA, I don't want this rock star thing turning into a circus. Are we all clear?"

♪♪♪

"Go ahead and have a seat next to your friend there."

Jackson reached down, grabbed Chris's left hand and cuffed him to the same handle on the bench that Pat was cuffed to.

"You guys just hang tight. We'll be leaving soon."

"For where, sir?" Pat asked.

"Downtown… Booking… Jail, my friend."

He closed the glass door and walked away.

Pat looked at Chris. "Dude, what have we gotten ourselves into?"

"I don't know man, it looks pretty hopeless."

"We should have called the cops." Pat said, "We should have just told them everything."

"Why, what did you tell them?"

"I didn't say shit. That detective is a fuckin' dick. I told them I wanted an attorney. I was gonna try to call Ron Goldberg, but they say I don't get a phone call."

"You can call him from downtown. That's where the phones are."

"So I hear. Why, what did you tell them?"

"I told them that I fired the gun. I just didn't want them to blame you or Tina, so I just came clean."

"I knew that asshole was lying to me. He was trying to get me to admit to it. Fuckin' prick. You didn't say anything else, did you? That detective got in my face for not saying anything about where the drugs came from. They keep asking about the drugs. You didn't say anything about Tina and Carlos did you?"

"Hell, no. If Carlos ever found out we said anything, we'd all be dead for sure. I'll let a lawyer answer those questions. Fuck no. Dude, they were telling me they'd reduce the charges from murder to manslaughter if I told them about Carlos. I don't even think they have the authority to do that. I didn't say shit."

"Do you think Tina said anything?"

"Fuck no…little miss paralegal Tina? She more than anybody knows to keep her mouth shut. She's probably already figured out a way to get hold of Ron."

Pat and Chris both stared at the floor in silence.

"Dude," Pat started, "we'll be okay. Ron will take care of all this. We'll bail out. They have to let us bail out, right? You've been to jail before, right? What happens?"

"Pat, I went for a DUI. All they did was hold me for twenty-four hours in the drunk tank and kick me out. I'm not sure, but I think we have to see a judge before we can bail out. I guess that would be Monday morning."

"So we call Ron Goldberg from jail, right? How do we get the number?"

"I don't know, bro. I don't know anything about this shit."

The glass door to the cell opened and Moreno and Jackson stood in the threshold.

"So who is Carlos?" Moreno said with a smirk.

Pat and Chris looked at each other but didn't say a word.

"Look assholes, we already know. Your precious friend Tina is telling her side right now. You guys better start talking. Now who's Carlos, and how does Tina know him?"

Pat and Chris just sat there trying to avoid eye contact with the detectives. Moreno suddenly jumped in front of Pat, knelt down on the floor and threw his forearm into Pat's throat causing him to choke. Pat grabbed at his forearm with his free hand but was unable to do anything to protect himself.

Jackson stood directly in front of Chris.

"Don't even think about it…" he said.

Moreno began screaming at Pat.

“Who’s Carlos? Your fuckin’ connection? Some fuckin’ killer of kids? You idiots are going to prison for some kind of dope dealer? You better talk, you fuckin’ pussy!”

Pat’s eyes were watering. He couldn’t speak or cry; all he could do was gasp for air. Moreno pushed harder against his throat. He was beet red and starting to flail around in an effort to get air.

“Talk, you fuckin’ pussy! Talk now!”

“He can’t!” screamed Chris, “You’re choking him! Let go of him!”

Moreno turned to Chris, his face red with anger.

“Then you better say something before I kill him then because I don’t give a fuck!”

Pat swung his free hand wildly and Moreno grabbed it and slammed it against the wall. Pat’s eyes were now bulging out of their sockets. He struggled for breath.

“Go on you pussy, talk!” screamed Moreno, spit spraying from his lips.

“You better say something, Chris…” shouted Jackson, grabbing Chris’s collar with a large hand and pushing him against the concrete wall.

“Stop! Stop! Let him go!” Chris pleaded.

Moreno pushed harder and upward under Pat’s jaw. Pat’s eyes began to roll back.

“Okay, okay,” pleaded Chris, “he’s a drug connection from Mexico. Tina dealt with him! The drugs are his! Just let Pat go! Please!”

Moreno pulled back his arm back and Pat fell forward, coughing and heaving. He tried to fall to his knees but couldn’t, the cuffed wrist, which was now bleeding, was holding him back.

“What’s his last name?” Moreno said, in a freakishly calm voice.

“We don’t know…he lives in Mexico. He’s Mexican Mafia.”

“How do you get hold of him?”

"We don't…Tina did."

♪♪♪

Detective Elizabeth Hunter walked into the room and sat across a metal table from Tina. She was very attractive, long straight blond hair, piercing blue eyes and perfect ivory skin. Tina would have preferred the standard bull–dyke lesbian cop to this lady; her beauty was intimidating.

"I've already told you," Tina said firmly, "I know my rights and I'm not speaking to you without an attorney present. If you want any information from me, you need to let me call my attorney."

"Listen Tina, we already know about Carlos and your dealings with him. We also know about the police evasion, and we know about Garrett Kinglsey. I'm just here to try to make you understand the severity of the charges against you."

Tina's mouth went dry and her whole body tingled. *How the fuck do they know about all this?*

Detective Hunter continued, attempting to use Tina's knowledge of the law to her advantage. "We have pretty much figured out the whole story, we just need to fill in a few blanks, and we figure once you hear the charges you might be a little more apt to cooperate with us."

Tina sat silent — not by choice — she was too shocked to speak.

"We've got a list of drug charges ranging from possession to sales to trafficking. We've got you for accessory to murder, obstruction of justice and attempting to cover up a crime scene. The DA is going to add evasion, reckless driving, assault and attempted murder on a police officer for an accident you caused during your little romp through Pacific Beach. Tina, we understand that you know your rights, and you do have the right to have an attorney present during questioning, but I also need to inform you that your friend Ron Goldberg was also raided during last week's NTF sweep and has been indicted on charges of his own. I doubt he'll be able to help you from where he is."

She's got to be lying...This can't be happening... "I don't believe you. I want to call my attorney now."

Detective Hunter set her cell phone down on the table. "Go ahead, feel free to use my phone."

Tina picked up the phone and dialed the number to Ron's offices.

"Law Offices, this is Cherie..."

"Cherie, it's Tina. Where is Ron?"

Cherie's voice raised an octave.

"Tina, oh my God, haven't you heard? It was all over the news. The police raided our offices. They say they connected Ron to some drug dealers or something and they're holding him downtown without bail!"

Tina just sat there, staring.

"Tina? Tina, are you there?"

"Yes...Yes Cherie, I'm here..." Tina could barely get her words out. "Cherie listen, is anybody taking over for Ron in the interim?"

"Not yet Tina, the police have closed the office and seized all of our files. I'm only here because they needed somebody to work with them. Tina, I don't know what we are going to do... without Ron here I..."

Tina hung up. She set the phone down and just stared at it.

"So my darling, we can give you a chance to scare up another attorney — I'm sure you know someone else — or we talk. Or we can go ahead and send you off to the women's detention facility and you can wait to use the phone until after you get booked in. My bet is you'll want to talk before you get processed, 'cause I don't think you'll be getting out."

Tina was finally at her wit's end. She couldn't even cry anymore. She wanted to give up, go to sleep and wake up from this nightmare.

"What do you want me to do?" she growled.

"Tina, I just want to know two things. Who is Carlos, and where can I find him?"

"You already have those answers…"

"What do you mean, Tina?"

"You have my phone."

Detective Hunter left the room, closing the heavy steel door behind her. Tina suddenly felt very cold and very alone. In a strange way, she wished Detective Hunter would hurry back. She looked at her reflection in the two-way mirror. She knew it was the reflection of a dead person. She wondered how long it would be until Carlos's people got hold of her, Pat and Chris in jail.

Detective Hunter opened the door, sat down at the table and set Tina's cell phone in front of her.

"Show me, Tina."

"Wait. Before I do anything, I need you to promise me a few things."

"Go ahead…"

"I need you to promise me that this is all you are asking me to do, and that immediately after that I can call an attorney from here, on your phone."

"Done."

"And I need you to promise me that I, Chris and Pat will all be put into protective custody. I'm sure you already know why."

"That's not my call."

"Then you get nothing, and I take my chances at the women's jail."

"I'll see what I can do…"

"That's not good enough. You need to promise me."

"Okay, I'll get you into PC."

"All three of us. Promise."

"Okay, I promise."

♪♪♪

"Okay boys, let's go…"

Moreno uncuffed them from the bench and cuffed their hands behind their backs.

"Anyone need to use the restroom before we go? It's probably the last time you'll have a private restroom for a long time."

Moreno and Jackson walked Pat and Chris through the office, down a long corridor and outside into a parking lot. It was now about ten AM, and the morning sun was blistering. The officers simply put on their sunglasses, those coming down off drugs were not as fortunate. Two uniformed San Diego police officers were waiting next to a black and white police car.

"Here you go, officers. Be careful with this one, he's a rock star!"

"No shit," said one of the cops. "Watch your head there, Mister Rock Star."

Moreno bent over and peered into the back seat at Pat and Chris. "Well guys, you're officially off to jail. I'm sure these two officers will take very good care of you. Have a nice life." He slammed the door shut.

Pat gazed out the left rear window as they got on the freeway and started toward downtown. After what seemed like hours of handcuffs digging into his bloody wrists, the car finally came to a stop in front of a huge set of iron gates emblazoned with the six-point star logo of the San Diego Sheriff's Department. The giant gate reminded Pat of something that might be at the entrance to heaven. Or hell.

As the gates slowly opened Pat glanced to his left and was blinded by the flash of a camera. Three or four other photographers ran up to the police car, snapping pictures and banging on the windows. The officer in the passenger seat hollered into the car's loudspeaker system.

"Back off! Back off now!" He turned to the driver. "Where the fuck did the paparazzi come from?" He then looked back at Pat. "I guess you really are a rock star. I'm impressed."

The gate opened and the officers drove in. It got darker and darker as the giant gates slowly closed behind them; their eyes needing a moment to adjust to the change. It was more or less a small parking area with a second set of equally giant gates straight across from them for exiting vehicles, bars to the left, and a long plain cement wall to the right. A Sheriff's Department bus sat idling diesel fumes into the stagnant air. There were some vending machines against the wall, as well as what looked like a two-way mirrored window and a huge green sliding metal door with a small window situated at the far right. A sign displaying the regulations regarding officers carrying weapons into the jail hung next to the door.

"Okay guys, welcome to jail. Hop on out."

The uniformed officers escorted Pat and Chris up to the door and pressed a buzzer. The door slid open with a groan. They uncuffed Pat first and shoved him up to a window that reminded Pat of a movie theater box office.

"Shoes, belt, wallet, jewelry including piercings, and empty your pockets," said the monotone woman behind the window, who was dressed in the green uniform of the Sheriff's Department.

"Yes, Ma'am," said Pat, wishing he were completing this procedure for airport security in some tropical location.

Chris took his turn and the officers walked them through a metal detector and into a small room. They were then instructed to place their hands on the wall and were patted down by the largest sheriff's deputy they'd ever seen. The officers walked up to a window and exchanged two file folders for two plastic wristbands. The deputy placed the wristbands on Pat and Chris, scanned them with what looked like a supermarket scanner, and unlocked the next door with oversized keys.

"Hasta la vista, gentlemen," announced one of the officers, "hope you enjoy your stay at the gray bar hotel, rock star!" The cops then turned and walked back out the other door. The deputy led them across a hallway, unlocked another door, pushed them through the threshold, and without uttering a single word, he locked the door behind them.

♪♪♪

"Tina, I know you won't believe me when I tell you this, but I like you, and I'm going to make this as easy on you as I possibly can."

Tina sat and stared at the wall.

I'm just going to ask you some yes or no questions. You don't even have to answer me, just nod yes or no. Is that okay?"

"Do I have a choice?"

"Tina, I've seen your history. I don't happen to believe you to be a bad person, I think you've just bitten off quite a bit more than you can chew. The same goes for your friends. I'm honestly trying to help you. You don't have to believe me, but I'm going to do what I can for all of you."

"Can we just get on with it?"

"Okay. Tina, as far as you know, is Carlos Castillion tied to the Mexican Mafia?"

Tina nodded yes.

"Did you smuggle the drugs in the truck across the border for him?"

Tina nodded again.

"Tina, did you do it because he threatened your life?"

Tina began to cry.

"Yes…" she sobbed.

"Did he also threaten the lives of your friends?"

Tina nodded as she wiped her eyes.

"Was the shooting victim at Patrick Pearson's house tied to Carlos, and was he there to pick up drugs?"

Yes, again.

"Tina, were you or your friends at any time knowingly in possession of the drugs for yourselves, whether for personal use or to sell, or were the drugs strictly owned by Carlos?"

Tina began to cry again.

"They belong to Carlos."

"Was the shooting an accident?"

Yes, again.

"Tina, is Carlos's phone number in your phone?"

Tina nodded.

Detective Hunter picked up the phone and held the phone's small screen in front of Tina's exhausted face.

"Is this the number?"

Tina nodded.

♪♪♪

Harrington, Moreno, and Jackson were sipping coffee and happily cutting it up around one end of the conference table. Across from Moreno was a senior officer from the Narcotics Task Force. Assistant District Attorney Carol Hutchins sat at the head of the table with her briefcase open, shuffling through paperwork. Detective Hunter hurried in and sat down.

"Excellent, Ms. Hunter is here," said Captain Harrington. "With some good info no doubt."

"Absolutely, Captain."

Harrington turned to the ADA. "She's just finished up some questions with Miss Stickney. This should put the icing on the cake."

"I hope so. I'm not too thrilled about being here on a Sunday," said the ADA, "Go ahead Ms. Hunter."

"You can call me Liz, Ma'am. Anyway, it appears that the shooting at the Pearson residence was entirely accidental."

"Is that right?" said ADA Hutchins, raising an eyebrow toward Harrington. "I thought second degree and accessory to homicide were already agreed upon? I didn't come in on a Sunday for an accidental shooting."

"This is news to me, Carol," said Harrington. "Please elaborate, Liz."

"Well sir, after interviewing Miss Stickney, I determined that she was forced to smuggle drugs for the Arellano-Felix Drug Cartel due to threats on her life and on the lives of Pearson and Martinez, from the man we know as Carlos Castillion, who is very well connected to the victim and the Cartel. The shooting could even be categorized as self-defense due to the fact that the shooter had zero knowledge of the drugs, which was the reason the victim was there in the first place. The victim also had a weapon, which was later recovered by the Sheriff. He was on Pearson's property, was assumed to be a burglar, and was shot with a legally registered weapon. The only one with the knowledge of the drugs and the smuggling operation was Miss Stickney and had she said anything, she'd have been killed by the Cartel."

"This is bullshit," interrupted Moreno, "those idiots are fucking drug addicts who were trying to make a quick buck by smuggling dope. They killed a guy! They aren't getting out of this shit. They need to be taken off the street."

Hunter turned to the ADA.

"Pearson has a clean record, Martinez has two misdemeanors and Stickney has a bunch of traffic tickets and a domestic violence charge she got probation for. These are not career criminals, they're victims of circumstance."

"Come on, Liz, you can't be serious?" said Moreno. "She led the SDPD on a high speed chase through Pacific Beach for God's sake!"

"Just a minute, Lou," said ADA Hutchins holding up a finger and turning back to Detective Hunter, "Liz, how did Tina get wrapped up with this guy in the first place?"

"I'm sure that the NTF can verify this..." Elizabeth looked over at Narcotics Task Force Lieutenant Michael Morgan. "You see, Tina was the girlfriend of Garrett Kinglsey, a dealer they raided the same day as the chase. It was he who was affiliated with Carlos Castillion. The NTF knows all about Castillion and Kingsley. They brought Kingsley in for sales in an attempt to get closer to Carlos. Tina was an accidental casualty in that operation."

"Why didn't I know about this, Liz?" asked Harrington.

"I wasn't sure about the connections, and you and Jackson already had the confession, so I just chased this myself."

"You know I wanted to know about the drugs, Liz."

"I'm sorry sir, but nothing was confirmed until after I talked with Tina and Lieutenant Morgan today."

"Mr. Morgan, is all this true?"

"We've been on to Castillion and Kingsley's drug activities for months now. The raid on Kingsley and all of the other raids we conducted were done in an effort to get more information on the Tijuana Cartel. Kingsley wouldn't talk out of fear of retaliation or being killed in prison. Make no mistake guys, Castillion isn't just affiliated, he *is* the Cartel. He has connections everywhere, all the way up to the Arellano-Felix brothers themselves. But he's slick; we have never been able to get all our ducks in a row at the right time, but it seems now we might. We are ready to drop a list of indictments on him, but we need somebody who has dealt with him to testify. And we need him in custody first."

"That's why this all works out sir," Elizabeth continued. "Stickney's in some serious trouble. We can cut a deal with her, a non-violent criminal, and get her to testify against Carlos for extortion, trafficking, smuggling and conspiracy. It may not be murder, but the NTF will have their man and be a step closer to winning the war on drugs. A cartel connection will be cut off, and these kids can get a more fit punishment."

"These are not just kids, Liz," Moreno interrupted, "these are adults who knew exactly what they were doing, and they didn't call the cops!"

"They're naïve, Lou. That's what I meant, and you know it."

"How did you come up with this theory Liz?" asked Harrington.

"Just a hunch. They didn't seem like bad people, just misguided. I thought somebody else had to be pulling the strings. The two worlds colliding; it just didn't make sense."

"And it still doesn't," charged Moreno. "You're giving these scumbags way too much credit! They knew exactly what the fuck they were doing! Martinez shot a guy in cold blood over drugs! They need to go to prison."

"Actually," continued Hunter, "what they do need is protective custody, and to speak to the ADA directly before they lawyer up. We need them to help us catch the one who is really behind all this. Tina's already waiting in the interview room ready to make a deal. What's up with Pearson and Martinez?"

"Those dopes are already downtown," said Moreno. "They're being booked as we speak."

"On what charges? This is all part of the same case!" Elizabeth turned to Captain Harrington. "Why would you file charges on them and not Tina? Why wasn't I told what was going on?"

"Tit for tat, I guess," said Moreno.

"Fuck you," said Hunter.

"Hey, knock it off you two. Lieutenant Morgan, what does the NTF intend to do at this point?"

"We are literally in place to take down Carlos as we speak. We have good intel that says he is traveling across the border into San Diego today. We can snatch him up anytime and open the indictment. All we need is the girl to agree to testify, and we'll pick him up. We are confident we can get a conviction"

"Pearson and Martinez will have to corroborate and agree to testify," added Elizabeth. "We need them to talk to the ADA."

"Too late my dear," Moreno taunted, "they're already being processed. You'll have to meet with them downtown."

"You've put these kids' lives at risk, Lou! Carlos probably has a hit out on them already! They have to be in PC or they're gonna be dead before we can even talk to them!"

"Oh well, another taxpayer dollar saved."

"You're a real dick, Moreno…" Hunter turned to Harrington. "Can't we just pull them out of there?"

"Liz, once they're in the Sheriff's custody they're pretty much lost in the shuffle until they actually get housed. At that point, they are permitted legal visits."

"How long will it be till they're housed?"

"Usually takes between six and eight hours."

"They'll be killed."

"Listen, we'll get to them when we can, Liz. In the meantime, you and Carol talk to Tina and get her to agree to testify – Carol? All this work for you?"

"Absolutely," Carol answered. "On Monday we'll get down to the courthouse and re-file charges before those kids see a judge. We'll go with involuntary manslaughter on Martinez, and criminal negligence on Pearson. We'll wait to see what happens before we file any drug or gun charges. We need to contact the Sheriff and have them moved to protective custody as soon as possible. I'll decide what charges to file on Tina after I talk to the DA's office tomorrow morning. Mr. Morgan, you have the full cooperation of my office. Proceed with your operation and bring Carlos in. Nice work, Detective Hunter."

"Thank you, Ms. Hutchins."

♪♪♪

"Please Steve, you gotta get me out of here!"

Patrick was huddled up against the wall in a futile attempt to hear on the phone. The clamor of people arguing and telling stories of their arrests in the concrete and glass echo chamber was unbearable.

The twelve by twenty-foot holding cell was completely full of drunks and drug addicts; some of which had been throwing up and others who had been in fights and were bleeding all over the place. The metal benches were all occupied, and people were sleeping on the floor. One of the two stainless steel toilets that protruded from the wall was overflowing, and the smelly brown water was quickly approaching Pat's stocking feet. The whole place smelled like urine.

"Patrick, you need to understand that it's Sunday, and there is nothing I can do until tomorrow morning. I'll get you an attorney as soon as the sun comes up, but they're not going to let us post bail until you've seen a judge. Have they told you what your charges are? Do you have a case number or a booking number or something?"

"No, not yet. There's a number on my wristband... Steve, all they've done is fingerprint us. They just keep shifting us from cell to cell. This is unbelievable. Steve, I can't handle this!"

"Patrick listen, you know what I'm going to say. You made your bed, now you have to lie in it. I'll get you an attorney as soon as I can, and we'll post bail as soon as we find out what's going on. Until then Pat, you're just going to have to tough it out. Now give me the number on your wristband. Maybe I can look it up on the internet."

"Okay, it's 708849211. Did you hear that? Steve, I can barely hear you!"

"Yeah, I got it. I'll find you an attorney, and I'll try to get some info on your charges and court appearance."

"Okay, Steve."

"Pat, just be careful in there. We'll get you out and into a rehab, okay?"

"Yes, Steve, yes. Hey, can you call Christine and tell her what happened? Tell her I'll call her when I can?"

"I'll alert all the appropriate people, Pat."

"Thanks Steve, I…"

The phone went dead. A sheriff's deputy was unlocking the door.

"Parker, Pearson, Martinez, Ruiz, Salazar. Come on down!"

Pat shook Chris awake from his slumber on the floor.

"Hey, come on, they called our names."

Chris got up and they exited the holding cell.

They were taken through a sliding metal door and into a long rectangular room with several Plexiglas windows, with another sliding metal door at the opposite end. It looked like a check cashing joint you'd find in the ghetto.

"Parker, window number one, Pearson, number two, Martinez, number three, Ruiz, number four, and Salazar number five. When you are done, go to the back wall, and assume the position. Pat was already familiar with the position. Face the wall, as close as possible, hands on it, as high as possible. Pat walked up to window number two.

"Pearson, Patrick Samuel?" asked the person behind the glass.

"Yes."

"Read the charges against you and sign it at the bottom." She handed Pat a piece of paper and a pencil.

As Pat began to read, butterflies appeared in his stomach.

```
HS 11377     POSSESSION OF CONTROLLED
             SUBSTANCE
HS 11378     POSSESSION OF CONTROLLED
             SUBSTANCE FOR SALE
HS 11379(a)  IMPORT OF CONTROLLED
             SUBSTANCE
HS 11379(b)  TRANSPORT OF CONRTOLLED
             SUBSTANCE
```

HS 11352	TRAFFICKING CONTROLLED SUBSTANCE

As he continued, they became bats.

PC 11370.1	POSSESSION CONTROLLED SUB/FIREARM
PC 12021.5	ILLEGAL FIREARM/VEHICLE
PC 12022	POSSESSION OF FIREARM DURING COMMISSION OF A FELONY
PC 12026.2.5	ILLEGAL TRANSPORTATION OF FIREARMS
PC 12022.53	POSSESSION OF FIREARMS DURING COMMISSION OF (PC187, PC189.5)
PC 187	MURDER SECOND DEGREE/ACCESSORY
PC 189.5	VOLUNTARY MANSLAUGHTER

By the time he was finished, they were albatrosses.

"Ma'am, are you sure this is correct?"

"That's the charges. If you have any questions, refer them to your lawyer or public defender tomorrow when you appear in court."

"But…"

"I'm not the one that filed the charges sir, I just need to know if you understand your rights and you understand the charges filed against you. Do you?"

"I…I…I just…"

"It's a yes or no answer sir."

"I…Yes, I…"

"Thank you sir, please sign the bottom."

He signed the document, and she pulled off the pink copy, handed it to him, and instructed him to stand at the wall.

"But Ma'am, I…"

"Hey!" The sheriff's deputy yelled at him from behind him, "Get up against the wall!"

Pat turned around.

"But sir, I…"

"Get on the wall!" He started toward Pat, hand on his nightstick. He grabbed Pat by the shoulder and shoved him toward the wall. Pat stopped himself from falling into it with his palms. The deputy kicked his legs open, pushed his hands above his head and held them with one hand, and put his forearm into his head, pushing Pat's face into the wall. Pat winced in pain.

"I don't have time for your shit. You shut the fuck up and do what I tell you."

"Yes, sir," Pat muttered.

Slowly everyone in the room finished their paperwork and were led into the next room. The room had some shelves on one side, another sliding door on the opposite side, and had a red line painted on the floor directly down the center. Five paper shopping bags were laid out on the ground on the other side of the red line.

"Gentlemen, listen up," said the deputy, "I need you to stand with your toes on the red line, in front of a paper bag. Next, remove all of your clothing. Time to get naked gentlemen – do not make me ask twice! Place your clothing inside the bag in front of you. You will then get to meet Deputy Coheed, who will be making sure that you aren't bringing any contraband into this lovely institution of ours."

"This is unbelievable…" Pat said under his breath.

"And humiliating too, isn't it?" replied the deputy. "You don't like it, don't come to jail!"

At that instant, a hand grabbed Pat on the shoulder.

"Okay, tough guy, turn around."

Pat was standing face to face with the deputy, who had on rubber gloves and was holding a flashlight between his teeth.

"Open your mouth."

Pat opened his mouth, and the deputy stuck in his finger and felt around inside his cheeks.

"Turn to your left."

He checked inside and behind Pat's left ear, pulling Pat's hair out of the way.

"Turn to your right."

Same procedure.

"Turn away from me, bend over and cough."

"Please, sir…"

"The extent that I search you is directly relative to the extent that you cooperate. Now bend over and cough."

Patrick did. At that moment he realized just how low a person could sink.

"There," said the deputy, removing his rubber gloves, "that wasn't so bad was it?"

Pat's entire body was in pain from trying not to cry.

Deputy Johnson handed Pat a felt tip marker.

"Write your full name and booking number on the paper bag."

"Booking number?"

"The number printed on the only item left on your body, stupid."

Pat copied the number off his wristband onto the brown paper bag.

"Shirt size."

"Uh…large?"

The deputy tossed him two shirts, one white and one blue. They both read SD Jail on the back.

"Pants."

"Thirty-three?"

The deputy tossed him a pair of pants, a pair of briefs, and a pair of socks.

"Gentlemen, when Deputy Coheed is done with you, get dressed. Then assume the position at the back wall."

Pat pulled up his pants, and they barely hung on.

"Sir, these pants don't fit, they're too big."

"This ain't a fashion show. On the wall."

At this point, Pat knew better than to question the deputies any further.

The deputies finished with the others and shuffled them all into another room where they were issued a foam mat and a blanket. They were then jammed into another cell, where they waited another hour or two.

A huge tattooed man had been staring at Pat ever since they'd been in the last holding cell, making Pat very uncomfortable. He jabbed an elbow into his sleeping friend's side.

"What?" Chris murmured.

"Dude, this guy over there is freaking me out."

"So? What do you expect? We're in jail. Everyone is a criminal or a weirdo…"

"Oh fuck, he's coming…get up man…"

"Hey, brother, are you Patrick Pearson?"

"Yeah."

"Wow, I thought that was you! I'm a Blacklist maniac, bro! You guys fuckin' rock!"

"Thanks."

The guy held out his hand. "I'm Kerry Parker. Big fan."

"We probably shouldn't broadcast that here, if you don't mind…"

"Nice to meet you. No problem man, I got your back." He reached across to Chris. "You are…"

"I'm Chris. We're friends."

"Obviously. I've been watching you guys since you came in, I just couldn't believe it was you. What the fuck are you doing in here, anyway?"

"It's a long story."

"Shouldn't you be in protective custody? You're a celebrity."

"Thanks for the vote of confidence. I don't know where I'm supposed to be. This shit is killing me."

"First time?"

"Yeah."

"Yeah, first time sucks for everyone, brother. Doesn't get much better the second or third time either. You'll get through it. The worst is over. They'll be taking us up to a housing module soon."

"What's that?"

"It's where you'll stay 'till they've decided what to do with you. In your case you'll probably be housed with non-violent crimes like DUI's and shit. I can't imagine you guys did anything terrible."

Pat and Chris looked at each other and sighed.

"No shit? What did you guys do?"

"It was an accidental shooting," Pat said. "A guy was breaking into my truck."

"Accidental? Then why are you guys in here with jail clothes on? Guys that do shit by accident don't go to jail."

"There were drugs involved."

"Ha! No shit! The rock star life, baby!"

Wow...

"That's pretty fuckin' funny."

"I'm glad someone is having a good time."

"Hey, man, let me tell you something. God has a plan for all of us. Shit happens, good and bad. You gotta accept it. Acceptance will get you through this. The sooner you realize that the easier this will all be."

"Where are you going to be housed?" Pat asked Kerry.

"Probably a high power mod. I'm in for armed robbery and it's not my first time. I won't be with the celebrities and DUI's, that's for sure."

"Okay, gentlemen," a deputy said as the door slid open. "Let's go upstairs."

They crowded into a large elevator, about twenty at a time, and went up several flights into what looked like a gymnasium with no basketball hoops. You could see a glimpse of daylight through some thin windows up by the ceiling.

"Get comfortable," said Kerry. "We're going to be here a while."

"What is this place?" Chris asked.

"Last stop before your new home. They're figuring out where to house everybody right now. It takes a while. I'd get some sleep if I were you, especially if you're coming down off shit like I am. Goodnight."

Kerry spread his mat out on the floor, laid back and put his blanket over him. Pat and Chris did the same. Soon they were all sleeping.

♪♪♪

A commanding voice shouted over a loudspeaker.

"Armstrong, Blake, Gonzales, Jackson, Parker, Pearson, Martinez, Vasquez, ... roll up!"

"Hey, Patrick, wake up!" said Kerry. "They're calling your name! Grab your shit!"

"Did they say Martinez?" asked Chris, rubbing the sleep from his eyes.

"Yeah, we're all going to the same place. You guys must have really fucked up to be going with me."

They grabbed their mats and blankets and shuffled to the door.

"Okay, guys," said a deputy, "you're going to 5B. In the elevator."

The deputy placed them in the elevator and pressed 5. The door opened up to what looked like a huge glass animal display at a zoo. Only behind the glass were not animals, but people. Or maybe they were animals. It was yet to be seen.

A deputy stood at the door to the giant glass room.

“Parker, you’re in bed 16B, Pearson, 17A, Martinez, 17C, Jackson, 17B, Armstrong, 11C, Gonzales, 21B, Blake 15B, Vasquez, 16A. Welcome home, gentlemen.”

He opened the door to the module. The noise was incredible. Every surface was either glass or concrete and everything echoed. It sounded like a Laker game. There were metal tables with stools that were fastened to the floor downstairs, and rows of metal bunk beds upstairs. On one side of the huge room there was a bank of six telephones, and on the opposite wall was a TV inside a cage mounted about fifteen feet off the floor.

“C’mon upstairs. Sounds like we might be neighbors,” Kerry said, leading them up a flight of stairs. “The numbers are on the bunks – just find yours, put the mat on it, and that’s your rack.”

Pat laid his mat down, climbed onto it and tried to pass out. The noise was inescapable. It was agonizing, how tired he was and how the constant clamor prevented him from the sweet escape of sleep. Just as he finally drifted off, another announcement came over the loudspeaker.

“Chow time, line up for chow and count. Chow time.”

“What is this shit?” he asked Kerry, who was right across from him in the next row of bunks.

“Dinner time. Before you get into line for food they have to scan your wristband. They do it four times a day. Keep track of you.”

Pat scanned the concrete walls. “Where the hell would we go?”

The three of them walked down the stairs and got in line. The deputy scanned their wristbands, and they got in line for dinner. After they got their trays and drinks, they looked for a place to sit.

“Hey, over here…” Pat sat down next to one of the guys they were booked in with. In fact, his bunk was above Pat’s. Pat remembered his last name as Jackson.

“Hey, man, how ya doin’?”

Jackson looked as if he'd just seen a ghost. Kerry stepped up behind Pat and pulled him up off of the seat by his shirt.

"Pat, get up. Dude, you can't sit there," Kerry then turned to the black man. "Sorry, he's new."

The black man just nodded.

They walked to another table and sat down. Kerry turned to Pat.

"Bro, you can't sit at a table with a black dude. This is jail. You'll get beat down by your own people for that."

"My own people? Are you serious? I'm not racist!"

"Neither am I."

"But you just said I can't sit with a black guy…"

"Brother, in here you do as the Romans. You have a lot of learning to do. This is *not* the rock star life. There's rules. You can only sit with your own race here. Except for Southsiders and whites, they can intermingle. It's jail politics."

"Southsiders?"

"Latinos who speak English. There are two separate groups, the ones who don't speak English are Piasas and don't associate with Woods. Woods are white. That's what you are."

"Wow."

"Just follow my lead around here. If they sense weakness they will take advantage of you quickly. You have to keep a very low profile."

Pat shrugged and went back to focusing on his dinner, as lack of food had made him ravenous. He was oblivious to the many sets of eyes locked on him. As he grabbed for his milk, he looked up. He was mortified.

"Kerry, why is everyone looking at me? Dude, I didn't know about the seating thing. I'm not a racist, man! I just didn't know!"

"Brother, that's not why they're looking at you," Kerry pointed to the TV on the wall.

The TV on the wall was tuned to CBS. The volume could actually be heard due to the fact that the inmates were eating their dinner.

"This evening on Entertainment Tonight... Patrick Pearson of Blacklist booked into county jail in San Diego...The guitarist and lead vocalist is reportedly being held on charges ranging from drug possession to murder. Only ET has the exclusive pictures of Patrick being driven to county jail in the back of a police car..."

Pat's jaw hit the floor.

"I'm Mary Hart...more on that story and the Amy Fisher interview coming up on ET after this."

The room went silent for a minute or two, then the noise began to slowly resume.

"That had to be awkward," said Kerry.

"That's just fuckin' great." Pat replied.

"So, murder?" He turned to Chris, "That make you a murderer too?"

"It was an accident," said Chris.

"You guys want to tell me about it now?"

"Yeah, I suppose."

"Hey guys, don't be bummed...I'll pay for dinner, order whatever you want." Kerry chortled in an effort to lighten the mood.

A Hispanic man with a spider web tattooed on his face stood up from a few tables over, threw the remainder of his dinner in the trash and turned in his meal tray to the trustees. He walked over to the phones and waited. He wanted to be the first one on the phone when the cops activated them after dinner. He waited. The last tray was turned in, and the deputies switched on the phones. The man dialed.

"Jose, it's Spider." He spoke in Spanglish. "Que onda loco, let me talk to Carlos...Si...Hey, Carlos, the rock star and his friends are here...Yes, I'm sure it's them, pinche fresas. They just showed his picture on the pinche TV... si guey...Okay, I'll get it done manana when they send us out to the pinche yard…si…don't worry Carnale, it's already done."

FIFTEEN

THE SHINY BLACK Mercedes-Benz sailed up the freeway toward downtown San Diego. Carlos always had the car washed before entering the United States – he felt that it fit in better and he liked to flaunt his success in front of the American people.

"Jose, I don't know why we trust any of these fucking Americans! This fucking puto steals from me again and again! I'm going to make an example out of him this time, carnale."

The puto that Carlos was referring to was a man by the name of Sal Foley, a CPA and money launderer for the Cartel, who had an office downtown.

Carlos was already livid about the raids in San Diego that had netted hundreds of weapons, thousands in cash and millions in drugs. The subsequent arrests and deaths had the Arellano-Felix brothers furious. The only apparent positive that came out of the messes was the fact that the rock star and his perros were now in jail where Carlos could easily get to them.

As if all that had transpired in the last few days wasn't enough to worry about, now Sal Foley was telling him that the ATF and FBI had put a freeze on two American bank accounts used to convert gun money. It appeared that all the money would be lost. Carlos disagreed with Mr. Foley's assessment of the situation, hence the formal visit to his office.

"DEA, FBI, NTF, ATF! How many police agencies do these fucking Americans have? They steal my guns and my drugs… Now this pinche cabrone steals money from my accounts? This gringo is dead, Jose. How could my money just be seized like this?

He must be working with the FBI. No mercy this time. I want to see him beg."

"Yes sir, Mr. Castillion,"

Jose pulled off the freeway, and they made their way through the downtown streets to a huge glittering glass building.

Fucking Americans. Their decadent pride will be their demise.

Jose parked the car in a metered space directly in front of the building, and the two of them walked through the front doors and straight to the elevators making eye contact with no one. They checked their pistols in the elevator on the way up to the fourth floor. Jose installed a silencer.

"I want him to admit he worked with the FBI, and I want him to beg for his life before we kill him, Jose."

"Yes, sir."

The elevator doors opened into a large hallway. A double door on the left hand side had a plaque next to it reading Foley and McGregor, Financial Consultants.

Jose pushed open the doors, and the men walked in. The lobby was empty, and nobody was behind the reception desk. There were two leather sofas and a coffee table garnished with a few fake palms, a door to the right and two doors directly in front of them, one being behind the reception desk.

"Hello?" Carlos called into the open door that led back into the offices.

No answer.

"Jose, you look behind the door over there. I'm going to walk back into the offices."

Carlos cautiously stepped through the door and peered into the office area. There were several desks with computers on them and three empty offices along the back wall. A glass-encased conference room was situated in one corner of the room, and another office — this one with its door closed — was in the other.

Hand in his jacket and on his pistol, he cautiously approached the office with the closed door. The plaque on the wall next to the door read Sal Foley. Carlos turned the knob and pushed open the door. Sal was sitting at his desk crunching numbers and was noticeably startled when his office door opened.

"Holy shit! Carlos, you scared the shit out of me! What are you doing here?"

Carlos pulled the pistol out of his jacket and aimed it at Foley's chest.

"Tell me more about my money, you fucking dog!"

"Carlos…I…I…the FBI has seized the account…I told you…"

"Shut up! I'm tired of you Americans stealing from me! Who are you working with?"

"Carlos, I'll show you the warrants. I don't have any control over this – we need to involve our attorneys. It's going to take time to sort out…"

"Fucking liar! All you gringos do is lie and steal from me!" He pointed the gun into Foley's face. Foley's bald head began to sparkle with beads of sweat.

"You tell me who you are working for, or I'll shoot you in your face!"

Suddenly a voice was heard from behind Carlos.

"Drop your weapon now!"

Carlos leaned over the desk, the gun not more than six inches from the terrified accountant's face and whispered.

"You're dead. You're all dead."

"Drop your weapon…I'm not asking again!"

Carlos slowly stood up straight, letting the pistol hang by its trigger guard on his index finger, and raised his hands. He let the pistol fall to the carpeted floor.

"Put your hands on your head and turn around slowly."

Carlos placed his hands on his head and very slowly turned to face the voice.

An officer in a suit jacket holstered his gun. Two other officers that were dressed in full armor with NTF embroidered across their chests kept their weapons trained on Carlos. The plain clothed cop smiled.

"Carlos Castillion, you are under arrest for extortion, trafficking, and conspiracy to commit murder. Lace your fingers behind your head and kneel down please."

As Carlos began to kneel in front of Foley's desk, one of the uniformed officer's head exploded with a thump, as if an invisible hammer had swung down and crashed into the side of the man's face. Blood, hair and brain matter splattered all over the doorframe. Foley screamed and dove under his desk.

Carlos stood up and kicked the plain clothed officer in the stomach, knocking him off balance and sending him flying backwards onto the floor in the main office. The second NTF uniform dropped to the floor as more bullets could be heard whizzing by. Carlos dove over Foley's desk falling on the floor right next to Sal.

"I told you, you were all dead."

Carlos stretched under the desk and grabbed his pistol off the floor, and in one fluid motion swung it out from under the desk, pressed it against Sal's forehead and pulled the trigger. The accountant's head split open with a loud bang. His body went instantly limp, and he fell forward onto Carlos.

Get off me you pinche cabrone…

Carlos pushed the dead accountant's body aside, got on his knees to the side of the desk and looked around its edge.

The corner of the desk exploded with a loud snap – wood splintered and flew everywhere.

Carlos put his gun around the corner and squeezed off three shots. Bullets were whizzing by his head so close that he could hear them even over the ringing in his ears from the unsilenced weapons.

"Mr. Castillion!" Rang out Jose's voice, "Come on, let's go!"

Carlos quickly stood up from behind the desk. Both uniformed officers were down and not moving, bloody puddles slowly soaking into the carpet around their heads. The plain-clothed officer was also on the ground face down. Carlos stared for a moment. He liked to know just who it was that would go to so much trouble to catch him. He started toward the body.

"No, Mr. Castillion, we have to go now…" Jose grabbed Carlos by the shoulder and whisked him away from the fallen cops and toward the exit. The officer slowly lifted his head, pulled his pistol out from under him, aimed and fired.

Carlos didn't feel the pain at first, just a thump, as if somebody had thrown a rock at his head. It knocked him a little off balance. He reached up and put his hand on his head. Blood. Then the pain. It seared through his head. He turned around, and he and Jose both emptied their guns into the injured officer.

Jose took Carlos's arm and threw it around his neck, partially carrying Carlos out into the hall and toward the stairwell. He kicked the stairway door open and started down the stairs, Carlos in tow.

Carlos could feel the blood beginning to drip down his face. Jose kicked open the emergency exit door that led onto the street, and let his eyes adjust to the bright sunlight. Sirens could be heard approaching from all directions. He got his bearings and ran with Carlos toward the Mercedes. He opened the door on the passenger side and helped Carlos into the car, just as the first police cruiser rounded the corner. Jose slammed the door shut and slid across the hood to the driver's side, simultaneously reaching for a fresh clip in his pocket and releasing the old one out of the pistol. He opened his door and jumped in, fumbling for the keys in his jacket pocket and trying to reload his gun at the same time. Momentarily stunned, Carlos wiped the blood from his face and stared at his hand.

"Mr. Castillion, I need your help… The police, sir."

Carlos shook himself out of the stupor and got a new clip out of the glove box, shoved it into his pistol and racked it back.

"Don't worry Jose, they're not taking us today."

He aimed at the approaching police car and fired six rounds, each going straight through the car's windshield. The car swerved left, careening out of control over the sidewalk and into the side of a building. He then spun around the other way and fired through the rear window, stopping a police car behind them.

Jose managed to start the Mercedes, and they screeched away from the curb and down the street toward the freeway entrance, dodging traffic and disregarding any traffic laws. Carlos looked back through the Mercedes' rear window, wiping the blood that was running down his face. He turned to Jose.

"Jose…"

"It's just a scratch sir, you'll be fine."

"Thank you, Jose, I…"

The driver's side window exploded in a deafening crash. Jose slumped forward onto the steering wheel, dark red blood spurting from his head.

"Jose! Jose! No!"

The car sped out of control through traffic.

Carlos's eyes began to water.

No, you fucking pigs…no…

He shook Jose's body in a total panic.

"Jose! Jose!"

The Mercedes continued across the lanes, headed straight for a bus stop and a wall. The rear driver's side window shattered.

Carlos reached across and released the door handle, pushing Jose's body out into the street.

You fucking pigs…I'll fucking kill everybody.

The car began to slow as it clipped a bus stop bench, took out a series of newspaper dispensers and finally came to rest on the sidewalk, its right side scraping down a wall in a shower of sparks.

The shots sounded as if they were coming from every direction. The rear window exploded, then the two passenger windows. Carlos huddled on the floor of the passenger seat, covered in shattered glass, bloody and shaking.

I'll get you, you fucking dogs, somehow, I'll get you...

♪♪♪

Little Carlos was rolled up in a tight little ball, his father Hector's arms were around him. Hector had one hand over his mouth. He struggled a little – it was difficult to breathe. His father looked down at him and put his forefinger up to his lips.

"Shhh..."

Carlos stopped struggling. He could hear the footsteps coming toward them – shuffling through the sand. A flashlight beam was moving through the leaves of the bushes. He was in a state of terror.

They'd been on the road for several days, and they were hot, thirsty and hungry. All that kept Carlos's father going was the promise of better things to come in the United States. Hector Castillion had relatives in San Diego who had been working on an avocado ranch in the small town of Valley Center, and Hector was promised a job and a place to stay when he, his wife and Carlos got there.

They had driven their own car from Mexicali to Morelos Cuervos, where it was handed over to the coyotes as partial payment for the human smuggling service they were providing. From there, they were taken in the back of a four-wheel drive vehicle to a dry river wash and dropped off. They'd been on foot ever since.

His father had been instructed to take enough rations for three days, and to travel only down the wash, and only during daylight hours when it was hotter than 90 degrees. The Border Patrol was using new technology called infrared detection, therefore travel by day was safer. During the day, the high-tech thermal imaging devices were useless, and it was much too hot at this time of year for the agents to patrol too deep into the blazing desert.

They'd packed fresh clothing in a duffel bag that they would change into as they approached the Imperial Sand Dunes State Park on the United States side of the border. At the designated place and time, a man out for a cruise in a dune buggy would pick them up in the dry riverbed. Appearing as a family out for a day of off-road fun, they'd casually roll up to the highway, hop into a motorhome and be on their way to San Diego. The motorhomes coming from the State Park were almost always waved through the checkpoint, so they'd be home free.

Carlos, his father, and his mother, had hunkered down for the night in a thick nest of bushes and trees. They were trying to cool off enough to get some sleep when his father heard an engine off in the distance. The engine had stopped at what seemed a few hundred feet away, and now the voices and footsteps could be heard clearly in the quiet of the vast desert night. The Border Patrol.

"Come on out, we know you're out here!"

Carlos's mother began to sob.

It always made Carlos very sad to see his mother cry, and he'd seen it a lot.

Carlos and his mother Carlita were very close and spent a lot of time together while his father worked – in fact, Carlos was named after her. His mother was much younger than his father, was very attractive and was actually from a wealthy family from central Mexico. When she left Monterrey to be with Hector her family had disowned her, as Hector was not the type of provider her father believed she should marry. Hector naturally vowed he would give her a good life and planned to do it in the United States. They just needed to get there.

His father put his arm around her head and his hand over her mouth to hide her crying. He could see a man with a dog approaching in the full moonlight.

"Come on spike, go find 'em…"

The jingling of a dog collar followed, and Carlos's father knew there would be no place to hide. He stood up and stepped out of the bushes with his hands in front of him. The dog that fortunately was still leashed, began to go wild.

"Hey, Roy, I got 'em! Over here…go get the truck…"

"All right, Jim."

"So what have we got here?" said a man waving around a shotgun. "A little wetback family? Long walk for you fucking idiots."

Hector immediately knew this was not the Border Patrol he was dealing with; this man was dressed in a white undershirt, long shorts, and military boots.

"Get down on your fucking knees."

Carlos's father gestured that he did not understand.

"No comprende, Señor."

The man put the shotgun barrel up to Hector's jaw.

"I said, on your knees."

Hector understood. He said something in Spanish to let his family know that they had better follow along.

"Empty your pockets…"

Once again, the gesture for "I don't understand."

The man patted his own pockets in an exaggerated manner.

"Your pockets, empty your fucking pockets amigo! Dinero!"

Hector turned his pockets inside out. He had four hundred dollars in American currency. The man took it and stuffed it in his shirt pocket.

"Hey motherfucker, don't look at me like I'm the fuckin' thief, you wetbacks steal from us every fuckin' day!"

The man then pulled a length of rope out of his backpack and tied Hector, Carlita and Carlos's hands behind their backs, leaving them on their knees.

A truck came bouncing through the sand, coming to a stop directly in front of them, the headlights all but blinding the small family. The driver got out of the truck. He was a very large and ugly man with spiky red hair and bad teeth. He was dressed entirely in camouflage.

"Well, goddamn, looks like we found ourselves a pretty one! Cut her loose, Jim…"

Jim pulled a knife from his belt and cut the rope from Carlita's wrists. She stretched her arms.

The man walked over to Carlita and cupped her chin in his hand, forcing her to look up at him. He could see beads of sweat sparkling on her breasts in the light from the truck's headlights.

"Hola, mamasita…Boy, I sure like the view from up here."

She turned her head away from him.

"Don't you turn away from me, you little bitch!" He grabbed her hair and forced her to look up at him. "You're going to do what I say. Now get the fuck up!"

He pulled her up off of her knees by her hair. Carlos's father jumped up. The red-haired man turned, pulled a large revolver out of his jacket pocket and pointed it at Hector.

"You got a problem with that, Jose?"

Hector stopped and began to back up. The man with the shotgun kicked him in the back of the legs, dropping him back to his knees. Carlita began to cry, and Carlos was now crying as well. The man shoved Carlita up against the truck. He put the barrel of the pistol under her chin and leaned very close to her face. She could smell his disgusting breath.

"You are a hot little bitch. You want it, don't you?"

He reached down with his other hand and grabbed the top of her dress, and yanked it down, breaking the straps and exposing her breasts. Hector began to stand again and cursed in Spanish. The other man hit him in the face with the butt of the shotgun.

"You got a death wish, boy?" the man said, putting the barrel up to Hector's cheekbone. "Might do you well to stay put and shut the fuck up!"

The red-haired man pushed Carlita back down to her knees.

"You're gonna suck my fuckin' cock," he said.

Carlita turned her head, sobbing. The man unzipped his fly and exposed himself, just inches from Carlita's face. She sobbed uncontrollably.

"No...please, no..."

Hector tried to get up, and the other man pushed him down into the sand, jamming the shotgun's barrel into his cheek and cocking it.

"You're gonna fuckin' die, boy."

The red-haired man shook Carlita by her hair

"What's the matter, you don't like me? You're gonna like this..."

He picked her up by her hair and took her around to the back of the truck and threw her into the truck's bed.

Carlos remained on his knees, listening to the screams for help from his mother. He looked to his father, who was on the ground with the barrel of the shotgun digging into his face. The man with the shotgun was laughing. Carlos couldn't take any more of his mother's screaming and pleading for help. He jumped up and ran around to the other side of the truck.

The red-haired man had his pants down around his ankles and was on top of Carlos's mother. Carlos ran up to the man, his hands still tied behind his back, and bit into his buttock as hard as he could.

"What the fuck?" The man screamed in pain, spinning around and hitting Carlos so hard that it knocked the wind out of him. Carlos coughed and wheezed as the shotgun man dragged him by his collar back over to where his father was.

Over the next few minutes, his mother's screaming finally began to die down. The ugly red-haired man brought her back over to where Carlos and his father lay in the sand and threw her to the ground. He bound her hands behind her back.

"How was it?" asked the shotgun man.

“Not the best, but not bad…” The man then pulled a walkie-talkie out of his pocket. “Civilian patrol six to Border Patrol control, do you copy?”

“Copy civilian six.”

“Good evening. We’ve got three bogies in custody, copy?”

“Copy that, six, what’s your twenty?”

“About 32.66 by 114.95. About 2 miles south of 116, in the riverbed, copy?”

“Ten-four, we’ve got a transport in the area, he’ll be there within ten, copy?”

“Ten-four. We’ll be ten-twenty-three.”

“Ten-four. Thanks for your help, Roy.”

“No problem, just being a good American.”

Carlos looked at his mother. All the color and spirit seemed to have been drained from her. She stared into the distance as if looking into another world. Carlos began to cry again.

“What’s your problem you little pissant?” said the ugly man.

Carlos just cried.

“You want to cry? I’ll give you something to cry about!”

The man unzipped his fly and laughing began to urinate on Carlos’s father.

As the man zipped up his pants, another set of headlights appeared on the horizon. As they drew closer, the vehicle was recognizable as the Border Patrol. The truck came to a stop, and two agents got out.

“Whatcha got, Roy?”

“Found ‘em in the wash. The male was a little unruly so we had to secure ‘em. They’re all yours.”

The agents opened the back of the truck and loaded Carlos’s mother into the truck.

“Goddamn, this one smells like piss.”

“Yeah, I know. Musta scared the piss out of him!”

They all laughed. Carlos's father was loaded into the truck, followed by Carlos. As they drove away, he could see out the back through the metal cage. The red-haired man was waving to him

"Bye, bye, my little amigo!"

Someday I'll get these Americans...Someday I'll kill everyone.

♪♪♪

Carlos reached over to the door handle on the driver's side and pulled himself over the center console and into the driver's seat. He turned the key, and the engine sputtered to life.

Oh, Jose...

Staying hunched down, he stomped the accelerator and people dove for cover as the banged up Mercedes roared down the sidewalk, taking with it anything in its path. Carlos poked his head up and attempted to make a quick assessment of his situation. The police were scrambling to get back in their cars to resume the chase. The freeway loomed ahead, but he'd never get anywhere in this car. He steered to the right down an alley, bouncing off dumpsters and weaving through discarded boxes. He blindly shot out of the alley, across the sidewalk into the next street, T-boning a pickup truck with a brain-numbing crash. Carlos was thrown into the steering wheel as the airbag deployed and hit him square in the face. Traffic screeched to a halt in both directions. People screamed and ran for cover as Carlos staggered out of the totaled Mercedes and ran down the sidewalk with his pistol in plain sight.

Trying to shake off the dizziness from the impact, he turned and darted down a cement corridor between two buildings, trying doors and looking for any place to hide. He came to a parking garage, jumped through some hedges and over a short wall into the structure. He located the elevator and pressed the up button, looking over his shoulder with his gun ready for anybody who might have seen where he'd gone and followed. The elevator's bell rang, and the doors slid open. Nobody was inside. He stepped in and pressed the button for the fifth floor – or the top of the structure. He checked his appearance in the mirrored walls of the elevator as the doors closed.

Carlos grimaced as he pulled his hair back from his forehead. Jose was right, it was just a scratch, but it had bled a tremendous amount. He pulled the emergency stop button. He took off his jacket and shirt, shaking out the broken glass and setting them to the side. He removed his undershirt, and spitting on it, wiped as much blood off his face as he could. He actually looked pretty good at first glance. He put his shirt and jacket back on and stuffed his bloody undershirt into an inside pocket. He then released the emergency stop button.

The door opened on the fifth floor of the parking garage and an attractive woman in business attire was standing at the elevator doors. Carlos looked past her for any signs of life and saw nobody else on the floor.

"Are you okay?" she asked, "I heard the alarm going off."

Carlos pulled out his pistol, shoved it into her side with one hand and covered her mouth with the other.

"Where is your car?" he quietly asked her, never removing his hand from her mouth.

She pointed to the lot, her eyes popping out of her head in surprise.

"Let's go," Carlos said, "and don't fucking scream."

They walked over to a white Nissan Pathfinder. Carlos led her to the driver's side with one hand on her shoulder and the other holding the pistol that was stuck in her rib cage.

"Unlock it and get in. Don't do anything stupid or I'll kill you."

She chirped the alarm and unlocked the doors. She sat in the driver's seat, and Carlos got into the back seat behind her.

"Give me your purse."

"Please don't hurt me…"

"Just give me your fucking purse."

Carlos dumped the contents out onto the back seat. He found her cell phone, took out the battery and tossed it out the window.

"Listen to me carefully. I've killed many people, and I will kill you unless you do as I say. Do you understand?"

"Y...yes..."

"Bueno. Start the car and drive us out of this parking garage and to the freeway where you will go south. Do not stop for anybody, including the police. If you do, I'll shoot you and find another car. Do you understand?"

"Yes."

"Good. Now go. I'm going to lie down. I have this gun pointed right at the back of your seat, so don't fuck with me."

She backed the SUV out, drove out of the garage and onto the street, heading for the freeway entrance. She turned to say something to him.

"Don't look back here, keep your fucking eyes forward."

She turned her eyes back to the road.

"Uh...whatever your name is... the police have the street blocked ahead."

"Make a U-turn and find another way to the freeway."

She did as he instructed. She drove through the downtown streets, watching the police activity around them. She got on Broadway going east and worked her way through the traffic to another freeway entrance that was free of the police.

"I'm getting on the freeway now."

"Good."

"Whatever your name is...where are we going?"

"You're taking me home."

"Um...you're not going to rape me are you?"

"I would never take sex from a woman without permission."

"But you've killed people?"

"Yes."

"Why?"

"Business."

"Is this business?"
"No."

Sixteen

"PEARSON, LEGAL VISIT*...Pearson, legal visit...Come down to the module door..."* yelped the annoying voice over the loudspeaker.

Awakened by the sound of hearing his name, Pat rolled over on his bunk. "Fuck, what the hell was that?" he asked nobody in particular.

Pat was in pain. Every muscle in his body was cramped. He tried to wipe the sleep from his eyes, but still couldn't fully open them.

"Bro, get up," answered Kerry, "they're calling you for a legal visit. It's your lawyer or somebody important. Get up, Patrick."

"What time is it?"

"Eight o'clock. Anybody who can get in to see you at eight o'clock sharp has some clout, bro. Get the hell down there."

Patrick sat up in his bunk and looked around the dorm. All of the inmates were quietly snoozing around him in spite of the bright fluorescent lights beaming down from the ceiling. Pat's head was ringing.

God, I need to get high...

He flopped back down onto his pillow.

"Patrick! Get up!"

"Okay, geez..."

He stood up, slipped his shower shoes on and shuffled down the stairs to the module's door. His head throbbed. He was freezing. He stood and waited, nearly falling back asleep where he stood a few times until eventually, a deputy opened the door.

"Follow me, Pearson."

They walked down a long corridor to several visiting rooms. The deputy unlocked a room and motioned Pat in. The small room consisted of a metal table and four metal chairs, two on either side of the table. The walls were a dingy beige color, and there was a speaker with a button next to it on the wall by the door.

"Press that button when you're done," the deputy said and locked Pat inside.

Pat sat down in one of the chairs. He was uncomfortable, his muscles ached, and he felt as if there was a greasy film over his whole body. He put his head in his hands and rested his elbows on the table, closing his eyes. He wished he could sleep forever. The lock on the door soon rattled him out of his daze. The door opened, and Steve walked in with a woman. She wore horn-rimmed glasses and had crazy gray hair. She looked like a female version of Einstein.

"Hey, Pat. How you holding up?"

"Steve, you've got to get me out of here."

The gray-haired woman quickly interrupted.

"We got here as quickly as we could, Patrick. I'm Sheila Williams, I'll be defending you."

"Great. When do I bail out?"

"It's not going to be that easy Patrick."

"Well, it's your job to make it that easy. I'll pay you whatever you want, just get me out."

Steve chimed in. "Look Pat, Sheila's the best in the business, but the charges are very, very serious. It's going to be complicated."

"Steve, man, I'm coming apart in here. I don't feel good. I'm fucked up," Pat said, wiping tears from his eyes.

"You're coming down off of the drugs," Sheila said. "You're a tweeker who needs help."

"Don't call me a fucking tweeker, and don't start preaching to me. You don't even know me! Just do your job and get me the fuck out of here!"

"I know you better than you think, Patrick." She opened her briefcase and took out two pictures and set them side by side on the table. "Look at these pictures Patrick. This one was given to me by your parents."

"What are you doing talking to my parents?"

"Look at yourself in this one, Patrick. You're healthy, full of life and ambition."

"So what?"

"Look at this one Patrick. This is your mug shot."

Pat stared at the picture in front of him. He looked like death. He had dark bags under his eyes, and his skin was pale white. The lines in his face were exaggerated, and his cheeks were so sucked in that it made him look like a prisoner of war. He truly looked like an old man. He began to sob.

"So what...why the fuck are you showing me this shit?"

"Because Patrick, you need to face the reality of what you have become. You are a serious addict Patrick, like it or not, and you've sunk as low as you can go. You are in serious, serious trouble. I will keep you out of prison Patrick, but you're going to do this my way, or I'm not helping you."

"I can get any fuckin' lawyer I want. I don't need you..."

"Pat, this is how it's got to go," said Steve, "We've spoken to the band, your parents, Christine, everyone. You promised you'd get help. We're holding you to that."

Pat's head felt as if it was going to split open. It was so cold in the room.

"Fuck, okay, whatever. Just get me the fuck out of here!"

"You need to admit you have a serious problem," Sheila said, "and promise that you are ready to deal with it."

"I said whatever."

"Patrick, you need to say the words to me, or we move no further."

"What is your fucking problem, lady? You're supposed to be my lawyer! I pay you! I call the shots!"

"It doesn't work that way when you are in this deep. You stand to lose everything you have ever worked for, Patrick. You need to ask for help and make a commitment to follow through. And you're not doing this for your band who you've screwed, your friends who you've lost, your family who you've alienated, or even your son and fiancée who you've completely neglected. You need only to do this for yourself. Should be easy to say, Patrick, as self-centered as you are."

"Fuck you…" Pat sobbed, his head back in his hands.

"I'm telling you right now, Patrick, that as you go down the long road to recovery, you are going to hear a lot of this. It's tough love, Patrick. I will save your life, but you need to promise me that you'll do your part."

"Okay, I fucking promise."

"Good. I hope you are sincere because if you are not, this is all for nothing."

Sheila put an empathetic hand on Pat's shoulder. "Listen Patrick, you're scheduled for arraignment today at ten AM. As soon as we leave here, I'll be going to speak to the DA to see what is going on, but I've got to tell you Patrick, it does not look good for bailing out today. You have a murder charge and a lot of gun charges. It may not be feasible to set reasonable bail at this hearing. You may have to wait for the pre-trial conference for us to work a deal. You'll have to just tough it out. You'll be okay in protective custody."

"When do I go to protective custody?"

"You're supposed to be in protective custody. Let me see your wristband…"

She gasped when she saw the blue wristband.

“Patrick, just hang tough till ten. I’ll straighten this out at the arraignment hearing. We’ll get you out of general population.”

“Please…I’m sick…just get me out of here…”

“Patrick, you’re going to be okay. I’ll see you in the courtroom at ten.”

“Steve, what about Chris? We’ve got to help him too.”

“I figured you’d feel that way, so Sheila will be defending him too. But you’re paying for it, and he has to go to rehab as well. Same terms, man.”

“Okay. Whatever.”

“Patrick,” said Sheila, “he is going in front of the same judge as you this morning. Let him know I’ll be meeting with him just before his appearance.”

“Okay. Can you get him into protective custody too? I don’t want us to be split up.”

“I’ll do what I can, but he’s not a known celebrity like you are. I may not be able to do for him what I can do for you.

“But the Mexican Mob might be after us. Isn’t that a good enough reason?”

“That probably is. Like I said, I’ll talk to the DA, and I’ll see what I can do. Patrick, you just have to be strong. You guys *will* come out of this better people.”

“Whatever.”

“Do you have any questions for me?”

“No.”

“Fine. I’ll see you at ten.”

She pushed the button on the wall, and a deputy opened the door. He first escorted Steve and Sheila out, and then returned for Pat. He walked Pat back to the module and let him inside. Everybody was waking up, and the noise was becoming worse. Pat walked up to his bunk, flopped down, and rolled over onto his back, covering his ears. Chris and Kerry both stared at him with quizzical expressions. He closed his eyes.

“So? Come on! What happened?” Chris asked.

"It was Steve and our lawyer. She'll be meeting with us before our arraignment this morning. It's at ten. They'll probably be calling our names any time now."

"Our lawyer? Dude, how am I going to afford a lawyer?"

"I've got you covered. But we're both going to rehab. She's a bitch, and she's adamant about it. It's the only way."

"Fine with me, I'm done with this bullshit. Thanks bro. I don't know what I'd do without you."

"No sweat, dude. We need each other to get through this."

They were suddenly, yet predictably, interrupted by the barking of the module's loudspeaker system.

"Attention…the following bodies have court this morning at ten o'clock. Be at the module door at nine. Abrams, Alfonzo, Darcy, Garner, Michaels, Pearson, Martinez, Salazar. Be ready at nine. Don't' make us come looking for you."

The message was then repeated in Spanish.

"Well, good luck guys," said Kerry. "Wish I could afford a hotshot attorney."

"Think positive my friend," Pat replied. "That's what you've been preaching to me."

"Yeah, it's easy to preach, tough to live by when you've been through this a dozen times."

"You'll be okay. We'll all be okay."

♪♪♪

"Okay guys, you know the drill. Hands in your waistbands, single file, no talking."

They walked down the corridor toward the elevators.

"Everybody stop and face the wall. Left hand up high, right hand behind you."

A deputy walked down the line and scanned all of their wristbands.

"Pearson, Martinez, take two steps back."

Pat and Chris stepped back two steps.

"Turn around and face the opposite wall. Keep your hands up high. Everybody else into the elevator."

Pat and Chris looked at each other.

"Dude, why are we being separated from everyone else?"

"I believe I said no talking!" bellowed a deputy. "Look at the wall and shut up!"

As the other inmates were sent off into the elevator, Chris and Pat were handcuffed together.

"You two don't give me any trouble, okay?" said a deputy assigned exclusively to them.

"Yes, sir..." replied Chris and Pat in perfect unison.

"Okay then. Down the hall to the elevator on your left. No talking."

The deputy walked them into the elevator and escorted them down to the second floor, where they disembarked and walked down a huge, long marble hallway, occasionally passing what appeared to be hurried and preoccupied attorneys and businessmen. The deputy led them to a wooden bench and sat them down.

"Don't make me chain you to this bench, okay guys?"

"Yes, sir..." they replied in the same harmony as before.

The deputy poked his head into a door and asked for Ms. Williams. The lawyer came out into the hallway.

"Hi Patrick, good to see you." She turned to Chris. "Christopher, I'm Sheila Williams, I'll be representing you both in this matter. How are you holding up?"

"I'm okay, I guess, under the circumstances," Chris said with a slightly relieved look. Pat nodded in agreement.

"Well, gentlemen, there's been some very interesting developments in the case. You two may be the luckiest dope addicts on the planet."

"What happened?" asked Pat.

"Well, it seems that through some surprisingly good police work that you boys may be cleared of numerous charges, including the murder charges. However, this will require that you cooperate with the police and the district attorney. You may be asked to testify in court, against a well-known member of the Mexican Mafia, who I'm sure you two already know as Carlos Castillion."

"No way. He'll kill us!"

"I think you should be more worried about what happens to you if you don't testify. You remain in jail and possibly face prison on murder charges, conspiracy at the least. Carlos will have no problem getting to you in prison. The Mexican mob runs the prisons. But, if you agree to the terms, you'll be sent to rehab immediately in an undisclosed location. It will be secret and secure – nobody will be able to get to you. It won't be a celebrity rehab either. You are looking at six months to a year of residential treatment."

"Six months to a year? Are you crazy? What about my career?"

"Your career will be there when you are well again."

"Well again? I'm not sick! Look, I can get off the drugs. It won't take a fuckin' year."

"Look, Patrick, you know I'm not here to make deals or argue semantics with you guys about this. You will go to rehab for the amount of time deemed by the court as the appropriate amount as part of your probation. You will complete it, too. Both of you will. Carlos Castillion will be convicted in the meantime, and you can put all of this behind you and start a new life. I should probably tell you as well that your cohort Tina Stickney has already agreed to the same terms. We're saving your lives here, guys. This is what it's going to take. That's the offer. Live free or die in custody."

"Living in a rehab isn't living free, and we're dead either way."

"Patrick, I want you to understand something. I don't do this for the money. I do this to save the lives of people I feel deserve it. I do my research. I've been in close contact with your family, and with Chris's sister. I'm doing this for your families that want you back. You don't have to listen to me, guys, but understand that if you don't, you are on your own. You will die, either at the hands of someone else or from the drugs. Take the help that is being offered to you. It's time to change the direction of your lives for good. Pat, *you* already promised."

Pat and Chris looked at each other. They clasped hands and looked back at Sheila.

"Okay. We'll do what it takes."

"You're making the right decision, guys. Now, we are meeting with the Assistant District Attorney and the Judge. The deal has already been made, we just need to sign some paperwork, and then you will appear in the courtroom strictly as a formality. Once inside the courtroom, you both will plead guilty to one charge. Patrick, you will plead guilty to possession of a controlled substance, and Chris, you will plead guilty to involuntary manslaughter. You both will get convicted on a joint-suspended sentence pending the completion of the drug program and probation. It's all a formality."

Sheila turned to face Pat. "Patrick, there will be media in the courtroom. I want you to ignore them. I brought a change of clothes for you, and the deputy will be escorting you to a bathroom so you can change into clothes that are more suitable for the cameras, but you will ignore them. Don't even look in their direction, okay? This arraignment will be quick and to the point, and they'll have nothing new to report. Understand?"

"Yes."

"You'll have court again on Friday morning for sentencing, and the media is barred from that hearing so that your rehab location can be kept secret. Beds at the rehab will be available on Friday afternoon, so you will be in protective custody until then.

The Sheriff will be taking you out of your current housing and moving you into protective custody tonight, probably around ten PM. Recovery Street — that's the name of the rehab — will be picking you up from jail Friday evening. You're getting out guys. Do you have any questions?"

"What about my home? My career?"

"Steve and your agent are taking care of everything. You and I will be visiting with him tomorrow morning to iron out power of attorney details, and you'll see him again on Friday before you are admitted into Recovery Street. I'm also arranging for Christine and Chris's sister to come down on Friday too. It may be the last time you can see them for a while. Anything else?"

"I guess not." Patrick looked at Chris and smiled. "We're getting out, bro!"

"I know," Chris said, wiping a tear from his eyes.

They both looked at Sheila.

"Thank you."

"I'm telling you both right now, I've taken care of everything, and I don't want you two to worry about anything but getting better."

"Okay."

"Oh," added Sheila, "one more extremely important thing…do not discuss this deal with anyone in your housing module. If this info gets to the wrong people before you are transferred to protective custody, you'll be known as snitches. In jail, that's lower than a child molester. Keep absolutely quiet. Do you understand me?"

"Yes, Ma'am," Chris said as Pat nodded his head.

"Okay then…" Sheila turned to the deputy. "Officer, if you'd be so kind…"

The deputy removed the cuffs and walked Pat and Chris through the doorway that Sheila had come out of.

Pat looked around the room, subconsciously rubbing his sore wrists. Every inch of the room was trimmed in hardwood that framed built-in bookshelves containing hundreds of law books. In the center was a giant oak conference table with several chairs around it, and a recording device in the center. The back wall featured a stained glass hanging of the scales of justice, framed by the United States and California State flags. Sheila sat down in the first chair on the left, and several other people Pat didn't recognize were seated around the table. A person Patrick did recognize sat at the far end of the table, her arms folded in front of her. Tina.

"Pat!" She jumped and ran over to Pat and Chris, and they embraced in a three-way hug. The deputies quickly pulled them apart.

"Okay that's enough of the reunion," said the man sitting at the head of the table. He had white hair, a long face and wire-rimmed glasses. "Let's get going here."

The deputies seated all three defendants.

"Thank you, your Honor. For the record, I am Assistant District Attorney Carol Hutchins, representing the People of the State of California, to my right is Sheila Williams, representing the defendants, who are all present, and we also have Detective Elizabeth Hunter present, as well as Captain Mike Harrington, and Lieutenant Michael Morgan of the Narcotics Task Force. Presiding is the Honorable David P. Lundquist. The following is in regard to case #SDC 38760115, case #SDC 38760256, and case #SDC 38760250, the people versus Patrick Samuel Pearson, Christopher Luis Martinez, and Tina Marilynn Stickney."

"Please continue, Ms. Hutchins," said Judge Lundquist.

"The People and counsel for the defendants have agreed to amend the original charges presented, pending agreement with the defendants to cooperate in tandem with the District Attorney's office and the office of the Narcotics Task Force to assist in apprehending and convicting named suspect Carlos Castillion, of the Arellano-Felix Drug Cartel, who is currently under investigation by the Narcotics Task Force and under indictment by the San Diego District Attorney's office, per case #SDC 30112577."

"Is this guy in custody yet?" asked the Judge.

"He slipped through our fingers this morning," answered Lieutenant Morgan, "and we lost a few men in the process. But we're working with the Mexican government to bring him to justice, and mark my words, it will happen."

"I just want to make sure that this deal is going to benefit the people. We need to move forward swiftly if we make this agreement."

"Your Honor, if I may," Detective Hunter interjected, "I investigated this entire case, and my findings were in total correlation with the NTF's investigation and in complete accord with the DA's office. This deal will seal Castillion's fate once we have him. And the defendants are truly not responsible for the death of Armando Romero. The investigation has proven the shooting to be accidental. Their punishment must fit their crime."

"Thank you for your input, Ms. Hunter. I will approve this deal in good faith that the People will benefit. Is Ms. Williams in agreement?"

"Yes, your Honor."

"And the amendments, Carol?"

"Case #38760115, the People versus Patrick Pearson, the following charges are to be dismissed: HS11350, HS11379a and b, HS11352, PC12021b and PC12021.5, PC12022, PC12026, PC187, and PC189.5. The defendant will plead guilty to HS11378, possession of a controlled substance."

"Mr. Pearson, are you aware of your rights, and that by pleading guilty you are waiving your right to a trial?"

"Yes, your Honor."

"And are you aware that you will be testifying on behalf of the People as part of your guilty plea agreement?"

"Yes, your Honor."

"And you are doing this of your own free will; nobody has coerced you or threatened you in any way?"

"Yes sir."

"Mr. Pearson, how do you plead?"

"Guilty, your Honor."

"Let the record show that the defendant has signed the document I am holding and that he has entered a guilty plea in accordance with the document. Please make the amendments. Next, Carol?"

"Case #SDC38760256, the people versus Christopher Martinez…"

Carol Hutchins read the list of charges to be dropped, and a similar agreement was made with Chris. The same was done for Tina.

"Okay. Thank you everyone. I'll see you all in court." The Judge got up and left the room.

"Okay gentlemen, and lady," said Sheila, "we need to sign a few more documents for the DA's office, and we'll go to court. We're making this short and sweet due to the media in the courtroom."

A series of forms in triplicate were set in front of them by Carol Hutchins. Pat tried to read the print. His eyes wouldn't focus. His head was throbbing.

"All it says, in legal mumbo-jumbo, is that you agree to testify in the Castillion case when you are subpoenaed. Go ahead and sign it, and we'll move into the courtroom."

Pat, Chris, and Tina signed the forms, were each given a copy, and Pat and Chris were cuffed together and led through a back hallway to a bathroom. The deputy handed Pat a paper bag and uncuffed him from Chris.

"Change into these clothes. And make it snappy."

Pat slipped into a pair of black slacks and a button-down shirt. There was also a pair of dress shoes and a tie in the bag, but no socks. He left his jail-issued sweat socks on. He sloppily tied his tie. It was too long.

"Okay, let's go..." the deputy announced and walked them handcuffed together back down the hall and into the adjacent courtroom. Camera flashes blinded them as the deputy sat them down on a bench inside a cage on the right side of the courtroom and removed the cuffs.

"Good luck, guys." The deputy locked the door to the cage. Pat looked out through the mesh at the circus behind the short wooden barrier that divided civilians from those intertwined in the legal system. He could hear camera lenses clicking all around. He put his hand in front of his face. He wanted to curl up into a ball and die.

"All rise, the Honorable David P. Lundquist presiding."

Judge Lundquist walked in donning a robe and requested that everyone be seated.

"Case numbers SDC38760115, 38760250, and 38760256, the people versus Patrick Samuel Pearson, Christopher Luis Martinez, and Tina Marilynn Stickney."

The deputy opened the cage and hurried Pat and Chris to the podium. Cameras clicked throughout the room, and a flash went off, annoying the judge.

"Ladies and gentlemen, that'll do with the cameras," the Judge said in an irritated voice. "Ms. Hutchins, have we reached an agreement in this matter?"

"Assistant District Attorney Carol Hutchins, your Honor. Yes, the people have reached an agreement with the defense. In the matter of the people versus Patrick Samuel Pearson, the People agree to the guilty plea of Health and Safety code 11378, possession of a controlled substance."

"Miss Sheila Williams representing the defendant, your Honor. The defense agrees."

"Mr. Pearson, do you understand the charges against you and do you understand your rights as a defendant?"

"Yes, your Honor."

"Very well, how do you plead?"

"Guilty, sir..."

"The court recognizes that the defendant has pled guilty to HS11378. We'll see you back here on Friday for sentencing. Good luck, Mr. Pearson."

"Thank you, sir."

♪♪♪

"Damn brother, every time I go to court it's an all-day deal!" exclaimed Kerry. "You guys are in and out in three hours?"

"Yup," said Chris, "and we'll be outta here for good soon."

Pat shot Chris a 'too much information' kind of look.

"Well done, gentlemen, well done." Kerry turned to Pat. "Hey brother, you don't look so good. You okay?"

"Yeah, I'm just so damn tired...and I can't sleep in this fuckin' place. Plus I feel so cooped up. The air is stagnant in here. I can't breathe."

"He never did do the comedown thing very well..." added Chris.

"Just lie down and rest your eyes brother," Kerry said, "we'll go outside when they call for yard time."

"Yard time?"

"Yeah, recreation they call it. They're required to give inmates the opportunity to exercise. They give us half an hour outside on Monday, Wednesday and Friday, but you gotta be one of the first twenty or so to line up."

"Cool...wake me up then." Pat rolled over and pulled his blanket up over his head. He was sleeping soundly minutes later.

"So tell me Chris, what's the story on you guys? What happened in court?"

"I can't talk about it."

"Did you make some kind of deal?"

"Dude, seriously, I can't talk about it at all."

"Come on Chris, we're friends, right? I've helped you guys along this far."

"Bro, we don't really know you that well, and even if I did, there's other people around…" Chris motioned to the guys sleeping in the next bunk, both Piasas who more than likely didn't speak English.

"Come on brother, those guys don't speak a lick of English. Fill me in. At least tell me what your charges are."

"All right, look man, we made a deal. A good one. I got involuntary manslaughter for the accidental shooting of the guy who was breaking into Pat's truck and Pat's getting possession. We're both moving out of here and into protective custody tonight, and we're getting out on Friday."

"PC? You better keep that to yourself. People will think you snitched."

"It's just because Pat's a celebrity, nothing else."

"Still…people around here wouldn't understand that."

"That's why I know you'll keep it quiet."

"Of course, brother, you should know that."

"I guess. I gotta use the bathroom."

Chris got up and walked toward the filthy tile area that loosely represented a restroom. There were six open shower stalls and four toilets lined up on a tile wall with small tile barriers between them. Nothing was private. Chris walked up to a toilet and lowered his waistband to pee.

"Que onda, ese…What's up fucker?" said a voice from behind him.

Startled, Chris quickly cut off his stream and turned abruptly. A wiry Latino man with a mustache and shaved head was not more than a foot away from him. As if he wasn't naturally intimidating enough, he also had a spider-web tattooed on his face. His eyes appeared to be halfway closed, and he spoke in a slurred manner that made Chris's skin crawl.

"H…hey…How's it goin', man?" Chris stuttered.

"Why don't you roll with your own people, ese?"

"I'm not sure what you mean…"

"Southsiders, holmes. You're fucking Mexican. You need to roll with your own people, not the pinche Woods, cabrone."

"Um…okay, I didn't know…"

"Where you from, ese?"

"El Cajon?"

"No, ese, where you *from*?"

"I'm not in any gang or anything if that's what you mean."

The guy put his hand on his Chris's shoulder and squeezed uncomfortably tight.

"You better fuckin' get right, bitch, you know what's good for you."

"Okay…I will."

"So ese, you friends with the rock star?"

"Yes."

"You pinche cabrones make a deal?"

"No."

"You answer fast, ese. Like you know exactly what I'm talking about. Like I said before, bitch, you better get fuckin' right."

The guy gave Chris a forceful shove, turned and walked away. Chris tried to force his stomach back down out of his throat. He didn't know what to do.

Just a couple of more hours, Chris…

He walked back over to their bunks and sat down across from Kerry.

"What's the matter, brother? You look like you just saw a ghost."

"Dude, that guy over there, the Latino dude with the spider-web on his face, he told me to get right."

"What?"

"He said I needed to roll with my own people."

"Chris, you'd better just do it. Go hang with the Southsiders, bro."

"Kerry, I don't know what a Southsider is. And I don't even speak Spanish!"

"You're Mexican to them, and if you don't remain loyal to your race in here, they'll take it personally, and they will fuck you up."

"Kerry, it gets worse. He asked me if me and the rock star had made a deal."

"Brother, if they think you are a snitch, then you've got bigger problems than just hanging out with your own people."

"Kerry, what do I do? Look, they're all looking over here right now!"

"Take it easy brother, don't panic. I'm gonna talk to the Woods rep, and maybe he can talk to the Southsider rep."

"Woods rep? Southsider rep? What the fuck does all that even mean?"

"You're really lucky brother. I go way back with the Woods rep. He's a patched member, and he's cool. The club sticks together. Just lay down on your bunk. Let me handle this."

Chris's heart was racing.

I don't know anything about jail politics...Please God, just a few more hours...

Kerry walked over to a huge white man with a long gray beard who was tattooed from head to toe. The two of them embraced, then walked downstairs to a table and sat down.

They glanced upstairs at Chris every so often during their conversation. Chris tried not to watch but couldn't help it – he was scared and confused. The biker gestured to another man; a Latino man with shiny bald head and an equally tattooed body. He sat down at the table with Kerry and the other man, the three of them engaged in a brief discussion. Moments later Kerry left the table and returned to his bunk where he took a seat facing Chris.

"Okay brother, they're going to leave you alone. I explained to them that you are a short-timer and that you didn't know the rules. I also told them you were leaving on Friday. The Latino shot-caller said he'd call off the dogs. Understand though, that if there is a fight or a race riot, your loyalty must be with them. You have to fight on their side, or they'll kill you. It's stupid, I know, but that's how it works in here. Anyway, for now just mind your own business, don't talk to anyone and you'll be okay."

"Thanks Kerry," Chris said. "We really owe you someday."

"No sweat, man."

Pat rolled over in his bunk and opened his eyes.

"What's going on?" he mumbled.

"Nothing important…how you feeling?"

"I have a fucking headache."

"Why don't you go down to the window and ask the cops for some Tylenol?"

Pat sat up. "Can I do that?"

"You can try," laughed Kerry.

"I'm going to." Pat got up out of his bunk, wrapped his blanket around him like an old woman and slowly shuffled down the stairs toward the deputies' window.

"He's so fucking naïve," said Chris, chuckling a little. "Kerry, I need you to promise me something."

"Shoot."

"Promise me that if anything happens to me you'll look after Pat. He's pretty helpless sometimes."

"I think I can do that."

"Thanks again for everything, bro."

"Like I said, no sweat."

"Recreation yard…" howled the loudspeakers, *"yard time, yard time, first twenty customers at the door."*

"Hey, let's go," said Kerry. "Tell Pat just to stay down there. He'll be first in line."

Chris yelled to Pat to stay put, and he and Kerry ran down the stairs and got into line with him at the door. The door opened, and a deputy began to count heads as he scanned wristbands.

"...eighteen, nineteen, twenty. That's it gentlemen, everybody else back to your racks. He had stopped on Kerry. Chris didn't make the cut.

"Hold on, dep, I don't think you counted right, he should be twenty..." Kerry said, pointing at Chris.

"Oh really? You a fuckin' mathematician?"

"No, sir. Just trying to help."

The officer recounted, and Chris was excluded again.

"Sorry Einstein, your friend stays."

Another voice spoke up in front of Kerry.

"Hey, it's cool man," said a Hispanic man, stepping out of line, "I'll stay back."

"Thanks, man," said Chris.

"Get right, ese..."

Chris gave Kerry a troubled look.

"Don't worry about it, brother."

"Okay sports fans, single file, hands in your waistbands, mouths shut! Enjoy your time at half hour fitness."

They all followed the deputy down a corridor, up the elevator to the roof and out into what looked like a helipad enclosed in a large steel cage. The sun was beginning to set behind the buildings across the street drawing long dark shadows on the cement platform, and the chain-link cage glowed a rusty red color in the evening light against an overcast sky. A deputy stood at the only door next to a Coke machine and watched as the inmates began to walk around the yard in circles. Pat breathed in the fresh air.

"This is it? Walking in circles?"

"There's no running allowed, and it looks like they haven't installed the basketball hoops I requested yet," joked Kerry.

They began to follow suit and walk around the perimeter of the yard.

"Why the Coke machine?" Pat inquired. "That seems a little out of place up here, doesn't it?"

"Some guys get a soda card with their stores."

"Stores?"

"You really haven't been to jail, have you? 'Stores' is the jail commissary. People have friends or relatives put money into an account, or on their books, as it's called, and you can buy things from the commissary. They have stuff like candy, soup, toothpaste, chips, and soda cards, which work like a credit card in the soda machine. Don't worry, you guys won't be here long enough to need stores."

"We won't, will we?" Pat said sarcastically, looking at Chris.

"Dude, Kerry's on our side. He's cool."

"Whatever, man. I need a drink."

Pat, still wrapped in his blanket, strolled over to the drinking fountain.

"Man," said Kerry, "he really is naïve."

"I know."

They continued walking around the small yard.

♪♪♪

"What's up holmes? You the rock star?"

Pat turned from the drinking fountain to face a man with a spider-web tattooed on his face.

"Yeah," Pat said as he extended his hand, "I'm Patrick Pearson. My band is Blacklist."

"They call me Spider, ese... So tell me rock star, why the fuck are you in jail?"

"It's a long story."

"I trust you won't be here too long, eh?"

"Hopefully not."

"So, can I get your autograph before you leave?"

"Sure, of course."

"I better get it right now, eh?"

"I don't have anything to write with."

"Don't worry, I do."

Spider reached behind his back.

♪♪♪

"Chris, are you noticing something strange?"

"Like what?"

"You better go to your people, Chris."

"They're not my people. And why?"

"I'm serious. All of the ese's have their shirts off and have them wrapped around their knuckles. Something's about to pop off, bro."

"That spider-web guy is out here too, I saw him in line."

"Where is he?"

"There, over there talking to Pat. Oh fuck…"

♪♪♪

"This is for fucking with Carlos," Spider snarled as he thrust the knife toward Pat. As Pat put his arm up to block it, the blade sliced across his forearm in a spray of bright red blood. Pat screamed in pain and recoiled in shock as Kerry jumped Spider from behind, threw him to the ground and attempted to wrestle the knife away. Spider jammed an elbow up into Kerry's rib cage and forced him onto his back while twisting his wrist free of his grip. The knife came down across Kerry's cheek tearing through the skin from his eye down to his mouth. Kerry pounded a knee hard into Spider's groin, and he rolled over and onto his back, holding his crotch and groaning in pain as the weapon clattered away.

Kerry tried to recover and wipe the blood out of his right eye as Pat backed further away in a panic holding his wounded arm. Blood was spurting out from between his fingers.

Chris leapt on top of Spider as he recovered the knife and swung it toward Chris. Chris met the swipe, forcing the dagger to the ground and causing sparks as it scraped along the concrete. Chris climbed on top of Spider, who forced the blade between them and looked Chris directly in the face.

"Pinche puto, fucking snitch…You're fucking dead."

He pushed up on the knife with all his might, the blade inches from Chris's face. Chris pushed downward, the two of them shaking as their muscles strained against each other. The knife came closer and closer to Chris's face and began to dig into Chris's chin. Blood ran down the blade of the knife, and into Chris's fist causing it to slip. He lost his grip. Spider's hand slipped free, and he plunged the blade into Chris's throat and pushed up. Chris's eyes opened wide with surprise.

Spider's head violently snapped back leaving a spray of blood behind from the blow of a deputy's baton.

"Everybody on the ground!" the cops hollered, "On the fucking ground!"

Officers in riot gear came streaming through the door launching a smoke grenade and firing rubber bullets at anyone who was still standing in the small yard. Inmates panicked. It was pandemonium.

Kerry, holding his cheek, rolled over on his side and looked into Chris's eyes.

"Take care of him…" Chris whispered as blood poured out of his wound and mouth.

"I will, brother."

Pat ran over and grabbed Chris's shoulders, trying to pull him up away from the chaos.

"Come on, Chris, we gotta move… Come on, man, let's go…" Chris could not move.

"Chris, get up. Come on man! Oh God, Chris, please! Oh God…Please God, no!"

Chris looked up at Pat, dark red blood gurgling from his neck.

"Rock star life, bro, we did that shit..."

Pat put his hand on Chris's neck, tears pouring down his cheeks. "Chris, come on, man, you're gonna be okay…"

Chris's eyes rolled back.

"Chris, come on man, come on! Chris! Oh, God, no!"

Chris's body went limp in Pat's arms.

"*No, Chris!*" Pat cried, "*Chris no! Goddammit, no!*"

As Pat tried to stand, the swift swing of a police baton knocked him back to the ground. Darkness followed.

SEVENTEEN

A STUNNING REDHEAD lay back on the brown leather footstool, totally naked with her head in Pat's lap. She handed him the pipe, and he took a long, deep hit. As his lungs filled, he could feel the familiar rush come over his body. His mouth tasted like sugar. He fell into an overstuffed leather chair as if he were a part of it and gazed into the eyes of the beautiful redhead as she rolled onto her side.

"Damn, Linda, I thought I'd never see you again. Tell me, how it is that you're here, anyway? I haven't seen you since we played in Phoenix."

She batted her long eyelashes, looking up at him with her big blue eyes. She brushed his hair out of his face.

"Does it really matter how I got here? Doesn't it only matter that I am here?"

"Where's Chris, Linda?"

"Don't you worry about that," she said, reaching down between his legs and massaging him. "You just enjoy this!"

She stood up and straddled him, her milky white skin glowing in the soft light. She moaned as he penetrated her. He let his head fall back and closed his eyes. She began to ride him.

Oh yeah...Linda...Maybe it was all a dream...Thank God...

He lifted his head off the chair's pillow and laced his fingers behind it, staring into her eyes. She moved slowly up and down on him, holding onto his arms. She began to dig her nails into his forearms. It hurt, particularly on his right forearm. He tried to reach over with his left hand to remove her tight grasp on his right arm, but his left arm would not move. He closed his eyes again, and the alarm on his watch began to chirp.

Shit, I'm late...Late for what?

When he opened his eyes, she was gone. The chirping had gotten louder, and it was making his head pound. Things were spinning in the darkness. He tried to put his hands around his head, but his left arm would not move, and the pain in his right was excruciating. The chirping would not cease. He cried out loud.

"What the fuck is going on? Help! Where am I?"

As his eyes began to focus, he realized he was behind a curtain. He felt trapped. A bright fluorescent light blinked on from the ceiling, temporarily blinding him. He tried to shield his eyes from the light with his right arm, then grabbing at his left in fright. The room was closing in on him.

"Where am I, goddammit? I can't move my fuckin' arm!"

A nurse opened the curtain and darted to his bed with a sheriff's deputy close behind. The constant chirping from a heart monitor was increasing in rate and volume.

"Mr. Pearson, calm down. You're all right..."

"Where am I? Why can't I move my arm? What's going on?"

"Your arm is handcuffed to the bed Mr. Pearson."

Pat looked down at the cuffs, then at the deputy, then back at the nurse.

It wasn't a dream...

"Where am I? What happened?"

"Mr. Pearson, there was a riot in the jail. You were seriously injured. You're at the hospital. You really need to calm down Mr. Pearson..."

"Where's Chris?"

"I'm sorry Mr. Pearson, I don't know who you are referring to."

"Tell me what happened to Chris! Tell me now!"

The deputy stepped forward.

"Get the fuck away from me! Tell me where Chris is!" Tears began forming in Pat's eyes.

"Mr. Pearson, you need to calm down. You have some serious injuries."

The pain suddenly hit Pat like a wave. His head throbbed. The chirping from the machine was making him crazy.

"God, my fucking head."

He lifted his right arm to his forehead, and pain shot through him. He could feel a bandage around his head. His face contorted. The nurse pulled a syringe from her jacket and inserted it into the IV.

"Mr. Pearson, please try to relax and get some rest.

"Please, just tell me where my friends are…"

"I'm sorry Mr. Pearson, but I don't have that information."

Pat began to feel dizzy. "I just…I just need to know…Chris and Kerry… What happened…"

"Mr. Pearson, you need to rest now. Somebody will be here in the morning to talk to you."

Pat laid his head back on the pillow. He felt relaxed and fell into the hospital bed as if he were part of it.

♪♪♪

"I'm really sorry, Patrick."

Sheila tried very hard to be comforting – she was the only person who had access to Pat. He simply stared as if looking out a window, though there were no windows in the small hospital room. His head pounded and his arm hurt, but the physical pain paled in comparison to the pain he felt in his heart.

"It's my fault. It's all my fuckin fault. Chris would still be here if it weren't for me."

"Pat, you cannot blame yourself for this. You don't need any more weight on your shoulders."

"You're the one who told me how I've fucked up everything from my band to my family. Looks like I've caused my best friend to die too."

"So you're going to throw yourself a pity party? Patrick, you have a lot of emotional issues you will have to plow through in the next few months. You have to be strong. And I know recovery, Patrick. I was an alcoholic. Helping people like you is one of the things that keeps my eyes open, and my body sober. You're taking the first and hardest step, going to the rehab."

"Give it a fuckin' rest already, will you? I've had about enough of your bullshit recovery lectures! I'm not going to the fuckin' rehab."

"Patrick, you have to go to the rehab. Take the only good that's come out of this situation – that you won't have to go back to jail. You'll stay here a couple of days, appear in court, and then leave for Recovery Street directly from the hospital."

"I don't know if you heard me. I'm not going to rehab. Not without Chris. As soon as they take these fucking cuffs off me, I'm going someplace where nobody will find me. I'm going to find an island or something. I'll go to Mexico."

"You're thinking irrationally, Patrick."

"You'd fucking think irrationally too if you just lost your best friend!" screamed Pat. "Now get the fuck out of here and leave me alone!"

A deputy poked his head in the door.

"Everything okay?"

"No, it's not okay!" Pat yelled, "I've killed my best friend! I've lost my fucking freedom! Things are not okay…I need to get high…"

Pat was crying hysterically. Sheila gestured for the deputy to leave and embraced him.

"Patrick, I know it all seems overwhelming right now, but as the good book says, this too shall pass. I've lost loved ones as a result of my addiction and I blamed myself too. But we move on.

And you will. You have lots of important people in your life who love you, Patrick. Your *fans* love you – how many people can even say that? You are a very blessed person. You're going to be okay."

The door opened, and a nurse walked in.

"Good…Can I please have another shot?" Pat whimpered.

"I'm sorry sir, but the doctor has said no more shots are needed. I can give you some Tylenol with Codeine."

"Great…I give up."

"Take the Tylenol, Patrick," said Sheila.

"Whatever."

Pat gulped down a couple of tablets.

"I just have to check his stitches," the nurse said.

"Fine," said Sheila, "can you just give us a minute?"

"Okay, I'll be outside," the nurse said as she walked out the door.

"Patrick, on Friday morning the deputies will be here to take you back to court. Your sentencing will be at nine. After court, you'll be brought back here and guarded until Recovery Street gets here to pick you up. At that time your custody status changes from the Sheriff's Department to the Probation Department, who have *allowed* you to be in Recovery Street. You need to understand that you are technically still in the State's custody until you have completed your rehab and your probation. A joint-suspended sentence means that if you screw up — like you leave the rehab — you will do the original sentence which for possession is three years in prison. Do you understand that?"

"Yes."

"Good. Friday will be the first day of the rest of your life, Patrick. You'll look back on this and be amazed that it ever happened." She paused. "I've got to go now, please rest and get ready for Friday."

"See ya…" Pat mumbled.

Sheila left, and the nurse came in and pulled the bandages off of Pat's head and arm.

"How's the pain on a scale from one to ten, Mr. Pearson?"

"I'm okay… Two…"

"Your stitches look good."

"Groovy."

She continued re-dressing the wounds and bandaging.

"So, I understand you'll be leaving us for rehab on Friday?"

"I'm not going to rehab."

♪♪♪

"Good luck, Patrick."

"Thank you, your Honor."

Patrick walked back and took his seat in the cage. All he had to do now was wait until the rest of the day's sentencing was completed, and then he'd be whisked away back to the hospital, where he'd wait for the rehab to pick him up.

And then at the first sign of real daylight, I'm fuckin' outta here…I'll call Christine…She'll pick me up, I'll get all my shit, and I'm off to Mexico…

Pat had a surfer friend who owned a beach house in Rosarito. He figured the guy would have no problem letting him stay down there indefinitely.

I'll go to Rosarito, and I'll find that fuckin' Carlos… I'll handle this shit myself… Chris will not die in vain…

As the wheels of justice continued to turn, so did the wheels in Pat's mind. Other cases were heard as Pat continued contemplating his plan.

I'm already off the dope – all I have to do now is stay this way… I'll find Carlos, deal with him, and return to the United States… What's the worst that could happen? I'll be clean…they'll just give me another rehab… Three years…they won't give me three years…I'm not a criminal – I'm just a guy who was in the wrong place at the wrong time… I'm just a guy who liked to party…And I've stopped and gotten clean…they can't convict me…I'm a fuckin' rock star…

The last case wrapped up, and Pat was escorted to a meeting room down the now familiar marble hallway. The deputy led him into the room, sat him down at a table and took a seat next to him.

"You know, Pearson, I've been watching you closely the last few days, since your friend was killed. I want to offer you my condolences."

Pat was floored. None of the deputies had ever said anything but 'shut up' to him.

"I kinda looked into your career a little bit. You have a good life ahead of you, Pearson. You don't belong in jail. You're a good person like a lot of these guys. Shit happens to all of us. My sister was an addict. She got her life right. Has two kids now; doin' great. I hope you do the right thing and get your life together Pearson."

"Wow, thanks Deputy…"

"I'm serious, Pearson, don't be a repeat customer. I don't ever want to see you around here again, okay?"

"You won't, sir."

"Good."

They sat in silence for a minute.

"Deputy?"

"Yeah?"

"Will justice be served in my friend's death?"

"The killer's dead, Pearson, he didn't make it. I guess you could call that justice, but you have to understand that that prick was already dead anyway. He had nothing to lose. That's the life he chose. I doubt it mattered to anybody if he was killed. You want to honor your friend, Pearson? Get your life right. And help others to get their lives right too. That's what my sister does. Do it *for* your friend. Don't become a statistic."

Pat let the comments soak in.

"Thanks, Deputy."

"No sweat, brother."

Brother... Wow...I wonder how Kerry is...

Sheila opened the door and came in.

"So, Pat, are we happy? You're getting out of custody today."

You have no idea...

"Yeah, I'm happy."

"Well, we've got one little complication. We sent you up to the hospital to hopefully dodge the media, but it seems that they're on to us and have set up shop in front of the building, so you're going to have to slip out the service entrance this afternoon."

"Whatever it takes..."

"The deputy will have your belongings and will turn you over to Recovery Street, who with the help of the hospital security will take you out the service entrance to the parking garage, and you'll be on your way. For your safety, nobody can know where you are going, Patrick."

"Hell, I don't even know where I'm going!"

"It's in downtown LA."

"Okay..."

"This could be the last time we see each other for a while, Patrick. Do you have anything you need to ask me at all?"

"Actually, I have a request."

"What is it?"

He looked at the deputy.

"I want you to help somebody like you helped me. I'll pay for it."

"I'll see what I can do..."

"No, I'm serious. I want you to help this guy. He's a two-striker, but he's a good man. He saved my life. Get him to Recovery Street. I will pay anything you want."

"Like I said, Patrick, I'll see what I can do. What is his name?"

"Kerry Parker."

♪♪♪

The deputy opened the door to the hospital room.

"Pearson?"

"What's up, Dep?"

The deputy undid Pat's handcuffs and handed him a brown paper bag. The bag had Pat's name and booking number written on it in his handwriting.

"It's your property from when you were booked in. Go ahead and change into your street clothes. The rehab is here for you."

Pat's mouth went dry.

"Okay, sir."

Pat went into the bathroom and began to change into his clothing.

This is it...I'm out of here!

He zipped up his pants, pulled on his shirt and got his shoes and socks on. He turned to look in the mirror.

*Don't become a statistic...*He thought as he felt the stitches on his head. *Do the right thing and get yourself right...fuck that, I'm going to Mexico...*

He turned, opened the door and stepped out of the hospital room. The deputy was standing with two men – one was blond and pudgy with a pockmarked face, the other was a tall black man with huge ears and big lips. The white guy was signing some paperwork for the deputy on a clipboard. The black man put out his hand.

"What's up man, I'm Lester, and this is Dave. We're from Recovery Street."

"Hey, I'm Pat. Pat Pearson."

"Oh, I know who you are, Mista Rock Star!"

"Easy, there Lester," said the white guy. "Pat, I'm Dave. Glad to meet you."

"Likewise."

"Okay, I guess we're ready to go."

"Patrick," said the deputy,

"Yeah?"

"I don't want to see you again."

"Thanks, Dep."

The three men walked down the hall past the nurses' station to an elevator and descended to the lobby. The sun shone in through the glass doors to the front of the building. Pat could see a couple of TV vans parked out in the driveway. Hospital security directed them into a back hallway and toward the rear entrance.

"How long were you in jail?" asked Dave.

"About a week."

"That's it? A week? I should be as lucky!"

He should be as lucky? What's that supposed to mean?

"It was quite a week."

They continued down a long hallway, through some double doors and out onto a loading dock. There was a warm breeze blowing and the air smelled of the ocean. Pat breathed it in.

"Okay, the parking garage is right over there," said the hospital security guy. "Good luck to you."

They started down the steps.

"You want a smoke or somethin'?" Lester pulled out a pack of Kools. "That's the first thing I wanted when I got out."

When I got out? Out of what?

"No, thanks."

Pat looked around. There was a main street up the drive in the distance.

Okay, here we go…

Pat started down the drive toward the main street.

"Hey man, our car is this way, in the garage," said Dave.

"I'm not going with you."

"Oh shit, here we go," Lester said.

"You're not serious, right?" said Dave.

"Sorry to make you drive all the way down here."

"You know that as soon as you are out of our sight," Dave said, "we have to call probation and they issue an arrest warrant, right? And I really hate those fucks. Please don't make us do that."

"I'll take my chances."

"Patrick," Dave continued, "don't do it man. You will end up with your original sentence plus a violation. Believe me, I know. You'll do a year in county and then your full sentence. It's not worth it, man. This is your chance to get your life right and help a few others in the process. Give our program a chance."

Get my life right...Fuck, do all these people read from the same script?

"I'll be fine. See you guys later." Patrick turned his back and started walking. Dave called out after him. "Patrick, this program will save your life. We care about you, man."

"You're paid to care about me."

"Paid? Shit, we're drug addicts just like you."

Pat stopped. "I'm not a drug addict."

"Then we're *partiers* just like you. Call it what you want."

"So, you are recovered guys that became counselors, right? You're the worst kind."

"Dude, you got us fucked up!" Lester chimed in, "We ain't counselors. There ain't any counselors. Our program is run by the residents. We're all fuckin' dope fiends!"

Run by the residents? That can't be true...

"You're thinking it can't be true," Dave said, "but it is. Patrick, everyone in the program has one thing in common – we're all sick of the bullshit that goes along with using dope. You really need to just give us a chance, bro, you got nothing to lose. The doors aren't locked. You don't like it, you can leave anytime."

Leave anytime? That can't be right either...

"Look," Dave continued, "what we do know is that if you walk away right now, you'll be caught and you'll catch a violation. You'll do your time. If you come with us, you can scope out the place and stay if you like or leave if you like. It's a win/ win for you. So come on, let's go."

Pat stared at the ground.

Fuck, what do I do? I don't want to go...why can't Chris be here...

"You don't understand," Pat yelled back to Dave. "I just lost my best friend. We were going to do this together. I can't do this without him."

"Do it without him? Shit, you should be doing it *for* him."

Pat began to cry again. He'd been an emotional wreck; a side effect of sudden sobriety. He wiped his nose. Dave started up the driveway toward Pat. "Bro, I won't lie to you – this is going to be the toughest thing you've ever done. But you're going to do it. And it is worth it. You're worth it. Now let's go."

Just then a guy with a camera ran down the drive, snapping pictures and hollering Pat's name. Pat turned. He got in between Pat and Dave.

"Patrick, just a few questions…Please…"

Pat turned and tried to walk around the guy toward Dave and Lester.

"Patrick, what was that you were saying about rehab? What happened to you in jail? How bad were you hurt?"

"I can't talk to you right now."

The guy jumped right in Pat's path.

"Come on, Patrick, give me something. Are you going to rehab? Why were you crying back there?"

"Leave me alone, man. I can't talk to you right now."

He stepped in front of Pat, bumping into him. Another reporter was rounding the corner with a tape recorder in his hand, followed by another.

"Come on man, are you going to rehab?"

"Listen, motherfucker," Lester said as he spun the reporter around to look him in the face, "you're going to be going to rehab for your broken motherfuckin' bones if you don't back the fuck off!" Lester shoved the guy to the ground. "Now get the fuck out of here!"

The reporter scrambled to his feet and backed his way toward the corner of the building, snapping pictures as he retreated. The stampede of paparazzi was slowed by what they'd witnessed but not deterred. Lester grabbed Pat's arm, and the three of them ran into the parking garage.

"Thanks man," Pat said to Lester.

"That's how we do it at Recovery Street. Watch out for my new brother."

"So, we're all cool?" said Dave, "You're giving us a chance?"

"Yeah, I'm giving you a chance."

Though Pat didn't smoke much, he bummed one before getting into the car.

EIGHTEEN

THEY EXITED THE Hollywood Freeway at Vermont Avenue in Los Angeles. The air was hot and heavy and the evening sky was turning a dull auburn. The smell of Los Angeles permeated the car's A/C unit.

As they pulled into the driveway of the facility, Pat had to squint due to the amount of light emitting from the marquis bulbs under the awning. The building was huge and immaculate. Pat was reminded of Las Vegas.

"Well, here we are," said Dave, "Home sweet home."

"This is it?"

"Yup. Not bad, huh?"

"No. Not bad. I thought this wasn't a celebrity place. How much is this costing me?"

"Not a dime, my friend."

"Who pays for it? The government?"

"We're self-supporting."

"Self-supporting? What does that mean?"

"You'll find out soon enough."

They walked in through the glistening automatic glass doors into a huge marble atrium with a fountain in the center. A man in a tie and jacket sat behind a big marble counter staring into a computer screen.

This can't be it…this is a hotel…

They walked up to the front desk.

"What's up Dave," the guy behind the desk said. "This our newest addition?"

"I'm Pat. Patrick Pearson." Pat reached out and shook the man's hand.

"Nice to meet you, Patrick. I like your band."

"Thanks, man."

"Not too often we get celebrities here."

"I'm just like anyone else, bro."

"We'll see...Go ahead and have a seat on that bench over there. Somebody will be with you shortly."

"Shouldn't I contact somebody about getting my things here?

"You won't need anything."

"Well, I'm gonna need my clothes and toiletries, right?"

"Nope."

"Well, I'll definitely need some cash, right?"

"Nope. You're money's no good here."

What is that supposed to mean?

"Just have a seat on that bench."

The man again pointed to a hard wooden bench just to the left of the desk.

"Okay, sure."

Pat sat down and looked around. There was a tremendous amount of activity going on, none of which seemed to be recovery related as far as he could tell. Crews of people were cleaning the atrium, well-dressed business people were walking back and forth looking at paperwork and carrying clipboards, and more people were out on the veranda sitting at tables having discussions. People barely made eye contact as they scurried about like they were all in a huge hurry.

This can't be the rehab...these people seem like they're at work...

The cleaning crews worked their way through the entire atrium, scrubbing every surface. The place sparkled.

Must be the hotel staff...Maybe the rehab is part of the hotel...

Minutes passed and then tens of minutes. Pat became uncomfortable on the hard bench.

What is going on? Do they know I'm here?

He walked up to the front desk.

"Excuse me, who am I supposed to see? Do they know who I am?"

"Have a seat sir, they'll be with you shortly."

"Can you call them?"

"Have a seat, sir."

Pat sat back down. An hour had passed.

This is bullshit...Where are these people? What kind of rehab is this? I should just walk out of here...

He walked over to the front desk again.

"Excuse me, what is going on?"

"Have a seat sir, they'll be with you shortly."

"Dude, you've been saying that for an hour and a half!"

"They will be here, sir. Please be patient."

Pat sat back down.

Fuck this...I'm outta here...

He eyeballed the doors.

I can't leave...I'll go to prison...I gotta give this a chance...

It had been nearly two hours.

Dammit, what the hell is going on?

Totally frustrated, he put his head back and closed his eyes.

"Mr. Pearson?"

Finally... "Yes, I'm him..."

Pat turned to find himself facing a small, balding white man with a fuzzy gray mustache and glasses, and the biggest black man he'd ever seen off a football field.

"Hi, Patrick, I'm Bill, and this is Kittridge."

"Bill? Like Big Book Bill?" Pat offered, making a feeble attempt at some AA humor.

Bill looked at Kittridge.

"Hardly. You want to follow us please?"

They walked around the corner and into a small room. The room consisted of a sofa and a small high-backed chair. There was a small coffee table between them with a box of Kleenex on it.

"Have a seat, Mr. Pearson." Bill motioned to the chair and shut the door.

"Well, Patrick, you already passed our first test, sitting on that bench."

They left me there on purpose?

"That bench tells us a lot, Patrick. It tells us that you want to be here, it tells us that you have patience, and it tells us that you aren't stupid enough to leave. You do want to be here, right?"

"Yes."

"Good. Let me tell you about this room. This room is called the Vatican. It's sacred ground. Hopefully, this will be the only time you ever have to come in here, but chances are it won't be."

Pat had no clue what this man was talking about.

"Let me ask you something, Patrick," Kittridge started. "Why are you here?"

"To get my life right and help some other people along the way?"

Kittridge laughed. He laughed hard. "Sounds good, Pearson! Help some other people! Sounds real good! Where'd you come up with that? Your attorney tell you to say that shit? Someone you know that's in recovery somewhere? Sure didn't come out of your sorry-ass little brain!"

Pat sat quietly.

"The correct answer would be 'to complete my probation and avoid going to prison.'"

What's with these guys?

"I'm sorry?"

"Listen rock star, the act stops here. Nobody in their right mind goes to rehab to help other people and most don't even go to help themselves, especially when they've got some money, as I'm bettin' your ass does. Your money's no good here. So you can drop the fuckin' act. You're here for selfish reasons – we already know that. Don't try to kid yourself or us, Patrick."

"Look, I was just trying to…"

"Impress us? Don't try to impress anybody here, you can't. What you will do, however, is leave whoever you thought you were at the muthafuckin' door, because you ain't that person no more. What you are is a lowlife, scumbag drug addict just like the rest of us. You get that shit, rock star?"

"I…I guess…"

"Good. It'll be a lot easier if you do."

Bill stepped in. "Here's the deal, Patrick. We ask only two things of you. We ask that you do whatever we ask of you and that you trust our system. Can you do that, Patrick?"

"Whatever you ask?"

"That's right. Whatever we ask of you. This is important Patrick. If you can't do that, you might as well leave now."

Well, I guess they probably tell everyone that comes in here the same thing…

"Okay, I'll do whatever you ask. And I'll trust the system."

"Good. We've got three rules, Patrick. No drugs, no violence and no threats of violence. Break any of those rules, you're gone. Out the door. Everything else here is a guideline. Understand?"

"I think so."

Kittridge took over. "I hope so. Now let me give you a warning about one guideline — seein's how you were a rock star and all that — it might help if I spell something out for you right now. Do not fuck with any of the women. You may not have physical contact with any woman, including your significant other if you have one, for at least the first four months of your stay. Do you understand that?"

They're fuckin' kidding, right?

"Four months?"

"I may as well tell you now that you ain't having contact with *anyone* from the outside world for three months. Not your girl, not your mama, nobody. Not your fuckin' goldfish. Do you understand that?"

"How can I not talk to anyone? That's crazy, what if I need something? In fact, I need to call my manager and my agent. I need to sort some things out before I'm admitted in."

"Call my muthafuckin' *agent*?" Kittridge mocked sarcastically. "Don't you worry; we got everything you need here."

"Don't you think three months is an awful long time? What about my family?"

"Shit...You've dissed them so many times they won't even notice you're gone." Kittridge turned to Bill. "I love these muthafuckas. They go into rehab and all of a sudden they act like they're used to calling their mamas every night!" He laughed and turned back to Pat. "But if you really want to make a call there's a pay phone down the street at Denny's...Go ahead and handle your business, rock star. But you better make your next call to your probation officer."

What kind of mind games are these guys playing? They're worse than the cops...

"I'm not sure I'm clear on what are you saying..."

"We're saying that you are already in. You're here. There will be no outside contact, no drugs, and no women. That's it. We own you now. Do you understand *that*?"

"Look, I..."

"Either you do or you don't. It's very simple. The door is right out there. I'm sure the probation department would be more than happy to put you back in jail where they can actually make some money off you. Please, feel free..."

Kittridge motioned to the door.

Pat was a nervous wreck. He wanted to leave, but he couldn't. These guys had him going out of his mind.

"Look, okay...I'll do what you say. I'll go with it. I understand."

“Well, all right then! Welcome to Recovery Street. Go ahead and strip down.”

“What?”

“It’s a precaution,” said Bill, “same as jail. If you do what we ask of you, this will be the last time you ever have to do this.”

Pat stripped down and was thoroughly searched by the two men. It was equally as humiliating as the last time.

“Okay,” said Bill, “get dressed and let’s get you to the barber shop.”

“Barbershop? For what?”

“Gotta lose them golden locks,” Kittridge laughed.

Pat had had long hair since he was about ten years old. In fact, he had not even trimmed his hair in over five years. He believed it was the key to his rock star image, and that it gave him power. He crossed his arms like a defiant child.

“No way.”

“What do you mean, no way?”

“No way, I’m not cutting my hair. It isn’t necessary. I’ve always had it long.”

“Well, guess what? It’s time for a much-needed change.”

“Not happening. Doesn’t have anything to do with recovery. Not gonna happen.”

Bill looked at Kittridge.

“I can’t believe this shit is starting already. This one’s going to be a pain in the ass. Do you want to tell him, Kit?”

“I’d love to.” Kittridge turned to Pat. “Patrick, this is the last time for a long time that anyone is going to know you as a rock star. You said you would do anything we asked of you, and you’re going to drop the muthafuckin’ bullshit rock star image! *Now get the fuck into the barber shop and sit in the fuckin’ chair!*”

Startled at the tone and volume of Kittridge’s voice, and the proximity in which he stood, Pat stood up and walked with them to the small barbershop. He reluctantly sat in one of the chairs.

"Okay," Bill laughed, "will that be a number one, two, or three?"

"Just get it over with."

He watched in horror as Bill sheared off his precious locks. Long lengths of hair fell to the floor in bunches.

"Look on the bright side, Patrick, think of all the money you'll save on conditioner."

Pat did not laugh.

"Well, there you go. What do ya think?" Bill spun him around to look in the mirror. "I think you look a little like a light bulb with ears from behind."

Kittridge again laughed heartily. Pat was sickened.

"All right," Bill said, "let's get you upstairs."

They walked down a long carpeted hallway to an elevator and ascended to the fourth floor, where they entered a locked room. The room was full of piles and piles of used clothing. It looked like a garage sale.

"Have a seat, Patrick...What size waist are you?"

"Thirty-three."

"Better get you thirty-sixes; you'll probably gain some weight here."

Great. I'm gonna be fat and bald. That'll make for a great picture on our next CD...

Bill tossed him seven pairs of underwear, and seven pairs of pants.

"Can I get some different pants?" Pat asked, "these look like what somebody working at a gas station would wear."

"Sorry, man. You want better pants, you gotta wait."

"Wait how long?"

"Oh, about three months or so," Kittridge said, laughing his hearty and now annoying laugh.

They then tossed Pat seven of the ugliest shirts he'd ever seen. Some of them had holes in them. Pat was appalled.

"These shirts are faded and torn," he said.

"You ain't gonna be in any beauty contests," Kittridge laughed.

They went on to provide Pat with equally crappy shoes and socks. Lastly, he was given a toothbrush. Pat packed it all into a black plastic trash bag.

"You hungry, Patrick?" Kittridge asked as they rode the elevator back down to the first floor. "Need anything to drink? Smokes? Anything like that?"

"Not really…"

"Getcha food and drink while you can. Lights out is in half an hour."

They walked down the hallway to another elevator, this one taking them further downstairs. They stopped by a linen closet for bedding on their way to room 110. They walked into the room, which consisted of a small bathroom with a tub and three beds. Each bed had its own nightstand and reading lamp. There was a large etched glass mirror hanging over a chest of drawers and a huge picture window looking out into a garden.

Not bad…I've stayed in hotels that were much worse…

"Where's the mini-bar?" Pat joked.

"I'm glad you got a sense of humor," Kittridge said, "because you're gonna need it. Sure you don't want to go upstairs for something to eat or drink?"

"No, I'm cool…I'll just chill here."

"Suit yourself. Be on the floor to serve breakfast by six."

Six? I haven't gotten up at six in about ten years…

"How will I wake up?"

"Don't worry; your dorm leader will get you up."

Dorm leader?

"Well, Patrick," said Bill, "welcome home."

They left, closing the door behind them.

Pat stood up and looked into the big mirror. His buzz cut was so short that it made him look almost bald. The lines on his pale face seemed more pronounced, and the dark rings under his eyes were almost purple.

I used to be Patrick Pearson – now I'm Uncle Fester...

He looked down at his bright blue polyester pants with a hole in one knee, and his stained used-to-be-white T-shirt. He had a bandage on one side of his head, and another around his right arm, not to mention the miscellaneous scrapes and bruises. He looked like a homeless man. He stepped back and lay down on his mattress, reflecting on the last two weeks of his life.

How the fuck did all this happen?

Without making up his bed, he cried himself to sleep.

♪♪♪

"Hey, wake up man!"

Pat rolled over and pulled the blanket over his head. The reading lamp above his head clicked on.

"Dude, you gotta get up, man!"

Pat peeked out from under the blanket.

"What time is it?"

"Five-thirty."

"You can't be serious."

"I'm your dorm leader. You want to shower before going up on the floor? That's why I gave you a half hour extra..."

"No, I'm good..."

"Okay, man. I'm going up. I like to be early. If I were you, I'd get in that habit too, because they don't tolerate lateness around here. Make sure you're in the dining room by six, bro. Just take the elevator up to one, walk down the hall and past the atrium area, and you'll run right into the dining room. Cool?"

"Yeah, cool."

"Okay, man. See you at breakfast."

Pat rolled over and went back to sleep.

♪♪♪

Kittridge yanked on the blanket, causing Pat to roll off the bed and onto the floor.

"What the fuck, man?"

"Get the fuck out of bed goddammit!" Kittridge threw the blanket back down on top of Pat. Pat scrambled to his feet holding the blanket in front of him.

"Geez, I'm sorry, man. Don't I get a little slack? It's my first day…"

"You'll get a little slack in three months or so. Now getcha fuckin' clothes on and brush your fuckin' teeth. It's time for work."

Work? What is this shit?

"Are you going to watch me?"

"Yeah, I'm going to watch you."

Kittridge watched Pat get ready and escorted him onto the main floor and into the dining room. It had a huge high ceiling and giant windows that looked out over a freeway below. There were probably twenty or thirty tables that workers were frantically wiping down. It looked more like a restaurant or cafeteria than any rehab dining room. Pat guessed once again that it must be part of the hotel. Looking around he felt a little tinge of hunger. Kittridge walked him up to a guy holding a clipboard who was leaning on one of the tables. Kittridge pulled a suit jacket off one of the chairs and worked into it, then began to put on a tie.

"Here you go Mario…he's all yours. I gotta go. This muthafucka's made *me* late for work."

Kittridge turned to Pat. "I'll deal with you after work. Have a nice day."

He hurried off leaving Pat facing the guy holding the clipboard. He was of medium build, with a dark complexion and short, spiky black hair. He looked Pat up and down.

"Have a seat, Patrick. I'm Mario."

"Sure." They both sat down.

"Let me explain a couple of things to you. Get you oriented a bit."

"That'd be nice…"

"You are on what we call the maintenance crew. We keep the facility clean. We work from eight to five with two fifteen minute breaks and a one hour lunch, but you are also required to be on the floor at six AM because we also serve breakfast and clean the dining room immediately afterward. Same goes for lunch, dinner and ten o'clock snack time. All in all, you are putting in a good twelve-hour workday, six days a week. The other guys will help you get acquainted."

"What do you mean? I'm working for the hotel?"

"Patrick, there is no hotel. This is our home. You work for the foundation. We're a self-supporting, non-profit rehab center. The only one of its kind."

"So I just work all day? When do we have AA meetings and stuff?"

"We don't do twelve step bullshit. AA is for people who can't handle their lives without having a place to cry about how tough it is. That's not the way we operate. There's no church, no AA, no therapy, nothing to blame your addiction on, and no crutch to fall back on. We believe that when life gets tough, you get up and go to work anyway – like the real world does. And we don't believe in relapsing. You use drugs, get the fuck out. We don't need you. In fact, we don't believe that you are addicted, we believe that you are a lazy asshole who would rather avoid life's challenges by getting high than by dealing with reality. And, you've probably been doing it that way your entire adult life, at the expense of other people's feelings. Ask yourself how many people you've hurt. Think about it. This program is all you, bro, learning about who you are and becoming a responsible, practical, taxpaying member of the workforce who is considerate of others."

"Dude, it's not like I don't know how to work hard. I'm pretty successful."

"Yeah, and you came this close to pissing it all away. You're looking at prison, man. How successful is that? Let me ask you this… when is the last time you did anything, including a full day's work, without being high?"

Pat couldn't remember a time when he wasn't on something.

"I don't know…"

"Well, John and Mary Q. Public, the normal people out there who make their living legally, and buy your albums, do it without being high every day. That's what you need to be. You have any kids?"

"Yeah, one boy. He's great."

"How would you know if he's great or not? You ever see him straight?"

"No." Pat looked at the floor looking like he was going to cry.

"Hey, man, me neither. I was on drugs twenty-four seven."

"You're not a counselor?"

"Fuck no! I'm a dude who got here a couple of months before you."

"So now you are like, my boss?"

"Exactly. But I already went through everything you will, so I've got a little insight. That's how it works around here. People who have been here awhile help the newer guys. Dude, this place works wonders. Look at Kittridge. Armed robbery. Fuckin' crackhead. Now he pretty much runs the facility."

"Wow. You can run the facility after a few months? What, did he get voted in or something?"

Mario laughed. "Dude, he's been here for six years."

"Six years? Why?"

"He likes to give back. He likes it here and wants to save some lives before he leaves."

"This place is a trip."

"You don't even know. Okay, enough bullshitting. Time for work."

"Yeah, okay… but can I get some breakfast first?"

"You missed it. Sorry, you have to wait for lunch. Be on time tomorrow and you can eat. Now go grab that mop over there."

♪♪♪

Pat sat at the dinner table finishing up what proved to be one of the best meals he thought he'd ever had. At least the best he'd had in a few weeks. He rubbed his sore, tired feet. They'd been working all day; cleaning, mopping, raking leaves in the garden, wiping windows; Pat was exhausted.

"So what happens after dinner?" Pat asked to a couple of fellow maintenance crew guys whose names he couldn't remember. One of them answered.

"We clean up the dining room real quick, then we go to a group session for two hours, then we get a little free time. There's a TV room and a library, pool, and ping-pong, or you can just go to bed early. That's what I usually do. Five-thirty comes pretty damn early!"

"I hear that."

Mario walked over to the table.

"Hey Patrick, I need you to come with me, bro."

"Okay."

They walked out through the atrium to the front desk.

"Have a seat on that bench."

The bench he was referring to was the same bench he sat on when he came in. Patrick got a bad feeling in his stomach.

"Why am I sitting here?"

"Just have a seat, bro; someone will be with you shortly."

Not this again…

Pat sat and waited. And waited. People were walking by in groups, laughing and talking. Pat waited. After a half hour or so, he could barely keep his eyes open.

This sucks... What the hell is going on?

He put his head in his hands and closed his eyes.

"Mista Pearson!"

Startled, Pat looked up. Kittridge.

"Follow me, Pearson…"

They walked around the corner into the Vatican room. Pat took a seat in the uncomfortable high-backed chair. Bill was also waiting.

"Well Patrick, looks like we're off to a rocky start."

Pat sat silent.

Kittridge started in. "Look muthafucka, you're to be on the floor for work at six! You understand?"

"Yes."

"You better understand. We don't tolerate this bullshit! You ain't getting special celebrity treatment! There ain't no fashionably late around here! Get the fuck out of bed when your dorm leader tells you! You got that?"

"Yes."

"Good. You got two hours extra duty."

"What does that mean?"

"It means while all of your peers are sleeping or watching TV, you are going to be wiping windows. Now get the fuck out of here and go to your group."

♪♪♪

"Hey, we got a new guy in our group."

There were about twenty people circled in chairs around the perimeter of a plain white room.

"Anyone want to explain the rules of the group to the newbie?"

"I got it…" a guy said, "Stay seated while the group is on you, and keep your hands in your lap. That's it."

What kind of rules are those?

"Okay then, let's talk to the new guy," said a tall, ugly guy with sleeved arms. "What's your name, bro?"

Doesn't anyone recognize me? Do I look that fucked up with this haircut?"

"I'm Pat. Patrick Pearson. From Blacklist."

"Yeah, I heard you were here…"

Somebody else said, "You're Patrick Pearson? Damn brother, you're a fuckin' mess. You sure don't look like that in your videos!"

"Thanks a lot," Pat said, "but I don't really feel like sharing…if you guys want to give somebody else a chance."

"He doesn't feel like sharing!" Everyone laughed. "Well, *Patrick Pearson of Blacklist,* I guess you don't really know how the groups work around here, do ya?"

"I just got here last night."

"Well then, let us introduce you to the group. Tell us how you got here, and don't be shy about it."

"I don't know… We were just trying to score something to party with, and things got out of hand. I got arrested and was sentenced to this program."

"Wow, sounds simple. You didn't hurt anyone, right? In fact, you're pretty much a victim of circumstance, huh?"

"Pretty much."

"You know what dude, you better wake up. I've seen dickheads like you come in and out of here over and over. Rock star life, right? Because you're a fuckin' rock star, you think you are above the law? Fuck you, punk!"

Pat was stunned. He was unable to speak.

"Yeah," Somebody else chimed in. "I can see your arrogant bitch-ass attitude coming a mile away. Your mommy probably told you that you were special, huh? You're just a victim, right?"

People began laughing. Pat was frozen.

"So, you get in too deep, rock star? Couldn't handle what went along with the party anymore? What a fuckin' pussy!"

I don't deserve this... "Hey, I just got into some trouble."

"You got any family, rock star, you a daddy?"

"Yes."

"When's the last time you were there for them, you piece of shit? I bet you choose your fuckin' drugs over anything! You probably see your kid high on shit! Real nice example, dickhead! Here's a pop quiz, asshole, how many lives have you destroyed so far?"

Pat was quiet.

"Hey, anyone buttfuck you in jail, pretty boy? You did go to jail, right? Or did they send you to a women's jail?"

The room roared with laughter.

"I don't really want to talk about jail."

"Whoa, the rock star did get buttfucked! They grab you by your hippie hair and ride you like this?" The guy talking made motions of wrapping hair around his wrist and gyrated his hips like he was having sex doggy style. The room was in stitches. Pat felt sick.

Why are these people talking to me this way? They don't even know me! "You know, I lost a friend in there. You guys might want to cut me a little slack."

"Oh gee, we're real sorry, we don't want to upset you... What happened? You get him killed cause of some stupid scheme you cooked up? Some easy dope score?"

Pat began to cry. Nobody had ever talked to him in this way. *They can't talk to me like this...fuck this...* He began to stand up.

"Sit down!" The whole room yelled in unison. "We're not done with you yet, asshole! Go ahead, cry like a little bitch! Damn, we hurt his feelings!"

"You people are unbelievable," Pat sobbed. "You take everything from me, cut off my hair and strip me of my identity, then sit there demeaning me."

"Waaaah!!"

Pat began to get angry.

"You people don't fuckin' know me. Nobody's ever talked to me like this, and you can't either! I'm a fuckin' rock star."

The room erupted in laughter.

"He's a rock star!"

People were hooting and hollering.

"Damn baby," said a fat black woman that was missing some teeth, "I still think you're sexy, Mista Rock Star! Specially when you get all hot and bothered like that!"

The laughter was uncontrollable. People were falling out of their seats. The assumed leader of the group caught his breath.

"Whoa, okay, okay everyone…that's enough on the new guy. Patrick, go ahead and take five. Mario, go with him. Whoo, that was awesome. All right who's next?"

Pat and Mario walked down the hallway and outside onto the veranda. Pat walked up to a railing and leaned on it, wiping his eyes.

"Was all that shit really necessary?" he sobbed. "I'm not staying here. Nobody talks to me like that."

"Patrick, you have to understand something, none of that was personal. We don't have traditional therapy here, Pat. They're going to beat you up and tear you down my friend, and in the process, thoughts and emotions will surface that you need to think about and confront."

"A little empathy would be nice."

"You'd be surprised just how much empathy was behind everything you just heard. What you're looking for is sympathy; someone to feel sorry for you. We've all been where you are and worse. We know what you are going through.

All those career recovery assholes out there that go from one rehab to another – it's because they still can't deal with reality without crying to somebody constantly, or worse, using drugs. Around here you get beat down, and you deal with it. And if your head is fucked up over it, somebody reminds you that it's not that serious in the grand scheme of things, then kicks you in the ass and tells you to get up and go to work."

"You guys are pretty ruthless."

"Once you get to know everyone, you'll be ruthless with them, and they'll be even worse with you. Then afterward, you'll have a cup of coffee and a couple of laughs together. Everything about you is out there on the table, and they won't have anything left to tease you about, and you will have nothing to hide. It's very liberating. It will be all in your past. At the end of the day, you'll be tough, and you'll learn to deal with life as a grown up without the help of AA, or a therapist, or drugs. Does that make any sense?"

"I guess so."

"It's a trip, but it works. I can't tell you how, but it does."

"How long have you been here?"

"Just under six months, but I'm going to stay longer."

"Have you gotten in any serious trouble here?"

"Hell, yeah."

"What happened?"

"Did my extra duty and moved on. A lot of hours. Hundreds."

"Damn."

"Patrick, you're supposed to get in trouble. People in the real world fuck up all the time; they have challenges. But they deal with them instead of using dope. You'll be able to do that too, but you have to re-learn life. That's why you face your challenges in here where there are no drugs, and practice it before you return to the outside world."

"Sounds logical."

"Believe me, you give it a few months here, and not only will you not need drugs anymore, you won't be able to imagine life any other way. You'll be hopping up out of bed early in the morning ready to seize the day."

"I'll believe that when I see it."

Seriously bro, you'll learn how to work without it, party without it, fuck without it, everything! And you won't be able to imagine how you used to get through life *on* it. For you, wow...you'll probably be twice the musician you were. Your career will soar."

"That sounds good. Hey, what were you into out there?"

"Sometime you and I will share that stuff, but not here. We don't tell war stories here, we only look forward."

"Gotcha."

"You cool now? Let's go back to that group. And you tell those assholes just how fucked *they* are."

"You got it, man. Thanks."

After the group ended, Pat spent two hours wiping windows in the atrium for his tardiness, during which time he was forbidden to talk to anyone. His head was full of thoughts about Christine and Tommy, his parents, his band and career, Tina...and Chris. Thoughts he had a lot of difficulty getting out of his head.

He checked in with Mario as the second hour finally passed.

"It's midnight bro, I'm done."

"Cool. You okay, Pat?"

"Yeah."

"All right then, goodnight. See you tomorrow."

"Night."

Pat was slowly working his way across the atrium area toward the elevator when he heard something. It was music. Not like on the radio or TV, but definitely some form of live music. Somebody was playing a guitar. He changed course and followed the sound to a black guy who was sitting on a chair plinking at the strings of a beat up old Taylor.

"Oh, hey…you wanna play? I was going down to bed anyway." The guy handed Pat the guitar.

"Sure. Thanks, man."

Pat set the guitar on his leg and strummed. He checked the tuning and intonation. It was workable. After a little fine-tuning it sounded pretty good. A few people gathered around. Pat played and sang; much to the enjoyment of the small audience. They joined in and sang along to the familiar tunes until they were too tired to sing anymore. For the first time in weeks, maybe months, Pat's troubles seemed to fade. At least for the moment.

♪♪♪

Pat looked at the clock.

6:57? Oh fuck…

He jumped out of bed, threw his clothes and shoes on and ran for the elevator. He charged down the hall through the atrium and into the dining room, where the rest of his crew were already hard at work serving breakfast to other residents.

"Mario, I'm sorry bro! I don't think the alarm went off. My roommate said he was going to set it!"

Pat's dorm leader walked by going the other direction, chiming in without breaking stride. "I woke you at five-thirty, and you went back to sleep! It's on you brother!"

Shit…

"Well," said Mario, you missed your breakfast again. Come with me."

They walked over to the bench.

"Have a seat, Pat."

You gotta be fuckin' kidding…

Pat sat down and waited.

"Word has it that you were up putting on a little concert 'till three AM last night..."

Damn, was it that late?

"I'm sorry Kittridge, I just lost track of time. It won't happen again."

"Goddamn right it won't happen again, cause if I catch you touching or even looking at that guitar, you'll be wiping windows for six months."

"Wait, why, what does the guitar have to do with anything?"

"That's your comfort zone. It's an escape for you. You're not gonna escape shit."

"Come on, man..."

"Come on nothing. And, Mr. Pearson, you can start your four hours of extra duty tonight after work."

"Four hours?"

"Wanna go for eight? Be late again."

Fuck...

"Now go get to work."

Pat's day dragged on. And on. That night after he did his extra duty, he went straight to bed. With no escape from himself.

♪♪♪

"Hey, Patrick, come in here! You gotta see this!"

Pat had managed to roll out of bed half an hour early this morning and was on his way to the dining room to grab a cup of coffee before work. He wasn't planning on being late again. He altered his course and poked his head into the TV room at the request of the person calling out to him. "Check it out, bro!" said the guy, pointing to the TV.

"Welcome back to Good Day L.A.," said news anchor Steve Edwards, *"Jillian will have weather in a few minutes, but right now let's go to Dorothy Lucey who as usual has all sorts of exciting news in the world of entertainment. Dorothy?"*

"Thanks Steve. At the top of the list today, or we might want to call it the 'Black list', is rocker Patrick Pearson, who has apparently had quite a wild ride since the wrap-up of the band's spring tour, according to the new issue of Us Weekly. Pearson was not only arrested on drug charges in his hometown of San Diego but was reportedly directly involved in a riot at the San Diego jail that claimed the lives of two people. The Us Weekly article reports that Patrick was seriously injured and that his personal assistant and close friend Christopher Martinez was killed in the riot. The pictures you are seeing, which are courtesy of Us Weekly, were taken outside of Scripps Memorial Hospital in La Jolla, just north of San Diego. You can clearly see the bandages on Patrick's head and arms. The magazine also reports that Patrick was released from the hospital to an undisclosed drug treatment facility. The Blacklist camp has issued a statement saying that Patrick is in good shape and high spirits and that they are confident that he will be able to deal with his personal issues and be back in time to complete the band's new album, which is slated for Christmas release."

"Wow," responded co-anchor Jillian Barberie, *"I'm a big Patrick Pearson fan! Did you say his personal assistant was killed?"*

"That's been confirmed. Two people were killed including his friend, and our local affiliate in San Diego, XETV has also confirmed that the riot was caused by a gang member who attacked Patrick."

"Does anyone know which rehab he is in?"

"No, according to the magazine, they're keeping it very hush-hush."

"Well, my heart goes out to Patrick," said Jillian *"If you're listening, Patrick, get better soon!"*

Everyone in the TV room turned and looked at Pat. He was embarrassed.

"Love ya Patrick," agreed Dorothy, *"And good luck! Next when we come back, pop princess Britney Spears receives two Grammy nominations..."*

Without saying a word, Pat backed out of the TV room and resumed his trip to get coffee.

♪♪♪

Carlos picked his phone up and answered. "Bueno?"

"The rock star is in rehab."

"How do you know this?"

"It's on the television. Where are you?"

"Tijuana."

"Channel eight."

"Canale ocho! Ahora!" Carlos bellowed across the grimy bar.

The bartender jumped up and put the TV on channel eight from San Diego.

"New information obtained by News Eight reports that the riot at the downtown jail last Monday night was reportedly started when a known gang member attacked rock star Patrick Pearson of the band Blacklist, who was reportedly being held in custody on drug charges. Pearson's personal friend Christopher Martinez of East County was killed, as was gang member Eduardo Espinosa, although the actual causes of both deaths are still under investigation."

"I'll tell you how he was killed! That fucking rock star killed him!"

"Pearson was moved to Scripps La Jolla and released a few days later to an addiction treatment center that has yet to be disclosed. Mr. Pearson was the subject of a recent article by Us Weekly, which reports that he is in good condition and high spirits."

Carlos slammed his fist down on the table, causing the drinks to spill.

"That fucking puto has caused the deaths of two of my men! I want him fucking dead!" He looked at the other men around the table. "You find him and kill him! I want his fucking head!"

NINETEEN

TINA RAN AS fast as she could. It was difficult — her legs felt heavy — as if she was running in quicksand. She could see the doors in the distance down the long corridor, but no matter how hard she ran they seemed to get further and further away, to the point of disappearing into a fog. She couldn't breathe. She felt a hand pulling on the back of her blouse. She was pulled backward and fell, hitting the back of her head on the hard concrete floor. She tried to roll into the fetal position, but her pursuer had control of both her wrists. She kicked, but it turned out to be futile. Carlos jumped on top of her and slammed both her wrists to the floor.

"You're going to like this, puta..." he snarled.

He withdrew his knife and cut through Tina's blouse exposing her breasts. She tried to hit him, but her arms would not move. She tried to scream, but her mouth would not open. She could hear her voice inside her head, but she could not form words.

Carlos placed the blade across her neck.

"Die, puta."

She worked up everything she had and let out a loud shriek. Carlos stood up as the fog became darkness, forming all around him and engulfing him. She was confused; it was like the shadows came alive and swept him up. She screamed again as the darkness began to submerge her like rising water.

"Tina!" exclaimed her roommate Jenny. "Tina, wake up!"

Tina sat up in her bed, gasping for breath. She was shaking and disoriented.

"Tina, it's Jenny," she said in a soothing tone as she put her hand on Tina's arm. "You're fine. You're at California Ranch. It was just a dream."

"Oh my God, Jenny," she sobbed, "when are these dreams going to stop?"

"It's okay, T, it will just take time. You will be fine. It's a process."

"I know. It just sucks," Tina said as she regained her composure. "What time is it?"

"It's time to get up anyway. Let's get ready for breakfast. It looks like it is going to be a beautiful day."

It was a beautiful day, and the California Ranch Christian Recovery Center was a beautiful place. Nestled back in the hills of east San Diego County, the ranch was as pretty as a postcard. The grounds featured several small buildings with six private rooms each. In the center was a huge flagstone courtyard, shadowed by two huge oak trees and flanked by the great room and cafeteria on one side, and the chapel on the other. All the buildings were of a rustic feel; huge beams and natural wood created a relaxing setting. There were large lawns, stables, and a huge pasture, where two horses were playing and rolling on the ground.

Tina considered herself very lucky to be accepted – California Ranch was exclusive. Her faith in God as a child had helped her find the right words to convince the interviewers that the program was right for her. She was very serious about her recovery and her connection with God. Her progress had been exemplary.

She and her roommate walked across the courtyard and into the great room, where other residents were enjoying breakfast. They got their food from the buffet and sat down with Pastor Mike.

Pastor Mike was a kind man in his late forties. He was in very good shape. He wore wire-rimmed glasses and had a touch of gray around his sideburns, giving him a scholarly look. He had been running the program for over ten years. Not only was he a dedicated man of the church, he was also very educated, and had a gift for helping people struggling with addiction.

"Good morning ladies," welcomed Pastor Mike. "You sleep okay?"

Jenny looked at Tina. Tina gave her back a sarcastic stare.

"I slept fine until morning," Tina offered.

Jenny looked at her again.

"Okay..." Tina continued, "Pastor Mike, I cannot seem to get free of the dreams. I woke up screaming again this morning." She began to tear up. "It's really hard… I don't know what to do."

"Tina," Pastor Mike said, "Come with me…"

Tina and Pastor Mike finished eating and walked out to the stables. They saddled up two horses as Pastor Mike probed about the dreams, clearly theorizing that there was some trauma that Tina was dealing with.

"Tina, what brought you to the Lord when you were young?"

Tina looked uncomfortable. "I don't know…my parents were churchgoing people."

"Why do you get anxious when I ask? Is there more to it than your parents taking you to church?"

"No, not really."

They mounted their horses and led them along a trail to a small stream, continuing the conversation along the way.

"What was your dream about this morning?"

Now she felt very uncomfortable. "I'm a little uncomfortable talking about it."

"So, don't tell me. Tell Jesus."

"This feels like confession."

"Does it? Because it feels to me like we are just horseback riding."

Tina laughed a little.

"Tina, the only reason I do what I do, is that I feel like Jesus works through me. I do not judge. I am here to help. Jesus is here to help."

They stopped by the stream for the horses to drink. There was a hitching post near the water, and they tied off the horses and sat under a shade tree. The air was warm, and the sun reflected on the water. Tina felt relaxed.

"It was about a drug dealer," Tina offered. "He was chasing me."

"Was it a memory or a situation you went through in the past?"

"Not really… you know, dreams are strange."

"A place you recognized?"

"No, I was somewhere else. A long corridor. With doors at the end. I couldn't reach them."

"What kind of doors? What did they look like?"

"They were double doors with windows. Like you'd find it a school…" Tina stopped. She remembered. She began to cry.

"Tina, are you okay?"

"It was my school," she sobbed. "A boy tried to rape me there. He chased me down that hall… he was killed… I feel like it was my fault."

"The drug dealer?"

"No, this was when I was a child. The drug dealer is the reason I ended up in rehab."

"I suspect the drug dealer *isn't* the reason."

"My dreams are all mixed up," Tina wept. "The kid was hit by a car while chasing me. I felt that God did it to him… for me."

"Tina, you are carrying a lot of burden for what happened in the past. Your past is behind you. Gone. It is simply imagination at this point. Because it is not real. Nobody can change it, nobody can make it go away, but it is irrelevant. It's only the future that matters. Feeling guilt is a waste of time. Especially for something you have no control over. And the drug dealer? That's your former life."

"I suppose."

"Tina, I want you to close your eyes. Relax your body. Feel the sun on your face. Let your shoulders fall limp. Relax."

She did as instructed. She felt calm.

"Imagine a door. A huge, thick wooden door. On the side you are on, is this day. The stream, the sunshine, green grass, blue sky. Calmness. On the other side of the door are all your fears and nightmares. You can see them churning. The drug dealer, the rapist, drugs, death, fire, darkness. Close the door. Bolt it shut. You are a new creature in Christ. You are reborn. Your life is fresh, new and alive. You believe in yourself, and you feel the power of the Lord. The door is closed. Never to be reopened."

Tina imagined.

"Now you walk away. The door fades. The further you walk away, the more it disappears into the distance. It is gone. All you see is blue sky and green fields where the door was. Jesus has removed your past. Jesus has removed your sins. You are new."

Tina smiled. She felt reborn.

"Tina, from this day forward, the Lord's light is in you. You are brilliant. You are beautiful. You are unstoppable."

"Yes, I am."

♪♪♪

Kittridge poked his head into the room. "Hey guys, got a couple of new people joining your group tonight." He motioned for the two new residents to come in and join the group.

"This is Julie Eisenberg and Kerry Parker."

Holy shit! Kerry!

Pat began to get up to hug Kerry but thought the better of it.

Knowing this place, they'll have some stupid rule about us knowing each other...

Pat decided to stay in his seat. Kerry didn't recognize him immediately due to his fabulous new haircut. He and the new girl found seats and sat down.

"Well," said the group leader, "no sense in wasting any time; let's talk to the newbies. So Kerry, what's your story?"

Pat felt bad for Kerry. He knew what was coming.

"You mean like what did I do to get here?"

"Yeah."

"Assault and armed robbery, twice. Tried to run from the cops. Did a couple of minutes in the State Pen. Got a few strikes."

"You say that like you're proud of it."

"I've been around the block a few times."

"So you think you're some kind of fuckin tough guy because you can scare people with a gun? That make you a tough guy? What you are is a fuckin' pussy that *hides* behind a gun!"

"Excuse me?" said Kerry, totally flabbergasted at what he was hearing.

"There *is* no excuse for a fuckin' loser like you, tough guy! Look at all your stupid jailhouse tats and shit… Are you tryin' to look scary? Ooooh! You think you're scary? The only thing scary about you is the fact that you think you have some kind of right to do that shit to people. What gives you the right, anyway? What, was your daddy mean to you when you were a baby or something?"

"Don't talk to me about my father! You don't know me!"

"Ooooh, looks like we hit a nerve!" another guy chimed in.

"Poor baby, did your daddy hurt you? So now you get to take it out on normal people? Like the world owes you something for what happened to you when you were a little fucking kid? Fuck you, punk!"

"Fuck you, brother!" Kerry screamed. "What kind of fuckin' place is this? I don't have to sit here and listen to this!"

"Then jump out the window, pussy!"

The room began to chant. "*Jump, jump, jump.*"

"Oh, the big tough guy, he's a victim! Waaahh!"

Everyone joined in with the crying noises and began laughing at Kerry.

"Waaahh, waaahh, waaahh!"

Kerry finally recognized Pat, the only person who wasn't laughing. Kerry shot Pat a confused and questioning look. Pat did his best to let him know through subtle sign language that keeping his cool would be the best move, and Kerry seemed to understand.

"I don't know what kind of therapy you people are trying to run on me, but it's not working. You're just pissing me off," Kerry said.

"Oh, geez, are we pissing you off?" said another guy. "Are we pissing off the poor little victim in the big ol' tough guy body? Geez, we don't want to do that, he might get a gun and steal our watches!" The room began to roar with laughter. "You know, with that bald-ass head you kind of look like a big ugly Gerber baby with tattoos. Poor little Gerber baby…Waaahh!"

Kerry was speechless. Never since his father had anyone made him feel so low.

"Waaahh, my daddy hurt me! Waaahh, I never grew up! Waaahh! It's my daddy's fault I'm fucking *worthless*!"

Worthless?

That did it. Kerry was fuming. He began to stand up with the intention of hurting somebody. Pat jumped in front of him.

"Kerry, no, you can't get up!" Pat turned to the group leader. "Hey, he's had enough; let me take him outside for a break."

"You're right, Patrick. Go ahead, you guys take five."

Pat gave Kerry a shove toward the door and out into the hallway. Kerry stomped down the hall in silence; fists clenched and veins bulging out of his neck. Pat opened the glass doors, and they walked out onto the veranda.

"What is this fucking place, Pat?" Kerry said through his teeth, still shaking and breathing heavily.

"Relax, man, it's not personal, they do that to everyone, especially when you're new."

"It's fucking bullshit, brother. I'm gonna fucking smash somebody."

"No you aren't, bro. It's all good. It's their way of getting your emotions all heated up."

"Well, that part works."

"A lot of it works. This place is a trip. Hey, gimme a hug, man!"

They embraced.

"How long have you been here?"

Pat thought for a moment. "Shit…I guess it's been about three months!" he said with a big smile.

"No shit?"

"Yup. Wow. Time really does fly around here. And it does get better as time goes by. I'm doing pretty well now, unlike when I first got here. I had a little trouble acclimating to the program, but now I'm getting more privileges and stuff. I've even got requests in for visits and to play guitar again. I think they're going to let me!"

Kerry couldn't believe what was coming out of Pat's mouth, and the fervor with which it came.

"Privileges? Let you play guitar? What is this, some kind of grade school?"

Pat laughed. "Sometimes it feels that way. But it's all for a reason. You gotta trust the program."

"So I hear."

"Seriously dude, it's truly working for me. I feel like a new man."

"I don't know, brother. I'm not as mellow as you are. I'm not sure I can handle this shit."

"Kerry, I'm going to explain it to you, just like it was explained to me."

♪♪♪

"Patrick, come on in and have a seat."

Pat walked into the Vatican room and sat down.

"Lot nicer when you're not in trouble, right?" said Kittridge.

"Yes it is…"

"Well, Pearson, how do you feel about your stay so far?"

"I feel good about it."

"So do we," said Bill, pushing his glasses back up to the bridge of his nose. "We see a lot of changes in you. Good changes. And we think it's time for you to move up to the next level."

"I won't argue with you."

"I didn't think so," said Bill. "Patrick, you're off the maintenance crew. We're giving you a job. We think you've got some great communications skills – you have the gift of being a very easy person to like, Patrick, and for that reason, we're going to put you in the Corporate Relations Office."

"Awesome… What is it?"

"Well, we stay afloat not only by the businesses we run but through donations. Large donations from corporations. It will be your job to ensure that we keep a good relationship with our current corporate donors, as well as finding us new ones."

"I think I can handle that."

"Good, Patrick. It means you'll be getting some new clothes. Business attire."

"Sweet."

"We've also decided that you may have phone contact with your…what is she, your girlfriend or wife?"

"Let's say fiancée."

"Okay, your fiancée and your son, and we've approved you for a visit, to take place sometime next month."

"Thank you. That's great."

"You may also play guitar, but do not let it distract you from everything you are doing to improve yourself and your relationships."

"No problem."

"Patrick," Kittridge said in a firm tone, "we're dead fucking serious. Do not make us take it away from you. Music is not to be your focus, and we will take it away again if you fuck up. Understand?"

"Yes. I understand."

"Good. You have the weekend off. You earned it. Enjoy your weekend, and we'll see you at your new job on Monday morning."

"Thank you, guys, I really appreciate it."

♪♪♪

"Yeah, bro, I can play music again too," Pat proudly exclaimed.

"That's great, Patrick," said Mario as he picked a card up off of the deck. Kerry slapped one down.

"I still can't believe you have to ask for permission," Kerry half-laughed.

"It is what it is."

"Hey Patrick, the Recovery Street Halloween Bash is coming up at the end of next month. Why don't you do a show? People would dig that."

"What's the Halloween Bash?" Kerry asked.

"Dude, when Recovery Street parties, we party hard. We just do it without drugs and alcohol. Teaches us how to have fun without – you know? So every holiday we have a huge bash and Halloween is usually the best one. We build a haunted house, have a dance with a professional DJ and usually hire a live band too. Former residents come, and people can invite their families and kids. It's sick."

"Sounds cool."

"It is. But I'm thinking we don't need a band this year. Patrick could do an acoustic set." Mario looked at Pat. "What do you think?"

"Will they let me?"

"Yeah, they'll let you! Will you do it?"

"I don't see why not. I guess it would be cool."

"Awesome. What do you need to make it happen?"

"Not too much…a couple of nice guitars, amps and a PA system – a board with an effects loop and some outboard gear. I'd need a decent monitor system, and an audio engineer."

"Outboard effects loop and an engineer?" Mario laughed. "I don't even know what that is! Dude, you're at a rehab!"

"You know, a main system, stage monitors, and a sound guy… I guess I could mix it myself if it's just me. I'll need some time to adapt some songs."

"You do that, and I'll come up with a PA. Patrick Pearson from Blacklist! This will be the best Halloween yet!"

♪♪♪

"Mommy took me to the fair. We went in the bumper cars, and I got to drive. I crashed everyone!"

"Wow, sounds like fun."

"Daddy, I want my own car."

"I think you're a little young for your own car, sport."

"Daddy, I have a kitty too. He wants to meet you. When are you coming over?"

Pat felt the familiar twinge of guilt that ran congruent with every conversation that he'd ever had with Tommy. The guilt of never being there in the past, and the guilt of not being there now. The only difference at this point was that Pat was clean, sober, and dead set on beginning a new life with Tommy and Christine. But how do you explain good intentions to a three, wait, four-year-old?

Holy shit, he's had another birthday… And I missed it…

"I'll see you soon, kid," Pat said.

"When Daddy? How many days?"

When did this kid develop the concept of time?

"I tell you what…you and Mommy can come over to my place in LA. It's a new place. I'll talk to your Mommy about it. Definitely this month."

"How many days is that?"

"It's about thirty. It'll be soon, buddy, really soon."

"Can I bring the kitty?"

"I don't think so, sport."

"I love you, Daddy."

"I love you too, son. Let me talk to your mommy."

Pat listened to Tommy hollering for his mother. It made him smile. Christine picked up.

"Hey, Pat. Are you okay?"

"Actually, I've never felt better, with the exception of not seeing you and Tommy."

"That's great, Pat."

"I miss you terribly."

"I miss you too."

"They've approved you and Tommy to come up and visit this month. When can you do it?"

"Pat, I don't think I want to bring Tommy up there. I'm not sure I want him to see you in that environment."

"Why not?"

"It's a rehab, Pat. He's only four."

"Exactly. He's only four."

"So what are you going to tell him, Pat? How do you explain rehab and the fact that you aren't allowed to come home with him? How do you explain that to a four-year-old?"

"I don't know."

"I know you don't Pat, and neither do I. I don't think I want him to see you until you come home."

"Come on, Christine…"

"Pat, do you know that every time you leave after seeing him that he cries himself to sleep? It's because you never come back when you say you will. I'm not putting him through that."

"I'm sorry…Look, Christine, I've changed. It's not going to be that way anymore."

"That remains to be seen."

"But baby, I need to see you too."

"Pat, you don't need to see me, you need to get laid. You always come back to me when you are lonely. Aren't there any hot groupie chicks there?"

"Christine, it's not like that anymore. I want us to be a family."

"Pat, I haven't even heard from you in over four months. You go to jail, then rehab…what the hell am I supposed to think? You can't expect me to believe you want to settle down and be a family just because you call me and tell me that! Are you sure you aren't getting high in there?"

"Very funny."

"Seriously, Pat. You have to see my side of this. You've screwed me over repeatedly for years. How can I trust you based on a phone call? I want nothing more in this entire world than to become a family with you, but you have to prove yourself."

"Well, you have to come up here and see how I've changed."

"Listen, Pat, I'll think about it. But I'm not bringing Tommy. Not to a rehab."

"Fine. But I really want you to come up."

"Look, Pat, I really don't know. I'm not sure I want to see you there."

"Christine, please…"

"I know you are used to getting what you want, Pat…"

Shit, not these days…you have no idea…

"…But I'm sorry, I don't want to put myself through it either. I cry myself to sleep a lot too, Pat. You have a lot to prove and a lot to make up for."

"What do you want me to do?"

"You'll figure it out."

"But Christine, I love you."

"That too remains to be seen."

♪♪♪

It was a beautiful, sunny and clear fall day. The sky was a bright blue, and the Hollywood sign looked like it was so close you could touch it. Autumn leaves fell from the trees in the warm wind.

Pat walked out of the building and took a deep breath, closing his eyes. The fresh air energized him. He opened the door to the small, white Hyundai sedan and took a seat behind the wheel, gripping it and stretching out his arms. He turned the key, put the car in gear, and drove out into the busy Los Angeles traffic on Vermont Avenue.

"You know Kit, it's a trip how one appreciates the small things after being cooped up for a while."

"Amen," answered Kittridge.

"The fresh air, the sunshine, driving a car… I feel like a school kid."

"Hopefully you'll learn to keep appreciating the small things in life long after you leave this program, my friend."

"Oh, I will. I certainly will."

"You been studying all that literature about the program?"

"Yes, sir."

"And you got the promotional package in the back seat in your briefcase, right?"

"I'm ready to go, boss!"

"Good. Your appointment is with the public relations manager of Tri-Com Corporation in Sherman Oaks at one-thirty, and I've got Valley Paper Products in Woodland Hills at two. I'll take the car to Woodland Hills and be back to pick you up as soon as my meeting is over. Then we'll head back to the house and grab some lunch."

"Sounds good. What does Tri-Com do?"

"They're a networking service provider out of the UK. In other words, I don't know what the fuck they do. Just put on that rock star smile and dazzle them with how brilliant our little program is. You'll get their money."

They both laughed as they got on the 101 freeway and headed up the hill towards the San Fernando Valley. They passed the Hollywood Bowl on their left, and the Gibson Amphitheater on their right.

"I've played there," Pat noted. "Hollywood Bowl *and* the Gibson."

"Lemme ask you something…what makes somebody so successful like you want to piss it all away? Shit, I grew up in the ghetto. Never knew any other way. You had rich parents and a good career. Fucked it all up. Why?"

"Pussy. Same as you."

"Pussy?"

"Yeah. Why did you have your first drink or hit? To be cool? To fit in? Why did you want to be cool? To get laid."

"When you break it down like that…you're probably right."

"Hey, I always had a self-esteem thing when I was young. It was all about getting laid, and girls didn't like me when I was a kid. So, I had to be the coolest of all. Drugs made me cool, just like playing music did. That's why I started playing guitar and singing – to get laid. It wasn't some divine calling. And remember, it's a whole lot easier to get laid when the other party is on drugs too. Sex, drugs and rock n' roll go together. It's the rock star life, baby!"

"Amen to that," said Kittridge.

"Anyway, you start out that way, and then you realize one day that you can't function without the drugs. At that point, you're fucked."

"Let me tell you something else, Patrick," Kittridge said, "pussy will also be the death of you."

"How so?"

"That's why niggas relapse. They're trying to get laid, so they go where they used to go for the pussy. Next thing you know, they're using again. You can't go back to your old scene."

"I'd be inclined to agree with that."

"Pussy will get you into more trouble than anything else in this life or the next. But life ain't all about getting laid. There comes a time when you gotta grow the fuck up."

"That's why I intend to get back with my fiancée and my son. Settle down."

"I hope so, rock star, cause with all the temptation you're gonna face out there, you better keep your muthafuckin' head on straight."

They pulled off the 101 onto Ventura Boulevard and continued west.

"I will, Kit. I just have to convince my girl of that."

"What you need to do is prove it to her. Keep that ass out of trouble."

"Amen... I'm done with the drama."

"We'll see…"

They parked in front of a large glass office building. Pat grabbed his briefcase and hopped out of the car. Kittridge walked up, straightened Pat's tie and gave him a playful smack on the shoulders.

"Good luck, Patrick. See you right here in an hour or so."

"Cool. Good luck to you, too."

♪♪♪

Pat walked out of the building's foyer and into the sunlight. He smiled. The presentation had gone perfectly. The manager of public relations was a young woman who was familiar with Pat and his band, and he told her the story of where his life had gone wrong and how Recovery Street had helped him to get it back on track. He went over the literature with her, and she was very impressed. All in all, Pat was able to solicit a cash donation of eight thousand dollars. He was elated.

He stood outside the building waiting for Kittridge. Ventura Boulevard was busy with afternoon traffic, and there were cars parked along both sides of the street. A white GMC Suburban stood idling at the curb a couple of car lengths to Pat's right. He began to shuffle toward it, anticipating its departure and figuring it would open up a space for Kittridge to pull in. There was a bench there, and Pat took a seat.

A very attractive woman with long blond hair and a pretty face was sitting in the passenger seat of the Suburban. She glanced in Pat's direction, giving him a nice smile. Pat smiled back. The woman did a double take then suddenly jumped out of the truck and began a quick stride toward Pat. The driver of the truck, a medium-built black man, ran to the back of the Suburban, tore open the back doors and grabbed a TV camera.

You've gotta be kidding...

Pat stood up from the bench and casually walked back toward the building he came out of. The woman followed him.

"Patrick, Patrick Pearson, is that you Patrick?"

Pat kept walking.

Oh fuck...I can't talk to this bitch! Where the hell is Kittridge?

Pat looked over his shoulder at the street, straining to see if the little sedan was anywhere around.

"Patrick Pearson! It is you! Patrick, just a couple of words! Please!"

Pat put his hand up in front of his face. The man obviously already had the camera on.

Oh man, I can't be an asshole...nobody's seen me in months...should I talk to her? What the hell do I do?

Pat stepped inside the building's front doors. The woman followed right on his heels, having absolutely no problem with causing a scene.

"Patrick, Patrick, just one minute… please." Her voice echoed through the granite and glass foyer.

Pat turned around.

"Okay, I'll talk to you. Just step back outside, I don't want to make a scene in here."

"No problem, whatever you like. Can we just get a short interview?"

"Look, Miss…"

"Amy Powell, Access Hollywood."

"Miss Powell, I'll give you a short interview, but it's got to be quick and private."

Amy motioned to a small courtyard between some retail stores.

"Could we just talk in that courtyard over there?"

"Sure. But when I say we're done, we're done."

"No problem, Patrick."

They walked over to the courtyard and took up a space in a corner. Amy grabbed a microphone with the Access Hollywood logo on it out of the bag that her cameraman had slung over his shoulder and positioned herself next to Pat. She fixed her hair.

"Okay, are we ready, Mike?" she said to her camera operator.

"Yeah, go ahead…"

"This is Amy Powell reporting from Hollywood. I'm here with an exclusive interview with Patrick Pearson from the rock band Blacklist. Patrick, it has been reported in the media lately that a man was killed at your Encinitas home. Is this true?"

Whoa, where did that come from?

"Hold on, Amy, let's start this over…" Pat said, putting a hand up in front of the camera. The camera guy lowered the camera, obviously frustrated.

"Patrick…"

"Wait a minute," interrupted Pat. "Look, I can't comment about any legal aspects of what happened with the incident at my home or in jail or anything like that. I'm in rehab right now, and

I'm not supposed to be speaking to the media at all. If you want me to tell you simply how I'm doing I'll do that for you, but nothing more."

"That's fine Patrick, we can do that."

"Fine."

"Mike, are you ready?"

"Yeah, go ahead Amy…"

"I'm Amy Powell, and this is an exclusive interview with rocker Patrick Pearson."

♪♪♪

The room went completely quiet. Everyone stared at the TV until Kerry exclaimed out loud. "You gotta be shittin' me! How the fuck?"

"Well Bill," Amy said, *"you probably know all the rumors about the shooting at Patrick's San Diego estate, the allegations of Mexican Mafia involvement and the deaths of his best friend and another inmate at the San Diego County Jail. Rumors have been circulating about the fate of Patrick, and the band as well. Unfortunately, I was not able to get any answers to those questions, but I did manage to speak to a very cheerful Patrick Pearson about his current situation and what the future may hold for he and Blacklist."*

Bill, Mario, and Kerry sat in the TV room watching in total amazement.

"I'm here with rocker Patrick Pearson. Patrick, you've been out of the public eye for a while and are rumored to be in a treatment program."

"Yes, Amy, I'm currently in treatment, and I'm feeling great. It's been a life-changing event."

"How the hell did Pat do an interview with Access Hollywood?" laughed Kerry.

"I don't know," said Bill, "But he'll be very sorry he did."

♪♪♪

Christine came rushing out of the bathroom. Tommy was sitting on the bed with toy cars and trucks scattered all around him. He was screaming at the top of his lungs.

"What's wrong, sweetie? Why are you screaming like that?"

"Daddy, Daddy!"

Christine felt terrible. The phone conversation with Pat had obviously affected him – but yet he didn't seem to be crying.

"Honey, your Daddy is away at work for a while. I'm sure he'll call again soon."

He looked up at his mother. "Daddy, Daddy, he's here!"

"Tommy, your Daddy's not here. But we can maybe go visit or something."

"No Mommy, there…look…"

She turned to the TV and nearly jumped out of her skin. There he was. He had short spiky hair and was dressed in a business suit. She was surprised Tommy recognized him. He looked filled out and healthy. She cleared the toys out of her way, sat down on the bed next to Tommy and watched.

"Patrick, you look fantastic. What's with the short hair and suit?"

"It was just time for a change, I guess."

"How far along are you in your treatment, and what can we expect from you and Blacklist in the near future?"

♪♪♪

"Oh my God, it's Pat!" Tina screamed in delight to nobody in particular.

"Patrick Pearson?" Acknowledged Jenny. "I thought he was in jail."

"No, we got out."

"What do you mean, we?" Jenny questioned. "Do you know Patrick Pearson?"

"Shhh!" Tina turned up the volume on the TV.

"Right now I'm just focusing on working out my family life with my fiancée and my four-year-old son. I look forward to getting back to work with the band, but right now my family has to come first, and I ask for everyone to respect our privacy. Thank-you for your time Amy, I have to go."

"Tina?"

"Oh, wow, I guess you didn't know," Tina said with a smile, "we were arrested together. Yes, we are longtime friends."

"I think you need to share a little more, Tina."

"It's a long, long story."

"We have nothing but time."

♪♪♪

"Anyway, regardless of all the rumors circulating in the tabloids, Patrick looked and sounded great, and I believe we'll be seeing big things from Blacklist later this year."

Carlos sat on the balcony of his Playa De Tijuana Costa Azul home overlooking the beach. Two men sat across from him on the sofa, and his wife, who had just pointed out the latest gossip news on the TV, sat on Carlos's lap.

"Thanks, Amy for that much-needed update," said the show's host. "*Now some other news from Hollywood..."*

Carlos mashed out his cigar and lounged back in his chair. He looked at the two men sitting across from him. He smiled.

"The rock star has a family. A little boy. Find them."

TWENTY

IT NEVER REALLY leaves a performer completely, but like anything, with practice, it can be controlled. It can also be the catalyst that drives the mind and body into performing way above expectations. Either way, every artist starts out their career performing by the skin of their teeth, their body teeming with adrenaline. A drink or a hit off of a joint will relax the nerves and give the illusion of control when quite the opposite is true. The sad part is that the doping up eventually causes every performance to feel monotonous and carefully planned out. Somewhere along the way, the thrill is lost completely.

For the chosen few who have felt the electricity of live performance, the loss of the rush can be mentally catastrophic and at that point more often than not the performer winds up looking for a new way to satisfy the hunger that is left behind. For some, extreme sports and the like may fill the void. Sadly for most, it is usually increasing the amount of drugs that winds up being the replacement for the original catalyst.

Patrick could not remember the last time he had stage fright. He stood up on the balcony above the facility's main ballroom watching the crowd milling around below. His stomach was in knots.

I've played stadiums before...why do I feel this way?

The Recovery Street Halloween Bash had attracted a few hundred or so people, mostly residents, graduates and their children. They were all dressed up as ghosts and ghouls and were happily dancing to the DJ and enjoying the free refreshments.

Colored lights had been strategically placed around the ballroom, and fog machines completed the creepy ambiance.

Geez, I pretty much know everybody here...what am I worried about?

"Yo, Patrick, What's up?"

Pat jumped when the hand touched his shoulder.

"Hey, Mario, shit, you startled me!" Mario was dressed like a vampire.

"Sorry, bro. When are you gonna play?"

"I don't know. Soon..."

"Hey, what's up with you? You look nervous."

"Dude, as strange as it sounds, I am. I mean, I've played hundreds of shows in front of thousands of people, but this has got me all tripped out. I don't get it."

"Well, when's the last time you played sober?"

Now that's a good question...

"Honestly, I can't remember. Probably back when I was a kid. Definitely before Blacklist."

"How did you feel before a show back then? Before you were a rock star?"

"Like I wanted to throw up before every show."

"Welcome back!"

Pat thought about it for a moment. The adrenaline, the rush he'd lost so long ago, the feeling he'd been chasing for years. He wasn't sure he wanted it back.

"This is going to be a big step for you. This is your first performance without being high on something. Are you feeling it?"

"Truth be told since you pointed it out I'm even worse. Fuck man, I usually have my band. It's just me and an acoustic guitar! I've never done this before. I don't even have a soundman! Shit, how am I supposed to do this without a soundman? This is bullshit!"

"Pat, relax, it's just for the other residents."

"No, man, it's not that simple. I'm a perfectionist, dude. I'm unrehearsed! I haven't performed in months! This isn't how you do a show! I don't have a clue what it's going to sound like out there with no soundman… There's no lighting… No production… No proper planning… I don't know, man…this isn't such a good idea."

"Dude, calm down. You're Patrick Pearson, bro! You've got this nailed. This is small-time compared to what you're used to."

I don't know Mario…this isn't going to work, bro. I can't take the chance that I might suck."

Mario started laughing. "Oh my god, you're killing me, bro! When I came to rehab, I never imagined in my wildest dreams I'd be trying to talk the mighty Patrick Pearson into playing a show for a bunch of drug addicts! This is fuckin' classic. I cannot wait to tell my kids about this one!"

"Shut up, asshole."

"Dude, seriously. They're a bunch of dope fiends and little kids! They'd love you if you went out there and played the kazoo! Now suck it up, use your fear and go out there and find the fuckin' zone. If you can't do this now, you may as well never play again."

Pat stared out at the crowd for a minute.

The zone…

Mario was right.

"Okay, man. It's on…"

Pat walked deliberately down the stairs to the DJ and told him to cut the music after the next song. He took the stage, pulled up a tall bar stool and sat down with the acoustic guitar on his knee. His mouth went dry and his core was quaking. He remembered the feeling.

The DJ faded the music out, and Pat looked out over the heads of the people to the back of the room; an old trick for stage fright that he learned back in school from his trumpet teacher, Mr. Left. '*The crowd perceives you as looking at them, but you are really making eye contact with nobody, leaving you able to focus*.' He remembered an episode of the Brady Bunch where Greg was told to imagine the audience in their underwear. He laughed to himself and pulled up the boom mike to his face.

"Hi everyone, welcome to the Recovery Street Halloween Bash. I believe I know most of you, but if not, my name is Patrick Pearson."

His fingers were shaking. He took hold of the fretboard and began to play the beginning to the Black Crowes hit "She Talks to Angels".

"She never mentions the word addiction..."

"In certain company..."

The notes flowed effortlessly. He looked directly at the crowd. They smiled and stared open-jawed.

"She'll tell you she's an orphan..."

"After you meet her family..."

Pat looked straight into the eyes of a beautiful girl. She looked into his. He smiled, and she returned it ten-fold. The crowd began to cheer, and it gave him goosebumps. He kicked the stool out from under him to the back of the stage and strummed the guitar hard with everything he had. He embraced the zone.

♪♪♪

The body and mind never really forget a habit even if the habit was left behind years and years ago.

Back in the days when Pat played in nightclubs, after a set he would automatically beeline for the bar to get a stiff drink. Fortunately, at Recovery Street, the drinks were pretty soft, though comforting just the same. He stared into the mirror behind the bar and cupped his glass of orange soda.

"It was fuckin' incredible, dude! People in the real world would've paid a hundred bucks a pop to see that! I wish I'd have sold tickets!" praised Mario.

"Thanks, man," Pat said, without turning from the mirror.

Pat was pre-occupied by another face in the mirror. It was Julie, staring back at him. Julie, the newest resident at Recovery Street. Julie, the same girl with whom he'd made eye contact throughout the show. Julie, who after this show, for this moment, Pat was infatuated with. Old habits do die hard.

Pat got up from his barstool and walked over to where Julie was sitting.

"Hey…"

"Hey, Patrick."

Julie had the biggest blue eyes Pat could remember ever seeing. In contrast, her long curly chestnut hair made her face seem to glow. Her perky breasts appeared to be straining to get out of the tight, low-cut blue shirt that he imagined she must have picked out because it matched her eyes. The thick mascara and the cute little kitty ears and tail she had on as her Halloween costume had Pat floating in her presence.

"Did you like the show?" Pat asked, as he always asked.

"Of course. Seeing you up close like that was nearly a dream come true for me."

"So you're familiar with the band?"

"I've been a fan for years. In fact, it's kinda hard to believe I'm talking to you right now. Everyone else is so matter-of-fact around you because they've been living with you for a while. I just got here, so I guess I'm still a little starstruck."

Pat was eating out of her hand.

"Hey, I'm just like anyone else. I get into trouble too."

"Why are you here, Patrick?"

"The rock star life, baby."

Her eyes were sparkling.

"You partied too much?"

"Way too much. The rock star life can spin out of control sometimes. I needed a break from it all."

"Wow, I'd imagine you would."

"So let me ask you…How'd a beautiful girl like you wind up in a place like this, if I may be so bold as to use the oldest cliché in the book, which I might add, is absolutely accurate in your case."

"You are so sweet. I made a few mistakes, same as you."

"Like what?"

"You know, none of that is really all that important. We're here now, and some kind of weird destiny has brought us together in this place, at this time."

"I agree one hundred percent. Say, do you wanna get some air?"

"Sure. I'd like to go out for a smoke."

"Please, allow me."

Pat pulled back her barstool for her, and the two of them made their way through the crowd and up the stairs, through the atrium and out onto the veranda. They could still feel the thumping of the music downstairs. It was clear and crisp outside and the moon shone down into the gardens below; the reflections dancing off the leaves of the exotic plants and palms. A light breeze blew through Julie's hair as she leaned back against the railing.

"What an incredible night," Julie said, as Pat scrambled to find some matches on one of the empty tables. He lit her cigarette for her.

"Yes, it is."

"You know, I've seen your concerts on TV and stuff, but that, Patrick, was the greatest performance I've ever seen. Just you and your guitar. It was so sexy."

"I didn't feel comfortable at all until I saw you. You made the show happen. I'm out of practice and out of my element without my band. I felt very vulnerable up there until you smiled. Then I knew it was okay."

"Vulnerable. I'd have never guessed. You emanate confidence."

"Thank you."

“I never thought in a million years I’d be standing here, over a beautiful garden, on a beautiful night, having a conversation with Patrick Pearson. Especially in a drug program.”

“Life is crazy, isn’t it?”

“It really is.”

“Has anyone shown you the gardens?”

“No, I really haven’t seen much of the outside of the building at all. I’ve been pretty depressed, being in a drug program and all, so I haven’t really ventured out yet. I’d love to see them though.”

“Please, allow me to show you around a little, my darling.”

Pat took her hand, looking over his shoulder to see if anyone was watching them. Everyone was downstairs in the ballroom partying, save for the guy behind the front desk, who was heavily engaged in a conversation with a graduate.

They slipped down a set of Spanish tile stairs with carved concrete handrails that led into the gardens. At the bottom of the stairs were several paths that led through a tropical paradise that would rival any five-star hotel. Low voltage lighting beamed up the trunks of palm trees, making all the plants glow softly in the dark.

The pathway led them down a hill and over a small footbridge that straddled a pond fed by a waterfall. They continued around a corner to the back of the building, which was covered with ivy and immersed in palms and other tropical flora and fauna.

Julie stopped, looked up into Pat’s eyes and ran a hand through his short bushy hair, down his cheek, and across his chin, bringing his face down to hers. They kissed deeply and passionately, grinding their bodies together.

Pat put a hand on her breast and began to softly caress her. She ran her fingernails down his chest in reciprocation. Sliding his hands down and around her hips, he then picked her up off her feet as she wrapped her legs around him. They kissed hard, their tongues entangled with passion.

Pat quickly looked around and saw a small corridor leading to a door that appeared as if it had never been used. It was dark and isolated. They ducked out of sight into the cement cubbyhole.

Pat pushed her up against the wall and kissed her again, holding her hands above her head. He worked his way down her neck to her chest as she moaned with delight. He moved a hand down and lifted her shirt and bra up over her head and began to suck on her perfect half-dollar nipples.

"Patrick…Oh my God…"

"Baby, you're so beautiful…"

"Patrick, you make me crazy…"

"You do the same to me, baby…"

She reached down, unzipped his jeans and began to massage him. He instantly became rigid.

"Oh my God, Pat…You're so big…"

Never get tired of hearing that one…

He unzipped her pants and let them fall to her ankles. He kissed her breasts, her stomach, and down to her panties, which he pulled down to her knees using his mouth. She squealed.

She stepped out of her pants, and now completely naked against his body, wrapped her legs around him and began to lower herself onto him.

"Oh, Pat, I never do this… Only for you…"

Never get tired of hearing that one either…

They began to move together, in rhythm to the music off in the distance. She rode him hard, trying to hold in her cries of delight. Everything around them disappeared. Nothing else mattered.

It was just the two of them melting together into one, in total ecstasy. Then together at once, they climaxed.

♪♪♪

"Have a seat on that bench, Patrick."

Pat sat down.

Oh God... do they know? Do they know about me and Julie? Shit...how could they know?

He nervously crossed his legs then uncrossed them.

Nobody was around...and there were only two people on the veranda when we got back...they just said hi...nobody seemed to miss us...Maybe they're just going to ask where we were... That's it...They don't know shit...They'll just try to interrogate me...

He put his hands in his lap and looked at the clock.

Fuck, it's only been ten minutes?

He tried to get comfortable but couldn't. He just kept squirming.

Maybe it's just about the interview...They never talked to me about that...Yeah, that's what it is, the interview...Kerry said they saw it on TV... That's it...

Half an hour. One hour. Two hours. Pat was becoming a wreck.

God... they know about Julie... They must know... But how? She'd never tell...would she? Shit, I really don't even know her... No, she wouldn't tell... But why am I on the bench and she's not? Maybe she did tell... Oh man, I'm such a fuckin' idiot...what have I done?

Three hours had gone by. It was now ten-thirty, and everybody was going down to bed.

Somebody must have seen us... Dammit ... Shut up Pat! It's probably nothing...then why would you be here for three fucking hours? Why are you talking to yourself? Shut up!

Everybody went down to bed. The lights in the atrium dimmed. The front desk attendant left his post. Pat became tired.

This is so fucked up...what in the world am I going to say? They have to know... I've been here all night... and where is Julie? Why isn't she here? No, it can't be about her, or she'd be in trouble too... It's the interview... Man, when the hell are they going to deal with me? I'm getting delirious...

He tried to stay awake, but his eyes kept closing.

Why'd I do it? I shouldn't have done it... But she's so hot... But not that hot... Not for all of this... I'm so tired...

Pat let his eyes close and finally drifted off. A vivid dream woke him.

Dammit, why did I do it? This is unbelievable...what are they going to do to me? I should just leave... screw this place... wait, what am I thinking? Why do I care what they do to me? It's only wiping windows - that's the worst that can happen to me... Oh, man, the groups... I'll never hear the end of this... I can hear 'em...rock star this and rock star that... I can't handle that... Shut up, Pat, yes you can... It's only words... It's better than prison... wait, you don't even know if they know yet! Why are you giving up? Tell nothing...Even if she told, admit nothing... stick to my guns... Oh fuck...this is ridiculous... God help me...

Pat laid his head back in despair.

Fuck, I give up...I'll just admit it and get it over with... take my lumps... won't change what happened... Damn, why did I do it?

"Pearson, let's go..."

Kittridge. They walked into the Vatican room. Bill was sitting there waiting.

"So Pat, you got anything you want to tell us?"

Maybe I should just cop to the interview... Act like that's all I've done... That's what they want, for me to slip up, to squirm... I'll just cop to that, they'll punish me for it, and that'll be it. Nothing else... they don't have anything solid on me anyway...

"Pat?"

"I'm sorry...are you referring to the interview on TV? I'm sorry. I didn't know what to do! They just cornered me. I had to tell them something, it would have looked way worse if I'd just run from them...I was real vague about everything, and I made it real quick. I didn't know what else to do! I'm sorry."

"Yeah? Why didn't you tell us about it?"

"I don't know... I was afraid of getting in trouble I guess."

"Afraid of getting in trouble. Interesting. Are you still afraid of getting in trouble, Patrick?"

"I don't know…what do you mean?"

"I mean you just came clean with us, and we didn't hit you or anything, right? Don't you think that honesty is the best policy?"

"Yeah, I suppose…"

"Good, we do too. I'm sure you feel like you've gotten a load off your mind, right?"

"Sure…"

"Is there anything else?"

"No, I don't think so…"

"You don't think so?"

"No. There isn't."

"Okay Patrick, I guess there isn't."

Kittridge got up and opened the Vatican room door.

"That's it?" Pat asked.

"That's it," said Kittridge.

Pat walked out of the room and turned toward the elevators.

"Hey, no Patrick, this way. Back on the bench."

"What?"

"Have a seat."

"But…"

"But nothing! Have a fuckin' seat."

Pat sat down, and Kittridge and Bill walked off toward the elevators. Pat was in shock.

What kind of mind game are these fuckers playing? This is bullshit!

It was now almost two AM Patrick was losing his mind.

Fuck, they know... they have to know... why didn't I just tell them when I had the chance? Dammit, now it's going to be worse! Fuckin' honesty, the best policy... Fuck me! Why do I do this shit to myself...? Goddammit Pat!

Pat put his head in his hands. It felt like it was going to explode.

Dammit, why do I do these things? I didn't need to fuck her! I love Christine anyway! Why didn't I just wait? What is wrong with me? Why can't I just grow up?

Pat continued to exhaust himself mentally until he finally fell asleep on the bench.

♪♪♪

"Pearson, wake up." Kittridge lifted Pat up by his shirt and walked him into the Vatican room.

"You got anything else to tell us?"

Oh, fuck, just say it... there's no use...

"You mean about Julie?" Pat reluctantly muttered.

"Yes, we mean about Julie, you stupid fuck! What the hell is the matter with you, Pearson?"

"Look, I'm sorry..."

"Sorry for taking advantage of someone you don't even know? Sorry you broke the fuckin' rules? Or sorry you got caught? Which is it, you fuckin' dipshit?"

"I'm sorry for all of it."

"We told you the rules! Don't fuck with the women! Don't you think there's a reason we tell you that? You think we make up rules for fun? You think the fuckin' rules don't apply to you? You think you are above it all now because you played a little rock show?"

"No, I..." He started to tear up.

"So you're tough enough to fuck a girl you don't even know and lie to us about it, and then you have the balls to sit there and cry like a little pussy? Man up, muthafucka!"

"I didn't lie to you about it..."

"Not telling us is lying! In fact it's worse! You sat there like you didn't know what the fuck we were talking about and looking at us like we were stupid, you dishonest little prick! You better understand Pearson, if you are in this room, then we already know! You need to tell the fuckin' truth! The first time!"

"I'm sorry..."

"We don't give a fuck if you're sorry! Let me tell you something about Julie. Do you know why she's here?"

"No..."

"I know you don't! You don't even know her! She's here because she was turning tricks on the street to support a heroin habit! She fucked rich guys and robbed them! And she came here for help! To get better! Now you come along and drag her right back down into the shitter. You're a fucking trick!"

"But I..."

"Shut up! You don't care about anyone but yourself! What was all that bullshit you were telling me about getting back with your fiancée and starting a family? You've fucked her over again too, you selfish prick! Did you think about her and your son while you were fucking Julie?"

"No, I..."

"You got on the stage at the party and fell right back into your fucking rock star bullshit! Thank God there were no drugs around! If Julie had some drugs, no doubt you'd be right back where you started! You are far from better, Mister Pearson, far from better! You just proved that to everyone! You are still a selfish, thoughtless, piece of shit dope addict! Grow up, you asshole!"

Pat was bawling.

"I wouldn't have used...I wouldn't, I swear! I'm sorry! I didn't mean to hurt anybody!"

"Nobody ever means to hurt anybody! But you did. You hurt your fiancée, your son and somebody you don't even know. You are truly a worthless piece of garbage."

"I'm sorry... I'm fucking sorry..."

Bill and Kittridge let Pat cry it out for a minute or two. They toned it way down.

"Listen, Patrick, do you see how easy it is to fall back into your old behavior? You and I had this talk in the car, about pussy being the death of you, how life isn't all about getting laid and how you need to grow up. Patrick, you were this close to using drugs even though nothing was around. It's the behavior you have to question."

"I know…" Pat said.

"Patrick, you have the right idea, the right attitude, and the brains to make your life better than you ever imagined. You must, however, practice it every day. And I trust after all of this, you might see old behavior coming and be able to recognize it and stop it before it happens. Consider yourself very lucky it happened here, Patrick. If you were out there, you might have just lost your family you were trying so hard to earn back."

"You guys are so right."

"You also have to remember the other parties involved have problems too and be more sensitive to the possibility that you might be hurting them. Julie did not deserve this. She'll be severely disciplined just like you. And it's your fault. You may have set her way back in her recovery."

"I know…I'm sorry, man. I really am. I just didn't think."

"No, you didn't. But next time you will. And rest assured it may save your life."

Pat sat and thought in silence for a minute.

"Now, Mister Pearson, what you will do, is hold yourself accountable for your actions, admit you made a mistake, take your punishment and move on. Are you cool with that?"

"Absolutely."

"You've got what we call a thirty-day contract. No free time for thirty days, just extra duty. And no leaving the house for thirty days. You'll work in the office here. No guitar, and you've lost your visit."

♪♪♪

"Hey, babe."

"Pat, I'm so glad it's you! How are you?"

"I'm okay. How are you and Tommy?"

"We're great! He misses you so much, Pat. I do too."

"I miss you too. This place is crazy. I can't wait to get out. Just a few months to go."

"We went with Steve the other day to check on your house. The gardeners have been there every week, and the maid has been dusting and watering the plants inside. The house actually looks fine. Tommy ran around in the garage getting into your cars, Pat. It was so funny."

"Man, I miss my life. Or let me re-phrase that, I miss my home. My life was a joke."

"It's really nice to hear you admit that, Pat. I can't tell you how proud of you we are. And your mom and dad too - I guess you talked to them. They're so happy, Pat. All they've ever wanted is for you to be okay."

"I know. I love them very much. I love you guys too. Let me say hi to Tommy."

"Okay…"

Tommy got on the phone.

"Daddy, we went to your house! I drove your cars!"

"You did? Which one do you like best?"

"I like the red one, Daddy. It's fast!"

"Yes it is. You've got great taste, my boy."

"I didn't taste it, it's a car!"

"That's not what I meant." Pat laughed. "Forget it. Are you taking good care of your Mommy?"

"Yes, Daddy, she says I'm her prince."

"You're my prince too."

"Mommy says we're going to see you soon. In days."

"Really? Um, I don't know about that, son, let me talk to her…"

"Okay, Daddy! Love you!"

"Love you too, sport."

Pat could hear what sounded like the phone being tossed across the room. He smiled.

"Pat?"

"Hey…"

"I guess he told you before I could. Being at your house made me rethink things a little. I've decided that we will come up and visit. We're planning on this weekend!"

Oh man…

"Um, babe, that plan is… has… changed a bit."

"What are you talking about?"

Be honest… hold yourself accountable…grow the fuck up…

"Babe, I kinda got into a little trouble over the weekend."

"Oh Pat, what happened?"

"It's no big thing; I just have to wait another month for visits."

"Pat, what did you do?"

I'm gonna regret this…

"Babe, I kinda got caught with a girl. But it was nothing. It's all over. It was a stupid misunderstanding."

"Pat, stop right there. I don't want to hear any more."

"Babe, it's no big thing. I'll see you next month."

"I doubt it, Pat. You are truly unbelievable. Even in a rehab… Will you ever fucking grow up?"

"Babe, I am. That's what it's all about. Honesty! And I'm being honest with you!"

"Pat, you are a selfish child. Honesty! Good God, Pat… you'll never grow up."

"But that's exactly what I'm doing! You just need to trust me."

"Trust you? Pat, every time I begin to you pull a stunt like this. I give up. I'm done. Geez, even in a rehab!"

"Babe, come on… I'm really trying…"

"It's not enough, Patrick. You have to earn trust."

"I will."

"I don't think so."

"Babe, I'd do anything for you…"
"Goodbye, Pat."
"You'll see… I'll prove it. I'll prove my love for you!"
"Goodbye, Pat"

TWENTY-ONE

IN THE YEAR 1987, the R.J. Donovan Correctional Facility, named for the late California Judge and Assemblyman Richard J. Donovan, was constructed in the southernmost portion of San Diego County. Built less than two miles away from the Mexican border, the prison had an overwhelming Hispanic population, most of which were affiliated with drug cartels and street gangs.

Originally designed as a training and work-oriented facility, the intention was to provide comprehensive vocational, academic and industrial programs to help rehabilitate inmates before integrating them back into civilian life.

Of course, anyone who lived there might offer a different opinion of life in the facility. The prison had weathered countless lockdowns and riots, most of them racially motivated. It was not unusual for a person to die in custody, but the truth of the matter was that it is one of the nicest prisons in California.

Garrett lay on his bunk, reading an old issue of Us Weekly that he got from his cellmate whose wife frequently provided him with semi-outdated gossip mags.

Holy shit! This cannot be true…

Garrett was astonished at what he was reading.

> …Sheriff's deputies confirmed that the riot began at around 5:00pm after inmates had had their dinner.
>
> "It's a normal activity; we do it [recreation] every other day," said Sgt. David Blakely of the

San Diego County Sheriff's Department. "Nothing seemed out of the ordinary. We knew that Pearson was in our custody, but nobody in general pop is given preferential treatment. He and Martinez blended in, so nobody could have foreseen what would happen next..."

The inmates were led single file into the small outdoor yard for their tri-weekly recreation period. Patrick, Christopher, and about twenty other inmates began power walking around the small enclosure.

That's when witnesses say that Eduardo Espinosa, who went by the street name of Spider, attacked Patrick as he went for a drink of water. A fight broke out between the three men, resulting in the deaths of Christopher and Eduardo. Patrick narrowly escaped with life-threatening injuries that landed him in the hospital for almost a week. The fight also set off a racial riot that resulted in multiple injuries to inmates and Sheriff's Deputies alike and caused a two-day lockdown of the entire San Diego Central Jail.

Further investigation of the incident by the Sheriff's Department and the CDC uncovered facts suggesting that the fight that incited the riot was not racially motivated at all but was instead an attempt at retaliation by the Mexican Mafia for a shooting that occurred earlier in the week at Patrick's Encinitas home.

The San Diego Sheriff's Department has confirmed that the shooting did occur and that Patrick and Christopher were arrested on charges related to the shooting that were later dropped. The two men were held on drug charges, and Patrick was later released to an undisclosed rehabilitation and treatment center, rumored to be in the Los Angeles area. Christopher was to be released to rehab with Patrick the same day, but sadly his untimely death would change those plans.

Patrick Pearson's music career began back in the late 1980's with...

Oh, God...Chris is dead? I don't believe this...

Garrett rolled over on his back, staring at the underside of the bunk above him. He'd cut out all sorts of pictures of hot women from the gossip mags and pasted them into a collage under the bunk.

God rest your soul, Chris...

He closed his eyes for a moment, thinking back to the last time he'd seen Pat and Chris. Remembering an outrageous night in the hot tub, he smiled to himself. A loud banging on his cell door jolted him out of his reminiscing.

"Hey, Kingsley! You got a visit in fifteen minutes!"

A visit? I don't have any visits scheduled...who is visiting me today?

Garrett got up off of his bunk, grabbed a blue denim prison shirt and a pair of jeans out of his footlocker and put them on. He looked into the scratched up metal mirror on the wall and splashed some cold water on his face. He glanced out the partially open door toward the yard as he toweled off. It looked like a chilly day. Didn't matter much in this place – he was just happy to be off of the reception yard and into his own cell.

He slicked back his hair with some gel and put on his tennis shoes.

Maybe it's my sister...she said she'd be coming down in the next few weeks... that'd be nice...

He straightened his bunk, wiped down the sink and grabbed his fur-lined denim jacket. He walked out into the corridor, feeling the bite of the December air. It was still early and fairly chilly outside, so not too many inmates were out on the yard yet. He could see a crisp blue sky and a slight wind kicking up dust outside through the mesh-covered windows.

I can't get over Pat and Chris... What really happened?

He walked out onto the yard, squinting as the bright sunlight hit his eyes. The wind was cold and dry, and he noticed a slight smell of smoke in the air that seemed to occur everywhere around the beginning of winter.

As he began to cross the dusty common area, he thought about what a nice soccer field could have been placed here. Of course, they'd stopped watering the grass years ago to save water, so all that remained was a hard, bumpy dirt lot, with a few remnants of a baseball diamond at one end. Sad. He looked up at a tower. He could see the reflection of himself walking in the two-way mirrored glass.

Fucking assholes... he grumbled to himself.

He continued across the yard, hands in his jacket pockets, nodding good morning to the usual suspects. Although Garrett pretty much kept to himself in Donovan, he was a part of the Aryan Nation. Outside the fences, Garrett was an equal opportunity businessman, his clients only needing to have one thing in common, cash. But inside, clicking up was essential to his survival.

As he continued along the fence toward the sallyport gate for the visiting center he took the long way around a group of Southsiders, who were eyeing him up and down as he passed. Though the Southsiders and Aryans did form an alliance against Blacks, Piasas and Nortenos should a race riot occur, Garrett still avoided them like the plague. The sheer number of Southsiders intimidated him. He'd been here before, in 1996, at this exact spot, fighting for his life as one after another took their best shot at killing him until his own race had stepped in. The fight resulted in one death, sixteen injuries and a week-long lockdown. Just the sight of the Southsider prison gangs made him nervous and scared.

The sallyport gate slowly slid open, and Garrett was ordered via loudspeaker to continue down the dirt path toward the visiting center's rear entrance. Once at the visiting center, he found his way to a holding cell and waited. After about a half hour, a gun-toting redneck guard opened the door.

"All right, Kingsley, let's go…"

Garrett got up off the bench and followed the CO down the hall to the visiting room.

"There you go…Table number three. I'll be watching your ass."

Garrett was astonished.

Carlos?

♪♪♪

"Wow, I've never seen such an entourage show up for a resident's visit!" said Kerry.

"I know. It's like a little party down there," said Jim, a three-year resident.

"Happy Thanksgiving and Merry Christmas, Pat!" his sister exclaimed. "How are you?"

"I'm great! Better than ever!"

"You look fantastic!"

"So do you…I've really missed you!"

Pat sat back down and smiled from ear to ear. He looked around him at the throes of people who had driven hours to visit him on the first Sunday of winter.

On his left were Steve and Mike; and even Jay had made the drive up. Steve had dragged along Pat's personal agent and accountant Leo as well.

On Pat's right, were his mother and father, his sister and her husband, and Christine. Tommy was naturally sitting on his lap.

“Patrick, you look so good with your hair shorter,” Pat’s mother said as she brushed it to one side, attempting to make his part straight. He squirmed in his seat like a child.

“Come on, cut it out, Mom!”

“I agree,” said Christine, “You look way better. Younger.”

“Well, thank you both very little.”

“Seriously,” said Steve, “it’s a miracle what you’ve transformed into. It’s hard to believe you are the same person. Now let’s talk a little business so we can get out of here and leave you to visit with your family.”

“Sounds good. What’s up?”

“When is your actual graduation date?”

“I’ll be out on Super Bowl Sunday. January 28th.”

“That’s perfect. We’ve booked Studio West in San Diego for February to put the finishing touches on the record and pushed back the tentative release date to March or April. Are you guys okay with that?”

“Good with me,” said Pat “You guys?”

Mike and Jay both agreed. Steve continued.

“We’re going to schedule a press release for the first week of February. Leo has spun this thing so that the media is champing at the bit.”

“It’s incredible!” Leo chimed in, “It’s like every gossip magazine is running a ‘Where is Patrick Pearson’ piece this month for their ‘year in review’ issues. I’ve been stringing them along with little tidbits for weeks. The timing will be impeccable, with the interest of the media in Patrick’s story, he,” he turned to the other band members and gestured excitedly around with his hands, “and you guys will be getting more free publicity for your album than we could have ever bought. While the hype is still hot, we release a single or two, and then launch the whole thing in April or May before this stuff cools down. Patrick, you’re gonna be a household name.”

“And,” Steve added, “we’ll set up a summer tour to boot.”

"Hey, Steve, can we take a little time to decide on the tour? I need to have some family time." Pat looked at Christine. She broke eye contact and looked at the ground.

"Yeah, okay, we'll take the touring thing slow…make sure you're fully ready. No problem."

"Patrick, you do need to get some income flowing in, just keep that in mind," said Leo.

"The album," Pat said.

"Patrick, you know how long it takes for album money to kick in even if it does sell well initially. And with the internet, everything has changed. You guys need to do appearances and get on the road. Promote. I'm not saying today, just keep it in mind."

"Okay."

"Okay, Pat, we're gonna take off and let you hang with your family," Steve said. "It's been great to see you. We're really proud of you and look forward to going back to work."

"Me too."

There were hugs all around, and Pat walked Steve and the guys all out to the front of the building.

"Let us know about Super Bowl Sunday. We'll send a car for you whenever you're ready."

"Yeah, we'll see. I may get a ride from Christine or something."

"Whatever's clever. See you soon."

"See ya."

Patrick strolled through the atrium area and back out to the veranda where his family waited. Pat's mother and sister fawned over him as he played with Tommy. His father was naturally a bit more skeptical of the recovery process. Christine seemed disinterested and preoccupied. Patrick felt they needed some alone time.

"Mom, can you guys watch Tommy for a few minutes? I'd like to take Christine for a walk through the gardens."

"Of course, honey."

Pat took Christine's hand and led her down a pathway, taking care to make sure it did not lead to a certain spot that he was familiar with. She kept looking back over her shoulder, leading Pat to do the same. Something seemed to be capturing her attention. Julie. She was on an upstairs balcony casually observing Pat's visit from afar.

"So, is that her?"

"It doesn't matter."

"I'm just curious."

"It never mattered before."

"Yes, it did. You just didn't give a shit. And you weren't sober."

"Yes, that's her. And I haven't really talked to her since."

"She's been watching us all day, Pat."

"I'm a celebrity, Christine. Lots of people watch me."

"Not in here. Not like that."

"Babe, it takes two. She's just one. I'm not into her – I'm into you."

They walked along the pathway, looking up through the treetops at the blue sky.

"Do you know how many times before you've told me those exact words?"

"It's different now. My head is clear. I have a new direction."

"Your head was clear when you decided to bang that girl, Pat."

"But I wasn't better yet."

She laughed uncomfortably. "So you're better now? And I should just put all of my trust in you because a few months later you say you are better?"

"I know it sounds strange, but it's true. You must make mistakes in order to recognize and avoid future ones."

"Pat, do you have any idea how many times you've hurt me in the past?"

"That's a redundant question; there is no way I could answer that. What I do know is that I'll never hurt you again. We can move on."

"I've told you Pat, it's not that easy."

"Tell me then, what do I have to do? You want flowers or something? You want to go on a vacation? Diamonds? What do I have to do?"

"Come on, Pat. This isn't something you can throw money at. A heart takes time to heal. And time is what I need."

He pulled her close. She was trembling. He gave her a soft kiss.

"Look, I love you, and that's the truth. You need me to prove it…I'll prove it. Wait and see… I will prove it."

♪♪♪

"Carlos! Hey, man, what brings you to the pinta?"

"I was visiting a business associate at the County Jail and thought I'd stop by and say hello. I have to thank you for not rolling over."

"You should know, man, I don't fuck around."

"This I do understand. For that reason, I've put a thousand dollars on your books."

"Wow, Carlos, thank you!"

"How is your family? Your father and sister still have the jewelry business in Pacific Beach, yes?"

"Yeah, they're fine… not very happy with me, though, as I'm sure you can imagine."

"Yes, prison is tough on the family. It is hard when you cannot be there to make sure your family is safe. You must feel like your hands are tied."

"Oh, it's not that…they do fine without me. They're just disappointed in me."

"But it is hard when you are in here." He motioned around at the mesh-covered windows, heavy metal doors and armed guards. "One likes to be there to protect one's family. And it can't be done from in here."

"Yeah, I guess that is true."

"Would be a shame, should something happen to your family while you are in here. While you are powerless to do anything about it."

The elation over the generous donation to Garrett's prison account suddenly began to fade. It somehow did not seem as much like a friendly gesture it did a few minutes ago.

"Yes, you're right, it would be awful." Garrett began to feel very uneasy. "Carlos, is there a problem of some kind?"

"Why do you ask? Is it that obvious?"

I forgot what a mindfuck this guy can be. I wish he'd never showed up here...

"Carlos, you should know I have your back. If there is some kind of problem that I'm involved in, let me know about it, and I'll fix it."

"Well, since you mentioned it, there is something that has been troubling me for some time now. A problem I would like to deal with, once and for all."

"Anything Carlos. Name it."

"You have some friends that I have had a problem with. A rock star and his sidekick, and a girl named Tina."

You've got to be fucking kidding me...

"A rock star and his sidekick?" Garrett said nervously.

"You do know these people, yes?"

Garrett's stomach was doing summersaults.

"Um...I...I assume you are talking about Patrick Pearson and Chris?"

"And the girl, you know who I'm talking about, yes?"

"Tina, yes."

"These fucking perros are responsible for the deaths of three of my men, including Jose. And it is your fault as well. The fucking cunt came to me dropping your name."

"Carlos," Garrett whispered, looking around him to see if anyone might be listening, "what the fuck are you talking about?"

"Your friend Tina came to me saying she was to continue your business for you. Then her friend the fucking rock star shot one of my men during a business transaction and stabbed another of my men in jail. He caused me to lose millions in drugs and guns, and this fucking puto still walks the earth. I want him dead. And the fucking puta too. We already got his sidekick."

My God, it was Carlos... He killed Chris...

"Carlos, there must be some mistake. You can't seriously believe that I had anything to do with any of this. And Patrick? He wouldn't hurt a fly..."

"Don't worry, I will let you and your family live." He leaned in close to Garrett. "If you cooperate."

Garrett swallowed hard and asked the inevitable question.

"So what do you want from me?"

"You know these people. You tell me where I can find them."

"I don't know where to find them Carlos, I've been in prison. I know even less than you! All I know is what I've read in the tabloids."

Carlos leaned in even closer to Garrett, inches from his face. He grabbed his hand, gripping it hard enough that it hurt. He watched the guard from the corner of his eye. The guard did not move.

"You listen to me, you fuck. I run this fucking place. If I give the word, you'll be dead before you can get back to your cell. Comprende amigo? You tell me how to find them."

"Honestly, Carlos, I don't know... I guess Pat's in LA at some rehab!"

"I know that you fucking idiot. I too can read. The rock star has a wife and son. I want to know where they are."

"I don't know Carlos, I've never met her."

"You know nothing about her?"

"Carlos, Pat was just a customer. I don't know his family."

Carlos stared at Garrett long and hard. Then he smiled. A disgustingly smug smile.

"Okay, Garrett, I understand." He looked over at the guard and smiled. "I guess our business is finished. Good luck to you. And to your family." Carlos got up to leave.

Garrett was petrified. He knew full and well that if he didn't give Carlos something, he'd never see his family again. And his own death would not be without pain.

"Carlos, wait…"

Carlos slowly turned and sat back down.

"Si? What is it?"

"Look Carlos, all I know is that they live in Lakeside."

"Lakeside. It's a big place, carnale."

"Somewhere near Wintergardens Road. That's all I know."

"Oh, I think you know more than that. And I think if you don't want to see your huevos hanging in front of your face as you die, you'd better tell me her name."

"Her name is Christine."

"Her whole name."

"I don't know, Carlos, I swear to you."

Carlos paused, massaging the bumps on the side of his head that the stitches from the gunshot wound had left.

"And where do I find Tina?"

"She was homeless. Living with me at the time."

"Who was she living with before you?"

"Her husband."

"His name?"

"Craig."

Carlos stared at Garrett, his eyes piercing with anger.

"Craig Stickney," Garrett said. "He owns a restaurant."

"Where?"

"Somewhere in La Jolla."

"What is it called?"

"The Pier. It's on the beach."

Carlos's expression slowly went from a scowl to one of his sick grins. Garrett preferred him when he was scowling. He was more readable.

"You see? You know plenty. And I was worried that you didn't."

"Carlos, I really think you might be making a mistake. I know Pat and Tina, and they're not the killing types. It's got to be a big misunderstanding. You really should reconsider. I think you are directing your revenge at the wrong people."

"Oh, it's not revenge, carnale, it is business. I don't intend to kill the rock star right away; I intend to get the money for my drugs and my guns first. Only then shall I kill him."

TWENTY-TWO

THE CHILLY OCEAN breeze blew right through Lisa Stickney's dress as she locked the front door of the restaurant. She ran and jumped into the passenger side of the silver Mercedes-Benz C300.

"Did you set the alarm, hon?" Craig Stickney asked.

"Yes, just like I do every night, hon," Lisa answered with a hint of playful sarcasm in her voice. She reached for the knob to turn on the car's heater.

"It's not warmed up yet…"

"Doesn't matter…"

Craig smiled to himself. She always turned the fan on, blowing cold air into the car before the heater was warm. It was one of the very few things they disagreed on, and he thought it was cute. He loved her very much. Getting married to Lisa had changed his life. What a contrast to his first marriage.

Craig put the car in gear, and they left the parking lot and headed up the hill toward home.

Maybe he was just too young and irresponsible when he married Tina, maybe they both were. He wasn't quite sure why they had married and wasn't entirely sure what had happened to end it. He didn't know what "tweeking" was, or what this whole Crystal Meth thing was all about. All he knew was that suddenly — it seemed like overnight — they had no interest in each other at all. Tina seemed obsessed with what she said was her career, though he never saw any results from the work that she claimed to be busy with as she stayed up all night on the computer or out all night at God knows where. She even became more and more unattractive to him though he couldn't pinpoint why. She hadn't gained weight or anything like that – he just felt uneasy around her. He later found out through mutual friends that she'd been doing Methamphetamine and Cocaine behind his back and hanging out with some questionable people. Then he cheated, and she disappeared.

The only contact they'd had after that was regarding finances and property. Tina didn't have any family to speak of, so she was pretty much dependent on him to work everything out. The divorce had been easier than he had anticipated. She almost seemed like she was too tired to fight him for anything and she certainly did not seem to be hurt emotionally. She had strayed off in a direction that he'd never understand. But he did love her at one time and would always be there to help, even though it usually was some crazy state of affairs he would inevitably have to bail her out of. Thank God Lisa was such a patient person.

Lisa. His ultimate Godsend. How destiny had brought them together, he'd never know but would always be thankful for. They had been inseparable since day one. They had the same ambitions and dreams, the same wants and needs, the same spirit and sense of humor. Every part of his life changed when she walked into it. His business was thriving, his new home was beautiful, and this new Mercedes she talked him into buying… Wow, what a machine.

He stepped on the gas and raced up the winding Mount Soledad streets, almost giggling to himself like a kid with a new toy. He looked over at her in the passenger seat noting the equally big smile on her face. They were perfect together.

He pulled into the driveway of their new modern home and stopped the engine. Except for the dim glow of the white stucco house in the moonlight, it was dark all around them. The city of San Diego glittered below over the side of the hill. It was truly a sight to behold.

"Fantastic night, huh?"

"It's only going to get better, my love," she said, kissing him softly on the lips, reaching into his lap and stroking his package. "This car makes me horny."

"Babe, the neighbors might be watching."

"Good thing you got the dark tint."

"I don't know if I can get hard out here, babe."

"Well, let me see if I can help you with that problem…"

She took off his seatbelt, and unzipped his pants, smiling at him as she went down. He laid his head back against the headrest and closed his eyes.

He never noticed the truck pull up behind them.

♪♪♪

"It's been real, and it's been fun, but it ain't been real fun!" Pat laughed, using the oldest joke in the book. The small crowd of new residents in front of him and the older residents standing around the perimeter of the room all laughed with him.

"Seriously, this place has changed everything about me. I have direction now, a new wholesome direction. I'm going to live an honest life and reap the benefits."

"When do you graduate?"

"A week from Sunday."

"Are you sure you are ready?"

"Absolutely."

The group of newer residents began to ask more probing questions.

This'll be great practice for the first press conference…

"So, Patrick, what makes you think you won't do dope the minute somebody puts it in front of your face backstage at a concert or something? You know it'll happen."

"You are right, it probably will. But if I realize what Pat is capable of and think out my decision before taking any action, I'll be able to make the right choice. I'm not an addict who joneses for a fix anymore, that shit is out of my system, so I have plenty of time to think rationally before making a choice. It's all about choices."

"So if things aren't going your way out there, like you get depressed or something, you think you'll still be able to make the right choice?"

"Absolutely. I have total confidence that I can live my life any way I want."

"What about all your rock star friends? Hollywood parties and shit?"

"I intend to be more of a family man, and I'm fortunate that none of the other guys in the band party like I did. They just have a couple of drinks and that's it."

"Do you think you will be able to party normally like that? Stop after a couple of drinks?"

"I don't think in my case I have a deep burning need to get high like some addicts do, so yeah, I wouldn't rule it out for someday, but I can tell you, I'm taking things really slow. In fact, I opted not to tour this year."

"Did you get into trouble here? Did you get extra duty hours?"

"Everybody does, and I'm no exception."

"What was the worst thing you did?"

Pat looked across the room at Julie, who was smiling.

"I had an incident with a girl."

"That's that rock star shit!" somebody touted. The room filled with laughter.

"Yeah, call it what you will, but I did it, I paid for it, and I learned from my mistake."

"What did you learn? Not to get caught?"

The chuckles continued throughout the room.

"That's funny. Seriously, we are very lucky to be in this environment. With a clear head, you can actually learn from a mistake. Out there when you were all fucked up, you didn't learn anything. Same shit over and over, day after day."

"Where are you going to go for support out there if you need it?"

"My family. And Recovery Street relationships."

"So your family took you back with no problem? Even though I'm sure you screwed them over?"

"Well, parents always love you regardless, and kids forgive fast. I guess my significant other may take a little work."

"She don't trust your ass, huh?"

"No, not yet."

"So what are you gonna do?"

"I'll find a way. She'll come around eventually; of this I'm sure."

"Are you worried that your past may come back to haunt you? Old friends? Acquaintances? Enemies?"

Pat thought long and hard about that one.

"I hope not. I really hope not."

♪♪♪

The driver's window shattered with a deafening crash, showering glass all over them. Lisa pulled her head up and screamed. In an automatic reflex, Craig put his left hand up to block whatever it was that was crashing through the window. A hand grabbed his wrist and slammed it down onto the car's door. It hurt badly.

The passenger door swung open, and a hand reached in and grabbed Lisa by her hair, pulling her out onto the ground. Another hand went across her mouth. Craig watched in horror as she was dragged away into the darkness. He turned to open his door and was hit in the face with something harder than a fist. He felt the teeth on the left side of his jaw dislodge. Everything began to go black as he was pulled from the car and dragged up the stairs to his front door, where Lisa stood with a hand across her mouth and a gun against her temple.

"Where are the keys?" an unrecognizable voice said.

She pointed back to the car. A third person went into the car, pulled the keys from the ignition and closed the car's door with a thump. He scurried up the stairs to the front door, unlocked it, and they were thrown onto the cold marble floor of their foyer. The door was closed and locked behind them. They were in shock and utterly disoriented.

She grabbed Craig, crying uncontrollably. Craig was coughing and almost limp in her arms; the blow from the butt of the pistol had made him both dizzy and nauseous. He was then kicked hard in the chest. Lisa became hysterical.

"Baby, oh baby, oh my God… Oh my God."

"Back up," a dark figure said to her. "Back up now."

She recoiled into a corner, her eyes wide with terror.

Another silhouette kicked Craig again. Lisa screamed.

"Shut up," said the first guy, pointing a pistol at her.

She did her best to comply.

"Get him up," the first voice commanded.

Two men grabbed Craig's shoulders and hauled him down some steps into the couple's living room and tossed him onto the floor. The room had huge glass windows overlooking a steep hillside. The entire city of San Diego glowed in the clear night.

"Get up," the first man said to Lisa.

She couldn't move.

"I said, get up," he repeated, this time putting the gun to her head. She slowly staggered to her feet.

"In there." He motioned her into the living room. She sat down on the floor next to her husband, who was curled up in the fetal position gasping for air.

"Please," Lisa begged, "just take what you want, but leave us alone."

The man in charge began to laugh.

"Really, we won't call the cops – please don't kill us."

"I have no interest in your home," the man laughed.

She was panic-stricken at his words.

"Please...don't rape me...we have plenty of money...please..."

Craig looked up at the men. He was crying and covered with blood. "Please..." he coughed, "leave my wife alone...I'll give you whatever you want..."

The man laughed even louder. The other men began to snicker as well.

"I want nothing you have! I have everything I need. You fucking Americans! You think you can buy your way out of anything!"

Lisa began to sob louder. "Then what do you want? Why are you here? Who are you?"

The man knelt down close to the couple, and put his hand on Craig's shoulder, looking him closely in the face. The smell of cologne made Craig even more nauseous.

"My name is Carlos. I'm looking for Tina."

"Tina?" Craig coughed, "I'm not married to Tina anymore."

"But you know where she is, yes?"

"No."

Carlos grabbed Lisa by the hair and pushed her face up against the living room window with a boom. Her face and breath made a cloudy mark on it.

"Now do you know where she is?"

"I'm sorry...I'm sorry...she's in rehab...her lawyer sent her to rehab..."

"Which one?"

"I don't know..."

Carlos pulled out his pistol and fired three rounds through the living room window, shattering it from ceiling to floor. The cold winter wind blew into the room as the echo from the blasts faded.

Carlos pulled Lisa up by her hair and positioned her in the open space where the window used to be.

"You tell me, or your wife dies."

"California Ranch," he cried blood spraying from his lips onto the white carpet. "California Ranch…It's in East County…She gets out tomorrow…Please…let my wife go…"

"She gets out tomorrow?" Carlos said in amazement.

"Yes…"

Carlos smiled.

♪♪♪

"Well, I heard some things about you before I came into Recovery Street like you might still be in some trouble out there," a guy said. "How you gonna deal with that?"

"I'm not sure what it is you are referring to," said Pat.

"Some magazine said the Mexican Mob is after you."

"I don't know what you are talking about."

"Are you kidding? Don't you read the gossip mags? You're all over them!"

"I've been in Recovery Street getting my life together. Besides, I don't read my own press. Never have."

"Well maybe you should, 'cause they're after you, dude."

"Yeah," said somebody else, "I heard that you shot a drug cartel guy and that they now have a hit out on you. I saw it on a TV show."

Pat swallowed hard. "That's absolutely not true. I never shot anybody."

"And then you stabbed someone in jail."

"Don't be ridiculous. And don't believe everything you read."

"But what are you going to do about it if they *are* after you? You can't hide forever. What if it is true?"

"Nobody's out to get me."

"I'm just sayin'…"

"Look, I don't know what any of this has to do with my recovery guys, we need to keep these questions recovery related."

"You might run into people from your past, that's all we're saying. We need to know how you intend to deal with that."

"Listen, it's all in the company you keep. I don't run those circles anymore. I'm a family man now, and nobody that's into drugs is gonna to want anything to do with me. I'm boring now, and I'll be absolutely forgotten by people in those circles. And I say good riddance."

"I don't know man, you'd better watch your back out there from what I heard."

Pat nervously looked at his watch. "Look, we're just about out of time, so if you guys have any more recovery related questions ask them now, otherwise this seminar is over."

Everybody got up and began to exit the room. Pat stood staring out the window. It had started to drizzle outside, and the freeway below was at a standstill.

"Hey brother," Kerry said putting a comforting hand on Pat's shoulder, "don't let those motherfuckers get to you. They're new and they're always going to try to stir up some kind of shit."

"Dude, I don't know. They might be right. I've been a little out of the loop. Those guys really might be looking for me."

"Ain't nothing gonna happen to you as long as I'm breathing."

"Thanks man, but haven't you already saved my life once?"

"Let me tell you something. About six months ago I was sitting in a holding cell in the downtown San Diego courthouse, waiting to enter the courtroom and face the judge for armed robbery. Again. My third strike. I'd already met with the public pretender who told me that at this point the best we could do was attempt to plead for five to ten years on an assault charge rather than a third armed robbery which would mean twenty-five to life. He didn't think it would work seeing as I also fled from the cops, but he said it was worth a try. So anyway, there I am, all fucked up from the jail riot sitting next to some smelly-ass hillbilly waiting to be read my fate. I'd just given up. I was hoping they would just put me away for life. At least I wouldn't have to steal for a living, look over my shoulder all the time and be a slave to the fucking rock the rest of my life. Three hots and a cot every day, right?"

Pat nodded as he continued.

"So, I'm sitting there, and this crazy fucking bitch comes into the holding cell, sits down and starts lecturing me on how I've fucked my life up, how it's nobody's fault but my own and I need to make it right. She starts talking about recovery and moral restitution and shit. She says I owe the world for the shit I've done. She tells me that she is going to get me into a program and that it is my last chance to be a human being. It turns out that she's some fucking hotshot attorney, and she rolls with me into the courtroom, throws down a bunch of legal mumbo-jumbo and the next thing I know I wind up here, in Recovery Street. I remember asking this bitch how I was supposed to pay her for this and she says, 'It's already handled - just get your life right'."

Kerry looked into Pat's eyes. "Brother, you wouldn't happen to know anything about all that, would you?"

Pat smiled. "Nope. Nothing at all."

"Well, that moment saved my life. I'm now looking at becoming a normal person instead of looking at life in prison. The way I see it, me and you are even."

Pat just looked out the window, smiling. The drizzle had given way to a soft rain.

"I'm going down to bed, man. Good night."

TWENTY-THREE

SUCCESSFUL RECOVERY FROM addiction works differently for different people. For the hardened criminal, harsh reality and tough love was usually the best detour from the road to ruin. Others may respond better to the support and fellowship of working the twelve steps with those that share similar beliefs. Some believed that God would take away their addiction and looked to the church for support, while yet others would religiously attend therapy sessions. No matter what method a person used to deal with their demons, they would all share one common necessity for making it all work – they had to believe in something. Whether it was faith in God, faith in the system, or faith in one's self, you had to have faith.

> *"Therefore, if anyone is in Christ, he is a new creation;*
> *Old things have passed away;*
> *Behold, all things have become new."*
> *II Corinthians 5:17*

Tina read the passage taped to her mirror that morning just as she had every morning – however that morning was special. Today she peeled the verse off of the mirror, folded it and tucked it safely into her pocketbook. She tossed the pocketbook into her purse and spread her suitcase out on her bed. Her roommate lay on the other bed watching.

"I am going to miss you so much, T," said Jenny.

"I'll miss you too. But don't worry, you only have a month or so to go, and we'll be together again."

"I know, but you've been there for me like nobody ever has. I just wish you weren't leaving."

"I have to. It's time for me to go start my new life."

"What time is Craig picking you up?"

"Nine."

"Is his *wife* coming with him?" Jenny said sarcastically.

"Probably. And it's okay Jen, she's actually a really good person, and they are good together. I'm very lucky that she's so tolerant of me. I wouldn't know what to do without them – all the people I know out there are druggies."

"So she's not mad at him for setting you up with the apartment and everything?"

"He's not setting me up, he's helping me out until I can get a permanent job. I've got two interviews this week. And I plan to pay them back every penny."

"Where are your interviews?"

"Both downtown. One's a receptionist job, and the other is a personal assistant. You have to start somewhere you know?"

"Are you kidding? I'd love to have either one of those jobs. You're gonna be great, T."

"I know. I'm really excited. Hey, help me fold this stuff."

They packed all of Tina's things into an old tweed suitcase, and the two of them walked out into the great flagstone courtyard. It was cold and gray outside, and a light mist hung in the air making everything appear wet and colorless. Tina could see her breath. They continued into the main building and walked into the great room where several other residents waited eagerly to see her off. Everybody was smiling, and the room felt warm and cozy.

Pastor Mike removed his spectacles and put them in his shirt pocket.

"Tina," he said, "you are an inspiration to everybody here, and you will be greatly missed. You've demonstrated to us the power of the Lord; as you have shown great maturity, integrity, and ambition. I have no doubt that with the help of the Lord, you will be a great success in any endeavor you may choose. We were lucky to have you in our house and look forward to seeing you again."

"Thank you so much Pastor Mike. I'm going to miss you all."

"Well, we expect to see you back here often for church services, right?"

"Of course. There's no church I'd rather attend."

"Let's do a quick prayer for Tina."

All hands were joined and heads were bowed.

"Lord Jesus, we come to you on this special day in praise. We come together in your name to ask that you bless Tina Stickney and guide her along the path of righteousness that you have provided for her. We ask that you watch over her and light her way with your brilliance. We ask that you protect her from evil and give her strength. We know that you are the truth, the way and the life and that the only way to God is through you, Lord Jesus, and we pray all of this in your holy name, Jesus Christ, Amen."

At that moment, as everyone raised their heads the wintry clouds parted, and a ray of sunshine reflected off the walkway in the front of the building, refracting the light through the glass doors and lighting up the entire room with a rainbow of colors. It was a sight to behold.

"Look, it's a sign…" said one of the group.

"I'd like to think so," Tina said with swelling eyes.

"Don't cry little sister," said another resident, "this is a time for rejoicing!"

They all embraced in a group hug.

"Okay…" Tina said as she attempted to compose herself, "I'm going to take my bags down to the curb. It's almost nine."

"What if he's late?"

“Craig’s never late. I’ll run back up for the last goodbyes after he gets here. I just need a little time to myself.”

Tina walked through the glass doors onto the front walk. She looked around at the mountains shrouded in the floating mist. The sun shone down in incandescent pillars of soft light, making the ground sparkle like it does after a spring rain.

She took a deep breath of the crisp air and descended the stairs, imagining that this might be what heaven looked like. She set her bags down at the bottom of the stairs and looked through the fog into the distance. A pair of headlights were shining brightly through the mist. Her heartbeat amplified. This was the first day of the rest of her life.

What is this? Did he rent a limo?

A long black Lincoln limousine cruised smoothly out of the fog like an airplane breaking through the clouds into the sky. It rolled to a stop in front of her.

Oh my God, this is so cool...

“Wow...” Tina said out loud as a man stepped out of the driver’s seat, put a hand on her shoulder and opened the rear door.

Brimming with excitement, Tina poked her head under the door’s threshold.

“Craig, you didn’t...” her voice cracked, and she froze solid.

“I’m sorry, Tina, Craig couldn’t make it,” said Carlos, waving a chrome .357 magnum in her direction. “Get in the fucking car.”

The man pushed her into the limousine, threw her bags in behind her, and the car sped away from the curb, disappearing into the mist as quickly as it had come.

Jenny stood in the great room gazing through the glass doors, her mouth hanging open with disappointment.

“She never said goodbye.”

♪♪♪

"I don't know," said Steve, "maybe you should. But you're going to have to pay for it yourself somehow."

"Dude, I'm the hottest thing to hit the tabloids this year and you can't get me a fuckin' bodyguard? There's other celebs out there running around with entire entourages! Bill it to the corporation. I'll pay it back eventually."

"Pat, I can't get it approved right now. We need to show more income before an expense like that will be considered feasible. You have to realize that you aren't fully trusted yet either."

"What about advances?"

"The advances are for the album. And your time in rehab set us way back. We can't get any more funds until the album is complete."

"What about my slush account?"

"We've been paying all your bills while you've been gone."

"I should have plenty of money."

"You'll have to talk with Leo about that. We also paid a ton of legal fees out of that account too, so there probably isn't much there. Pat, what is it that you are so afraid of anyway?"

"I don't know… These guys in here were bringing up all kinds of stuff they read and saw on TV. They said that the Mexican Mob is after me. What have you read?"

"Pat, you know how the media sensationalizes everything."

"I know…It's just that as soon as I graduate, I'll be more in the spotlight than ever before. It would be easy for these people to find me. What if they *are* still after me?"

"Who is it that you think is after you?"

"Carlos. He's the guy we were supposed to testify against, and they've never caught him, remember? And the guy in jail that tried to kill me… he said Carlos's name to me. I don't know, man… I just have a feeling that he might be out to get me."

"I don't know what to tell you, Pat, but if you feel that strongly that you need a bodyguard, you'll have to find a way to pay for it yourself for now and maybe you can get reimbursed later."

"Will you call Leo and see if it's in the cards?"

"Yes, Pat, I'll call Leo."

"Steve, I'm serious! I'm not just being paranoid. I've got a bad feeling, bro."

"I said I'd take care of it."

"Thanks, man."

"So are you gonna need a car to pick you up this weekend?"

"No, Christine's gonna come get me and then I'm taking her and Tommy to Disneyland on the way back to SD."

"Sounds fun. You staying overnight?"

"Planning to."

"I'll call my guy. We'll get you a comp suite at the Disneyland Hotel. Stay as long as you want."

"Steve, that would be awesome. Thank you."

"You sure you don't want a car? We can even have Christine and Tommy picked up at home in a nice stretch."

"Nah, it's cool. Christine's car is fine."

"Suit yourself. Hey, Patrick, I really want you to relax. Enjoy your family, get laid, do what you need to do. I want you all nice and fresh for media day and the studio."

"Dude, I can't wait to get back to work – it's going to be great. Best record yet, and best year yet."

♪♪♪

Tina was cold and shaking on the car's black leather seat. Carlos had not said a word since she had gotten into the limo, and she was not about to be the one to strike up a conversation. The silence was deafening. She could not see Carlos's eyes behind his dark glasses. He just sat there, twirling the shiny silver gun around his finger like some dime store cowboy. Tina could not take her eyes off it.

"So how was your stay at rehab, mi amor?" Carlos suddenly asked.

Tina didn't say anything.

"In Mexico we don't have rehabs. People can't afford them, and nobody cares that much. The Mexican people can't run away and hide like you Americans do. Everybody in America feels sorry for the drug addicts. I like the drug addicts just the way they are."

Tina shot him a cold glance, and then averted her eyes out the window. *I can't believe I just went through rehab to come out to this...* She wanted to cry. She wanted to go back to California Ranch. "What do you want from me, Carlos?"

Carlos sat back smugly in the seat across from her, still playing with the gun. He crossed his legs.

"I simply want what is mine."

Oh my God... Why the bullshit... "Of course you know I'm going to ask you what you are talking about."

He leapt across the car and pushed her down onto the seat, jamming a knee into her chest while putting the gun to her head.

"You fucking cunt! You want to know what the fuck I'm talking about? You and your rock star fucking boyfriend have caused me nothing but pain! You perros steal from me and kill my men, and you want to know what the fuck I'm talking about?"

He pulled the gun from under her jaw and hit her in the temple with the barrel. She cried in pain and tried to shield herself from another blow as Carlos continued his tirade.

"You fuckers! You killed Jose! You stole from me! You will pay! Do you hear me? Every last cent!"

He grabbed her by the hair and held her head in front of his face. He then began to speak in the eerily soft tone that she remembered as the most threatening sound she'd ever heard.

"I want what is owed to me. What is owed to the Cartel. Your fucking rock star boyfriend has money. I want it all. For the guns and drugs you caused me to lose. Then, I may consider letting you live."

He pushed her down onto her seat. She gasped for air between sobs.

"Tell me where I find the rock star's wife."

"I…I don't know…"

"Do not lie to me. I know she is in Lakeside. You will tell me where."

"Carlos, I don't know."

"You disappoint me. I'd hoped you would have helped me."

Carlos pressed a button on the seat, and the limousine's partition slid down.

"Stop the car."

"Yes sir, Mr. Castillion."

The driver pulled the car into an alley and came to a stop.

"Get out," Carlos commanded.

"Carlos…"

"Get the fuck out!" he screamed as a henchman opened the car's door and grabbed Tina by her arm.

"Come with me," he said.

Carlos stepped out after them and tucked his gun in his belt, and he and the driver followed closely behind Tina and the henchman. The air was frigid, and the wind was whistling through the alley.

"Stop," said Carlos. "On your knees."

She began to shake.

"Wait…please…I…"

"On your knees!" the man said and pushed her to the ground. She began to cry. Carlos faced her. He pulled the gun out of his waistband and held the barrel to Tina's forehead. Her bladder started to let go.

Father, why have you forsaken me?

"Please Carlos…please…I don't want to die…"

"Tell me where the rock star's wife is."

"I can't…I mean, I don't know…I was only there once…"

She could feel the warmth of her urine running down the inside of her thigh as she looked up at the gun's barrel. She prayed.

The Lord is my shepherd, I shall not want…

"You can take me to her?"

"I…I don't know…"

Carlos clicked the gun's hammer back with his thumb for effect.

Even now as I walk through the valley of the shadow of death, I fear no evil, for thou art with me…

"Take me to her."

"Okay…I'll try…I'll try…"

"Well, okay then. You should have said so before." Carlos said as he holstered the weapon. "We could have avoided this unpleasant situation, mi amor. Please get up."

♪♪♪

"Yes, Pat," laughed Christine, "I took Monday and Tuesday off, and yes, we'll be there."

"What time, again?"

"We agreed on nine, right?"

"Remember, if you aren't fifteen minutes early, you're late!"

"Who is this? Put Pat back on the phone!"

"I'm just excited."

"So am I."

"I love you guys so much."

"We love you too, Pat. I love you."

"It's about time you came around."

"We'll see how things go."

"Well, it's going to be great. We're going to Disneyland."

"What, is that some kind of metaphor? Whenever someone accomplishes something they always say they're going to Disneyland?"

"No, seriously, we're going to Disneyland. I want to take Tommy there for his first time, and I can't think of a better time than this. It'll be awesome. We've got a room at the Disneyland Hotel for as long as we want it for."

"Pat, that is so great."

"I thought so. So just be here tomorrow morning at nine sharp, and I'll be waiting. Wow, I can't believe it's tomorrow!"

"I know…it's crazy…are you doing anything special? Are they having a party for you or anything?"

"No, graduations are simple and common. Everybody graduates at different times, and it's pretty much done without any fanfare. I mean there'll be hugs all around, but nothing special."

"Well, I'll have something special for you. I hope the room is a suite."

"I'll make sure of it."

"Tommy's tugging at my leg. He wants to talk to you."

"Put him on."

"Hi, Daddy," Tommy said, "Are you coming home soon?"

"Sure am. I'll see you tomorrow, son."

"Yay!" Tommy exclaimed.

"And we're going to Disneyland!"

"Disneyland?" Tommy said in disbelief. "Really?"

"Yup."

"And you're taking me on the rides?"

"I sure am." Pat was amazed at how well Tommy was forming sentences.

"Daddy, you are the best Daddy ever! I can't wait to start the new life."

"What's that bud? The new what?"

"Mommy says when you come home that we're starting a new life."

Pat was speechless.

"Uhm…wow...is that right – well, if your Mommy says so, then it must be true."

"I can't wait to see you Daddy! I love you!"

"I love you too, son."

As usual, the phone sounded as if it had just been thrown into a dishwasher until Christine picked it back up.

"A new life, huh?"

"I sure hope so, Pat."

"Bet the farm on it."

"I don't know about that, but I do know that I'm really happy right now. Pat, I think everything is going to be okay."

"I assure you, everything is going to be great. See you tomorrow."

♪♪♪

God...Please forgive me for what I'm about to do...But I have no other choice...I don't want to die...

Tina stared at the scenery rushing by and silently cried to herself. The rays of sunshine that had managed to break through the clouds earlier that day had been replaced by a slow and steady rain. It was cold enough that the car's windows were fogging, and the tint made the day appear even darker than it was.

Please protect me... Tina looked down at her bags that the henchman had thrown onto the floor of the limousine. Her Bible was sticking out of the top of her tote bag.

"Would that book make you feel safer around me?" asked Carlos as he lit up a cigar.

She didn't answer.

"Go ahead, guera. Pick it up."

She reached down into the tote bag and extracted the Bible. She held it close to her chest.

"You believe that God made you stop using the drugs, guera?"

"It's not quite that simple."

"If you could see the things that I have seen, guera, you'd know that there is no God."

She held the Bible closer to her chest. "I respectfully disagree."

"Your Bible doesn't help you. Your prayer can't help you. The only reason you are alive right now is because I allow it."

"I respectfully disagree," she repeated, "God has a plan for everyone."

Carlos pulled the gun from his waistband and laid it on the seat.

"You think I couldn't just kill you right now?"

"You could, but you won't."

"What makes you believe that, guera?"

"Because it's not my time to go yet. God won't let you kill me."

"Don't fool yourself into having faith in something that is not there, guera. I could kill you anytime."

"But you won't."

Carlos laughed and looked out the window of the car. The driver was making a turn onto Wintergardens Road. Several apartment buildings were scattered on the left hand side of the street. Carlos rolled down the partition.

"Okay, guera," he laughed, "I'll let you live for now. Now tell Rico which building the rock star's wife lives in."

"I…I'm not sure… It was dark when I was here."

"Listen to me guera, you had better remember fast or I will prove to you right now that there is no God."

"Carlos…I…turn left onto that street…"

Rico followed the directions.

"There…that parking lot…this might be it…"

Please let me be wrong...

They pulled into a small parking lot with several covered parking spaces, most of which were vacant. There were walkways on all three sides connecting the parking lot to neatly manicured greenbelts that surrounded the brown two-story condominium units. Every building had four units, each unit with a small patio on the ground floor and a balcony above. Wood paneled walls that enclosed each patio blocked the view of the inside.

"Which one?" said Rico.

Lord, please forgive me...

Tina pointed to the building in the center of a grassy area.

"Second one from the left, I think."

"You'd better be sure, guera," Carlos said as he picked his gun up off the seat and pulled the slide back, cocking the weapon. "You better be goddamn sure."

"I'm sure," Tina said, although she wasn't. *I can't play this game anymore... I guess if I'm wrong, it's my time...*

Carlos tucked his gun into his waistband.

"Miguel, please come sit back here and keep Miss Tina company while Rico and I attend to business."

"Si, Señor Castillion."

Miguel stepped out of the passenger side of the car, got into the back and sat down across from Tina. Tina could smell him from across the car. She wanted to vomit.

"Don't give Miguel any trouble, eh?" Carlos sneered.

Tina just stared out the window as Rico came around and opened the door for Carlos, and the two walked off toward the building seemingly unfazed by the now semi-torrential rain.

"Que paso, Señorita," said Miguel, reaching across the back of the limo and placing a hand on Tina's thigh, "It seems we are alone."

"Fuck you..." Tina said, landing a shot directly to Miguel's testicles with the heel of her foot.

"Fucking bitch, puta!" Miguel screeched and backhanded Tina across the face. She was knocked out cold.

♪♪♪

Christine gazed through the peephole trying to make out who it was that was repeatedly ringing the doorbell. She didn't recognize either man.

"Who is it?" she called out.

"Hello? Miss Christine, my name is Carlos, and I'm collecting donations for the church. Could we please talk to you for a minute?" Carlos said in his best accent-free voice.

Church donations? It's raining cats and dogs out there...Maybe I should let them in out of the rain...

"Which church are you from?"

There was no answer.

"Sir, which church..."

The door crashed open, sending splinters of wood flying across the room. Christine fell backwards screaming and pulled a table full of knick-knacks over with her. The two men stormed in and slammed the damaged door behind them. Carlos dropped to the floor next to Christine and wrapped his arm around her head, covering her mouth with one hand and producing his gun with the other.

"Shut the fuck up or you die."

"Mommy?" said a voice from upstairs.

Ah, the boy...

"Listen to me puta, you make one sound, and you and your son are dead. Do you understand?"

She nodded yes, her eyes bulging with surprise.

"When I let you up, you will get what you need for you and your boy for a few days and put it into a bag. No questions. Just do it. Do you understand?"

She nodded yes again.

"Very good, puta. Now slowly get up. Do not make me kill you both."

They both slowly got to their feet, and Carlos slowly removed his hand from her mouth.

"Go... Get your things. Quickly."

Christine was in shock. Unable to move, she just stood there and whimpered. The wind and rain whistled through the mangled doorframe.

"Go! Now!"

She began to cry as she turned to go up the stairs.

"Rico, go with her."

Rico followed her closely as she went upstairs. Carlos scanned her living room. He picked up a picture of Christine, Pat, and Tommy together at what appeared to be a carnival. They were smiling and holding hot dogs.

Perfect American family... Today, your dreams are shattered, rock star...

He threw the picture to the ground, smiling as the glass cracked.

Banging noises came from upstairs, and Tommy began screaming.

"Rico! What is going on up there?"

"We're coming, Mr. Castillion."

Christine came down the stairs with a bag slung over her shoulder and Tommy in tow. Both were crying uncontrollably.

Carlos put the gun up to Christine's jaw.

"You stop the crying now and control that child."

Christine gasped for air as she attempted to curtail her sobbing. She knelt down in front of Tommy.

"Please Tommy, it's okay," she said between sniffles, "Stop crying…It's okay…"

Tommy gasped and whimpered.

"Listen to me," Carlos commanded. "There is a car out front. You will walk out that door, and straight to the car. You will not stop; you will not look around – nothing. Do you understand?"

"Why are you doing this?"

"Just do as you are told!"

Rico opened the door, and Carlos stuck the pistol into Christine's back.

"Go! Now!"

They all walked in tandem through the pouring rain to the waiting limousine. Rico opened the door and Christine, Carlos and

Tommy got into the car. Christine looked at Tina's lifeless body on the floor of the car.

"Oh my God... Is she dead? Is that girl dead? What are you doing to us?"

She began to cry hysterically.

"Miguel! What the hell happened here?"

"I'm sorry Mr. Castillion, she tried to escape."

Carlos felt for a pulse. "Get in the front, you fucking puto."

Miguel climbed out of the car and got into the front seat. Christine was still crying, and Tommy was screaming. It was a nightmare.

"Both of you shut up unless you want to end up like her! Rico, drive!"

Christine grabbed Tommy and pulled him close to her, trying to shelter him from the madness. They were both trying desperately to hold in the tears.

"Why...what...what is going on? Why are you doing this? Where are you taking us?"

"We're going on a little trip," Carlos said as he rolled up the partition. "A vacation."

"Please... What do you want from us?"

"Oh, I don't want anything from you. I want something from your husband."

"There must be some mistake... I'm not married...you have the wrong people...please, let us go..."

"The rock star...this is his little boy?"

"Pat? Are you talking about Pat?"

"Yes, Pat...Patrick Pearson...You have a lovely child, you and Patrick Pearson. Would be a shame if something were to happen to him."

"Goddammit, I don't know what is going on, but you better not hurt my boy!"

"If your husband cooperates with me, your son will be fine."

"Where are you taking us?"

"Like I said, a little vacation. But first, I must attend to some business."

Carlos reached into his jacket and pulled out a large serrated knife. He grabbed Christine by her hair and brought the blade toward her. She screamed.

TWENTY-FOUR

"I'VE BEEN CALLING her all morning!" Pat was in a panic. "She's still not answering the phone."

"Doesn't she have a cell phone?" asked Kittridge.

"No, just a home number… But she should have been here by now. It's eleven o'clock!"

"It's probably the LA traffic, man. Shit, it's raining cats and dogs out there. She'll be here."

Pat picked the phone up again and dialed Steve's cell.

"Steve, it's Pat."

"Hey Pat! I guess congratulations are in order! You must be on your way to Disneyland!"

"No Steve, I'm still here at Recovery Street. Christine hasn't arrived yet, and I'm getting worried. Dude, she's never late for anything."

"LA traffic, bro. It's pouring outside."

Pat glanced out the window and then back at Kittridge.

"Yeah, I know, but still… She hasn't answered all morning. She doesn't have a cell – what if she was in an accident? Do you have anyone in East County that can run by her house?"

"Pat, you're trippin'."

"Well, do you?"

"Pat look, it's probably nothing. Just traffic. What time was she supposed to be there?"

"Nine."

"Well, give her another hour or so. It's a long drive from San Diego – especially in the rain."

"But…"

"Pat, give her another hour or so and if she doesn't show up, I'll see about having somebody run by her house, okay?"

"Yeah, okay."

"Since when have you been so punctual anyway? Relax, bro, everything's gonna be fine."

"Okay man, I'll relax. But if she's not here by noon, promise me you'll get somebody to go by her house. And check the traffic reports for me. I'm gonna call the Highway Patrol."

"Pat, don't worry. I know you are excited and it's a huge day for you, but everything is fine. Just enjoy your day. You deserve it."

"You're right. I'll call you when she gets here."

"Sounds good."

♪♪♪

"We can't sail today Mr. Castillion, it's too rough outside, even for your boat, sir."

"I know that, you idiot! We don't have to leave today, but I want these bodies on the boat."

The rain hammered the car as they pulled through an empty hotel parking lot and up to the mouth of a long dock. Carlos's yacht was moored in the very first slip.

The boat was a beautiful seventy-foot Vitech twin diesel named "El Encantador de Dragon", or "The Dragon Charmer". The vessel was a personal gift from the Arellano-Felix family. It was probably big enough to brave the storm, but Carlos and Rico were not extremely experienced pilots, and the weather was brutal.

"Rico, you get Tina," Carlos barked over the din of the rain, "and Miguel, you get the other girl. I'll take the boy."

Carlos picked up Tommy's limp body, slung it over his shoulder and turned into the driving rain. It was much windier down at the waterfront, and the rain was stinging. He ran toward the boat. Rico had Tina's arm around his shoulder and was walking her down the dock. Miguel had his hands in each of Christine's armpits and was walking backward dragging her body across the wooden planks. Carlos put Tommy down on a sofa in the main salon and looked out the window at the absurdity. He jumped up and ran back out into the rain.

"Cabrone! Fucking idiot! Why would you drag her like that? Do you want people to take notice?"

Carlos picked up Christine and put one of her arms around his shoulder and instructed Miguel to do the same. They brought her inside the yacht and laid her on the floor. Carlos pulled his gun from his belt and smacked Miguel in the side of the head with the barrel. Miguel recoiled with an unhappy yelp.

"It's your fault we had to do this!" Carlos snapped. "If you hadn't made them hysterical we wouldn't be dragging them in here right now. Do you want me to throw you overboard?"

"Lo siento! I'm sorry Mr. Castillion!"

"Just shut up and go find some towels."

The boat suddenly rocked violently from the wind and the storm surge.

"Rico, are we tied down well?"

"Yes, sir."

"We'll need to go as soon as possible."

"As soon as the rain lets up, sir."

"I should have taken a fucking plane."

"You'd be in the same situation sir."

"Go park the car, then come back here and find out when this fucking rain is going to stop and when we can leave this fucking country. And keep the phone close."

"Yes, sir."

♪♪♪

Pat was thoroughly annoyed that the blinker's rhythm didn't match that of the windshield wipers. He'd been subconsciously tapping out different rhythms to the thumping of the wipers for almost the entire drive down the coast, but now as they waited to turn onto Encinitas Boulevard, the clashing tempo of the car's left turn signal had disrupted his cadence and thrust his troubled mind back into reality.

He'd done nothing for the last few days but anticipate how today would play out. Finally, the big day – released from rehab a new man! He'd be giving Tommy a big hug and Christine a big kiss, waving goodbye to his new friends, and stopping for a Caramel Macchiato on the way to visit his parents before introducing Tommy to the wonders of the Magic Kingdom.

But something had gone wrong. Very wrong. All Pat could do as he sat helplessly in the back of the car for the four-hour traffic-laden drive down the coast to Encinitas was contemplate all the horrible things that might have happened to them. Was it an accident? Did her car break down? Road closure? Did something happen to Tommy at home? Did she change her mind about everything? Or worse?

The car splashed its way through the rain-soaked streets and finally arrived at Pat's home. Pat thanked the driver and told him to add a hundred bucks to the bill for himself as he didn't have any cash on him. The driver thanked him, backed down the driveway and drove off. Pat watched as the taillights disappeared into the rain. He continued to stand there staring into the murky darkness feeling less than sure of anything. He shivered a little as he looked up at the cold dark house he called home.

The landscape around his home looked thicker and greener than he remembered; sort of jungle-like in the pouring rain. The wind shook the trees making him feel as though he was surrounded by an omnipresent being. He wished he wasn't alone.

He tried hard to resist but couldn't help looking down at the driveway for blood stains. There weren't any.

Was it eight, nine months ago? Seems like a different lifetime...

He slowly walked over to the garage and punched in his code. The door went up, and the lights flickered on. No blood stains in there either. The cars were just as he'd left them, however somehow tonight they looked old and dusty.

As he started into the house, his mind raced.

It wasn't supposed to be like this... Christine and Tommy were supposed to be here... This was supposed to be the happiest day of my life...

He walked from the garage and into the party room. It was immaculately clean; in fact, it looked rather sterile and unlived in. The cushions on the sofa were perfectly placed, and the big TV was eerily dark. He felt the tears coming.

Damn, Chris... I wish you could know how much I miss you, bro...

He couldn't see into the yard – it was now dark and raining in sheets. The sliding doors were like walls of blackness. Continuing upstairs he turned on all the lights, the TV, and the heat. The smell of dust burning off of the heater filled the house. He couldn't remember ever feeling so alone.

Well Pat, you're home...

As the house began to warm up, he shook off the cold and tried to organize his thoughts.

Okay...time to get back to reality...turn on the news, then a hot shower, a call to the CHP and all the hospitals, Steve, my parents, Christine's parents...

He took off his coat and went into the bedroom to toss it on his bed.

Then I'll take a drive over to her house...

Looking at his bed, he froze.

What is this?

It was a cellular phone. With something tied around it. He slowly stepped closer.

What is that?

He picked up the phone and in utter shock dropped it back onto the bed. It was wrapped in Christine's hair.

♪♪♪

"The neighbor across the way called and said she saw the door just flapping in the wind, and when she came over to close it, she noticed that the door frame was destroyed and the house was a mess. She then called us."

Detective Hunter looked around the apartment. "And why did you call me?"

"We lifted a couple of prints off a family photo frame that gave us instant matches," the sheriff's deputy continued. "Carlos Castillion was one of them. And it seems that you are in charge of the investigation on him."

"I am part of it…" She ran her hand down the splintered doorframe. "And who lives here?"

"Christine Johnston. Single mom. Works as a bank teller at the California Savings branch on Wintergardens. It's only about five minutes from here – we've got a deputy over there right now."

Detective Hunter slowly circled the room. She extracted a pair of rubber gloves from her pocket, pulled them on, and picked up a picture of Christine and Tommy in a Ziploc off the kitchen table.

"Who's the boy?"

"Tommy Pearson, four years old."

Elizabeth Hunter stopped dead in her tracks.

Pearson?

"Did you say Tommy Pearson?"

"Yes, Ma'am."

"Do you know who his father is yet?" she asked.

"We don't know yet."

"I do. And the other set of prints belong to…"

"Tina Stickney…" they both said in unison.

♪♪♪

Christine knew her eyes were open, but she could not see anything – dark, blurry shapes formed in front of her. Her head hurt. She went to rub it, but her arms would not move.

My God, what's happening to me?

She attempted to move again and this time felt herself fall over. As she began to weep, her eyes started to regain their focus.

From the floor, she could see a man in a white suit walking up a flight of stairs and turning toward her. As he stepped closer, he extracted a large knife from his jacket.

*Oh, God...Where is Tommy...*She tried to wiggle away.

The man knelt down and freed her hands from behind her.

She sat up and looked around, became dizzy and leaned back against a sofa. Another girl lay resting against the couch next to her; her head was flopped back and to the side in an unnatural position. Her eyes were closed, and one of them was black and blue.

The girl from the limousine...God...is she dead?

She turned her head further and saw Tommy lying on the couch.

Oh, Tommy...Oh God...

She put a hand on his face – he was warm and breathing. She turned to the man who was now sitting across the room behind a burlwood coffee table with his legs crossed, casually sipping a drink.

"Please…" Christine sobbed, "Somebody please tell me what is going on…"

Tina stirred but just stayed against the sofa with her eyes closed.

Thank God, she's alive...

"Of course, mi amor," Carlos replied, "What would you like to know?"

"Who are you, and where am I?" Christine asked.

"My name is Carlos. You are about to embark on a glorious vacation on my beautiful boat, my darling. Have you ever been to Mexico?"

"Why are you doing this?"

"I'm offering you a vacation in return for helping me to get what is owed to me."

"What are you talking about?"

"Your husband…he owes me a great deal of money. You and your son will ensure that I get it."

"Pat doesn't owe you shit…" Tina murmured without lifting her head.

"You shut your fucking mouth, panocha! Now that I have the rock star's wife, I have no more use for you! I should just kill you now!"

Carlos pulled out his knife and started toward Tina. Christine screamed. Tommy woke up and began screaming. Carlos put the knife back in its sheath and grabbed Christine by the neck.

"Cállate! Stop screaming or I'll knock you out again!"

Her screaming turned back to sobbing, but Tommy's amplified.

"Take the boy down to the stateroom!" Carlos hollered to Rico.

"No…No, please, don't hurt him…please…" Christine pleaded with Tommy. "Tommy, please be quiet…It's okay…please."

"Listen to me, all of you!" Carlos bellowed. "I own you! You are my property until the fucking puto pays me what I am owed."

Carlos had both women by their necks.

"When he pays me my fucking money you will be let go. Until then, you will do as I say!"

He was spitting as he yelled.

"If I don't get my money you all die! Comprende?"

Tommy's crying turned to shock, and they all stared at Carlos with fear in their eyes – just the way Carlos liked it. He pushed them away and sat back down, straightening his tie.

"Now as I told you, this is a vacation however short it may turn out to be. We'll be having dinner soon. Rico, take them and clean them up."

"Yes sir, Mr. Castillion."

♪♪♪

Pat stared in disbelief at the phone lying on the bed wrapped in long auburn locks. He wanted to pick it up but was unable to move. Just then, his own phone rang, making him jump out of his skin and scream out loud. He caught his breath and picked up the cordless handset of the piercing phone at the bedside table.

"Hello?" Pat said, his voice trembling.

"Pat, Steve."

"Steve, something's happened, man."

"Pat, I need you to stay calm. We'll find out what's going on."

"Why, what do you know?"

"Pat, you need to be cool…"

"I'm cool! Just tell me what the fuck you are talking about!"

"Pat, I called Leo and had him send his assistant out to Christine's house."

"And?"

"Pat, you've got to stay calm, okay?"

"I am! Just tell me!"

"Her door was boarded up. There was a notice on the door from the Sheriff's department about it being a crime scene."

"Oh, God…"

"Pat, I called the number on the door and spoke to a detective. Christine and Tommy are missing."

"Fuck!" Pat screamed as he hurled the phone across the room. He fell onto the bed, head in his hands, sobbing and staring through the tears at the cell phone on the bed. There was no doubt who would be at the other end of that phone. Hands shaking, he picked it up and removed the lock of hair. After carefully placing the hair back on the bed he picked up the phone and pressed the power button. The screen blinked to life, and he pressed the softkey for the contacts list. There was one number in the list. He took a deep breath and pressed send.

♪♪♪

"Pearson? Yeah, we spoke to his manager, and he gave us the contact info," said the Sheriff's detective, "is this the same Pearson that was involved in all that stuff last year in the tabloids? The musician?"

"The same," said Detective Elizabeth Hunter. She leaned back in an office chair across the desk from the young Sheriff's detective. She was a short stocky Hispanic woman. She had her hair tied back in a bun.

"You were involved in the investigation of that whole mess?" the detective asked.

"Yes."

"Is that how you were put in charge of the Castillion investigation?"

"I'm not the one in charge. We are working in tandem with the NTF."

"I'm impressed."

"I appreciate that. Now who was it that called you? I need details."

"Steve Stanford, Patrick Pearson's manager. He said he had a business associate go to Miss Johnston's residence when she failed to show up at a meeting with Mr. Pearson today. It seems that he was released from rehab this morning, and Ms. Johnston was picking him up. She never showed."

"Please continue…"

"When Ms. Johnston didn't show up, Pearson requested that somebody go to her residence to check on her and that's when the business associate found the notice we posted on the door to Miss Johnston's condo. She called Mr. Stanford, and he called us."

"Where is Pearson?"

"On his way home from rehab. He's in a limousine somewhere between LA and his home in Encinitas."

Elizabeth processed the information for a moment. "Okay, I'm going to have to take over the investigation from here. Keep trying to contact Mr. Pearson and when you do, tell him we need him here. Can I use your desk for a while?"

"I suppose. Sure."

"Good." She paused for a moment. "Listen, detective…"

"Salazar…Rosa Salazar."

"Rosa, this Carlos Castillion, he's a known lieutenant and chief enforcer for the Arellano-Felix Cartel. The NTF and the DEA have been trying to catch this guy for years. He's a killer. Carlos also tends to take things very personally – that's his weakness. Several of his people were killed last year in the mess with Pearson. I'm sure he's blaming Pearson, partially because he is a fairly high-profile celebrity. He probably can't stand the fact that Pearson is alive and the media rubs it in his face every time he turns on the TV. He's projected all of his anger onto Pearson. There's no doubt in my mind that he is responsible for the disappearance of Ms. Johnston and her child – I only hope that they are still alive and in the United States. My gut tells me that they are because Carlos will want Pearson face to face. But his narcissism will cause him to slip up. We can and will find him, but we have to keep the interests of Pearson and his family a priority. It's going to be complicated."

"It definitely appears so…"

"I'm going to bring my people down here. In the meantime, I need you to send a unit out to Pearson's home to pick him up. And,

I also need the exact whereabouts of Tina Stickney. I believe she too may be a target."

"I'll get right on it, Detective."

"Call me Liz."

♪♪♪

"Bueno?"

Pat was trembling. "Who is this?"

"Ah, it's the rock star! I was wondering when you would call!" Carlos said in a snide and elated manner.

"Where is my family?"

"Don't worry rock star, they are fine. We are on vacation. In fact, we were just sitting down to dinner."

"You listen to me, you son of a bitch – you'd better not hurt them!"

"No, you listen to me, you pinche pendejo. I've already hurt them. And I will hurt them more. Much more."

Pat was on the verge of losing it. "Why are you doing this? What the fuck do you want from me?"

"Ah, the magic question. I simply want what is owed to me."

"What the hell could I possibly owe you?"

"Your fucking life, you pinche culero. But I'll gladly take your money too. That is if you ever want to see your family again."

Pat could feel stomach acid in his throat. The conversation was agonizing. "How much do you want?"

"Four million should be fine."

"Four million dollars? For what?"

"I can't put a value on the lives of my men, nor on the disrespect you have shown the Cartel, cabrone. But I can put a value on the drugs and guns I lost. Can you put a value on the lives of your family, rock star? Isn't two million apiece a fair value for your lovely wife and son?"

"I don't have four million dollars."

"You are a rock star, you will find a way. Or your family will be dead."

"So help me, if you hurt them…"

"Oh really, cabrone? Why don't you listen to this?"

The phone dropped. Pat could hear Christine and another voice screaming…pleading.

Then the sound of Tommy screaming. Pat cringed helplessly. The phone was picked back up.

"Can you hear that, puto? Do you want more?"

The screaming in the background made Pat numb. "Please," he said softly, "please, I'll do whatever you want… I'm sorry…just leave them alone!"

"I thought you might feel that way, rock star. Now listen to me carefully. Keep this phone with you at all times. You get the money and you call me. I'll give you further instructions. And cabrone, if I even get a *feeling* you may have spoken to the police, I'll gut your wife and kid like pinche cerdos. Police equals dead, cabrone. I will have no problem killing your family like I have so many others. And even then, I won't stop until I find you and slit your throat as well. Killing is in my blood, puto."

Pat believed every word he said.

TWENTY-FIVE

DAVE MICHAELS, THE long-time editor of *Celebrity Weekly* Magazine slammed his fist down on his desk.

"Dammit!" He screamed at nobody in particular. "Are you fucking kidding me?"

Chris McAlister of the Baltimore Ravens had just picked off quarterback Kerry Collins to negate a fifty-nine-yard drive by the New York Giants in Super Bowl XXXV. Being originally from New York, Dave was livid. Baltimore was now leading 10-0.

Marco Holdman poked his head into Dave's office.

"What's going on in here?"

"The goddamn Giants! Baltimore is a fucking expansion team! This is unbelievable!"

"Well, here's some news that might you feel a little better – Patrick Pearson's out of rehab."

"How do you know that?"

"I got an anonymous call – someone from the rehab leaked it. He was released today."

"Which rehab?"

"They didn't say."

"What did they want?"

"Nothing."

"Come on…"

"On my life."

"Do you think it's true?"

"The timing seems right."

"Do you think anyone else knows about this?"

"Nobody as far as I know."

Dave turned away from the TV.

"So you're telling me that some anonymous source just dropped the biggest story of the year in our lap and asked for nothing in return."

"That's what I'm telling you."

"You've got to find a way to verify it. Call his management or his agent – whoever you have to. Inform them that we already know and make a deal that you won't break the story until they give the okay as long as we get exclusive rights. If they want to negotiate then negotiate. If they won't give you any confirmation, you are going to have to get it yourself."

"Yes sir."

"Find out where Pearson's home is and stake it out. Get some pictures. Maybe we'll get lucky. Take Steph with you."

"My pleasure."

"Now aren't you glad you came in on a Sunday?"

"You're just lucky I'm not a football fan."

♪♪♪

Pat just stared at the phone in his hand. He was numb. He couldn't cry anymore.

Okay, Pat...Keep it together, bro...we'll do this one step at a time...stay rational...

He set the phone down on the bed.

I'll call Steve... No, he'll want me to go to the cops. There's no way I can involve the cops...I've got to get the money myself...

He slowly walked into his home office and started up his computer. The desktop background came up with a picture of him, Christine and Tommy. He felt like putting his fist through the screen. Accessing the web, he typed in all the necessary information to view his bank accounts.

Total Available Balance: $392,490.13

Shit…four million? I don't even have four hundred…

Pat picked up the phone on his desk and dialed his agent.

"Leo, it's Pat."

"Pat! Hey, are you okay buddy? My assistant told me everything. I'm really sorry. Do the cops have any leads?"

"Yeah, Leo, I'm a little distraught. Hey, listen, I need to know just how much is in the band's corporate account."

"Is this for the bodyguard thing? I know Steve told you no, but in light of the recent events, I'll go ahead and authorize it."

"No, it's for something else… and my portfolio, what's in there right now?"

"Pat, what's this all about?"

"Leo, just tell me what I'm worth right now. I need to know what's there."

"Pat, tell me what is…"

"Leo, look up my fuckin' accounts!"

"Pat, relax, I'm going to my computer right now, but you need to understand that you can't pull personal money from the slush fund. It belongs to the corporation."

"Then *my* corporate account. And my portfolio."

"Pat, you've got about twenty grand in your corporate account. Your retirement portfolio is worth about four hundred, but you can't touch that."

"Twenty grand is all I have? Are you fuckin' serious? Where the fuck is my money?"

"Pat, we paid all of your legal fees, your bills, your mortgage; your lawyer was not cheap. You paid legal fees for three people, Pat.

"What's my house worth?"

"Your house?"

"Yes, my fuckin' house!"

"I don't know, a million or so."

"How can I get money out of it right now?"

"You can't…you'd have to sell or apply for a credit line… Pat, what the hell is going on?"

"Leo, I just need to know how much cash I have! Is that too much to ask?"

"You could probably create about a million if you cashed in everything. I don't know what you've saved personally."

"Goddammit!" Pat screamed and slammed down the phone. It rang again. He scooped it back up.

"Leo, look, I'm sorry man…"

"Hello? May I speak to Patrick Pearson?"

Whoa…who the hell is this?

"May I ask who's calling?" Pat said in the calmest voice he could muster.

"This is Detective Salazar with the San Diego Sheriff's Department."

"Uh, Pat's not here…"

"To whom am I speaking?"

"This is his, uh, assistant…Chris."

"Chris, do you expect him soon? I understand he is on his way home from the Recovery Street facility?"

"I don't know… I'm just taking care of the house…"

"Chris, it's very important that I speak with Mr. Pearson as soon as he arrives. Let me leave you my number."

"Okay, go ahead."

Pat pretended to take down the number.

"Okay, I'll let him know if I see him."

"Thank you. And Chris, can I get your last na…"

Pat hung up the phone.

Great… now the Sheriff is breathing down my neck…I cannot let the cops fuck this up worse…

Pat stood up and looked out the window. There was a pair of headlights coming down the rain-drenched street.

Fucking cops…

Pat ran across the room and flipped off the light switch. He squatted down and made his way around his desk to the window and peered over the sill. Sure enough, a Sheriff's car was slowly approaching the end of his driveway.

I knew it...

Pat looked into the hall. There were other lights on in the house. He crawled as fast as he could through the office and into the hallway, where he slapped switch after switch. He ran down the stairs into the party room and killed the last light he knew of.

Shit...did I close the garage door?

He scurried back up the stairs and looked out one of the front windows. The car had stopped right outside his front door, and two uniformed officers had already gotten out of the car. They were walking toward the glow of light coming from the open garage.

Oh, fuck me...

He lunged back down the stairs into the party room and felt his way through the dark over to the sliding glass door that led to the garage. The blinds were still drawn, but the doors were unlocked. He stood behind the glass doors holding his breath. He could hear the two deputies talking as they approached. Suddenly a flashlight beam illuminated the blinds just on the other side of the glass door.

Oh, please...carefully...

Crouching in front of the slider, Pat slowly reached up and held his breath as he began to turn the lock.

Please don't click...

The lock slipped into place just as a hand grabbed the handle from the other side. The door rattled. Pat quietly stood up as the two cops discussed looking under the blinds. He dove away from the slider and onto the floor in the party room just as a slit of light hit him in the eyes. He rolled behind the couch.

"Did you see that?" said a voice from the other side of the glass.

The flashlight beams raked around the room from under the blinds.

"See what?"

"I thought I saw movement in there."

The cops rattled the lock on the door.

"Mr. Pearson? It's the Sheriff's Department."

The cops moved back over to the front door. Pat sat up and let out a huge breath. They pounded on the door and rang the bell relentlessly.

"Mr. Pearson, San Diego Sheriff!"

"Mr. Pearson, are you home, sir?"

Pat sat on the floor in the dark. There was no way he'd be seen from the front.

"Mr. Pearson, please open the door!"

Pat heard some mumbling, and the cops trying the door. Then a flashlight beam shone right over his head into the room from the backyard. An officer had opened the gate and was coming up to the patio sliders.

Shit…

Pat dove up onto the hearth and rolled himself into a ball inside the fireplace. The flashlight swept the entire room. The officer began trying all of the sliding doors.

I thought my days of hiding from the cops were over…

Sweat dripped into Pat's eyes, stinging them and making him wipe his brow. He stayed curled up inside the fireplace.

The officer finally left the yard and walked back to the front of the house. The phone began to ring. And ring. His muscles were cramping. Then the ringing stopped. The knocking stopped. Finally, the sound of an engine starting and the cruiser driving away.

Pat rolled out of the fireplace and stretched his sore legs. He cautiously crept up the stairs and looked out the window. Nobody was around. He slithered through the dark back into his bedroom.

Too scared to turn on any lights, he felt his way into the very back of his closet, pushed aside all of the shoes on the floor, and pulled up the carpet. He pried up a floorboard with his fingernails and felt around. He pulled out a small .380 pistol from the space beneath the floorboards, lifted himself out of the closet and sat on the floor with his back against the wall.

I knew I might need you…

Pat climbed onto the bed, and holding the gun in his hands, began to cry. He cried himself to sleep.

♪♪♪

"Mr. Stanford," Elizabeth continued into the desk phone, "we sent a car over to his residence shortly after dark, but there was no answer. Our Deputies cannot access the home without a court order, so they didn't go inside, but they believe somebody had been there recently as one of the garage doors was left open. Have you heard from him at all?"

"Not since I spoke to the other detective, but his agent did. Pat called him in a panic earlier tonight asking about his net worth and how much cash he had on hand. He said Pat sounded hysterical and hung up on him. He'd been worrying about a bodyguard."

"His agent is the one who sent the girl to Ms. Johnston's home, right?"

"Yes."

"And you say Patrick was expressing fear of Carlos Castillion?"

"Yes, he was. I wish I'd taken it more seriously. I feel terrible."

Detective Hunter scribbled down some notes and gestured for Detective Salazar. "Steve, we believe Patrick's probably been contacted by Carlos Castillion and is either planning to run or to pay him ransom to get his family back. My guess is the latter. A really bad situation is unfolding right before us."

"What can we do?"

"First and foremost, we can't let Patrick try to take matters into his own hands. We need to find him or he'll get himself killed. Carlos is very, very dangerous." She tore off a sheet from her notepad and handed it to Detective Salazar. "I'm going to obtain a court order to access his home tomorrow morning. In the meantime we need you to let us know if he contacts you. Reason with him and ask him to call us. And please call us immediately with any information at all."

"Of course."

"Steve, Pat may already be in great danger. We really need your total cooperation in this matter, and we cannot let the media get wind of any of this or the whole thing will blow up in our faces."

"I understand...."

"Thank you Mr. Stanford."

♪♪♪

"Rico, take Tina and the child down to my stateroom."

"Yes, Mr. Castillion."

"Please, let me and my boy stay together," pleaded Christine.

"You will not be separated long. We just some time alone. Please, come join me on the couch."

"Fuck you."

Carlos smiled and pulled his coat back, exposing the pistol in his belt.

"I'll ask you again…please join me."

Christine reluctantly stood up from the table and walked to the sofa.

"You enjoyed your dinner, yes?"

"I'm not enjoying any of this."

"Please try to relax and enjoy yourself during this time. It will all be over soon. Try to make the best of the situation."

"Whatever."

"I am not an evil man, mi amor, I am simply a businessman. One must separate business from personal."

"You're a drug dealer."

"Business is business. I'm not so unlike anyone else. I'm a great success at what I do. I have nice things, lots of money and a good family. Is that so different from your husband? What is it that makes you love the rock star, mi amor? Could you not love me just as much in another time?"

Christine cringed.

"You are nothing like him. People love Pat. He is a star for good reason. He's talented, smart, and has a heart of gold. Whenever you see his face on TV, you just remind yourself that he is all of the things that you will never be and that he has all of the things that you will never have, you fucking piece of shit."

Carlos backhanded her across her face. She fell to the floor crying. Carlos grabbed her throat, choking her.

"You listen to me you pinche panocha… When he comes for you, I'm going to kill him while you watch. And after he is dead, you will die. Slowly."

♪♪♪

Pat opened his eyes. Two police officers stood above him.

"Patrick Pearson, you are under arrest for murder."

"What is this?" Pat exclaimed. "I never killed anyone! The police proved me innocent!"

The officers grabbed him and rolled him over onto his stomach and cuffed his hands. They pulled him up by his collar and led him into the hallway.

"You have the right to remain silent. Anything you say can and will be used against you in a court of law."

They shoved Pat down the stairs and out the front door. The sun was so bright it stung.

"I'm not a killer! I just finished rehab! I'm supposed to be with my family!"

"You have the right to be totally screwed. You have the right to beg for your life."

"What? What are you talking about?"

They pushed him out into the driveway where a police car was waiting.

"Watch your head, sir," the officer said as they shoved him into the back of the car. Pat looked into the front seat.

"There's been a mistake! I'm not a killer! You've got the wrong guy!"

The two cops got into the car. Pat put his head in his hands between his knees.

"Please..."

He lifted his head and looked up directly into the faces of Spider and Christine. Spider had a gun pointed straight at Christine's head.

"You killed me," said Spider "Now she must die..."

Pat clawed at the barrier between the back and front seats of the police car.

"*No!*"

Spider pulled the trigger, and the gun went off.

Pat woke up screaming to a loud clap of thunder. He wiped the sweat from his forehead and pinched himself to make sure this was reality. It was. And it wasn't much better.

Oh, God... What am I going to do...

Pat picked up the gun and walked slowly into the study. He sat down at his computer desk and stared out the window into the darkness. The rain was pounding. There was a silver SUV idling at the end of his driveway.

I'm so fucked...

Pat picked up the phone and dialed.

"Hello, Recovery Street, how may I help you?"

"Hi. Can I speak to Kerry Parker?"

"Who's calling?"

"It's Pat."

"Oh, hey Pat, let me see if he's on the floor. Hold on a sec…"

Pat waited anxiously trying to make out who was in the car parked outside.

"Pat! It's Kerry! What's up, brother?"

"Kerry," Pat sobbed, "I need your help."

TWENTY-SIX

"AND YOU ARE supposed to call him back?" asked Kerry.

"Yeah. I've got the phone right here."

"Do you have that kind of money?"

"Not even close."

"Damn. That's a crazy fuckin' dilemma, brother."

"Tell me about it."

"You know I love you man, but I don't really know what to tell you. I know I can't do anything from here. They'd never let me out of here to help you."

"Kerry…dude…I'm at the end of my rope. Please… can you talk to Kittridge? I don't know where else to turn."

"Of course I'll talk to him, but you know how this place is."

"I know."

"Hey, I'll do everything I can, brother. Let me call you back."

"Okay."

Pat set down the phone and looked out the window. The rain was coming down slowly and steadily, making it even more difficult to see who was in the SUV at the end of the driveway. He could see mist drifting out of the tailpipe, so he knew the car was running and there was definitely somebody inside.

He looked down at the pistol in his hands. His palms were wet with cold sweat. He instinctively wiped it off with the sleeve of his sweatshirt so the gun wouldn't tarnish.

My God…what has my life become?

He thought about all the parties he'd thrown in this house, all the women and all the drugs, wishing he could go back.

I thought everything was supposed to be better after rehab...why do I feel like putting this gun to my own head?

He began to wonder if there was any dope hidden in the house. The sound of the phone ringing nearly caused him a coronary. The caller ID read Recovery Street.

"Hello?"

"It's Kittridge."

"Hey, Kit."

"You and Kerry are a couple of goddamn fools, Patrick."

I knew it... There's no way they'll let Kerry get involved in this shit...

"But Kit, I just don't know where..."

"You're a goddamn fool to think that we wouldn't do anything to help you."

"You will?"

"Goddamn right. I'm putting Kerry back on the phone. He says he's got a plan. Probably won't work, but he's got one."

"Thanks, Kit."

"No sweat my brutha..."

Pat smiled and let out a sigh of relief as Kerry picked up the phone.

"Pat, you there?"

"Yeah."

"Hey brother, I got some ideas. Me and Kit are going to grab a car and come down. We told Bill that I had a family emergency."

"That's awesome."

"I need you to meet me in Escondido at my house. My uncle is there, but he's a little strange, so you really should coordinate a time with us."

"Tell me when to leave."

"We'll pack some shit and leave here within the hour. It'll take us two or three hours to get to there."

"I'm only about an hour away. I'll leave in two."

Kerry gave Pat his home address.

"Great. We'll see you there."

"Kerry, there's a car sitting in front of my house. I don't know if it's him. What do you think I should do? You think it's them?"

"Nah, it ain't them. If it was Carlos, he'd have already killed you. I'd just hang tight. You've got a gun, right?"

"Yeah."

"If they haven't tried anything by now, they probably don't even know you're there and are waiting for you to come home. Maybe it's the cops. I'd just keep a close eye on 'em until you are ready to go, and blast right past 'em."

"Blast right past 'em?"

"Are they blocking your driveway?"

"No…"

"You got a car, right?"

"Yes."

"Then fuck 'em! Blast right past 'em! They try to get in your way, take 'em out."

"Take 'em out? How?"

"Take 'em out of the car with your gun and put 'em on the ground."

"You make it sound easy."

"Nobody wants to get in a shootout, especially the cops. Just blast past 'em."

"Okay…"

"Be strong, brother. We'll see you in three hours. Everything is going to be okay."

♪♪♪

"You need to go home and get some rest."

"I'm fine," said Elizabeth, taking a sip of coffee. "You go ahead, Detective, I'll see you in the morning."

"Liz, what can you possibly do right now? You can't do anything legally until tomorrow morning."

“We’ve got to locate Carlos and Patrick.”

“Tonight?”

“Rosa, we’ve got people on Carlos all the time. So does the DEA. I cannot fathom how he keeps slipping away; it’s like the guy is a ghost. We simply have to find him before he finds Patrick or vice-versa. Somebody must have eyes on him. And Patrick Pearson… How does this guy just disappear? Technically he’s still in the custody of the probation department, and he’s taken one drive from rehab to his house! How the hell can we not find him? Carlos may already have him! This is insane.”

“I don’t know what to tell you, Liz. Do you want me to put a car outside his house? That’s really all that we can do without a court order.”

“Yeah, I guess so, put a car there. I’m sorry, I’m just frustrated. I just feel like this thing is going to explode before we can get a chance to stop it.”

Detective Salazar’s desk phone rang.

“Salazar. Yes, she’s here, hang on a sec.” Rosa turned to Liz. “It’s a Lieutenant Morgan from the Narcotics Task Force.”

Elizabeth smiled and took the phone.

“Hey, Mike!”

“Hi, Liz. I got your message about Castillion and the rock star’s family. Déjà vu, huh?”

“Mike, it’s a bad scene. We have to find Carlos.”

“Well, here’s the latest on him… He’s been doing his traveling back and forth by boat. We’ve got him locked down on land; his face is all over the border crossings so he can’t just come across undetected anymore. Our latest intel from DEA says he’s been on a yacht. We just don’t have the resources to go out into international waters after him, and we never know where he docks. He changes it up all the time. It’s a real pain in the ass.”

“Well, you must be able to find his boat, right? Isn’t there some kind of electronic identification or something? Can’t the Coast Guard find him?”

"It's not like an airplane where there are flight plans and stuff. He's hard to find. Believe me, if he were in the States, I'd have him right now."

"Can we get the Coast Guard involved?"

"Oh, they are involved; they know all about him but they can't just search thousands of square miles of water. If they do happen across him, he's as good as in custody."

"Does the boat have a name?"

"El something de dragon… It's Spanish for dragon slayer or something… I'll email you what we do know about the boat."

"Do we have anyone in custody who might know where he keeps it?"

"I'll check the list. You'll be at the Sheriff's office, right? I'll email a list of possibilities, and you can decide who you want the Sheriff to squeeze."

♪♪♪

Pat fumbled through the dark for some warm clothing. Pulling on a jacket, he slipped down the stairs and peered out the stairwell window. The SUV was still there. He continued into the party room and checked the time. Nearly eleven.

Gotta go…

He unlocked the sliding door and crept into the garage. He looked around the corner. Nothing had changed outside.

Looking across the garage at the selection of cars, he contemplated what he might need to '*blast right 'em.*' The old cars did not handle well, especially on wet roads, so it looked like the Viper was the ticket. He darted across the open door to the second bay and got into the car.

Okay…As soon as that door is up enough to fit through, I back out and punch it. They'll never catch me in this…

He reached up to the visor, pushed the garage door opener button, and started the car.

♪♪♪

Stephanie Baker pressed the seek button on the stereo, then turned the heat up. Marco was annoyed.

"We've been sitting here for four hours, Steph, nothing's going on. Let's go get a hotel."

"Yeah, right. Separate rooms."

"Why separate rooms?"

"You know why."

He looked her over. Long hair, big boobs, pretty face, the works. She was gorgeous. He truly hated working with her for that reason; he couldn't keep his mind on work around her.

And she always dresses like this... Fifty degrees outside and she's wearing daisy dukes and a belly shirt!

"Stop undressing me, Marco."

"I don't have to. Look at you."

"You should be used to me by now."

He doubted he ever would be. She was a great writer though, headstrong, and relentless when it came to pursuing celebrity stories. Probably the best talent that Dave had ever hired. And definitely the best looking. Marco turned the heat back down.

"Come on, Steph, let's get out of here. Let's at least go eat."

"Okay. You can take me to dinner, but then we're coming right back. It's going to be a long night."

"Great...."

Marco put the SUV in gear and turned it around in the cul-de-sac. He drove past the top of Pat's driveway.

"Wait!" Stephanie screamed, looking into the rearview mirror. "He's there! He's leaving!"

Marco turned around to look through the rear window. Another garage door had gone up, and a red sports car was backing out.

"Oh, shit!" Marco said, putting the SUV in reverse.

As Marco backed up, they could see the car coming up the driveway. Marco skidded to a stop, partially blocking the driveway and Pat's exit. The headlights on the car blinded both of them as they jumped out of the SUV.

"Get the camera!" Stephanie screeched as she opened her door.

Marco grabbed his camera, ran toward the Viper's driver door, and stopped dead in his tracks. Pat had a gun pointed directly at his face.

"Back off!" Pat yelled as the weapon shook nervously in his hands.

"Patrick!" Stephanie said with her hands up in front of her, "Patrick, I'm Stephanie Baker with Celebrity Weekly."

Pat pointed the gun in her direction.

"Celebrity Weekly? Are you kidding me? Get the hell out of my way!"

"We're sorry if we startled you, we just want to get a few words…"

Pat was momentarily stunned by her beauty.

"No… Move your car."

Marco snapped a picture. The flash was disorienting in the darkness.

"Look asshole, you take one more fucking picture and I'll shoot you where you stand! And move your car! I'm not fucking around!"

"Please Patrick, we just want a couple of words…" Stephanie pleaded as Marco continued to snap pictures.

Pat fired a round past Marco's head and right through the SUV's right rear window. Marco stumbled onto his backside and dropped his camera, holding his ears.

"Patrick, what are you doing?" Stephanie screamed.

"I told you, I'm not fucking around! Now get him out of my way!"

Stephanie pulled Marco up by his collar, and the two retreated up the driveway. Pat maneuvered the car around the SUV and sped off into the night. His tires screeched on the wet pavement.

Fuckin' paparazzi Assholes...She was easy on the eyes, though...

He turned left, and the car drifted sideways on the wet asphalt, narrowly missing a head-on with another car that was approaching from the other direction.

You've got to be kidding me... The Sheriff?

♪♪♪

"What happened here?" The deputy asked, inspecting the broken windows on the SUV.

"We're with Celebrity Weekly magazine," said Stephanie. "We were just sitting out here waiting for Patrick Pearson, and when he came out of the house he almost shot my photographer in the head! Then he took off."

"Pearson was here?"

"That was him driving away in the red car."

"Shit. You two stay put."

The deputy walked back to his cruiser and dialed his cell phone.

"Detective Salazar?"

"This is Salazar."

"It's Deputy Roman. I was assigned to watch Pearson's home. I just saw him leaving his residence."

"Did you stop him?"

"No Ma'am, there were two reporters in front of his home, and one was hurt. I stopped to help. I didn't realize it was Pearson until they told me."

"How did a reporter get hurt?"

"He says Pearson shot at him. He's just shaken up."

"Pearson shot at him? Holy Christ. Where's Pearson now?"

"He was leaving the area, probably heading through Encinitas. Nearly ran me off the road."

"Did you call it in?"

"Not yet, I wanted to call you first."

Deputy Roman could hear a discussion happening on the other end of the phone. Salazar came back on.

"Deputy, we'll call it in. You just deal with whatever situation you have there. What was he driving?"

"A red Dodge Viper."

"That should be easy to spot. Okay, we'll look it up and get a bulletin out. Thanks for your help."

♪♪♪

The obnoxiously red car rumbled slowly through downtown Escondido as Pat tried to make out the addresses on the houses.

Man, I can't see shit at night... My house party days are definitely over...there it is...

Pat recognized the familiar small sedan with the Recovery Street logos on the sides parked in the driveway. There was a fully dressed Harley Davidson chopper parked next to it.

If not for the car and bike, Pat would probably have assumed the house to be abandoned. The yard was unkempt and the paint was peeling everywhere. From what Pat could see, all of the windows had either plywood or foil covering them. The security door in the front was badly rusted, and the roof appeared to be covered with plastic. Kerry and Kittridge stepped out from around the side of the garage as Pat parked his car.

"Damn, nice ride," Kittridge said. "Rock star life's been good to someone."

"I suppose. What's up, guys..."

"Kerry's dropped this brother into the middle of Nazi nation," Kittridge joked.

"I told you, Riff is a good guy," Kerry interjected.

"Yeah, we'll see if I get noosed in the next hour."

They all embraced and moved into the garage. Pat gazed around in amazement as he stepped through the threshold.

The large garage was packed top to bottom with electronics and motorcycle parts. Computers, DVD players, stereo equipment and stuff he'd never seen in his life. There were tools, books, electronic testing equipment, and in one corner, amplifiers and guitars. The ceiling was covered with Harley Davidson regalia, a Nazi flag and the flag of the Confederacy. A giant of a man in a leather vest, with a braided beard, covered in tattoos from head to toe, stood stoically in the corner of the garage.

Through his uneasiness, Pat's attention was drawn to a particular guitar in the corner on a stand.

"Is that a real Les Paul?" Pat asked.

"As far as I know," Kerry mumbled. "Don't know much about them."

Pat walked over to the golden instrument and picked it up. He carefully examined the pickups and hardware, noting the bridge in particular. He ran his fingers down the fretboard, flipped it over and checked the serial number. He was astounded.

"Dude, do you know what this is? This is an early 60's Gold Top! This thing is probably worth like twenty grand!" He strapped it on strummed the strings. "Where the hell did you get this?"

"I know people."

Pat noodled out some guitar work. The biker in the corner was staring at Kittridge with his arms crossed until Pat began to play. The music distracted him until Pat put down the instrument.

"I guess you do…"

He pulled up one of the office chairs that were scattered about the garage.

"So, Pat," asked Kittridge, "how you holdin' up?"

Pat first put his head in his hands, and then looked up.

"Not so good, man, not so good. I just don't have the money to pay this guy. I can't even come up with half. I'm totally fucked.

The police can't help – if the cops were worth a shit, they'd already have him. They've been trying to catch him forever. Our original deal was for us to testify against the bastard. Obviously, they still haven't caught him, or I would have. The cops will just end up getting my family killed."

"So the cops can't help, and you can't pay him."

Pat's voice became unsteady.

"That would appear to be the case."

"Then we get your family back ourselves," Kerry said.

"How?"

"Once we find him, we'll figure that out. But we have to find him first. This Carlos fuck, you say he gave you a cell phone?"

"Yeah."

"Do you have it?"

Pat extracted the phone from his pocket.

"Right here."

"Then I can locate him."

"You can?"

"Well, I can't, but I know someone who can. He's pretty special. He can locate pretty much anything that transmits. We can find Carlos and save your family. Guaranteed."

The biker moved from the corner. Pat was startled, and Kittridge bristled.

"You ain't thinkin' 'bout taking them to Pops, are you?" he growled.

"Yeah, Riff, I was going to..."

"We didn't talk about helpin' no snitch. And we certainly didn't talk about helpin' no nigger."

Kittridge stood up. "What the fuck did you just say?"

They went toe to toe.

"I got no beef with you, brother," Riff said, "but the club may not feel the same."

Pat observed the patches on the back of Riff's vest. He recognized the pattern of a fully patched club member. The tension could be cut with a knife. He and Kittridge were inches from each other.

"Riff, these guys saved my life," Kerry said.

"I gotta watch out for the club first. And Pops is a club asset."

"Only because of me, Riff. You all wouldn't even *know* Pops if it weren't for me. I brought him in."

"You gonna explain these two to the club? Your loyalty to the club has to come before this shit."

"I told you, these guys saved my life. I owe them. *We* owe them."

"I don't owe them shit."

There was a long silence. Pat spoke.

"Please sir, my family is going to die."

"You're a fuckin' snitch."

"Riff, this is to the club's advantage," Kerry said. "The guy holding his family is Carlos Castillion. The Tijuana Cartel. They've been hurting the club for years."

"It's my child, sir. Please let him help me."

There was a longer silence. Riff spoke.

"If you weren't Patrick Pearson, I wouldn't even entertain this shit. If I turn my back, you answer to the prez if things go south, Kerry."

"I know Pops better than anyone, and I take full responsibility."

Kittridge and Riff still stood inches from each other. Their eyes never unlocked.

"I'm gonna walk out that door, Kerry. You're on your own, no club support," Riff said. "I will be back tomorrow. Be gone."

Riff walked around Kittridge, deliberately bumping shoulders with him.

"Muthafuck…"

"Kit, stop," Kerry stepped quickly in front of him. "Not now."

Kittridge backed off, and Riff left the room. As Kittridge cooled down, the sound of a Harley starting up and roaring away shook the garage.

"Well that was fucking intense," Pat said.

"That ain't exactly the words I would choose," added Kittridge, wiping sweat from his forehead. "Fuck that muthafucka. He better hope I don't see him again."

"I'm really sorry, Kit. I don't live that life anymore," Kerry said. "I don't see color or race when I look at someone, and you know Pat doesn't.

"Never have," Pat added

"I know, bruthas," Kittridge acknowledged.

"Listen," Kerry continued, "we gotta put that shit behind us and focus guys. It's time to see Pops.

"Man, what's the deal with this Pops anyway?" asked Pat, "What is he, some kind of mad scientist or something?"

"Something like that. Anyway, we find Carlos, then we take him by surprise. Get your family."

"Take him by surprise – are you serious? Come on man, he's a big drug cartel guy. How we gonna do that?"

"We'll cross that bridge when we get to it. First, you'll need to call him on that phone so we can find him. What should we say?"

"I don't know…I've been dreading that since I got the fuckin' thing. All I can tell him is that I don't have the money."

"That's it…you call him to say you have some, but not all. Tell him you need more time. While you are on the phone, we locate him."

"Dude, he'll know what I'm doing. And what do you mean locate him?"

"Let me worry about that."

"So what, you are going to triangulate the call?"

"Triangulate?"

"Yeah, triangulate."

Kerry laughed. “Where’d you hear that?”

“Dude, I don’t know, TV or something – gimme a break, man!”

“I’m sorry,” Kerry smiled, “but look, it isn’t really that far-fetched. You can tell Carlos that because it’s Sunday night, banks are obviously closed. You need till tomorrow at the least to get that kind of money. He should believe that.”

“That actually sounds reasonable.”

Nobody spoke for a moment.

“So that’s it? Pat asked, “I call him, you…find him… or whatever, and then what?”

“Once we find him, we’ll scope out the scene and figure out how to get your fiancée and son back.”

“I don’t know, Kerry.”

“Brother, we can do it.”

Kerry took a key and opened the padlock on a large steamer trunk.

“Besides,” he said, pulling out the biggest machine gun Pat had ever seen, “I don’t think we have any other alternative.”

“Lemme see that muthafucka,” Kittridge said.

Kerry tossed the gun over. Kittridge racked her back and laughed.

“Boy, you just full of surprises, ain’tcha?”

“One or two.”

Kerry continued to extract weapons from the trunk.

“You got ammo for this shit?” Kittridge asked.

“Does a squirrel have nuts?”

Pat became even more troubled. “Dude, I don’t know – you can’t just start a gun battle with the Cartel… My kid’s gonna be with them – at least I hope he is. This isn’t some kind of military operation.”

“Well, then we make it one. We logically find a solution to our problem and we execute, step by logical step, and we remain disciplined until the mission is accomplished.”

"You just make that shit up?" asked Kittridge.

"Kind of," Kerry turned to Pat. "Okay brother, are you ready to make that call?"

"I guess so…"

"Kit, you wait here. Pat, let's go."

"Where?"

"Inside."

♪♪♪

"Are you sure he's not with the FBI?" asked a muffled voice.

"No, Pops, he's cool. Please open the door."

The sound of locks being released from behind the door seemed to go on for several minutes until the door opened. If Pat was amazed at what he saw in the garage, what he saw in the house left him dumbfounded.

The house was a maze of wires and cables. Pat had seen some of the largest lighting and sound rigs in rock n' roll history from behind the scenes, but he'd never seen anything like this. The walls were lined with racks and racks of humming electronic equipment. It looked like NASA. In the center of the room, under the plastic sheeting that covered the roof, were an array of large satellite dishes and other bristling antennae. The energy in the room almost made his hair stand on end.

"Don't just stand there, come in…"

A crazy looking man with huge coke-bottle glasses and haggard gray hair grabbed Kerry and hugged him, pushed him aside, and commenced to locking what could be mistaken as the back door to Fort Knox. He reminded Pat a little of Doc Brown from Back to the Future. He pointed at Pat.

"Who is he? Where does he come from? What does he want?" The man asked in a panic.

"Pops, he's cool," said Kerry. "He's my friend. He's a musician."

"Oooh, I like musicians. You understand harmonics, don't you?"

"Well, yeah, I guess…"

"Harmonics are infinite! Frequencies go on forever! Multiplication of waves! It's the basis of all forms of communication! It's immeasurable by humankind! You understand! That's how we will find them!"

Find them? Pat knew better than to ask. "Yeah, harmonics are really something."

"Pops, please try to relax. We really need your help."

"What can I possibly do to help a musician?"

"Pops, we need the physical location of a cellular device."

"If I am to locate it, I need it to be transmitting!"

"I know, Pops, we're going to call it. Pat's got a phone right here. The call has to be from this phone only, Pops. The person at the other end must see only this number when we call it. The number to the phone we need to locate is in this phone's memory."

"You have the number? Whose phone is it?"

"Pops, we just want to know where it is."

"I'll find it for you."

Pops began flipping on monitors, pushing buttons and turning knobs.

"Give me the phone you want to call with."

Pat handed him the phone. Pops removed the battery, then the sim card. He inserted the card into a slot on some kind of card reader and handed Pat a corded telephone.

"Call it."

"Uh, I can't…the number is in the phone."

Pops began laughing hysterically.

"I guess we'll have to look it up!"

He turned a monitor to face him and began frantically typing on a keyboard. He spun the monitor back around to face Pat and pointed at a number on the screen.

"Is this it? Is this the number?"

"Yeah, I think so…"

"Dial it."

Pat took a deep breath and dialed the phone. After a few rings, Carlos's voice came over the phone.

"Bueno?"

"Carlos? This is Patrick Pearson."

"Do you have my money, cabrone?"

"Carlos, I can't get it tonight. The banks are closed. I need till tomorrow."

"You think I'm stupid, pendejo? Are the police listening?"

"Carlos, I swear, there are no cops. I just can't get the money until the banks open."

"You fucker… I'm going to kill them."

Pat began to panic.

"Wait, Carlos…Please, just listen to me!"

"You get me my money you fucker! If I see any police they're all dead! If I find out you lied to me, I will cut off one of your son's fingers. Every time you lie he loses another, comprende puto?"

"Carlos, I swear, no police. I just need to go to the bank in the morning."

"Manana, puto."

"Carlos, I prom…"

Carlos hung up.

Pat was drenched in sweat.

"Pops, did you find it?" Kerry probed.

"Something's wrong!" Pops screeched to himself. "Something's wrong! It's not on a cell tower or a landline!"

"What are you talking about, Pops?"

"It's not a cell phone! It's something else!"

"Something else? What?"

"It's from a satellite! It's coming from a satellite!"

"Pops, can you track it?"

"Stop distracting me!"

"Sorry, Pops."

"It's coming from Inmarsat! It's a satellite phone! It's a TT3064. 3064 alpha! The frequency is 1626.5 megahertz!"

"Pops, what does that mean?"

"It's not a cellular. It's ship-to-shore."

"Ship to shore?" asked Pat, "They're on a ship?"

"Yessir! On a ship!"

"A ship? Are you kidding me? I'm so fucked."

"Pops," Kerry pleaded, "can you locate the boat?"

"Who is this man? Why does he want your money?"

"Pops," Kerry interjected, "it's a long story… It's not important."

"What are you getting me into? Does this have to do with the government?"

"No, Pops, Pat just needs your help. Please locate the phone, Pops."

"No way! You get out of here now!"

"Pops, please!"

Pat, still shaken by the phone call, couldn't hold it in anymore.

"Sir," he cried, "a man has taken my family. For ransom. I can't pay it. You're my only hope for getting them back. Please, sir… Please."

Pops looked Pat in the eyes.

"You go to the police."

"We can't. He'll kill them," said Kerry. We just want you to find the boat. Please…"

"They better not find me."

"Pops, you are safe."

"I'll find the boat, you call the police."

Pat and Kerry looked at each other.

"Okay, Pops, we'll call the police."

"Fine, then…Now that I have the device, I can do anything you want."

Pops pulled up what looked like a radar screen on his main monitor.

"This is a vessel tracking plotter. I can use the sat phone as a transponder signal and input it directly into the program. It will use geo-imaging to give me the location and, since we were on the phone for a few minutes, it will also use the time displacement and signal duration to plot a bearing. Simple as pie."

Kerry and Pat just looked at each other.

"There it is. Right there."

As far as Pat could tell, the boat was off the shore of San Diego. It looked pretty far out. He didn't really know how to read it.

"Pops," Kerry asked, "how far away is the boat and where is it headed?"

"It's six miles out from the channel. It's going due east. You can plainly see right here."

Pat and Kerry looked at the screen and at each other again.

"Can you identify the boat's name or something?" Kerry asked.

"What am I, a freaking wizard?"

"Sorry, Pops."

He suddenly became agitated again. "You boys need to go!" Pops said, nervously putting Pat's phone back together. "I have work to do!"

"Pops, how long does it take to get to shore from there?"

"I don't know!" he exclaimed, pushing the phone into Pat's hand. "Depends on parameters! Factors! Velocity and wind speed and water current and juxtaposition! It depends on all kinds of things! Things I don't have time for!"

"Pops, can you just find out how fast the boat was traveling?"

"You people are impossible!"

Pops squinted at the screen and pushed his thick glasses back up to the bridge of his nose. He pulled out a calculator from under a stack of greenbar paper and typed in some numbers.

"Thirty-five knots. Forty-one miles per hour. Now you boys have to go!"

"Okay Pops… Thank you."

"Yeah, thank you sir…" Pat said as Pops pushed them out the door. The sound of clicking locks followed their exit.

"He's getting worse," Kerry said. "I'm not sure how much longer he can function in normal life on his own. The club watches out for him when I can't be here."

"Yeah, he's a bit out there."

They walked out of the house and into the garage. Kittridge had outfitted himself with several weapons and a bunch of ammunition.

"Look, I'm little black Rambo!"

"Hope you're not scared of water, black Rambo."

"Why?"

"They're on a boat."

"On a muthafuckin' boat?"

"I shit you not."

"Well, they're gonna have to dock that muthafucka before I do anything."

"Yeah, Kerry, what the hell are we gonna do now?"

"We're going to adapt. According to what Pops said, they'll be somewhere around Mission Bay in minutes. We gotta find out where."

"How are we going to do that?"

"There's only one way. We'll let them get into port, give Pops a chance to calm down, and you'll have to call Carlos again."

"And tell him what? You heard him! He'll cut off my kid's fingers if he thinks I'm fucking with him. I can't call him again. No way!"

"You can if you have his money."

"I don't."

"You can tell him you do."

"Dude, I can't lie to him. He'll kill them."

“It’s perfect. You tell him you have the money. He’ll tell you where to meet him. You say you are hours away from his location. He has no idea where you are, he’ll have to take your word for it and wait. During that time, we locate the boat, sneak up on him, and ka-pow,” Kerry smacked his palms together, “we get your fiancée and kid back and turn him over to the cops. It’s a done deal.”

“Dude, what color is the sky on your planet? You’re delusional! This isn’t a movie dude, it’s real life.”

“Gimme another option, Pat.”

“I don’t know …”

“We don’t have any other choice,” Kerry said as he turned to Kittridge. “You in, black Rambo?”

“Hell to the yeah.”

“Pat?”

Pat shot him a look of total despair.

“Like you said, do I have a choice?”

TWENTY-SEVEN

DETECTIVE SALAZAR HANDED Elizabeth another cup of the station's best coffee. She took a sip, cringed and set it down.

"Needs more sugar," she said, rubbing her temples. "Four hours of sleep just isn't enough." She got a scrunchie out of her purse and put her hair in a ponytail.

"Well, at least your court order came," Rosa said as she walked back over to the coffee station. "I just pulled it off the fax. Do you want to drive?"

"Are you kidding?"

The two detectives took the elevator downstairs to the parking garage and got into Rosa's plain black Ford Crown-Victoria. They rolled through a drive-through for a snack and some decent coffee and hit the highway. The morning sun rose behind them, and they were soon entangled in Monday morning rush hour traffic. Elizabeth put on her sunglasses and gazed out the window. This was the first time the sun had been out in days. It wasn't long before her coffee was cold and her eyes were closed.

"Liz, we're almost there," Rosa announced as she exited the freeway in Encinitas.

Elizabeth picked her head up off the window.

"Wow, I don't think I've slept in a moving car since I was a kid."

There was already a black and white waiting for them as they approached Pat's driveway.

"Good morning, Deputy. Anybody home?"

"No, Ma'am."

"Can we gain entry?"

"Yes, Ma'am."

The deputy picked up a tool bag from the trunk of his car. They walked over to Pat's front door and within minutes were inside. Elizabeth set her coffee cup and a copy of the court order down on the kitchen counter.

"Rosa, can you and the deputy look around downstairs? I'll go up."

"Sure, Liz."

Elizabeth slowly climbed the stairs and looked around. She stepped into the master bedroom, and there on the bed laid a knot of auburn hair. She slipped on some rubber gloves and picked it up.

Definitely human...Probably the girl's...

She dropped it into an evidence bag and continued to browse around the bedroom, opening drawers and looking through closets. In one closet she noticed all of the shoes in a pile. Shining a penlight into the closet, she found the carpet in one corner to be pulled up. She lifted the carpet, revealing a small compartment in the floor. Kneeling down closer she could smell the familiar scents of gun oil and powder. But no gun.

The study was across the hall from the bedroom. She picked a cordless phone up off of its cradle and checked the caller ID history. Several calls had been received last night, many from the same numbers. One she recognized as the Sheriff's Department. She took out her notepad and jotted down the other numbers. Taking out her own cell phone, she dialed the first of three numbers. It was the voicemail for the offices of Steve Stanford. She disregarded it and hung up. The next number was the voicemail for SLK Entertainment. She hung up on that one too. The third number was to The Recovery Street Foundation. She let that one ring as she tapped on the computer keyboard sitting at the same desk. The screen immediately lit up. His desktop was a picture of Pat, Christine and Tommy.

Nice family… She thought, looking at Pat's desktop icons. *Somebody's definitely been on the computer recently…*

The phone at Recovery Street picked up.

"Recovery Street, how may I help you?"

"Hello, this is Detective Elizabeth Hunter of the San Diego Police Department. Is there anyone in charge there that I might speak to regarding a former resident?"

"Let me see…can you hold?"

"Of course…"

Elizabeth put her phone on speaker and set it down on the desk, turning her attention back to Pat's computer. She opened Internet Explorer and clicked on the history button. Only three websites had been viewed in the last six months or so, and they had all been viewed last night.

The first page was Yahoo.com, which Elizabeth assumed was probably Pat's ISP homepage. The next two were United Pacific Bank, and Mapquest.com. She smiled.

"Hello? Who's calling please?" barked the speaker on her phone.

"This is Detective Hunter, San Diego Police. To whom am I speaking?"

"Hi, Detective… This is Bill Riker. I'm the facilitator here. What can I do for you?"

"Bill, I've got a difficult situation that I thought maybe you could help me with. I'm sure you are familiar with Patrick Pearson."

"Of course."

"I can't go into detail but I can tell you that we are having trouble locating him."

"Sweetheart, I can't even tell you if he was ever here or not. We're legally bound to anonymity."

"Look, Bill," she said in her most calming and seductive tone, "this number was the last one he called from his home last night.

I need to know who it was that he spoke with, and why. His life could be in danger Bill, and I could really use your help."

"I could find out who was on front desk duty last night and see if maybe they remember who it was that he talked to."

"Bill, that would be great."

"Detective, I hate to be a pain, as I'm sure you have enough to deal with, but is there somebody I can call to verify that you are who you're telling me you are? If, hypothetically speaking of course, say Patrick *was* a resident here, he'd probably have a lot of calls from paparazzi claiming to be everything from family members to bill collectors just to see if he was here. I just want to be sure you are legit, okay?"

Elizabeth agreed and gave him the necessary information to get authentication.

"Bill, call me back as soon as you have verified me. This whole thing is pretty time-sensitive."

"You have my word."

Elizabeth snapped her phone shut and walked back out into the hallway and to the top of the stairs.

"Hey Rosa… You guys down there?"

"Yeah Liz, we're at the garage door."

"Rosa, can you get a computer geek over here?"

"Probably. Why, what did you find?"

"Well, I think we can now be sure that Carlos has the girlfriend and the son, and Patrick has already been contacted. Patrick is either trying to get the money right now or worse, getting ready to do something stupid. He's also carrying a gun. The quicker you get the computer geek over here, the quicker we'll know where he went."

♪♪♪

Rico watched in amusement as Carlos attempted to auger the mammoth yacht into their private slip at the Dana Landing in San

Diego's Mission Bay. He couldn't see Carlos's face from where he was, but he could imagine it. The boat's transmission protested with a loud grinding sound as Carlos threw the boat into reverse to avoid hitting the dock opposite them at the public boat launch. Rico could hear him cursing in Spanish from the fly bridge. As the boat inched closer to the dock, Rico decided to put his sunglasses on so Carlos couldn't see the laughter in his eyes. Carlos's head appeared over the rail.

"Don't just sit there you pinche puto, jump down and get us moored!"

"Yes, sir…" Rico responded with a grin.

As most people who worked for Carlos did, Rico despised him. A lot of people died because of the chip on Carlos's shoulder. The chip was growing bigger and bigger - particularly since the arrival of the 'rock star' into their lives. Carlos's foolish pursuits of people he felt had wronged him made for sloppy business that inevitably his men wound up cleaning up. Rico knew by the fact they had docked that the next mess was imminent.

He secured the vessel to its moorings and walked back upstairs taking in his surroundings. Mission Bay was a beautiful place, though he doubted Carlos ever really appreciated it.

"Rico, it looks like the weather will be in our favor. Pearson will bring my money this morning. Because Miguel is too stupid, I will have him stay inside with our guests so when the rock star arrives, you will meet him and bring him on board. We'll depart, and once we are in international waters, we will kill all of them and dump them into the ocean."

"Yes, Mr. Castillion.

♪♪♪

"So, are you ready?"

"No."

"You just gotta do it, brother."

"I know. It's just…I mean…what if he catches on to what we're doing?"

"Pat, you make it short and sweet. 'I have your money, where do you want me to go?' He'll tell you, and during that time we pinpoint his location. Then we go down there and ambush his ass."

"You make it sound pretty easy."

"It will be easy."

Pat was becoming tired and annoyed. They'd only slept a couple of hours in very uncomfortable accommodations. "How can you be so sure, Kerry?"

"I've ambushed a lot of people in my day."

"And you got caught."

"Only twice."

"Out of how many times?"

"Four or five. Maybe."

"Nice odds."

"Yeah, you suck," said Kittridge. "I robbed all sorts of people. Never got caught."

"You're in a rehab too, black Rambo," Kerry jabbed, "and I doubt it was because you were such a master criminal."

"Don't go gettin' all emotional on me…"

"Look you guys," Pat pleaded, "we're all clean and sober now. We're fighting the good fight, using our skills for good instead of evil. We're probably sharper than we've ever been in our lives."

"We can do this," Kerry added as he turned back to Pat. "Brother, the clock is ticking."

"Fine. Let's go."

Pat and Kerry walked out of the garage and into the house where Pops already had the door open for them.

"Hey, Pops…You know we were…"

"Just get in…" Pops pulled the door closed. "I hear everything," he said angrily. "Kerry Eugene Parker, are you out of your fucking mind?"

"Eugene?" laughed Pat.

"You aren't some goddamn fighting force! You can't ambush anyone!"

"Pops, we have no alternative."

"You're a small-time crook. A two-time loser. You don't know anything about stuff like this! You call the cops. Is Riff aware of this?"

"Yes, Pops. And we can't call the cops. He'll kill Pat's family."

"You chance it!"

"We can't, Pops."

"Well, I'm not helping you get yourselves killed."

"Pops, we have to find the boat."

"No way. You want to get yourselves killed, you do it without my help."

"But Pops…"

"But nothing. Get the hell out of here."

Pops pushed them to the door and began unlocking locks.

"Pops, please…we don't know what else to do…"

"Get out."

♪♪♪

The guy didn't look like any computer geek Elizabeth had ever seen. He was tall and handsome, with long blond hair and piercing blue eyes. His bangs were tied back into a ponytail, the rest of his hair flowed over his shoulders. Elizabeth was smitten.

"Are you Detective Hunter? I'm Tim Valentino with IT forensics."

She put out her hand to shake, and he took it softly.

"Detective Elizabeth Hunter, San Diego PD. Call me Liz."

"Okay Liz, what can I do for you?"

She led Tim upstairs to Pat's computer.

"Last night the owner of this machine MapQuested something and erased the history. Can you get the address he looked up?"

Tim smiled. "Kid stuff."

Elizabeth's phone rang.

"Please excuse me for a minute."

"No problem," Tim said, already typing away on the keyboard.

"Detective Hunter."

"Hi Detective, it's Bill Riker, Recovery Street."

"Hi Bill."

"Well, I checked with the guy who was working the desk last night, and he confirmed that Patrick had called and that he spoke with a current resident. The resident's name is Kerry Parker. He and Patrick were the closest thing to best friends that you are allowed to have around here."

Elizabeth scribbled on her notepad.

"May I speak with Mr. Parker?"

"I wish you could, but unfortunately Kerry and another resident left late last night on a home visit pass. Family emergency."

"That's an interesting coincidence. Where did they go?"

"Escondido. I'm sorry, but I don't have an exact address."

Tim nudged her with his elbow and pointed to the computer screen.

"Thanks Bill…I have it."

♪♪♪

"Now what are we going to do?" yelled Pat. "We can't find the fuckin' boat!"

"You're just going to have to meet him."

"Meet him? Are you high?"

"You're going to have to tell him you have the money and meet with him. We'll be watching you. When you make the drop, we'll follow the person who picks it up right to the source. We'll be ready for anything."

"He's on a boat. How do you intend to chase down a boat?"

"With a Jet Ski."

"You're a retard."

"Why not?"

"Dude, this is ridiculous. I was willing to go along with your plan when we could find the boat and catch them off guard, but this? Chasing down a boat with a Jet Ski? I mean, come on, man, like they wouldn't be prepared for something like this? I've seen enough movies to know what to expect. And how do you know he will want me to make a drop? He might rob me!"

"He comes near you, and we'll be ready to rock! Perfect!"

"My last statement was intended as a negative. Shit just doesn't happen like that in real life."

"How do you know?"

"I don't…I mean, I just do…"

"Nobody really knows anything. You said it yourself…this is not a movie. We can be ready for anything. We have weapons, technology, a fast car; we'll get a Jet Ski…. We can do it, brother. Where can we get a Jet Ski?"

"I have one," Pat said reluctantly. "Actually, I have two."

"See? Everything is falling into place! We're meant to do this."

Pat began to consider the plan and then shook the thought off.

"No…No way! This is nuts! Kit, help me out here!"

"Sounds exciting to me," Kittridge said.

"Exciting?" Pat answered in disbelief. "Exciting?"

"Pat," said Kerry, "if you have a better idea, please, share it, brother."

Pat stood up and paced around the room. "Fuck!" he screamed. "Okay, say we come up with some plan. What about the money? They're going to want to see it…what do we do about that?"

"Good question. I guess we'd have to make fake money stacks. Like on TV. You know, paper with real bills on top. I don't even know what four million dollars would look like. What would we need? Duffle bags or something?"

Pat just stared out the window, not believing what he was hearing.

"Well," started Kittridge, "a million bucks would be ten thousand hundred dollar bills, or one thousand thousand dollar bills."

"Good math. Do they even make thousand dollar bills?"

"I don't know."

"We need to find out if we could get thousand dollar bills. What should we do, call a bank?"

Pat could take no more. "This is totally unrealistic!" he shouted. "Carlos knows there is no way a person can get four million bucks in cash! There's no way! A bank wouldn't give that to Donald Trump! He's just trying to lure me to him to kill me! We're all dead! There's no way any of this shit will work!" He began to get hysterical.

"Pat, calm down, bro… Take a deep breath."

Pat sat down and ran his fingers through his hair.

"Dude," he said between gasps, "I can't take this… I just got out of rehab… Now I'm trying to come up with some cockamamie scheme to rescue my girlfriend and son from a psycho drug dealer who obviously wants me dead? Oh God…"

Kerry knelt down next to Pat and put an arm around him, letting him cry it out for a few minutes.

"Brother, this is the time when you need to think rational."

"Dude, I'm an emotional guy anyway… this I cannot handle."

"Let me ask you this: say you did have four million, would you pay?"

"Of course."

"Then let's proceed as if you had the money. Let's follow those steps. Then at least we'll know what Carlos would expect. So what would you do? Call your bank?"

"I suppose."

"Okay," Kerry handed him the phone, "then call 'em."

"What the hell do I say?"

"You need to withdraw all your funds. Nothing more than that. Find out the procedure."

"Okay."

Pat found the number to his branch and made the call. Although the manager of the branch was something less than helpful, Pat did get the details on closing his accounts and converting them to cash.

"I can get two hundred thousand today, and the rest tomorrow, or all of it in the form of cashier's check. And, they have to report it to the IRS and the DEA. And the highest denomination is hundreds."

"Wow…that's interesting," Kerry observed. "Four million bucks would be four hundred stacks of hundred dollar bills. That'd take up some space. Probably weigh a lot too."

"Well I can't get four million bucks anyway, so what's the difference?"

"We need to make a choice. Do we assume that Carlos is well aware of the fact that there is no way to get four million cash, tell him what we *can* get and give him options on getting the rest, or plan B, assume he would believe we have the money, get four million in fake cash and give that to him?"

"I'd believe he's well aware of what can be taken from a bank. He's a member of a drug cartel. I'm sure he's dealt with this kind of shit before."

"I agree. So you're gonna have to tell him you can get… say, half a million and the rest in a check. And tell him about the IRS and DEA. See what he says."

"Dude…I don't know…"

"Pat, we're acting as if you are really trying to pay him. This is what would happen."

"I know…"

"So call him."

"Okay…"

God help me…

Pat dialed the phone.

"Bueno?"

"Carlos…"

"Rock star…Do you have my fedia?"

"Carlos, the bank won't release that kind of money in cash. I can't get it all in one day."

"Then your wife and son die."

"Carlos, please, I can get about half a million today. And I can give you a cashier's check for the rest."

"A check, eh?" Carlos began to laugh. "The rock star wants to write a check!"

"Carlos, there's no other way…The bank just won't give me any more than five hundred thousand. And they insist on reporting it to the IRS and DEA."

"I know that, you fuck! Do you think I swam over here?"

Pat did not know what to say to that.

"Listen to me, you pinche perro, you will bring me the cash, and the check. I will hold your wife and son until the check clears. And if it doesn't clear…"

Pat heard the sound of a woman screaming. He couldn't tell if it was Christine.

"Do you hear that, rock star? If my check does not clear, that will be the last sound from her you ever hear."

"Carlos, please, I'll bring the money…the check will clear…I promise…"

Carlos enjoyed hearing the desperation in Pat's voice. He knew he was pushing Pat over the edge. "Okay, rock star, I will trust you. You will meet my associate at the boat launch at Dana Landing. You will meet him beside the banos. You will meet him at four o'clock. If you are late, the deal is off, and they die. If you are not alone, they die, and if there are police, they die. Do you understand, puto?"

"I don't know where Dana Landing is… Where…"

"Find it, cabrone."

"But Carlos, I..."

"Buenos dias."

Pat felt as if he'd just been punched in the gut.

"So what was that?" inquired Kerry enthusiastically. "The Dana Landing boat launch?"

"Yes," Pat said, attempting to catch his breath.

"What time?"

"Four."

"Shit...we've got a lot to do!"

"I suppose..."

"Kit, you get all the weapons and ammo together and put them in the back of the car. I've gotta grab some gear and make Pat some money and a cashier's check."

"Make me what?"

"We gotta create some cash and a check," Kerry said, clicking away on his computer. "Shouldn't take me more than a few minutes."

"Okay..."

"The cashier's check is easy - I'll have that printed pronto. The money bands won't be too difficult either. Grab that paper cutter over there."

Pat did as instructed.

"We just gotta cut them to size."

Kerry's printer spit out a Bank of California cashier's check for 3.5 million dollars.

"My bank is United Pacific," Pat said.

Kerry shot him a look. "Really?"

"Sorry."

The printer then spit out a sheet of mustard colored bands with the $10,000 denomination printed on them, complete with the Federal Reserve watermark.

"Damn, dude, is there anything you can't do?"

"We'll see, brother," Kerry said, stuffing everything into a duffle bag. "Now, we only need fifty stacks with bills on top. So we'll need fifty hundred dollar bills, and five hundred singles. You should be able to come up with that, right?"

"I'd imagine."

"Great. Here's some other shit we'll need."

He handed Pat a couple of pairs of binoculars and some metal cases.

"Take these out and put 'em in the car. Let's go."

♪♪♪

Elizabeth and Rosa pulled up in front of what looked to be an abandoned house in Escondido.

"Looks abandoned," observed Rosa.

"Looks can be deceiving."

They walked up to the front door and knocked. No answer. They listened. Nothing. Cautiously they slipped through the side gate and around to the garage door. Locked.

"Looks like nobody's home," Rosa said. "Do you think it's abandoned? Maybe our address is wrong."

"Maybe..." Elizabeth stepped back over to the gate and checked the power meter. "And maybe not," she said, pointing to the whizzing wheel inside the glass bubble.

Visually inspecting the eaves of the house, she walked back around front until she spotted exactly what she was looking for. A camera. She began to wave.

"Whoever is inside already knows we're here. He's probably listening as well."

"Hello? Whoever you are, I'm with the police." Elizabeth held her badge up to the camera. "We're looking for Patrick Pearson and Kerry Parker. Neither of them are in trouble, we are just concerned for their safety. Please, if you can hear me, open the door. Their lives may depend on it... Hello? Is anybody there?"

Rosa found another camera on another corner of the house and repeated Elizabeth's words to it. They milled around for a few minutes and tried again.

"Please…they could be in danger… Please talk to us…" They both stared into the camera. "If you can't help us willingly, we'll have to get a warrant to enter."

Giving up, they began to walk back to their car when they heard a voice.

"Wait a minute, officers."

They turned to see where the voice was coming from but were unable to tell. They walked back to the front door and looked into the camera's lens.

"Sir? Are you there?"

"Yes. What do you want from me?"

"Sir, may we come in and talk to you for a minute or two?"

"No… Tell me what you want."

"Is this Patrick or Kerry?"

"No. Tell me what you want."

"Sir, we need to speak with you."

"Is this about my alien contact? Are you from the Feds?"

Elizabeth and Rosa looked at each other.

"No sir, we're with the Sheriff's Department. We're here about Patrick Pearson and Kerry Parker. Do you know them?"

"I'm doing nothing wrong."

"Sir, we're not concerned with you, only about Patrick and Kerry's safety."

"I knew they were in trouble. I told them no way."

"They were here?"

"Yes."

"You told them no way to what, sir?"

"I told them I wouldn't help them find that boat. No way."

Carlos's boat… thought Elizabeth.

"Listen sir, Patrick and Kerry are in danger. They are in way over their heads. Sir, please, if you know where they are, please tell us."

"Then you'll go away?"

"We'll go away."

"You will tell no one that you spoke to me? You'll tell no one about my contact with the aliens?"

Rosa looked at Elizabeth, who almost cracked a smile.

"Sir, we promise, may we just come in?"

"No way. They went to the Dana Landing."

They looked at each other again.

"Is that someplace where the aliens land or something?"

"No, it's someplace where humans launch boats, you idiots. Now leave me alone."

Elizabeth finally let out a chuckle. "Thank you sir, thank you for your help."

"Go away."

Liz and Rosa got back into the car.

"Wow..." said Rosa.

"You're not kidding," laughed Elizabeth. "Well, it looks like we've got an idea where Carlos's boat is. Where is Dana Landing anyway?"

"Mission Bay."

"I'd love to get SDPD down there, but if we do, we might be endangering everybody. We have to be discreet and feel this thing out."

"I agree."

"I'm going to call SDPD and have them put a negotiator and SWAT on alert, but we make no moves until we get more intel. Let's go."

♪♪♪

After getting the appropriate cash denominations from the bank, Pat, Kerry, and Kittridge stopped for coffee and then continued to Pat's home. Pat read the court order that lay on his kitchen counter next to a coffee cup with lipstick stains on it. Kerry and Kittridge slowly walked around Pat's home, their mouths hanging open in admiration.

"How big is that TV?" Kerry inquired peeking down into the party room.

"I don't know," said Pat, obviously more concerned with his current reading material, "Dude, the cops have been here. They're looking for us! We gotta get this done before they fuck everything up!"

"Don't worry brother," said Kerry, laying the duffle bag full of money on the kitchen counter. "We'll be fine. Let's sort out this cash, get whatever else we need and go. It's getting late."

"Man, this house should be on muthafuckin' cribs," Kittridge playfully commented. "Hi, I'm Mista Rock Star, Patrick Pearson…Come on in, lemme show you what's in my rock star fridge!"

Pat ignored Kittridge and concentrated on creating believable stacks of money.

"So where are the Jet Skis?" asked Kerry.

"They're around the corner of the garage. I don't know how we're going to pull them, though. I haven't seen my truck since I was busted."

"I still can't believe you had all this and put it all in jeopardy for dope," Kittridge said, checking out the kitchen appliances.

"Life's a funny thing, Kit."

"Sure is, my brutha, sure is…"

The money was laid out in an organized fashion on the counter, along with a dozen weapons. Ammunition was inserted, and the weapons were locked and loaded. A map of Mission Bay was also laid out on the counter. The three men sat down on stools.

"Four o'clock, right?"

"Four o'clock."

Kerry opened a metal suitcase, revealing several pieces of what appeared to be listening devices and radios.

"Pat, strap this around your waist and make it comfortable. This goes in your ear. Kit, these are yours. We'll be in constant contact. Kit and I will go early and scope out the scene. Pat, by the time you arrive, we'll probably have a plan."

"Probably? I thought you already had a plan?"

"That is the plan. We'll go now and then you arrive at four by yourself in that red-ass car of yours. We'll be ready to follow Carlos's henchmen right to him."

"What about the boat? What if they leave and we have to follow them? We need the Jet Skis."

"We need a truck."

"Let me go and see if my neighbors are home."

Pat jumped up and ran outside.

"You know Kit, the Jet Skis are the way to go because we'd look as if we had a reason to be at a boat launch."

"We gonna need some Jet Skiing clothes."

"Just shorts and t-shirts, right? I'm sure Pat's got some stuff."

"Shit…Look at us! We both outweigh him by a hundred pounds."

Pat came running back in. "The neighbors aren't home, but their truck is there."

Kittridge stood up. "Don't worry, I got this."

"What if it has an alarm?" asked Pat.

"I said I got this. Where are your tools?"

♪♪♪

"I don't think we fit in down here," said Rosa, who was dressed impeccably in a navy pantsuit.

"The Crown-Victoria doesn't help either," agreed Elizabeth.

The Dana Landing public boat launch was bustling with activity. Fishermen and boat enthusiasts were loading and unloading watercraft of all shapes and sizes and tourists were happily enjoying the long-awaited sunshine. There was no waiting for vehicles at the launch, but the parking area was packed just the same. A group of sweaty guys were taking advantage of a fish cleaning station near the bathrooms.

"Let's go over to the mall and do some shopping."

They hid the police car in the hotel parking lot and walked the perimeter of the small marina taking note of the various docks, gangways and yachts. The public launch not only featured the fish cleaning facilities, but also a temporary use pier that was a good twenty or so feet above the water until its end where it became a two-story foot ramp leading to the lower portion. People would moor their boats while they parked their trucks and then return to embark on their day trips. Private docks with hundreds of slips surrounded the public area on both sides of the little harbor. A hotel stood majestically to the west while a mall full of trendy tourist shops sat opposite on the east bank.

Elizabeth walked out of the dressing room of a little clothing store and admired her new dress in the mirror. She added an oversized handbag to the ensemble and paid for her and Rosa's new attire with the company credit card. The two picked out some folding chairs and a beach umbrella from the store next door.

"Looks like a nice day for some sun," said Elizabeth, stabbing the big yellow and white beach umbrella into the grass near the boat launch.

"Sure does. What do we do now?"

"We wait."

♪♪♪

"You're gonna be fine, brother," Kerry said from the window of Pat's neighbor's silver GMC pickup. "We won't let anything happen to you."

"Okay."

"When you get there, park someplace conspicuous, so they know you came alone, and leave the keys in the car in case one of us needs it in a pinch. Turn your radio on when you are about a mile away from the launch. Call us for a radio check, and we'll reply. When you get there, take out your earpiece and drop it down your shirt so they don't know you're wearing a wire. We'll still be able to hear everything, you just won't be able to hear us. Okay?"

"Right."

"Pat, we can do this."

"I guess."

"We'll see you down there, brother."

Pat watched the stolen truck drive away with the Jet Skis in tow.

I'm never gonna survive this...

TWENTY-EIGHT

"TURN HERE," KITTRIDGE said.

Kerry turned left and followed the signs to the boat launch. The lot was completely packed, and there was a line of trucks and trailers waiting to pick up their respective watercraft. Neither Kerry nor Kittridge were sure what the proper etiquette was for this type of situation.

"Go around through the lot and get in line," said Kittridge.

"Are we going to launch these things right now?"

"Yes."

They waited in line for a few minutes or so and their turn came up.

"Go ahead and follow what everyone else is doing."

"Sure."

Kerry drove the truck across the open area above the ramp, put it in reverse and began to back up. They hadn't gone ten feet when the trailer jackknifed.

"Goddammit!"

"Ain't you ever backed up a muthafuckin' trailer before?"

"Not really… not this small… I can't see the fuckin thing!"

"Use your mirrors."

"I'm stuck."

"You gotta go forward again."

"Shit…"

Kerry pulled the truck forward and tried again with the same results.

"Goddammit!"

"I told you to use your mirrors."

"You want to do this?"

"I could do it better than your ass."

"Just get the fuck out and guide me back."

Kittridge got out and used hand signals to assist Kerry in a successful third try. The trailer now sat fairly straight and just above the waterline. Kerry yelled out the window of the truck. "How far should I back into the water?"

"I don't know… till them muthafuckas float?"

"Should you start them first?"

"Me? I don't know how to start these things. I don't even know how to swim."

"Excuse me? When the fuck were you going to tell me that?"

"I'm telling your ass right now."

"How were we going to chase down the boat?"

"Whatcha mean we? I was just goin' along with the plan."

"Fuck me…"

Kerry jumped out of the truck and eyed the Jet Skis. He took a closer look at one of them. It had what looked like a round key on a lanyard.

"It looks like it's got a plastic key. Should I turn it?"

"You never rode one of these things before?"

"Not really."

"What kinda white boy never rode a Jet Ski?"

"This kind. I spent a lot of time in other places, you know?"

"Well, how were you planning on doing this?"

"I ride all kinds of motorcycles…How different could it be?"

"I never seen any motorcycle go on water."

"Well, we gotta do something."

Kerry tried to turn the key and it came out in his hand.

"Shit, did I break it off?"

"I don't think so. Stick it back in the hole and look for a button or something."

Kerry scanned the handlebars. There was a button and two switches. Kerry tried the button. The engine turned over with a roar but wouldn't stay running.

"Shit, it doesn't run!" He kept trying. Smoke was coming out of the rear end. A boater who was loading up a catamaran next to them couldn't help but notice the fiasco.

"Hey, you guys having trouble?"

"Yeah, it's our first time."

The guy looked them up and down. Kerry was wearing a button down shirt with a pair of shorts that looked two sizes too small, and Kittridge had on a golf shirt and trousers. Both were wearing shoes.

"You don't say?"

"Yeah, and it won't start."

"Well first of all, you better put it all the way in the water. You'll mess it up if it runs without water. Then you gotta turn on the gas here." He turned a knob on the center console. "The engine run switch is here. Turn it on and crank her over with the start button."

Kerry did as instructed, and the ski fired right up. He eased the ski off of the trailer, got alongside and attempted to get on. The ski flopped over onto its side, dumping Kerry into the water and onto the cement bottom. Kittridge laughed heartily.

"Fuck! How do you get on these fucking things?"

Kerry righted the ski, started it back up, and made a second attempt, this time holding the handlebars for leverage. As he slipped into the water again, he accidentally pressed the throttle, and the ski took off, crashing into the trailer and the other ski.

"Goddammit!"

"Hey, man!" a voice yelled. "You gotta have a life jacket on or the cops will stop you!"

"Thanks!" Kerry answered through clenched teeth.

"Brother," he said to Kittridge, "I think we may have to scrap the Jet Ski part of the plan."

"You think so?" said Kittridge. "I thought you just about had it that time."

"Fuck you."

♪♪♪

"Are you seeing what I'm seeing?" Elizabeth laughed as she lowered her sunglasses.

"You mean those two dopes down there trying to unload the Jet Skis?"

"Exactly. You notice anything strange about them?"

"You mean besides the fact that they can't back up a trailer, can't start their own skis, can't ride their own skis and the black guy is wearing pants?"

"I guess you did notice. Nice police work."

They both laughed.

"Let's keep an eye on those two. It looks like they might have given up on skiing for today."

"Who goes skiing after three on a Monday anyway?"

"Not these two."

The two detectives watched as the men loaded the ski back onto the trailer and drove up to the parking area. They later left the truck with duffle bags and began to circle the marina.

"It looks like they're looking for something."

"Like what?"

"I don't know…"

The afternoon sun had begun to cast long shadows across the marina and the mall area. Elizabeth lost track of the two men behind a boathouse.

"Come on, Rosa, let's take a walk."

They walked around to the east side of the cove and found the two men on top of a staircase looking out across the marina with binoculars. Each of them had listening devices in their ears.

"Well, I guess they found what they were looking for."

"What's that?"

"A vantage point."

"Are they looking for the same thing we are?"

"Good question."

♪♪♪

Carlos sat back in the captain's chair on the fly bridge of his vessel. His hostages were secured in the main salon, and his men were tending to his business. He closed his eyes and imagined the look on Pat's face. He imagined him coming on board the yacht, handing him the money and pleading for the lives of his family. He imagined tying them all up, taking them out to sea, killing them execution style and feeding them to the sharks. He smiled.

"Mr. Castillion, it's almost four. Do you want me to go down to the launch?"

"Yes Rico, go… and bring me back the rock star."

♪♪♪

A man in a suit walked purposefully toward the public launch. Kerry didn't see where he came from but did have a theory of who it might be. The man stood at the restrooms with his hands behind his back and his sunglass-masked eyes straight ahead, like a secret service agent on guard for the President.

"You see that muthafucka?"

"Sure do."

"Carlos?"

"Or a henchman."

"What do we do?"

"We wait, just like he is."

A noise chirped in Kerry's ear.

"Kerry, are you there? Are you guys there?"

Kerry and Kittridge looked at each other.

"Pat, is that you?"

"Yeah, it's me… I'm about to turn into the lot."

Kerry turned and looked over his left shoulder. "I see you, brother."

"Have you found Carlos?"

"Maybe… There's a guy in a suit waiting by the bathrooms. Not too many guys in suits hang around boat launches, so I figure he might be waiting for you."

Pat's voice became shaky. "Dude, I'm fucking scared out of my mind."

"Brother, I'm with you every step of the way."

The light changed, and the roar of Pat's car rattled the parking area as he pulled in.

♪♪♪

"What the hell is this?" Elizabeth exclaimed as the bright red Viper entered the parking lot. "Shit, it's Pearson!"

"He sure knows how to make an entrance…"

"We've got to get closer."

As they began to move, Elizabeth looked up at the staircase and straight into the eyes of the two men. She froze, unwittingly giving a look of acknowledgment. The men both nodded back awkwardly. Rosa grabbed her hand, and they walked quickly around the cove and entered the ladies' restroom. Standing perfectly still and silent, they listened.

♪♪♪

Pat pulled into the closest parking space he could find and killed the engine. He looked at his watch. Two minutes to four. He dropped the car keys on the floor and after a long look at himself in the mirror, took a deep breath, grabbed the duffle bag off the passenger seat and stepped out of the car. Walking toward the restrooms, he was nearly startled out of his skin.

"Pat, your earpiece!"

He frantically pulled the earpiece out of his right ear, stuffed it into his shirt and continued toward the restrooms.

The man in the suit. He felt his palms begin to sweat and his breath get short. He walked just to the left of the man, leaned against the structure and set the duffle bag down.

"You Señor Pearson?" the man in the suit asked in a heavy Spanish accent.

"Yes."

"Come with me."

"I have the money right here. Where is my family?"

"Come with me."

He grabbed Pat's arm and led him down the path toward the dock where Carlos's boat was moored. Pat pulled free of his grip but followed just the same. They walked to the first slip, in which sat the biggest yacht Pat had ever seen. On any other day, he might have been impressed.

"Get on."

Pat walked up the gangway and was stopped at the top by another Hispanic man who took the duffle bag and opened it. He took a look, zipped it back up and commenced to patting Pat down.

"No weapons, eh?"

"No," Pat said.

"No police?"

"No."

"Please, come on board. Mr. Castillion is waiting for you."

♪♪♪

"Come on, man, hurry up!" yelled Kerry as he bolted from the staircase and across the parking lot. He held his finger in his ear so he could hear what was happening. He stopped halfway across the parking lot for a look. It was now getting dark as the sun had just dipped below the horizon, but Kerry could still make it out. There it was, the biggest yacht in the marina, sitting there all day long: 'El Encantador…

♪♪♪

…de Dragon' "God, Rosa, it was there the whole time! Let's go!"

The two officers drew their weapons and held them low, cautiously stepped out of the restroom and made their way across the parking lot, taking up temporary refuge behind a parked Escalade.

"How are we going to do this?" whispered Rosa.

"I'm not sure, but I need to call for backup. There's no way you and I can do this alone. Shit! Where's my purse?"

"You must have left it in the bathrooms."

"Do you have your radio?"

"Wouldn't go with the sundress. I left it in the car."

"Dammit! Rosa, you have to go for the radio. I'm going to wait here until you come back in case something happens, and then we'll call SWAT. Go! Go now."

Rosa jumped up and ran toward the hotel.

♪♪♪

Rico led Pat onto the rear deck of the boat, and down through a small set of stairs into the main salon. Pat's body went numb at the sight. On his right, Christine, Tina, and Tommy sat on a white sofa with their hands and legs bound with duct tape. Their mouths were also covered. Tommy was looking at him and sobbing. On his left, behind a burlwood coffee table sat Carlos Castillion, sipping a drink.

Pat had never actually seen Carlos, but he knew exactly who he was. He could almost taste the evil emanating from him the minute he entered the room.

"Ah, Mister Rock Star! Finally, we meet!"

Pat stood there in silence, unable to avert his eyes from Christine, Tina, and Tommy.

"Please, sit down!"

Rico shoved Pat toward Carlos. Pat reluctantly sat down and set the bag of money on the floor.

"Mister Rock Star, how does it feel to see your family again?"

Pat said nothing. Carlos stood up and walked over to the other sofa. "You can see they are unharmed. We did have a deal, yes?"

Pat again did not answer. Carlos ripped the tape from Christine's mouth. It obviously hurt.

"In fact, this is a reunion of sorts. A time to celebrate! I understand you have just finished a rehab?"

Pat did not respond. Carlos ripped the tape from Tina's mouth and put his hand on her shoulder. "I remember telling your amiga that we don't have much empathy for drug addicts in Mexico. But in America it is different – so tonight, we celebrate our meeting, the reunion of your family and your completion of rehab!"

Carlos walked back over to the coffee table and pulled out a huge bag of Crystal Meth. Pure glass. He dumped it out onto the table. The glass shards shimmered in the light as the boat rocked softly. Carlos then produced a shiny glass water pipe. Pat could feel his mouth begin to water and his throat go numb. He stared at the pile of crystal.

"Mister Rock Star, please do me the honor of taking the first hit."

Pat broke his stare at the table and looked at Carlos. "No, thank you," he grumbled.

"I'm not sure you understand me." Rico put his hand on Pat's shoulder and squeezed. Carlos continued. "I insist."

"Look, I brought you your money. Give me my family, and you'll never have to see us again."

Carlos laughed angrily. "I offer you a celebration and you disrespect me? You disrespect me on my boat which was given to me by la familia? You disrespect me in front of my crew and my guests?" Carlos leaned over to Pat and removed his sunglasses, revealing the most evil eyes Pat had ever seen. "You will smoke that pipe."

"Carlos, I brought the money. Please, just take it and let us go…"

Carlos picked up the bag of money and set it down on his lap.

"You have done me no favors!" Carlos's voice began to escalate in volume. "This is my fucking money! Now you take the fucking pipe!"

Rico dug his fingers into Pat's shoulder. "Take it," he said.

Pat's hand shook violently as he picked up the pipe. Rico took out a lighter, sparked it and held it in front of Pat's face. "Do it."

Pat looked over at Tina and Christine. They were both crying silently. Tina shook her head. Pat took the lighter in one hand and the pipe in the other. Carlos unzipped the bag of money, reached inside and pulled out a stack of bills. He looked at Pat as he fanned the bills. "Smoke it."

"Fuck you," Pat said and dropped the pipe onto the floor. The drugs spilled onto the carpet.

Carlos stood up and threw the stack of bills into Pat's face. Pat recoiled.

"You pinche fucking perro! You do what I tell you!" Carlos looked down at the bills all over Pat and the floor. "Fucking unos? You bring me fake money?" He was spitting as he screamed. "You disrespect me and bring me fake money?"

Carlos pulled a chrome pistol from his belt and pointed it at Tommy. The child tried to scream through his duct-tape covered mouth. His face turned red in terror.

“No!” Pat screamed as he jumped in the way. Carlos pressed his pistol into Pat’s chest.

“Adios, puto.” He pulled the trigger. The blast threw Pat backward onto the floor. He grabbed his chest, gasping for air. Christine and Tina screamed. Rico gulped.

“Rico, go to the bridge and get us out of here! Miguel, untie our moorings! Now!”

As Rico and Miguel scrambled to their assigned posts, Carlos turned the gun on Tina and Christine. “I’ll dump you all in the ocean!”

TWENTY-NINE

OH GOD…WAS *that a gunshot?*

Elizabeth couldn't wait for Rosa any longer. She darted out from behind the SUV with her gun drawn and ran toward the mouth of the dock. She could see Miguel reeling in the mooring lines on the huge yacht. The engines started, and the boat began to drift away from its berth. Running as fast as her legs would allow, she gathered all of her courage and leapt for the deck, landing on her belly with her legs hanging over the gunwale. Her pistol clattered across the shiny floor and came to a rest under a bench. Trying to catch her breath and kicking frantically she pulled herself up onto the deck and crawled toward her weapon, as several deafening cracks pierced the quiet evening. She attempted to shield her face as wood and fiberglass splintered next to her head.

"Pinche puta!" Miguel yelled from the forward deck. He began running toward her with an Uzi.

She rolled out of his line of fire, retrieved her weapon and leaned back against the opposite side of the cabin. She tried to listen over her own labored breathing. She thought she could hear Miguel's footsteps coming around the far side. She quietly stood up staying tight against the wall with her gun low in front of her, finger on the trigger. As she slowly looked around the corner, she turned only to face the barrel of Miguel's Uzi, just inches from her face.

"Die, puta…"

♪♪♪

"Oh fuck! Did you hear that?" Kerry screamed in a total panic, "We gotta go in!"

Kittridge was already charging toward the yacht with an AR-15 in hand, but it began to move away from the dock. He stopped and looked back at Kerry.

"What the fuck are we gonna do now?"

They both watched helplessly as the boat reversed, and then began to move parallel with the public fishing pier and toward the exit.

"Kit, come on." Kerry ran back to Pat's Viper and got into the driver's seat.

"What the fuck are you doing?" Kittridge asked.

Kerry frantically searched the car.

Oh Pat, tell me you left the keys…center console… visor…floor!

"Come on, Kit, get in!"

"I don't like this, Kerry…" Kittridge opened the passenger door and attempted to squeeze into the small space.

Kerry started the car and revved the engine. The howl of the exhaust shook the trees. The dock was about a hundred feet in front of them. Kerry jammed the car into first and popped the clutch.

"Wow, she's got some juice!"

"I don't know Kerry, this ain't right…"

"Put your seat belt on!" Kerry yelled over the roar of the engine.

Kerry aimed the car straight for the mouth of the fishing pier and floored it. The yacht cruised alongside the pier. He kicked the car into second and in an instant, they were up to sixty miles per hour.

"Kerry, this ain't gonna work!"

The Viper flew over the sidewalk with a shower of sparks, through a chain link gate, and onto the pier. The wood planks rumbled beneath the car.

"Oh, shit!" they both screamed as the car smashed through the safety railing at the end of the pier and sailed through the air as the boat crossed in front of them. The lights of the hotel reflected off the car's shiny red hood as they flew off the pier and landed squarely on the upper rear deck of the huge yacht, crashing into the cabin and coming to rest in the mouth of the rear staircase down to the main salon in a shower of glass. The last thing Kerry saw before it landed were the surprised eyes of Miguel as the grille of the Dodge crushed him into the carved wood trim of the yacht's upper cabin door.

"Holy shit!" yelled Kerry as he pushed aside the car's airbag. "Yeah, motherfucker! You see that shit?"

Kittridge pried his frozen fingers off the dashboard and looked at Kerry. "Nigga, you are truly fucked up!"

The two men jumped over the car's doors just as automatic gunfire raked across the deck and plinked the trunk of the car. They took cover on either side of the wreckage. As the gunfire paused, they reached over the car's doors, grabbed their weapons and crawled around to the right side of the boat's cabin, coming face to face with Elizabeth who was still trying to shake off the fact that a flying car had just crushed her would-be executioner not more than a foot away. She gave a confused smile to the two men and ran for the front of the boat as they followed close behind, diving and dodging gunfire. They stopped at the forward staircase down to the main floor as more gunfire was showered down. They all huddled against the cabin catching their collective breaths. Elizabeth looked at the two men.

"Detective Elizabeth Hunter," she whispered, "but you can call me Liz."

More gunfire riddled the deck around them, making them cover their faces.

"I'm Kerry, and this is Kittridge. You can call us crazy."

♪♪♪

The crash had jolted the yacht hard, sending everything flying around the main salon and causing a beam to crack through the ceiling. It appeared as if the roof was getting ready to cave in. Tina and Christine were hysterical. Carlos stood up and waved his gun carelessly at them.

"Shut up! Shut up or I'll kill you right now!"

Christine and Tina cowered, Pat lay on the floor moaning in a pool of blood and Tommy squealed through the duct tape covering his mouth. Carlos reached for the intercom and barked into the microphone.

"Rico! What is going on?"

The engines could be heard struggling below, and the boat suddenly listed heavily to the starboard side. Christine, Tina, and Tommy all slid across the across the room, powerless to stop themselves due to the duct tape restraints. Christine knocked Carlos off of his feet, and Tina slammed her head on the coffee table. The structure's creaking and groaning nearly drowned out the sound of gunfire outside. Carlos stood back up, angrily kicked Christine and continued howling into the ship's intercom.

"Rico! Answer me! What the fuck is going on?"

"There's a car on the boat, sir."

Carlos paused for a moment as the forward door swung open and Kerry came through. Carlos put a bullet right into his abdomen.

"Shit!" He fell to one knee, allowing his pistol to slip from his grip and slide across the room before he collapsed to his knees in the doorway. Carlos grabbed Christine by her shirt, and dragging her behind him, he scrambled for the aft door, firing his gun randomly into the room as he as he tried to maintain balance on the sinking ship. Everybody ducked to avoid being hit.

"Come on, you fucking puta!"

"I can't," she cried, "my legs are tied."

Carlos pulled out his knife and cut the tape, grazing Christine's leg. She began to cry as her leg bled. He put the gun up to her temple. "Shut up, you stupid bitch! Now move!"

Carlos pushed Christine up the stairway. She stopped.

"Why are you stopping?"

"There's a car blocking the door. I can't go any further."

Carlos's jaw dropped as he stared in incredulity at the front end of a car at the top of the stairway. Miguel's beheaded body hung from the car's bumper dripping crimson blood down the steps, causing Christine to gag. Carlos grabbed her by her belt and pulled her back down.

"Go down! Downstairs!" He shoved her down the stairs to the bottom level.

"I'll be back for all of you!" he screeched, and again fired indiscriminately into the salon. Tommy was hit in the right foot.

Kittridge came crashing through the doorway from the forward stairs, tripped over Kerry's body and landed on the floor. "Muthafucka!"

Elizabeth followed Kittridge into the room. "Oh my God!" she screamed to Kerry who was clutching his hip, "Are you okay?"

"I'll be fine." He sat up and motioned to Pat. "Is he okay?"

Kittridge crawled over and put a hand on Pat's cheek. "Pat, it's Kit…you there? Hang on, man, you're gonna be all okay." Pat lifted his head and mumbled. "Stay with me, Pat…don't go to sleep on me."

"Help me! Somebody untie me!" Tina was screaming as Elizabeth made her way over to her.

"Detective Hunter?"

"Call me Liz," she said as frantically tore at the duct tape in an attempt to free Tina.

"Detective," Pat moaned, "my boy…he's shot…get my boy off of this boat…please…"

Elizabeth found Tommy and pulled the duct tape off his mouth, allowing him to breathe more freely through his tears. She then freed his hands and legs. Blood soaked through the hole in his shoe.

Suddenly the boat began to list to the rear. The engines surged, and then with a loud groan the boat stopped moving, and the engines ground to a halt. The boat had run itself aground. It creaked as it began to lean further backward. Everyone began to slide across the floor again. Kittridge stepped into the stairway and looked up.

"You girls get the boy off this boat. Don't go through the front stairs, Carlos will be coming back up that way since it's not blocked. You gotta climb over the hood of the car and escape off the back. Just be careful, there's still somebody up on the bridge. I'll stay here and look after Pat and Kerry. Get help!"

Elizabeth picked up Tommy and made her way toward the door and into the stairs. They climbed to the top of the stairs passing the bloody headless body and started over the hood of the car.

"Liz," asked Tina, "how did that car…"

"You're asking the wrong person."

"Oh, God!" Tina screamed as she looked into the dead face of Miguel perched on the car's hood.

"Sorry, I should have warned you about that," Elizabeth said shielding Tommy's eyes from the gruesome sight.

Elizabeth pushed Tommy up on to the car's hood.

"Don't look over there. Just climb over the hood and jump down to the floor, buddy."

Tommy made his way up onto the hood as the car began to slide to the right. The boat listed further. The car was going to slide over the side.

Elizabeth reached up and grabbed Tommy's hand as the car slid out from under him. The boat leaned more. Miguel's head rolled off the car, through a gunwale, over the side into the water.

"The boat's going to tip over!" screamed Elizabeth over the creaking and screeching, Grab the door!"

Tina grabbed the cabin door and clasped Elizabeth's hand. Elizabeth gripped Tommy's forearm as the car slid across the right side of the deck and lodged itself against the gunwales. The doorway was clear.

Elizabeth held onto Tommy, grabbed Tina's hand and they crawled out of the stairway and leaned back against the front of the cabin as the boat tried to right itself. More gunfire rained down.

"How are we going to get out of here?" Tina whimpered.

Elizabeth pulled her gun from her waistband. She whispered, "You two stay here against the wall. I'm going to try to see where he is."

She slid around the left side of the cabin. She tried to look up. A barrage of bullets came down again making her cower against the wall. Then she saw it. There was the gunman's reflection in the car's windshield. She could see him looking over the railing of the bridge. He had a handgun. He could only have about fifteen rounds or so before he would have to reload, and he was being very liberal thus far with his ammo. She would have to time this perfectly. She checked her own weapon to make sure she had enough of her own ammunition and took a deep breath

"Hey, you fucking asshole!"

Gunfire ensued so rapidly there was no counting the rounds. Bullets screamed down all around her piercing the deck and sending wood splinters flying everywhere. He paused and yelled something in Spanish, and she could see his reflection dropping one clip and pulling another out of his jacket. She jumped up and put one shot into Rico's chest. He shook, swayed forward and fell over the railing landing right at her feet. She jumped back in shock.

"Come on, let's go" Elizabeth yelled to Tina who had Tommy covered up on the other side of the cabin. "We have to go now!"

Tina pulled Tommy to his feet, and they joined Elizabeth at the rear of the boat.

"We're going to have to jump," Elizabeth said.

Tommy started to cry.

"Listen sweetie, you are going to have to be brave, okay? We have to jump into the water. Do you know how to swim?"

"Yes…"

"That's great, sweetie. Take my hand…" She led Tommy to the splintered wreckage that was once the rear of the yacht. The water was about fifteen feet down.

"No… it's dark down there!"

"We've got you."

They each took one of Tommy's hands.

"We'll go on three…one…two…three."

Tommy screamed as they jumped from the boat. As they swam toward the rocks, gunfire once again erupted from the fly bridge. Carlos.

"You fucking cunt!" he yelled. "You are dead!"

"Ow!" Tina screamed. She felt pain in her leg; she didn't know if it was something in the water or a bullet. She was having trouble treading water.

"Liz, take Tommy. I'll distract Carlos." Tina said, "It's me he wants. I have to go back."

"Tina, no…"

"Fuck you Carlos, you puto!" Tina screamed as she swam back toward the boat. Liz and Tommy headed for the shore.

Carlos threw Christine to the floor. He pointed his gun at her face. She put her hands up and sobbed.

"I'll deal with you later after all these gringos are dead, mi amor."

He could see Elizabeth carrying Tommy as she ran from the water into the darkness. Tina was nowhere to be seen.

I'll kill everyone.

Tina pulled herself up a rope ladder to the lower deck of the yacht. She thought might be able to get inside faster than Carlos could make it down from the fly bridge. She put her hand on her calf and looked at her palm. Blood. Then pain.

God, please help me… you're all I have…

She staggered to her feet and limped into the boat, finding the staircase. She fell to her knee on her good leg and peered up the stairs. Nobody there. She quietly made her way up the stairs into the main salon. Kittridge had Pat sitting up against a wall. He was holding a towel to Pat's chest, just above his heart. It was bright red. Pat was making wheezing sounds. Kerry sat with his back against the wall next to the doorway Tina entered through and almost jumped out of his skin at the sight of her. He too was covered in blood. She began to sob.

"What the fuck happened to you?"

"I think I got shot by that asshole," she squeezed out between sniffles, "How's Pat?"

"Looks like it went through his shoulder," Kittridge said.

"Is that good?"

"He's not dead."

"Then I guess so."

"He's lost a lot of blood," Kittridge said. "Did you call for help? Where's the cop?"

"Where's Tommy…" Pat slurred.

"She got Tommy to shore. I'm sure she's calling for help right now. But Carlos is still here. I distracted that asshole so they could get away but he'll be coming for me. For all of us. We've got to get out of here."

"Kit's gun slid back behind the bar," Kerry said, nodding in the correct direction, "See if you can find it back there."

As Tina looked for the gun, Kittridge helped Kerry to his knees. He winced.

"Can you walk?"

"I think so."

"Then you just get the fuck out of here. I got Pat."

Tina found Kittridge's weapon and limped back to Kerry.

"Go, muthafuckas, go!"

The two of them put their arms around each other's shoulders and worked their way up the forward stairs. Kerry gave Tina a push up the stairs.

"Go Tina, get up on deck. I'm gonna help Kit."

She nodded and cautiously crept up the stairs.

Kittridge kneeled and looked Pat in the face.

"Pat, buddy, we gotta go."

Pat nodded.

Kerry and Kittridge each grabbed Pat under his shoulders and pulled him up.

"We just gotta get up the stairs. Let's go…"

"You pinche putos are going nowhere!" Carlos growled.

They stopped in their tracks. Carlos was right behind them. Pat fell to his knees. Kerry and Kittridge slowly turned around. Carlos had a pistol pointed at them.

"I want to see the rock star's face! Turn him around!"

"No, Carlos! Don't even try it!" Tina had followed Carlos down the aft stairs and had Kittridge's AR-15 pointed at his back. Her hands were shaking.

"Ha! Come on, guera!" he said slowly turning to face her." You can't kill me! Killing is a sin! What would your God think of you?"

"God will forgive me."

"Are you sure about that guera? You made God a promise! You were reborn! You can't kill!"

Oh please God…please forgive me…I have no choice…

"Tina! Shoot him!" Kerry pleaded.

"Go ahead, guera!" Carlos pounded his hand on his chest. "Go ahead and kill me! And burn for eternity!"

Oh God…

"Drop your gun, Carlos."

Carlos quickly pointed his pistol into Tina's face. "Are you sure you can fire that gun? Can you do it before I do, guera?" he taunted, “Can you murder me before your God? Before I murder you?”

Oh God…Please help me…

“Tina, *shoot him*!”

“Oh, God,” cried Tina, as she pulled the trigger. It clicked.

Carlos grabbed the barrel of the AR-15 and ripped it out of her hands.

“Maybe your God watches over me, you fucking puta,” he screamed as he hit her square in the stomach with the gun’s buttstock. “Get the fuck over there with the others.”

Carlos grabbed her by her blouse and threw her over to Kerry and Kittridge who were barely able to catch her. She gasped for air. He threw the rifle aside and pointed the pistol at the back of Pat’s head.

“Turn the rock star around! I will shoot one of you at a time until you do!” Carlos was screaming like a dog that had treed a cat. “Look at me you puto! I want to see your fucking face!”

Pat mustered up every ounce of strength he had left. He pulled himself to one knee, then the other, and bracing on Kittridge, slowly turned to face Carlos.

“Why, Carlos... why?” he mumbled.

“This is not business, rock star, this is personal.”

“No, this is business,” a voice said as Carlos’s right cheek exploded in a pink mist. He stepped back and dropped the pistol. He was missing an eye and his face was a bloody pulp.

“Fucking rock star…”

The noise was deafening as his body contorted and was ripped to pieces by a barrage of bullets. He fell to the floor in a bloody lump. Everybody was on the floor. As the ringing sounds decreased and the smoke dissipated, two bikers with assault rifles slung low appeared through the smoke. They looked at Kerry.

“You always have club support.”

Kittridge looked up at Riff. “Thank you…”

Riff nodded to Kittridge and turned to walk away as Christine and Elizabeth pushed around them.

“The cavalry is on the way,” Elizabeth said as she surveyed the carnage. Sirens could be heard approaching.

Pat collapsed to the floor. Christine dropped to her knees, cupping Pat’s head in her hands.

“Pat! Pat…Oh my God, are you okay?”

She put his head in her lap

“Pat! Talk to me!”

“See, I told you I’d prove myself to you...” he wheezed as his body went limp in her arms.

“Pat? Pat?” Christine cried. “Pat, wake up! Please wake up!”

THIRTY

PAT PULLED HIMSELF up onto the boat's deck with his left arm; his right was too weak. The pain shot through his shoulder. Kerry offered him a hand.

"How was it, brother?"

"Fuckin' awesome," he replied as he reeled in the rope and the wakeboard.

"How's the collarbone feel?"

"Not bad… almost healed. You ready to try?"

"Not yet," said Kerry as he trotted over to a bench and tossed Pat a towel, "doctor says a couple more weeks."

Pat climbed up onto the upper deck and sat down next to Stephanie Baker, who was looking truly unbelievable in a green bikini. He toweled off his bushy hair.

"Thanks again for giving us the exclusive, Patrick. And thanks for the day on your boat."

The brand new fifty-foot cabin boat, affectionately named "The Dragon Charmer II" bobbed softly in the warm Mexican water.

"My pleasure. I figured I kinda owed you guys from the gunfire incident." Pat looked at the photographer. "Sorry again, man! How's the eardrum?"

"What?"

They all laughed.

"So, you say you were inspired to buy this boat by the drug dealer's boat?"

"Yeah, his was pretty nice save for the car on the deck."

“Car on the deck?” inquired Stephanie.

Pat glanced at Kerry, who was currently being playfully slathered with suntan lotion by Tina.

“Long story,” he smiled.

“Do you worry about further retaliation from the Arellano-Felix Cartel? Have you taken any precautions? Like a bodyguard?”

“Not that I’m in the know or anything, but word has it that both the police *and* the Cartel are glad to see Carlos gone. And who needs a bodyguard when I’ve got K & K security?”

Kittridge emerged from the galley with a giant sandwich. “That’s right, my bruthas! K & K!”

“Even though they’re useless out here. The brother still can’t swim.”

“Didn’t stop me from savin' your asses before!”

“You saved *our* asses?” Kerry interjected playfully.

“I’m the only one who didn’t get shot… The way I see it, I’m the hero.”

“Okay, black Rambo.”

“No muthafuckin’ appreciation…”

“So Pat, you have no fears moving forward?”

“Steph, since I was a kid, I’ve been fighting a war with my own life. I’ll never know why. I was selfish. I was careless. I was thoughtless. I put so many lives in jeopardy. I lost my best friend, and nearly my wife and kid.”

“Lessons learned?”

“Not on my own. I owe my life to the people at Recovery Street who taught me that it’s not all about me.” He paused to take in his surroundings. Tommy was on the bridge with Elizabeth, pretending to steer the boat. His eyes became misty. “Once I gave up the fight with my former self, my eyes opened. I learned to live again. I thank God for it every day”

“Wow, Pat,” Stephanie concluded, “pretty incredible journey. Do you have any words that you think could sum it all up?”

Pat looked out over the turquoise water. He glanced up at the bridge at Tommy and Liz. A diamond wedding ring sparkled on Christine's finger as she soaked up the warm sun next to him. He was surrounded by the best friends he had ever had. He smiled and sipped his drink, put on his sunglasses and laid back in his lounge chair letting the sun warm his face. He secretly pinched himself.

"It's the rock star life, baby."

ABOUT THE AUTHOR

Peter S Barnes is the author of ***Hard Rock***.

Barnes has an uncanny ability to translate his life experiences onto printed pages, often enlisting a cast of supporting characters that are based on real people. His books are written accurately and authentically. Being a native of Southern California, the people, places and cultures of the golden state and Mexico often find their way into the pages of his novels.

Peter lives with his wife Jennifer and their black lab, Lucy, on their ranch in Southern California.

COMING SOON

American Terrorist

A true band of brothers. Semper Fi.

Dave, Mike, Darnell & Gruff were part of the most recognized Explosive Ordnance Disposal unit in Afghanistan until a tragic mistake ended their reign of greatness.

Now stateside with various levels of PTSD, the group disbands and attempts to integrate back into normal Southern California life. Dave and Gruff go to work for the local phone company in Temecula, Darnell joins the FBI in San Diego and Mike becomes a loose cannon and free spirit on the streets of Venice Beach.

Still tortured by the acts of terrorism they see in the news daily, unable to escape the fact that their country is under siege and having taken an oath to protect it, Dave, Mike and Gruff decide it is time to take matters into their own hands. They devise a plan to take back their country. A plan to send a message. A plan to strike back against radical Islamic terrorism by destroying a mosque in retaliation for every terror attack. Now under the guise of family life, they activate their own personal domestic terror cell secretly destroying mosque after mosque in a dangerous back and forth game with radical Islam.

Frustrated FBI bomb specialist Darnell Stewart is repeatedly eluded by his suspects, never fully realizing that the men from his former unit that he is celebrating the Fourth of July and every other holiday with, are right there under his nose. The guys must stay one step ahead, conflicted and torn by the guilt of deceiving their brother in arms.

As Darnell gets closer, the stakes get higher. The American Terrorists become more frustrated and watch each other's morals erode as they play cat and mouse with their comrade and the enemy, with little empathy from the nation they love so much. They conclude that domestic targets are not enough, and decide to make the ultimate statement - attack Islam on its own soil.

Darnell and his team pursue his suspects through the Middle East, inching closer and closer until the final showdown.

Semper Fi.

Made in the USA
San Bernardino, CA
13 June 2019